IN THE

ARMS

OF

ONE

WHO

LOVES

ME

IN THE
ARMS
OF
ONE
WHO
LOVES
ME

Jacqueline Jones LaMon

ONE WORLD
BALLANTINE BOOKS
NEW YORK

A One World Book
Published by The Ballantine Publishing Group

Copyright © 2002 by Jacqueline Jones LaMon

All rights reserved under International and Pan-American Copyright
Conventions. Published in the United States by The Ballantine Publishing
Group, a division of Random House, Inc., New York, and simultaneously in
Canada by Random House of Canada Limited, Toronto.

One World and Ballantine are registered trademarks and the One World
colophon is a trademark of Random House, Inc.

www.ballantinebooks.com/one/

Library of Congress Cataloging-in-Publication Data is available from the
publisher upon request.

ISBN 0-345-44719-0

Text design by Debbie Glasserman

Manufactured in the United States of America

First Edition: July 2002

10 9 8 7 6 5 4 3 2

THIS NOVEL IS DEDICATED TO THE
MEMORY OF MY MOTHER,

JULIAMAE M. JONES
(1927–1999)

ACKNOWLEDGMENTS

I have seen so many prayers answered, so many mistakes forgiven, and I thank God for the continuous flow of blessings into my life. The evolution of this novel has been an experience unparalleled, and I am very grateful for the opportunity.

I thank the home crew for allowing me the time and space to endlessly commune with my characters: my husband, Dana (the clock started officially ticking on the night of Al Jarreau—the first twenty were the overture—let's put Mike on retainer!); my daughters, Winter Laike (you didn't think I was actually going to call you Monkey in public, did you?) and Linnea Patrice (my *PumpItUp* partner extraordinaire—*Got Tokens?*); my sons, Dana Carrington (I'm going to embarrass you 100 percent even if you are six foot two and cute as all get-out; you *are* the Booptiboo!) and Anton Harrison (the best all-around dancer that Hollywood has yet to see . . . wait a minute . . . has anyone actually *seen* Anton since school let out?).

Eternal thanks to my agent, Sara Camilli, and to my editor, Anita Diggs, for taking a chance on a poet. This team should charge tuition. Working with you two has been a dream-come-true and a superb education: so *this* is how you write a book! I am *so* ready to do this again . . . let's go!

Thanks to all the talented, hardworking people at Ballantine who made me look good in print: Luisa Ehrich, Elizabeth Hines, Melanie Okadigwe, Dreu Pennington-McNeil (for the mighty hot cover that even I keep twirling around and around), and Christine Saunders (for answering all my questions and keeping my book front and center).

Thank you to the readers of my early drafts: Cheryl Crowell, Leslie Anderson, Tess Snipes, and Imani Ma'at. You all gave me the courage and strength to dig deeper. A very special thank-you to Duriel E. Harris for reading my book in one sitting when I *know* she really wanted to go out and play, for helping me to reenter the poetry, and for being one heckuva good friend.

Thank you to my teachers: Jackye Cooper, Eleanor Hinds, and Catherine Southerland—for teaching me how to hold a pen; Mount Holyoke College, John Peck, Mary McHenry, Esther Terry, Horace C. Boyer, and Andrea Rushing—for teaching me why I should hold a pen; Cal State Consortium MFA, Carole Oles, Katherine Haake, Anthony Dawahare, Lynn Elliot, Paula Huston, and John Ferris—for teaching me the power of my pen in motion.

With love and gratitude to my Cave Canem family: Toi Derricotte, Cornelius Eady, Carolyn Micklem, and Sarah Micklem. Special thanks to Lucille Clifton, Sonia Sanchez, Tim Seibles, Harryette Mullen, Elizabeth Alexander, Nikky Finney, Nzadi Keita, Reginald Harris, Devorah Major, Honoree Fanonne Jeffers, Quraysh Ali Lansana, Mendi Lewis Obadike, Jacqueline Johnson, Tracie Morris, Sheree Renee Thomas, Cherryl Floyd-Miller & MonkeyBREAD.

Thank you, thank you, thank you to Charles H. Rowell and *Callaloo* for allowing me to participate in the writing workshops at the University of Virginia, Charlottesville. A very loving thank-you to Natasha Trethewey, whose conversations with me concerning dialect transformed and enlightened this work. Thank you to Thomas Glave, who reminded me that once a dancer, always a dancer . . . and that dancing words should always be grandly choreographed.

Thank you to the poets who gave me new breath on more than one occasion: Ruth Forman, E. Ethelbert Miller, Saleem Abdal-Khaaliq, and Tenejal.

Thank you to Troy Johnson of AALBC.com, *Black Issues Book Review*, Ron Kavanaugh of *Mosaic Literary Journal*, John Riddick of *Rhapsody* magazine, Peter J. Harris of *The Drumming Between Us*, and Yemi Toure of HYPE.

Many thanks to Marie Brown and Denise Stinson for our conversations on excellence.

Thank you to Tri Tran Photography, Sabina of FoxTrot West, and Rosario Schuler-Ukpabi of Oh! My Nappy Hair.

Thank you to Doctors Jackie Fisher, Katherine Barbour, Susan Lowry, and Dorothy Williams for affording me the privilege of teaching writing at Antelope Valley College.

With love to my people: Tiphany Jones (My Sister), the LaMon family, Lenore Belzer (My Moms on my Brooklyn side), Joseph Burr (My Pops on my DeKalb Avenue side), Alice Hankerson Wilson (My Auntie on my Grandmom's side), Ann Niswander Sorenson (My Sister on my Concord side), Russell Cooper (My Brother on my P.S. 3 side), Jim Goins, Lynn Reid McQueen, Leigh McQueen, Karen

LeRoy, The Brotzes, Mary Tanner (who cried the tears my momma would have cried), Bruce Spain, and the Lancaster Performing Arts Center, all 758 seats.

Thank you to the writers who unselfishly shared their time and wisdom: Lolita Files, Colin Channer, E. Lynn Harris, Eric V. Copage, Victoria Christopher Murray, Camika Spencer, Jenoyne Adams, and Timm McCann.

And then there's that Eric Jerome Dickey guy. Eric, I could not have done any of this without your constant encouragement and support for the last gazillion years. You were the one who looked at this woman's poetry and told me I should try a novel. You were the one who allowed me to interview you for four hours and helped me to find homes for the articles. You were the one who allowed me to see your works-in-progress and learn from your efforts. You were the one who told me it was time for me to start looking for an agent . . . and then told me to contact *yours*. How can I ever thank you enough for being mentor, friend, and teacher?

Thank you to my musical/creative inspirations: Luther Vandross (who taught me the value of artistic excellence, patience, and integrity in a magnificent way), Giancarlo Esposito (who, as a child actor, never refused this little girl an autograph, even after my umpteenth time watching him understudy in *The Me Nobody Knows*), and Tawatha Agee (for teaching me the bittersweet lesson of being honestly prepared when one steps up to the mike).

And to those whom I loved fiercely, who did not survive to see this work in print: Frederick W. Jones Jr., Louarthur C. MacDougall, Frederick W. Jones Sr., Hester Anderson, Peter D. Cox, and Laurie Elkan.

Thank you to all of you who will take the time out of your lives to read the words that I have written. There is no greater honor.

If I left you out, it wasn't intentional. Just know I love you. Know that I care.

God bless you all.

Early again. Maybe it was the fact that it was Friday and folks wanted to make it a long weekend. Maybe it was the premature spring-like weather that was encouraging the masses to call in sick. Whatever it was, Nia Benson didn't care. Days like these made a woman rejoice in her womanhood; days like these made a woman inhale and feel energy literally expand within her soul.

She had made the thirteen-mile bike trip with no incident, just wind in her face and glorious morning thoughts cascading down her back. No cabdrivers had given her the finger, no exposed cobblestones had caught her tires and made her fall. This had been the ideal commute. She locked the bike in the back room behind the vestibule and took the stairs briskly to the second floor.

"Nia, Nia, Nia . . . fabulous morning, isn't it?" No matter how early she arrived, Jonathan Feinstein always beat her to the office. His office. He strolled through the waiting area, adjusting the worn magazines, making flimsy, halfhearted attempts at knocking imaginary dust off the blinds.

"Hey, boss. Sure was a beautiful ride today. Did you ride in this morning, too?" Nia placed her black canvas backpack behind her desk in the reception area and mentally reviewed the calls she needed to place first thing. There was a photo shoot at eleven . . . a voice-over session at two. And a file folder full of rejections to deliver.

"Of course, I have to keep my Ivy League physique intact!" Nia laughed as he stretched out his maroon suspenders to fit a man twice his size. He took this fitness thing very seriously, encouraging all of his employees to incorporate some regular program into their day. When Nia started at Feinstein, he had given her a choice of accepting a local gym membership or the use of "company wheels": a ten-speed Peugeot to provide her daily transportation. It was no contest. She had no interest in being inside a closed space with a bunch of sweating strangers, had no desire to schedule a time to be active. So even in the rain, even in light snow, Nia navigated that bike over the Brooklyn Bridge, through the congested streets of lower Manhattan, to the East 70s.

It was the air. She always had to have the air.

Jonathan Feinstein, ruddy and clean-shaven, lived only seven blocks from the company offices, in a fabulous three-bedroom condo overlooking the East River. It was a distance that was close enough to walk on most days, but impressions were critical in the world of television commercial production, even from his side of the camera. If his employees saw him climbing on the bike day after day, they were more likely to support his policies and climb on their own bikes. And it worked. Jonathan was a well-liked, debonair, successful man creating success in a fickle industry. And he had his own definition of how success should manifest.

"Jonathan, let me go and shower before the day gets under way," Nia called as she walked to the production area, backpack in hand. "I'll be out in just a few."

"Take your time, take your time." Jonathan slightly adjusted the position of her chair behind the reception desk and strolled to his corner office, humming the melody to a catchy jingle he was creating.

Feinstein Films felt like home. She had done temp work here the summer before her senior year in college, and just absolutely loved it. It wasn't the business, it was Jonathan. She wasn't that excited about working in advertising or production, but she recognized the man to be a catalyst for success. She craved for herself the glow that seemed to follow him around. She didn't envision herself staying in the field of commercial production; she had always wanted to try her hand at public relations. But this job offered her exposure to the inner workings of the entertainment business and was giving her a much needed education in people. She loved the small company atmosphere, the hectic pace, the quirky personalities. The money? Well, okay, the money was downright awful, but at least she was able to pay her bills for the moment and keep smiling. At least she could keep Sallie Mae from knocking on her door in the middle of the night, demanding student loan payments at gunpoint. And it gave her the flexibility she needed to learn the ropes. So right after marching with the Class of 1980, she accepted the offer to come and learn the business in the position of "administrative assistant." Yeah, right. She was working as a receptionist, pure and simple, but it was something to put on her résumé.

And how many other jobs offered the perks this one did? Inside the shower stall of the models' dressing room, Nia gloriously inhaled the rising steam. The scent of her favorite vanilla oatmeal soap invigorated her, made her grateful for a new day. She loved getting here early enough to renew herself this way, loved the indulgence. It steadied her.

Nia emerged totally refreshed, dressed swiftly, and felt prepared to do her job. She approvingly checked herself in the full-length mirror and then made her way to the staff kitchen to get her morning cranberry juice. The daily bicycle rides to and from Brooklyn had served her body well; her waist was trim, her legs toned, her arms sculpted. Her black silk jersey dress only accentuated the positive and served as an elegant backdrop to the magenta silk blazer that graced her shoulders.

It was turning out to be a great day.

"Nia! My calls. Damn, I'm late again." Lisa hurled herself into the office. Lisa Gold was a blemished, short, and chunky blond, albeit drugstore blond, who was Jonathan's niece by marriage. She had recently joined the crew and was trying to learn the business, but was severely deficient in terms of tact and poise.

"Good morning to you, too. Three calls."

"Already?"

"Already. Tricia called about the permit for the Kensington shoot. She said she really needs your paperwork by ten and . . ." A look of severe panic took over Lisa's face.

"Oh my Gawd . . . oh my Gawd!" Lisa shouted and dropped her new leather briefcase down with a thud.

"Lisa, what's the matter?" Nia asked quietly. She knew full well what the problem was. The woman hadn't even attempted to get the permit completed. Nia had heard Jonathan reminding her several times during the past two weeks about the assignment, and several times she had heard Lisa tell him that she had the job under control.

"Well, I just don't have time to do it. I don't have time to do everything! If you knew about the deadline, and I *assume* you did since you seem to know all about my business, why didn't you remind me? Huh? Why aren't you *competent* enough to give me a simple reminder? I'm tired of having to deal with the *tacky* . . . *hired* . . . *help* who don't care enough about the company to give a woman a simple reminder."

No, she didn't.

Not this time, Nia fumed. She looked up at Lisa and observed this ranting and raving as though she were watching a silent film. None of the words coming out of Lisa's mouth mattered. Lisa was one of those princesses who had had everything handed to her—her job, her education, her car, her money, her opportunities, her life. Nia was not about to come to her rescue again. Lisa had received two raises in the four months she had been on the job, her own office, and use of Nia as her quasi-personal assistant. And in that same period of time, Nia had received no financial thanks, nothing to indicate they were grateful for her contribution to the company. Nia decided it was time Feinstein Films came to realize that Lisa was no grand company asset. It was truth time.

"Well, there's just no way in hell that I can get that permit done by ten! It's after nine now and I'm supposed to be at my shoot at eleven!" Lisa was sweating.

Nia refused to lose her composure.

"Lisa, isn't that Margo's shoot?" Nia crossed her legs and smoothed her hand over the waves of her hair that were conservatively caught into a bun at the nape of her neck.

"Of course it's Margo's shoot, *Neeta*, but I'm supposed to be observing things so that the next shoot can be more . . . well, you know . . . under my direction." Nia was not going to bite on the name foul up. It was so juvenile. And so typical of this woman.

"Well, Lisa, I believe you have several options open to you at this time."

"Which are?" Lisa placed her hands on her hips and looked down on her.

Thankfully, the phone rang. Nia slowly and gracefully reached for the receiver and picked it up on the second ring. After rendering the traditional greeting, Nia was grateful to learn that she was somewhat acquainted with the client on the other end. It was now chitchat time. She leaned back in her chair.

After a few minutes of polite conversation, Lisa's patience took a nosedive.

"*Nia! Get off the phone!*" Lisa hissed, baring her teeth, clenching her fists, and looking very much like a two-year-old in the midst of a full-blown tantrum.

"Er, Ms. Adelman . . . okay, okay, *Katherine* . . . can you hold for just one tiny moment? I'm very sorry, but there is something that seems to require my most immediate attention. I'll be right with you. . . ." Nia placed the call on hold and looked up calmly at the woman/child enraged.

"You're doing this on purpose. We are in the midst of a company crisis and you are doing this on purpose." Lisa opened and closed her hands, as though she were contemplating either playing a piano concerto or having a fistfight.

"I'm having a conversation with one of our clients. That is my job, you know. To answer the phones? I am functioning here as the *receptionist*, remember? And you are the talented relative who doesn't have a clue. Now, if you don't mind, I have a great deal of work to do . . . and looking at the time, dear, it appears that you do as well." Nia picked up her crystal desk clock and held it for Lisa to observe. It was nine forty-five.

Lisa picked up her briefcase and stomped off in the direction of her office. Seconds later, she heard breaking glass and a frantic Jonathan Feinstein running toward the sound.

"What's the problem! What's going on in here!" Jonathan flung open the door to Lisa's office, to see her standing there trying to piece together the gold-toned mug that had graced her desk.

"Uncle JonJon . . . that girl is such a *bitch!*" Every hair on Nia's neck stood immediately at attention. "Why did you have to go and hire a *nigga girl*, any damn way!" With that, Nia quickly directed Ms. Adelman's call to its proper party and activated the answering machine. There was no way she was going to sit still for that assault.

As Nia stood to go back and personally defend her race, her gender, and her state of adulthood, she heard Lisa's door slam and heard decisive footsteps coming in her direction. She met Jonathan in the hallway, halfway between Lisa's office and the reception area.

"Nia, calm down." Jonathan always presented himself as being perfectly in control. Even in the midst of crisis or calamity, the man knew how to exude a peacefulness that kept everyone on course. Like the master of a sinking ship, Nia thought.

"I'm very calm. I'm not the one who is smashing coffee mugs and throwing tantrums because I missed a reasonable deadline."

"Nia, I know you heard Lisa. I know you heard her say . . . er, uh, well you know . . ."

Nia was not going to let him off the hook. She wanted to hear him say it. Wanted to have him feel the indignation of having to repeat it. "No, tell me. What was the part I wasn't supposed to hear?"

"Lisa . . . in her anger only . . . well, she used the 'n' word." Jonathan was obviously embarrassed and angered that he was being placed in a situation where he had to articulate the epithet.

"Yeah, I heard her. Horrible thing, isn't it?" The ball was in his court now. Nia wanted to see how he dribbled.

"I'm getting ready to go into a brief meeting with Lisa. Please hold all our calls." Nia nodded and rolled her eyes at no one in particular.

He was going to *talk* to her.

"Consider it done, Jonathan. Consider it done." Nia walked back to the reception area and looked at the clock. It was nine fifty-eight. Nia deactivated the answering machine and took out her personal assignment log. The log was Nia's way of keeping track of the various assignments that had been given to her during her course at Feinstein, so that she would know in what areas she needed to develop, what particular skills she had yet to obtain. And it came in handy to her during moments such as these, when she didn't quite know why she stayed and took the abuse from this child. It was a map, showing her where she had been and where she still had left to go. And right now, she pored over every entry, every memo, every report copy and looked for comfort. But all she could hear was breaking glass and the words *nigga girl.*

The door to Lisa's office flew open and Nia heard Jonathan walk to his office and slam his door. Well. Nia looked at the phone system to see who was calling whom first, and heard her intercom buzzer ring. It was Jonathan.

"Nia, once again, my personal apology. As you know, we need to get that permit on the Kensington shoot completed. I can probably maneuver an extension for us. I need for you to handle it." This was the no-nonsense Jonathan who was responsible for getting the job done. Nia had seen this Jonathan bail his niece out time and time again. It was repulsive. Nia looked down at the assignment log she had left on her desk.

"That's Lisa's assignment."

He sighed. "I know this, Nia. But I need for you to get it out."

The hour had arrived. Nia thought about the late nights she had spent studying in college, about her mom and the two jobs she had held to see that Nia made it through. She thought about her student loan payment that was due in seventeen days. Good ol' Miss Sallie Mae. She looked at her log. And then she spoke.

"You know, I was just looking at all the things on my desk and what needs to be done. I'll be glad to rush the permit and type it up—can Lisa get the copy to me, say, in ten minutes?" She knew that was pretty much an impossible request, but she wanted to see how he maneuvered it.

"I'd really rather you wrote the copy." He sighed. "You, Nia, are the more eloquent writer." Nia could just imagine Jonathan sitting in his office, with his door closed, running his hand through his wavy silver hair while looking out over Third Avenue.

She was way too angry to be flattered. Flattery did not pay the bills anymore. Nia looked down at the Persian carpeting next to her desk while she tapped her gold pen on the blotter. Lisa had tracked dirt into the office.

"Lisa," Nia said as she took a deep breath, "Lisa is the assistant director in charge of site acquisition, Jonathan. I don't want her complaining about my usurping her position and authority. I'm sure she'll do the job for which she has become known. I'll be ready and waiting to type up the copy." Nia hung up the telephone gently. There. She could tell from the array of lights on the switchboard that Jonathan and Lisa were having a discussion. Nia got up and walked back to the kitchen to refill her cranberry juice. It was ten. And already she was tired.

"I heard that shit, Nia." Nia looked up from her pouring to see Mercedes standing in the kitchen doorway. Leave it to her to come right out with it. Mercedes was an ever-observant secretary over in accounting. An abbreviated, plump woman in her early sixties, Mercedes had been around the block a few times and had heard more than her share of insensitive remarks.

"Oh, yeah?" Nia sipped her juice and looked Mercedes straight in the eye.

"Damn right. I don't know how you keep struttin' . . . why don't you just haul off and let Miss Missy have it once and for all! Wham! Right in the kissa!" Mercedes balled up her stubby little fingers and made a tight fist that reminded Nia of a giggling Doughboy in a prize fight. She had to laugh.

"Yeah, she's always tryin' to get outta work and get everyone else here to hold up her corner of the world. I mean, that's bad enough, just by itself, but *nigga girl*? Oh, I wish she *would* come back here and say some racist mess like that to me! Ooo, chica, I would be on that gal like arroz con pollo!"

"You'd say something to her?"

"Shit yeah, I'd have to! I mean, I like it here and I like my job and all, but there comes a time when you just gotta do what's right for you. You can't be game playin' alla your life. You gotta mean somethin'. You gotta do what lets you get some sleep at night." Mercedes looked down at the floor, shook her head. "No, chica, I wouldn't let the boss's daughter treat me like shit. That just ain't in the job description."

"The boss's niece, Mercedes. Lisa is just the boss's niece."

Mercedes shrugged her shoulders. "Yeah, like that makes a damn bit of difference. Niece—daughter—second cousin twice removed—

it's all in the family. Listen, you know you're smart and you know you're quality. We all know you're doing her work. Everybody here knows that. I would go ahead and stand up for myself if I were you." Nia nodded. "So, whatcha gonna do? Huh?" Mercedes leaned in for the whisper.

"You are too much, you know that?" Nia laughed. She had learned early on that you don't confide in folks on the job. No matter what. Not even those who are supposed to be on your side. Not even those who seem to have your best interest at heart. Because everyone has a cousin or a sister or a best buddy down the block who needs your job in the worst way. So you learned to make the conversation work, without revealing a thing about your true feelings or intentions. Walls always had ears when black folk were concerned.

"Hey, let's say we go to lunch next Monday? Kinda catch up on the sorta stuff that we gotta catch up on, you know what I mean, Nia? We can go to the new Chinese buffet over on Lexington, you think? You check your schedule and we'll do it for real, okay?" Nia waved and walked away while Mercedes was still speaking.

"Deal, Mercedes. Let's do it."

It wasn't going to happen.

Nia walked back to her desk and found the blank permit application, along with Lisa's handwritten copy. She placed her goblet of juice down and began reading the chicken scratch that Lisa tried to pass off as handwriting. This was a piece of trash. Pure unadulterated trash. Nia pulled the cover off the typewriter and turned on the switch. But trash is not my problem, Nia fumed.

"My permit, Nia." It wasn't a question. More like a demand. A demand from an incorrigible child. Nia smiled sweetly up at Lisa and picked up the application and the rough draft. She extended her hand and passed them cordially to the incensed woman above her.

"Here you go. Jonathan told me that we got the extension. Just rush it on over and we should be out of the woods." Lisa snatched the permit and the draft, walked back to her office and slammed the door, without the least little thank you. Right.

Two moments later, Lisa threw her door open. "*Neeeeetaaaaaaaa! What kinda shit is this?*" Lisa stood in her doorway with her jacket on, holding the document, and looking like a stark raving lunatic. By the time Nia had gotten up from her desk and walked down the hallway, all the folks in accounting were lingering nonchalantly in the vicinity of the princess's door. Apparently Mercedes had spread the news and sold tickets for front-row viewing of the pending showdown.

"Is there a problem with the application, Lisa?" Nia stood, folded her arms, and prepared for battle.

"You're gawddam right there's a problem with the application, Neeta! It's full of errors! Big errors . . . little errors . . . gawddammit . . . look at this shit!" Lisa took the application and threw it in the direction of Nia's face.

"Lisa! Watch your language! And there's no need for you to get nasty when addressing a colleague." Jonathan came storming out of his office and stepped in between Nia and Princess Lunatic.

"A colleague, my ass! The bitch can't even type a decent letter and you want me to treat her as my colleague? Shit." Lisa glared at Nia as Jonathan picked the application up from the floor.

"You're out of line. Way out of line. Let's see here," Jonathan said as he glanced over the now-rumpled document, "Well, I see your point. Nia, this isn't your usual superb typing job."

"I prepared the application verbatim from the copy that was given to me. If there is a problem, perhaps you ought to take a look at the quality of the copy." Nia folded her arms and let her weight rest on the frame of Lisa's office door.

"Uncle JonJon, she is such a lying bitch! Can't you see that . . . she's just trying to cover her ass."

"Lisa, I'm not going to tell you again. Stifle the profanity." Jonathan looked at Nia for help out of an impossible situation, but Nia refused to return his look. "Where is the copy?" Jonathan sighed, stood there with his hand sticking out, waiting.

"It was perfect. So I'm sure she threw it away," Lisa whined as she plopped down in her navy leather chair.

Nia walked over in front of Lisa's desk and looked down on her. She looked commanding now, her black three-inch leather pumps gave her five-foot-eight frame the added dimension of stature that the moment demanded. "No, Lisa. I always keep a copy of drafts—in case of an emergency. Here, Jonathan, let me get it for you." Nia turned and walked back to her desk. Lisa sucked her teeth.

She picked up the file with the copy of the draft and her typing and returned to Lisa's office. Mercedes and her posse stood there silent, immovable. Nia walked past them as though none of them existed, and handed the copy of the draft to Jonathan.

Jonathan looked over the draft, then examined the application, then returned his attention once more to the draft. He looked at Lisa and began to say something, but opted instead to walk down the hall to his office.

"Nia, hold my calls. I do not want to be disturbed." And then Jonathan Feinstein slammed his office door again.

Nia turned quickly and returned to her desk, noting that it was nearly ten forty-five. The models would be arriving any moment for the photo shoot and Nia welcomed the diversion in duties. She walked over to the plants in the reception area and felt the soil for moisture. They didn't need watering today. Nia turned on the stereo to an easy listening instrumental station that would change the air in the place. There. Almost had the semblance of peace in the joint now. The phone rang loudly, intruding upon the ambience Nia was trying to create.

"Good morning, Feinstein Films. How may I direct your call?" Nia almost had a smile on her face to match the smile in her voice.

"Feinstein Films, indeed." A smooth, deep voice on the other end whispered to her suggestively.

Nia smiled for real this time. "Hello, Rome."

Jerome Duane Carrington. The man had always managed to bring a smile to her face. He had done this ever since her sophomore year at Baxter Academy, his senior year there. Attending Baxter had been wonderful for her, both academically and socially. Being the first black franchised academy in the New York City area, her parents had taken a gamble, but the quality of the instruction and the pride that was instilled in the students more than compensated for the lack of experience. Baxter was full of young black students who were there to learn not only the traditional academics but also their heritage. They exuded a sense of pride that one did not encounter every day. It was refreshing and very much needed.

"You know what today is, Nia?" Rome was whispering, and whispering for practical reasons, but his whispering always made her blush. His supervisors discouraged personal use of the telephone.

"I do believe that it's Friday, Rome." Nia looked down at the switchboard. There was no other telephone activity.

"That's right, sugar. And I want to see you just like I always do on every Friday night the Lord sends. Yes, I do . . . I surely do. Hmm, I have an urgent project to wrap up here that's going to require some overtime. But maybe later on this evening?" Nia tried to look professional as a familiar model entered the reception area. They nodded to each other, and Nia thought it best to wrap up the conversation quickly.

"Yes, that will be fine. I'll call you later with the details, but I'm thinking the later, the better." Rome chuckled knowingly, used to her switching demeanor while on the job.

"Yes, you do that, baby. Make sure you pay attention to *all* the little details. And just remember, it will never be too late for Rome. Later, dear."

Nia hung up the phone and announced the model's arrival to Margo, the director assigned to the shoot. Margo came out to the reception area and personally escorted the woman to Studio Area B, located just behind accounting. And then Nia's intercom buzzed.

"Nia, my office . . . now, please?" Curt. And then Jonathan hung up.

Nia turned the answering machine on for the second time that morning, picked up a steno pad and her pen, and walked down the hall to Jonathan's office. Something was wrong. Lisa was going to get the boot. Or there was going to be an assignment shift. Or maybe Jonathan finally realized the quality of her performance and was going to give her the much deserved promotion into public relations that had always been the carrot that propelled her onward. Nia smiled and forced herself to relax as she opened Jonathan's door.

"Come in, come in." Jonathan was worried. His brow was wrinkled and he was holding an unlit cigar. Jonathan hated smoke; he was a former smoker, but when he was nervous, he held that same cigar—for gesture's sake.

"Have a seat, Nia." Nia sat in one of the overstuffed black leather swivel chairs that faced Jonathan's antique mahogany desk. The photograph of his wife and their two freckled children stared at her from the credenza behind his chair.

"I'm just going to come out and be straight with you, Nia. We have to make adjustments." Jonathan ran his hands through his hair that now sported the elegant disheveled look. Had the cigar been lit, he would have long since burned up every strand.

"Yes . . . and?"

"Nia, we have to let you go." The words fell around Nia like tiny knives slicing her sensibilities and causing her to doubt her perception of reality.

"Me? No. You mean Lisa, *right?*"

"No, not Lisa. You. Nia, let me explain something to you. I am a businessman . . ."

"And I take care of business. I'm a contributor to the company and—" Jonathan cut her off.

"Yes, you are. But I'm also a family man. I have to go home at night. I have to face my wife and her family. I have to consider the entire picture. And," Jonathan sighed, "Lisa is . . . *family*. I'm truly sorry, Nia. If you need a recommendation, you know you have it." Jonathan looked helpless. "If there is anything I can do . . ." His voice trailed off beyond the whisper.

"I *will* be filing for unemployment."

"Of course."

Jonathan reached behind him, unlocked the top drawer of the credenza, and pulled out a tattered brown leather checkbook. He looked more than awkward, like a little boy who had been caught in a web of lies and had no clue as to how he could emerge whole and unconsumed.

He opened the cover and slowly began to write, glancing at Nia periodically. "This check won't be going through accounting. This . . . this is my *personal* apology to you. My *personal* thanks. I hope it helps." He leaned across the desk and placed the check in front of her.

Nia sat silently, refusing to be moved by his gesture—or the four zeros following it.

"I wish it could have been resolved differently."

Nia stood and smoothed her dress. Jonathan stood and puffed the virgin cigar. They looked at each other for a long time before Nia finally spoke.

"You know, this is *your* loss, Jonathan."

Their eyes never wavered from each other's. "Yes, Nia. Believe me, I know."

Nia finally broke the stare and looked at the floor. "Well, I guess this is it then."

"Sometimes you have to make some hard decisions in business . . . hell, in life," Jonathan said, extending his hand to her. "Feel free to come back after hours to clean out your desk. Less traffic. Less explanation. And the bike . . ." Nia only looked at his hand and smiled a feeble smile. She shook her head.

"The bike is yours, remember?" She tried hard not to smirk, but her tone betrayed her.

"I want you to take it."

Nia picked up the check and walked to the door. "No, Jonathan. I only take what's mine."

As she entered the reception area she heard stifled giggles behind her. A quick glance over her shoulder revealed Mercedes and Lisa at the other end of the hallway, whispering and sipping coffee like bosom buddies. Nia reached down behind what had been her desk, picked up her backpack, pulled out her tennis shoes, and walked out of Feinstein Films.

No matter what she later realized she had left, she knew she wouldn't ever be coming back to retrieve it.

Once outdoors, Nia looked at the people passing her on East 73rd Street. A delivery guy with greasy brown paper bags in a cardboard tray. Two teenage girls with pressed parochial school uniforms, giggling and singing "We Are Family." A disheveled woman fervently pushing a child's empty stroller, full of papers and other treasures of a nomadic life. People. All with places to go. All with purpose. Hey, it wasn't that bad, Nia thought as she bent down to tie her sneakers. Now she had the entire summer to herself with nothing to impede her beachcombing. And she didn't need that stank job anyway. They didn't appreciate her. Why, actually, she was lucky. Yes, lucky.

She was standing in the open air.

The sun continued to shine. She didn't even know where she was going. But Nia began to walk and give herself the motivational talk of all talks. It really was their loss. She had done what any righteous young black woman would have done. She had refused to be taken for granted. She had decided to make herself remembered for her principles. She had stuck up for herself. She ought to be mighty proud of herself. Now, if she could only stop crying, everything would be perfect.

Just perfect.

"Come on, man!" Reggie whispered frantically to the man at his side. "Give me the ring!"

A multitude of pockets is usually a good thing. But not today. Not here. Not now. Seth put his hand into each pocket of his black tuxedo jacket and couldn't even find a decent piece of lint. The sweat was forming on his brow. This was not funny.

He relived the moments just before walking into the sanctuary, just before following Reggie to his position at the altar. He remembered the moment when Reggie handed him the ring and told him to keep it safe. He remembered the thin whistle that had escaped his lips at the sight of the dazzling diamonds that graced it, the intricate platinum network that held them secure. He remembered the coolness of the metal, the substantial weight of it. He remembered he told Reggie how beautiful it was and how happy he was that his best friend had finally found a woman who loved him. And he told him there was still time for him to change his mind and reconsider, that even at this late moment, he was still a man with options. Then Reggie's hug and reassurances, the playful punch on his shoulder. That was all he could remember.

"Aw, Reggie, man, I had it right here just a minute ago . . . not to panic . . ."

Reggie looked at him, his eyes pleading, begging Seth to get over whatever barrier was keeping him from supporting this decision. And Seth saw the glance. He had known Reggie long enough to understand the subtext, his own eyes conveying apology and shame.

He didn't want Reggie to marry Crystal and he didn't understand why.

She seemed to be a nice enough woman. She wasn't *his* type, but then again, she didn't have to be. She was Reggie's choice and Reggie loved her and that was good. But every time they wanted to do something or go somewhere, Crystal would object. She would ultimately lose whatever argument would ensue, but there was always drama associated with Reggie's life beyond her.

"Let me tell you a well-kept secret: A little discord can be a positive, my brother," Reggie had told him once when he had brought up the issue, "leads to good resolution. Making up is a wonderful thing." They laughed about it then; Reggie shooting Seth on-the-sly winks to let him know he understood the game and could handle it for himself. But Seth remained uneasy in her presence, always feeling as though he had to constantly go through fire to maintain closeness with his friend, this man who had been his tether so many times in his life, as he had been in Seth's.

The minister cleared his throat.

The vest, he thought. Must've put it in the vest pocket.

"Seth, don't do this to me." Reggie was sweating profusely now; Seth could smell it. Or maybe he was smelling his own cool being blown.

"Reggie, I'm sorry. I-I can't seem to find the ring." Seth barely said the words in a whisper, but they carried, and you could hear the guests' mutterings travel straight to the back of the church. He heard Crystal suck her teeth, her crinolines rustle as she shifted and sighed. He had to fix this.

Seth turned to the minister and said, "Don't suppose you have an extra band hanging around, huh?" Reggie was seething and trying hard to keep from cursing out his best man at the front of this cathedral. The minister didn't crack a smile. Just glared at Seth and rolled his eyes toward the heavens.

He Couldn't Find The Ring.

"Here, man, use this until we can get this little ol' mishap straightened out, okay?" Seth removed his class ring. A big old bulky gold and onyx monstrosity. Reggie turned around and faced this man who used to be his best friend in life.

You could have heard a pin drop in the church. No one breathed. No one coughed. No one whispered or made a sound. And then someone laughed. Loudly. A woman. Somewhere over on the groom's side. Not just a little bit of nervous laughter either. This woman was laughing like she was at a Redd Foxx moviefest and all she was missing was a soda and an extra-large buttered popcorn.

Reggie turned first, and then everybody turned around looking for the woman behind the laugh. Everyone in the entire church was turning around. The mystery woman was safe from detection. Seth was impressed and smiled.

"You are dead meat," Reggie hissed, snatching the ring from Seth and turning toward his bride. "Honey, I'm so sorry about this."

Crystal looked up at Reggie, looked down at the ring, and whispered loud enough for Seth to hear, "I told you we should have eloped, baby. Your friend is such an incompetent. Let's just move it along, okay? The reception site is *by the hour.* . . ."

When the minister pronounced them husband and wife, she turned and glared at Seth before the kiss. He sighed and mouthed a silent apology. She rolled her eyes at him.

The reception was held at Gramercy Manor, one of the most opulent catering venues in all of Southampton. The guests were greeted by red-coated valets and individually escorted into the Grand Ballroom. Waiters scurried about, making sure no guest stood empty-handed for long. A local jazz trio provided vintage melodies that the grown folk remembered, like "Stella by Starlight" and "The Girl from Ipanema," throwing in recent releases by Earth, Wind & Fire, Stevie Wonder, and Lionel Ritchie to keep the youngsters happy. Laughter and good times were everywhere. It was a fairy-tale reception.

Seth stood at the entrance to the ballroom at Reggie's side, still trying to get Reggie to talk to him. "Man, it's all over now. Dried up and married! Hand over that little black book." Reggie continued to ignore him, smiling absentmindedly at passing guests. Seth muttered into the air. "Yeah, you always could hold a grudge."

Reggie turned and faced Seth, looking him dead in the eye. "You ain't seen nothing yet. Man, how could you do that to me?" Before Seth could formulate a decent response, Reggie walked away with an attitude, carrying a flute of champagne, looking as regal as Duke Ellington ever did, white tuxedo radiating. He strolled over and greeted some older women who were hovering near the center of the lobby, looking lost. Women with auburn wigs and sequined dresses. Women with hose that were way too light. Women with old furs that had heads and paws. Family.

"You know, Aunt Patti could have killed you on the spot." Seth didn't turn around, still engrossed watching the women with the little dead animal heads around their necks. And then Seth heard The Laugh. It started first as a giggle, and then blossomed into That Laugh. He quickly turned around.

"It was you!" Seth looked at the cinnamon-colored woman standing before him. She was cute and compact. Couldn't have been any taller than five feet. "You know, of course, that everyone is trying to figure out who you are."

She extended her hand to him. "Shhh. Don't tell my secret, okay? My name is Lauren. I'm Reggie's cousin, originally from Richmond. And I know, you're Seth. I've heard, um, lots about you in the past hour or so." And then she laughed That Laugh again.

"Oh, have you? Such as . . . ?" Seth asked for conversation's sake but wasn't sure he wanted to know all the gory details. He shifted his weight and shoved his hands deep into his pants pockets. "Hey, what's this . . . ?" Seth pulled out the three-carat diamond wedding band and stared at it, completely baffled. He had been through his pockets a gazillion times and there had been no ring, no symbol of forever to be found.

"Wow! That's quite a band you got there. Getting married?" Lauren chuckled.

"Hey, you want to? I'm dressed for the occasion and *I've* got the ring! And it looks like all of your family is here anyway." Lauren smiled. Then as quickly as she had smiled at Seth, her smile retreated, replaced by a sudden overwhelming darkness. Lauren looked at the floor, her mouth open, as though she wanted to say something yet suddenly lost the power to speak. "Whoa, I don't know what I said to do that to you, but I'm sorry; I was just kidding, okay?" She nodded and reservedly resumed her smile. "Cheer up; I'll be right back. I think I have an announcement to make."

"I'll wait for you." Lauren winked at him—half smiling, half not—and watched him as he walked away.

Seth walked up to the bandstand, took out one of his business cards, whispered and handed it to the leader of the jazz trio as they were winding down a particularly funkified version of Ramsey Lewis's "Sun Goddess." He motioned to a waiter to bring him a flute of champagne and held it high above his head.

"Okay, I have an announcement to make. A toast and an announcement. First, the toast. Reggie and Crystal: May you experience the kind of joy that comes from sharing the love of God, the ultimate Love. You both deserve it. You know, you guys look like the top of a wedding cake. All perfect and lacking in nothing." Seth looked over at Reggie, but he wouldn't return eye contact, just groaned something under his breath. Seth beckoned to his friend.

"Okay, buddy, up here. Right now. In front of family and friends. Wow, all two hundred or so of them. You and I have been friends for entirely too long to let a little thing like a lost wedding band come between us." The room became silent. Reggie glared at Seth.

"Reggie, you know he's right," Crystal pleaded loudly. "Go on. Go." Reggie looked down at his bride. There were tears in her eyes. There were tears in Reggie's eyes, too. About three carats' worth.

Crystal squeezed his hand and released him to go to the bandstand. She looked at her husband and smiled a beam of encouragement his way.

Reggie took the microphone from Seth and turned to face the crowd. "I know that everyone is feeling the tension that I've been feeling. I mean, this is the kind of thing that happens in bad movies. Not real life. Not my life anyway. But you know, I have such a beautiful bride"—Reggie wiped his eyes as the crowd sniffled and applauded—"and she has shown me that no matter what, love and friendship . . . and *family* . . . is what this day is all about." Reggie turned and faced his best man. "So, Seth, I just want you to know, I still have some serious issues with you. And the two of us, you know, we gonna have to talk this through, man to man—but that's a whole 'nother thing. And don't think I'm gonna let you off with just an apology either. You're gonna have to pay me back for this one . . . to the tune of . . . oh, never mind, we'll take care of those humongous details later." Reggie laughed through his tears, grabbed Seth by the shoulder, and punched him. "But I love you, man. You my brother. You family. And noth-ing—*nothing*—is ever gonna change that."

There was not a dry eye in the house. Folks were sniffling and blow-ing and boohooing all over the place. Seth took the microphone from Reggie. "Hey, man, I think it's time for a duet. The two of us, whatcha think? We can sing a little Brothers Johnson, throw in some Bootsy, if you down with the get down." Reggie glared at him, then laughed at the corniness of it all.

"Man, there is just no hope for you. You the corniest Negro I know, but you all right. You gonna be paying me a long, long time, but you all right." They hugged.

Seth turned to the bandleader. "Say, my brother," Seth asked while adjusting his wire rims, "you have any music-to-present-a-ring-by?" He pulled the ring out of his pants pocket and handed it to Reggie. Even the waiters were getting moist in the eyes, and they didn't even know the full deal.

Reggie took the ring and walked over to his bride. He knelt on one knee and took her left hand in his. "Baby, this is for you. With all my love. And all my devotion. And with everything true and real that a man can give a woman. *This* is for you, Crystal." Reggie removed Seth's class ring and replaced it with the glistening diamond band.

After kisses and tears and congratulations and more tears, Reggie walked over to Seth.

"Here's your ring back. I guess I should say thanks." Seth took the ring and put it back on his finger.

"So, Reg, I guess this means we ain't going steady no more, huh?" Seth tried to look all hurt.

"Man, you are such a sick individual. You really do need profes-sional help." Seth looked across the room and spotted Lauren.

"You are a great diagnostician. And I think I see all the help I need, too." Seth and Reggie looked at each other, Seth wanting to say more than the lump in his throat would allow him to say. "You be happy, Reggie." Reggie nodded, understanding.

"Go on. Looks like someone's waiting for you."

Seth looked at Lauren from across the ballroom, watched her while she was unaware of being watched. She was in conversation with another woman, nodding, laughing, just pleasantly engaged. There was something doe-like about her, something elegant and innocent, something beautiful and precious that he wanted to protect. She wasn't model-beautiful, but then neither was he. But she was beautiful. Lauren had a certain round quality to her, not fat, not obese, round. As though all the rough edges that life chisels in a person had been smoothed over by time and circumstances. When her conversation ended, Seth walked over to her, slowly and deliberately. She watched him approach and allowed her lips to form a smile. A genuine one this time.

"*You* are beautiful." As soon as he said it, he wished he hadn't; it sounded like such a cliché. He didn't want to come off sounding like he was on the prowl. He didn't want her to think that skin was all he saw of her.

"I don't know how to take that sometimes." Lauren stopped a passing waiter, took two champagne flutes from her tray, and handed one to Seth.

"Thank you . . . for the champagne. But I'm not sure what you mean."

"I mean: I don't know how to take your statement. 'I'm beautiful.' What's that supposed to say to me? How is that supposed to make me feel?"

Seth shrugged his shoulders, dumbfounded. He didn't know how to answer her questions. He wasn't sure how to address her concerns. "It was a compliment."

"Yeah, it was a compliment. Thank you. How would you feel if I walked up to you and told you I thought you were fine? What would you think I was saying?"

"I would think that you thought I looked good. I don't know . . . what are you trying to say?"

"Let me help you out. You would think that I was trying to tell you that I wanted to get with you. That's what you would think. You wouldn't think I was making a statement about your eyes or your clothing or your nice personality. You would think I was *hitting . . . on . . . you.*"

She had struck a nerve in him, seen through his facade, and stripped him down to the core. He smiled at her and sipped. "You're right. I would."

"I know you would."

"And I would love it."

"Oh, I'm sure."

"One question, though."

"Hmm?"

"You really like my eyes?"

Lauren laughed. "Mmm hmm, I do. When they're telling the truth, I do."

"Can eyes lie?"

"Not easily. Not as easily as the tongue does. But yeah, eyes can lie. Sometimes we train them to tell our lies and keep our secrets."

Seth thought about how much he had lied in the past, trying to get what he wanted out of impossible relationships. He was tired of trying to make relationships happen. He was tired of the games, the rules he had invented for himself to protect his heart. Whenever he felt on the verge of getting hurt he would pack up and get out of the way of the disaster, leaving women cleanly before they had opportunity to leave him. His behavior had earned him a reputation of being a stone-cold womanizer, a love 'em and leave 'em kind of man, a man who was always in control of his feelings. A man women thought could never give love.

He looked at her and watched her speak, watched her lips; there was so much truth oozing from her mouth that it hurt him. The lights in the ballroom had been dimmed, the mirrored ball lowered, and most of the guests were participating in a wicked "Soul Train" line to a Chic medley while the band went on a much deserved break. He didn't want to hurt her. He still thought she was beautiful.

"Sometimes it's easier to do that than to deal with the truth—sometimes."

Lauren took his hand and held it. "Yeah, I know that, too."

Her mood had changed, but so had his. He felt the urge to explain himself to her, to tell her the mistakes he had made in the past and to ask her forgiveness. But he knew he had said enough already, exposing more of himself than he cared to reveal to any woman he had just met.

His collar was feeling tight and restrictive. It was getting hard to breathe in this space.

"Come on, Seth. Let's go get some air." She had read his mind, or maybe she was just feeling what he was feeling. Either way, it was good. He squeezed her hand and she squeezed his back. They walked through a pair of white-enameled French doors in the corner of the ballroom that led out onto an outdoor mosaic pathway. They walked the trail between rosebushes and Grecian fountains, jasmine bushes and koi ponds, crossing a footbridge that led to an intimate thatched patio. A beautifully romantic patio that was illuminated by paper lanterns and strings of tiny white lights entwined in the surrounding magnolia trees. The fragrance was heady, thick with sweetness, and intoxicating. They could hear the band softly playing a hauntingly beautiful rendition of "Misty" in the background. No one else had yet discovered this space. And once alone, Seth realized he had no funny lines to deliver, nothing witty to say.

He was having a rap-free moment.

Lauren caressed the back of his hand, looking at the combination of her gentle fingers against his velvety dark skin. "That was beautiful, what you did in there, Seth. I can imagine how bad you must've felt."

"Oh, the ring thing. It was irresponsible of me. This is something that is going to haunt me for quite a while to come." Lauren squeezed his hand, sighed, and shook her head. Seth continued, "You know, I laugh a lot of things off. Try to make people see the brighter side all the time, but I know there was no excuse for what I did. When Reggie and Crystal think back on their wedding day, they're going to remember me and the tears I caused them. Not this beautiful night. Not the music the band played. Not the guests or the food. They're going to remember Seth, the best man who couldn't get it right." Seth turned away from Lauren, so she wouldn't see the effect facing the truth was having on him.

"You know something, Seth? Seth . . . what-is-your-last-name Seth?" Lauren pulled back her pencil thin braids.

"Jackson."

"You know something, Seth Jackson?" Lauren reached to touch his face.

"What's that?"

"You really flatter yourself," Lauren whispered, touching his cheek.

"Flatter myself? I don't think so." Where was this woman coming off, anyway, Seth thought.

"You do. You truly flatter yourself. Come here." Lauren motioned for him to follow her across the footbridge, back along the narrow path to the closed glass doors of the ballroom. "Look at them. Look at Reggie and Crystal." Seth looked at the couple. They were in the center of the dance floor, waltzing. Totally oblivious to everything and everyone around them. Crystal's veil created billows when she turned, framing her beaming face. "They don't see you. Or me. Or the waiters. Or the cute little printed matchbooks on the tables. They don't see anything but each other. They don't even see the *mistakes*, Seth. They are looking at this evening through loving eyes."

Seth looked at Lauren as she looked into the ballroom, her mood of blessing deteriorating into sadness. "Lauren?"

"Hmm?" Lauren continued to look at the newlyweds.

"Would you like to dance?" Seth extended his hand to her.

Lauren shook her head. "Thank you, Seth, but no. I'm not really ready to go back inside yet."

"Well, neither am I," Seth said, looking at her long natural nails and loving them. "I meant out here, on the patio."

Seth opened the door to the ballroom just a bit, to allow the music into their private fairy tale. It was scary how quickly they were becoming comfortable with each other, scary like a roller coaster approaching that first summit. She was touching him, penetrating his exterior and getting under his skin, just as many beautiful women had tried to do in the past. But this time, with this woman—this time he promised himself he would not run. He looked down at her, vulnerable and accepting this, and smiled.

"May I have this dance, Lauren?" She laced her fingers with his and walked to him.

He put his arms around her waist and pulled her close, deeply inhaling the scent of roses in her hair. She sighed, held him tightly, and allowed her face to rest on his chest.

Together they breathed.

There were crickets making love in the distance, but neither Seth nor Lauren noticed. There were newlyweds dancing, cutting cake, beginning a new life together. But here, in this quiet corner of the night, a new world was unfolding for another couple. Seth and Lauren had found each other.

"Lauren? Lauren? Oh, there you are!" Mrs. Montgomery came running over to the opened doors, beckoning to her niece. "Lauren, Crystal is about to throw her bouquet! All single ladies, please!" Patti Montgomery smiled approvingly at the sight of the couple dancing. "Well, this is nice. Hello, Seth."

"I'll be right there, Aunt Patti, thank you!" Lauren smiled, winking in return.

"Hi, MommaPatti!" Seth shouted out, but by then she was already gone.

"I guess I should go inside, but I really don't want to," Lauren admitted.

"Oh, go ahead. You might just catch the bouquet!" He walked her to the door.

"And if I did, would that be a good thing?" She looked him in the eye, searching.

"It might be a very good thing. You never know." Seth smiled.

"You're right. I guess you never know."

Lauren went inside and mingled with the other single women and excited little girls who were jockeying for position at the foot of the spiral staircase in the lobby area. Seth watched her move, then slipped inside and closed the doors behind him. There was something different about this woman. Something mysterious and captivating. Something he wanted to feel more of in his life. Something really good. A soft something. A something good for him.

Crystal appeared at the top of the staircase like a queen holding court. "All right, ladies! The time has arrived! When I turn my back, I want you all to rearrange yourselves so that no one accuses me of playing favorites, okay?"

Crystal turned and faced the cascading brass fountain on the landing above the stairs. The women laughed, whooped, and hollered, removed their shoes, pushed each other around, and found their ideal spots. "Ready, everybody?" And Crystal tossed her bouquet back over her head.

It drifted down, down, down the staircase, as if in slow motion, floating toward its rightful owner.

"Me? Oh no; this wasn't supposed to happen like this!" Everyone turned around and looked at the bouquet and the woman holding it. "No—no, wait . . . I was just walking by on my way to the ladies' room! Oh, Lord! How did this happen?"

"Looks like you are the next one to take that step, Aunt Patti!" Lauren laughed and hugged her aunt.

"Er . . . I don't think so." Uncle Rex came up behind them and snatched the bouquet out of her hands. "Here, Lauren, congratulations on a fine catch!" He took Aunt Patti by the hand and led her to the dance floor. "This married woman and I have some rug-cuttin' to do while those cats are still playing the good ol' songs!" They hugged each other, jostling and laughing all the way.

Lauren stood looking down at the white rose and orchid bouquet in her hands, oblivious to the women surrounding her talking about what was fair and what was not. It was such an elegant, understated bouquet. She closed her eyes and inhaled deeply. Held her breath and slowly exhaled. And when she finally opened her eyes, Seth was standing six feet before her, with his hand extended, smiling.

At the sight of him, Lauren started crying, threw the bouquet into the crowd of teeth-sucking women behind her, and ran into the ladies' room.

Three

NIA

So many people. And all of them in such a hurry. At times the sidewalk seemed to bulge with all the people, hustling and bustling. Storekeepers sweeping the sidewalk outside their doors, some washing the plate-glass windows through which passersby would peer. Nia watched them all. It was amazing; they all seemed very busy, very concerned with their activities. It wasn't as if any of this stuff mattered, Nia thought. After it was all said and done, after the last customer had come and gone, the last light turned off, the last key turned, the last deposit made in the bank, nothing that mattered about life would have changed. We would all just breathe in and out. We would all live for a time and then we would die.

Principle, Nia reminded herself. She was walking down this street, depressed and unemployed, because of Principle. She was no militant; in college, she had steered clear of all the questionable personal or political causes, denied herself any ties to organizations that might have made it difficult for her most conservative of dreams to later come true. A cop-out is what some of her classmates had labeled her. At the time, Nia had just laughed it off. She knew that if it ever came down to it that she would be able to stand for what was truly right in her eyes.

Guess that time is now, Nia mused. The fragments of the morning that had led her to this present played themselves over and over again, like an endless loop of home movie footage in her mind. Many had witnessed Lisa's going off and being the ignorant racist that she was; the entire office had heard her call Nia a *niggah*. And yet nobody came to her defense. Not one of those people rallied by her side, in public or private, and told her that they, too, would walk if she had to walk, that they were down for the cause, that they would also put their jobs on the line in the name of what was right. She had been forced to do this march by herself. She bit her lip in anger at the tears that she allowed to fall. This had been her day to take a personal stand. And she had. Thank God, she had. But all those people at Feinstein would see similar days in their lives, Nia knew. Maybe not now. Maybe not even at Feinstein. But they would all see their days. Days when a word or a look or a decision would be tossed at them for no reason other than to feed the fear of the one who had the power to hurl it. Maybe not because they were black, maybe because one was a woman and was made to feel inferior in an office full of men. Or maybe because one was the older person thought to have long since served his usefulness. Or maybe because one chose to live life as an openly gay man whose very presence challenged all notions of what it means to be a man in corporate America.

They have called us all *niggahs*, Nia thought; you all just don't know it yet.

And she thought back to the last time, the only other time in her life when she had heard that epithet hurled her way.

"Your name is Nia? For real?" Mickey McMurray had hollered, his blazing red hair in a short crew cut, his mouth full of silver braces flashing across the lunch table during her first day in seventh grade. She had been bused in from her neighborhood, getting up at four in the morning to meet the bus at five-thirty, and she was already tired. The questions had been endless all morning long, from students and teachers alike. Questions about the wave of her hair and her permanent suntan, the curl of her eyelashes, and whether she had known the Rev. Dr. Martin Luther King Jr. on a personal basis. All morning long she had felt as though she had been preparing to play Pin the Tail on the Donkey, as though she were being turned around and around while blindfolded and unsure of where it was safe to go. She wanted to scream and leave this distortion. To tell Mickey to stop asking her these really stupid questions and to go back to the world she knew and understood. But her parents had told her to be polite to everyone, and so she had smiled at Mickey and what looked to her like barbed wire in his mouth and nodded yes; Nia was her name, for real.

"That's pretty neat. Nia. I like that." He grinned at her without any warmth or joy in his eyes. His buddies at the table watched him in silence, taking tiny bites of their peanut butter and jelly sandwiches, sucking hard on the paper straws that had long since collapsed in their red-and-white milk containers.

"So, Nia . . ." She had stopped eating and held her own peanut butter sandwich with both hands, trembling. The other boys at the table had begun to snicker quietly.

"Yes?" She finally rested her sandwich on the plastic cafeteria plate, unable to hold it for the shaking of her hands, and looked down at the purple jelly as it oozed beyond the hardened crusts.

"So, we all wanna know. How does it feel to be a *niggah*? Hmm?"

She cried that crisp September day that was supposed to welcome her to this better junior high school, cried when she told the lunchroom monitor what had happened, cried when she was ordered to go to the principal's office, cried when her parents were called to come and pick up their most disruptive daughter. It had hurt so much to be the target of hate while she had been trying so hard to be liked. She wondered then what she had done to Mickey; maybe if she had smiled more or talked more or made him laugh more, he would have liked her, just because she was Nia. Nia with the pretty neat name.

Her parents had gone to the NAACP that very afternoon; together they staged a major protest in front of the school. There were people from her community who had taken signs on sticks and walked up and down the sidewalk outside of the school's main entrance. There were cameras, recognizable reporters from the six o'clock news, people with wild afros and black leather jackets asking lots of questions and demanding lots of answers. People with suits and bullhorns, shouting directions. Hundreds, literally hundreds, of people were singing "We Shall Overcome," holding hands and swaying. After two days of this,

the principal himself called Nia at home and apologized for the misunderstanding. He said that Mickey McMurray wasn't going to be at
their school anymore and it was all right for her to come back; he said
they really wanted her to come back. Her parents told her to think
about it; about what it would mean for her to return, what it would
mean if she stayed away. But Nia was still tired. Tired from the long
ride on the bus, tired of having to constantly explain herself. And she
knew that all of Mickey's friends would still be there anyway. And
friends like that stick together. She chose then not to go back. She was
a little girl who only wanted to be a student and learn, not to serve as
the teacher and teach them tolerance and respect.

Times were different now. For starters, Nia was a woman. Yet while
the circumstances had changed with the passage of time, so many of
the feelings remained intact. Raw and hurting. This time she knew for
certain that this was not her fault. She knew that she could no longer
deny herself in order to be accepted. Not at Feinstein Films. Not anywhere. It was a promise she had made to herself, a promise she had all
intentions of keeping.

It would only be true if she let it be true: Nia Benson was no *niggah
girl.*

She tripped, and bent down and tied her shoelace, tears falling on
the pavement in front of her. She had been crying so long that she had
become used to the feeling and she hated that. She stood, grabbed a
tissue from her backpack, and glanced at the window of the business
in front of her. Midtown Legal Defense. She walked to the glass and
looked inside.

An elderly woman sat in a waiting area, surrounded by three small
children and soiled brown paper shopping bags splattered with blood.
Her eyes were filled with a tearless despair devoid of hope; her hands
were as wrinkled and fragile as ancient forgotten parchment. Her stiff-
ened fingers clutched an ivory rosary, stroked it. The children leaned
upon her lap, rested on her knees, buried their faces in the fabric surrounding her shoulders.

Nia thought to go in. She had all the reasons to do so; she knew she
had a good legal case. She wiped her eyes once again and reached to
open the door.

A young Asian man came running to the door waving his hands

frantically, shaking his head. He turned the key on his side of the door, opened it, and used his body to block Nia's entrance.

"Aw, I'm sorry, ma'am. We had an emergency here this morning and I'm the only one here now. And I'm just swamped. Swamped right up to here," he said, placing his hand high above his head. "Can you come back tomorrow? I mean, we really are closed." The young man pushed his sleeves up above his elbows, readjusted the suspenders on his pants, and shifted his weight impatiently.

Nia glanced over at the woman in the waiting area. One of the children stirred and whimpered. The woman placed her hand on his back and patted it gently to an inaudible rhythm. "You're closed?" Nia asked.

The man glanced at the woman and faced Nia stoically. "Well, is this a matter of life or death, ma'am? This is an *emergency* situation here and it's for the safety of everyone concerned that we close today . . . *please.*"

Nia shook her head and tried to smile. "Sure. I'll come back later on."

"Tomorrow, ma'am. Things would be better if you could just come back tomorrow."

He didn't wait for a response, just closed and locked the door and began speaking to the woman in a harried kind of way.

She wasn't the only one in pain this afternoon. It was tragic, but somehow the knowledge of this gave her strength. If those children could sit and not cry, she, too, could go on. If the woman could be fortified by stoically looking ahead, so could she.

Nia continued walking, thoughts about injustice and revenge swirling in her mind. It was only right that they should pay for their behavior. Only right that they should suffer just as she had suffered. Isn't that why so many had walked the picket lines and rode the freedom trains and boycotted and paraded and exercised what little power they believed they individually had? All those people who had gone before her didn't go through all those injustices just to have her fail to exercise her painstakingly earned legal rights.

It was too much weight for her to bear right at that moment, to think that she had become another link in the history of her people, a page in the book of slights and degradations to blacks. She had to remain focused upon the personal, what had actually been done to her, the pain that she had personally endured.

Nia reached into her backpack and felt around for her journal. She needed to write.

She felt the coolness of the black-and-white marble-covered composition notebook on the bottom of her backpack, and looked around for a place where she could sit and spend some time writing. There were several restaurants, coffee shops, and luncheonettes, but they seemed too noisy, too busy for her today. Nia looked down the block, across the street, and saw someone exiting a cathedral. Remembering the vision of the ivory rosary in the hands of the woman, she walked with purpose down the block, across the street, and up the many granite steps that led the way to a massive door that stood open, ready to receive her.

"Welcome to St. Augustine's. Please, come in." The tiny woman smiled and nodded her welcome as she entered the vestibule. Nia returned her loving smile and felt her peace.

The cathedral was filled with marble and gold and polished oak, with tiny white votive candles burning in front of statues along the room's perimeter. Nia chose an empty pew toward the center of the cathedral, about twenty rows from front and back. She took deep breaths and centered herself; prayed for guidance and insight before removing her journal and gold mechanical pencil.

Today the words flowed.

She wrote of peace and pain and disillusionment. She wrote of anger and release and the plight of black people in the United States. She wrote of racism, wrote of her personal struggle, wrote of how things should be.

As Nia wrote, the tears flowed. And the more she cried, the more she wrote. She hadn't realized how much noise she had been making, moaning that had started without her knowledge, a low soft song that rose from her soul and embraced her, rocked her as a cradle would. She hadn't realized that the woman who had greeted her at the door had come and sat down in the pew behind her.

"It's good to cry. And I see that you're a writer. It's extra good to write and cry." The woman leaned forward in the pew and whispered into Nia's ear with a strong accent of some Eastern European land.

Nia was startled. She stopped crying, stopped writing. But she didn't turn around to face the woman.

"Writing is your blessing," the woman continued. "You must always write, always treat writing as your Gift. Honor it and it will honor you. It will free you . . . yes, you will find freedom within the words you write." The woman placed her hands upon Nia's shoulders and Nia calmly nodded her agreement.

She waited for the woman to begin recruiting her to join the church and donate money for special prayers to heal her pain. But when she finally turned around the woman was not there; the only thing remaining was a flyer on the pew. Nia picked up the paper and looked at the words of St. Augustine engraved at the top of the page: "To sing is to pray twice."

The flyer announced the formation of The Poetry Pause, a weekly gathering of poets dedicated to using their art to uplift and heal. They met weekly here at St. Augustine's; there was no charge to attend, no requirement to join.

Nia folded the flyer and placed it in her journal. It was a lovely idea, she thought, but she didn't think it was a group she would be interested in joining. Sharing her poetry was not anything she enjoyed doing. She was well aware of how her poetry could heal her pain, but she had not had good experiences when it came to sharing her words with others. In college, conservative professors with tenure had boldly told her that black poetry was artistically and academically inferior simply because it was black. She hadn't believed them but she hadn't stayed, dropping those poetry classes and opting for black studies and women's studies classes, in which she felt more at home. She made opportunities to write for herself, to hear poetry read, and that sustained her.

Back in her college days, the coffeehouses in town sponsored poetry readings on the weekends. Every Friday evening she cruised the crowded sidewalks, watching the men and women poets outside the cafés wearing the telltale costumes of jeans and berets or Indian gauze. She laughed openly as they argued semantics and politics, trying too hard to sound radical and hip, smoking brown clove cigarettes with foreign names. These same people who worked in banks and the most conservative of offices during the week, were now wearing wild, disheveled hairstyles and acting so very, very superior.

She thought it was hilarious.

The first time Nia actually stayed to hear one of the local poetry readings on one of those Friday nights was an eye-opening experience for her.

"Excuse me, I'd like a cup of coffee," Nia said to the tall blond waiter who was leaning against the wall, observing her. "All right if I sit here?" The waiter smiled distantly, as though he was a friendly enough person but just didn't speak English. She hoisted her tote bag of books onto the opposite chair and plopped herself down, not waiting for a more explicit response from this Nordic-looking hippie.

"Java? Hey, but of course, my sister. Java is what we do best, you know what I mean?" Nia was surprised when she heard his English, but confused by his reference to her being his sister. This lanky Caucasian dude was in no way close to being her brother, and Nia didn't quite know how to take the endearment—white folks just didn't do that in this town. "So, do you want Colombian? Espresso? Cappuccino? Latte? Mocha? You name it, my sister, and the beverage is *yours*." He spoke in a low, deep slur, as if she had awakened him after a long night of too many rounds at an open bar.

"Just regular—black." Nia wished she had gone to the luncheonette on the corner.

"Regular? Ha, ha, well, I'll just bring you a cup of our finest Colombian, my sister . . . java, that is,"—the waiter leaned in real close—"unless, of course, you had a different kind of *Colombian* in mind." Nia shook her head vehemently and reached for her bag of books.

"You know, maybe this wasn't such a good idea." Nia started to stand.

"Sit, my sister, sit. Relax yourself. Just a little coffeehouse humor. Besides, you can't leave just yet. The poetry reading is about to start and you don't wanna miss that, now, do you? *Lady is reading tonight!* No, no, I didn't think you did. So you just lean back, sip your java . . . have a good one."

Nia's discomfort didn't go away. She didn't like being around smoke, and it was so smoky in here that the air appeared gray. But she decided to hang around to listen to the poet. She doubted it now, in her present mood, but it could've been someone she wanted to hear.

After a while a barefoot woman in a long turquoise gauze skirt and a white embroidered peasant blouse walked to the tiny stage in the corner of the coffeehouse. She wore wire-rimmed granny glasses low on her nose, and jingled constantly from the armful of silver and turquoise bracelets on her right arm. She solemnly introduced herself as Lady Running Water to sprinkled applause, opened a maroon velvet journal, and began shouting a poem about some poor guy who seemed to have been in the wrong place at the wrong time. Nia cringed at the memory.

No, poetry readings were not for her. She didn't have the need to publicly display her private thoughts, as some people obviously needed to do. Nia gathered her belongings and walked slowly around the cathedral, pausing at each of the statues, allowing the glow of the candles to give her peace and a reason to smile.

She really did have so much for which to be grateful. Even with the morning's fiasco. She was still alive, still a woman who was able to make choices in her life, still allowed the privilege of hope. She thought about all the times in her life when she, too, had been required to make tough decisions, when her actions had made another person cry. The moments lined up in front of her, one at a time, to remind her of the pain she had inflicted on others. She recalled all the times she had uttered words of apology and all the times people had been gracious enough to forgive her. Maybe Jonathan had already received his appropriate punishment by what would happen to Feinstein Films in her absence. Maybe that realization was greater than anything she could ever achieve in a court of law.

As Nia walked into the vestibule to exit St. Augustine's, the woman who had greeted her was standing off in the distance. She waved.

"I will pray for you. Light a candle and pray. The other sisters and I . . . we will pray." The woman spoke to her in hushed tones.

"Thank you. I'll pray for you, too," Nia said, and she meant it.

"Is there anything special I should pray?" Nia looked at the small woman who stood looking so concerned.

"Would you pray that I do what is right? Would you pray that I do the right thing?" The woman smiled at Nia and nodded as she exited St. Augustine's Cathedral.

Outside on the street, the shadows intertwined with the early afternoon sunshine.

Four

SETH

"**L**auren, what did I do?" Seth stood talking to no one in particular and looking dumbfounded, trying to chase away the accusatory looks from the women in the lobby.

Reggie came up behind him, put his arm around Seth's shoulder. "It's not you. You didn't do anything."

"That's a pretty bizarre reaction to something I didn't do."

Reggie nodded and motioned for them to walk toward the main entrance. "I know, I know. Lauren, well, she's been through a lot, Seth."

Seth sucked his teeth and opened the glass doors. "Yeah, I gathered that. What happened?"

Reggie stuffed his hands in his pants pockets and blew air out of his mouth, fortifying himself. "Trauma. She'll tell you about it."

Seth nodded. He didn't push Reggie for more information; he wasn't sure he wanted to know. Part of him knew that this would have been the ideal time to step out of the situation, to jump on the first thing moving and get away from this woman and all of her issues. He knew his routine: Once a female started showing her crazy side, he would only allow himself to count to ten before he was history. But it was that very behavior that he was intent on changing. All of his exes who had been gracious enough to give him relationship advice in hindsight told him that his greatest problem had been that he never stayed around for the resolution; he was a man who always left ten minutes before the final scene of the movie because he was afraid he wouldn't like the ending.

And it was obvious that Lauren needed something. Something that perhaps he could give her. Something that perhaps he was sent to her side to provide. Maybe he was the man who was supposed to rescue her, to love her through whatever it was until she could find her way on her own.

He could do that, he decided. This time, he would try.

He took a deep breath and gave himself permission to care.

He hoped that a day would come when she would feel comfortable enough to share her history with him. He suddenly felt protective of her, wanting to preserve that laugh and that smile from the challenges of life. Isn't that why men married women, Seth wondered, to do all they could to keep pain away from their lives? It wasn't the first time Seth had thought about marriage. But it was the first time in a long time that he had thought about why he would consider taking that step.

"So, how does it feel to be a married man?" Seth strolled alongside Reggie as they walked the length of the parking lot. Seth had known this was going to be a hectic time, but he had really wanted to connect with Reggie before he and Crystal left for the city. The newlyweds were going to spend the night at the Plaza, the opulent hotel at the edge of Central Park, and take off for the Bahamas in the morning. Paradise Island.

"Man, oh man, oh man, my brother. This is some kind of wonderful." Reggie looked down at the ground as they walked, the deep waves in his jet-black hair catching the bright lights illuminating the parking lot. "She's a good woman, Seth. Put up with a lot from me. Yeah, a real good woman."

They walked silently, listening to the sound of the crickets and the surf in the distance, mixed in with the DJ who had taken over for a while, spinning dance music for the younger crowd. It had been a long time since Seth and Reggie had taken a silent walk, although that was once a common thing. When Seth was twelve and Reggie was ten, they had met not ten minutes away from this very spot. A crew of older, ignorant guys were pushing up on Seth, calling him Four-Eyes and Dork and Mister Peabody, and Reggie had stepped in. Reggie had been visiting for the summer, too, and wasn't about to take any grief from the local riffraff.

"You need to go and find something else to do, you know!" Reggie, then five feet ten inches and growing, had hollered at the chunkiest boy, pushing his chest out up against the bully's face.

"Wassit to you, huh? You don't even know this punk! He's a punk, that's all he is, jussa punk . . . like you!" And the boy made the terrible mistake of pushing Reggie and making him take a step backward.

Reggie shook his head as though he was stunned that something like this could ever have happened. Then he pulled back his left arm and released his fist with a ten-year-old's force right into the boy's right temple.

"He's my best friend and you leave him alone!" Reggie shouted over the guy as he lay on the ground.

The bully, Herbie was his name, actually ended up being a pretty decent guy after Reggie decked him. He came around a lot, supplying Seth and Reggie with Good Humor ice cream bars and Eveready batteries for Seth's transistor radio. But after that first summer, he just disappeared. The word quietly going around was that his parents had split up and had to sell the summer place.

Seth and Reggie had been pretty much inseparable since then, even through the hard times after Seth's father had died and he and his mom had to move to North Carolina for a year. Reggie's parents had included Seth in all their summer plans just as though he were their child as well. That summer in Southampton, Seth and Reggie became extra close, discussing girls and "gettin' some," fears and family, death and despair.

"Wish I had a brother," Seth said one night, as he lay in the bed looking out at the stars.

"Excuse me? And what am I?" Reggie sat up and glared at Seth in the other twin bed.

"You're my best friend. I mean a *brother* . . ." Seth's words seemed to drift into the darkness and just hang there.

"You *are* my brother. Best friend, brother, whatever. And if you don't shut up and go to sleep, you gonna be the best friend soaked with my water gun. You know what, Seth? Sometimes you can say some really stupid stuff, you know that, Seth?" Reggie hadn't shot him with his water gun like he said he would, but they did end up having a massive battle with the goose-down pillows. And they were both punished the next day for the feathers all over the room. Just like brothers.

Seth looked over at his newly married brother. Reggie seemed so contented, so peaceful. This happiness had been a long time coming, Seth knew. Even though Reggie had never had any problems getting the attention of the ladies, he struggled through relationships. It seemed that women became captivated by his height, generous good looks, striking demeanor, and stopped right there. And all of this would happen right around the same time that Reggie would walk away and quit trying. Seth had never understood.

"You and Barbara broke up? Naw, man! I thought you two were gonna hang in there for the duration. What happened?" Seth shoved down the last piece of cheeseburger during one of their late-night White Castle raids.

"Seth, women are peculiar. I can't be myself around them. It's not Barbara's fault—she was great. But women ask so many questions, and they want you to actually give them answers." Reggie played with his fries, which had long since turned cold and nasty, eventually popping one in his mouth.

"Yeah, man. It's called communication. It's this really odd behavior that girls like to engage in, you know?"

"Oh, shut up. You don't understand." Reggie threw a fry at him and missed. "I guess I just want a woman who will *know*—know who I am and what I need without my having to spell every little thing out to her. You know what I mean? Something like our relationship."

"We've been friends a long time, Reggie. You can't expect a woman to just be able to jump into your head like that. Besides,"—Seth leaned in close for the whisper—"you don't *want* a woman roaming around your head like that." Seth had exaggerated a wink at Reggie and Reggie had laughed. As the years went by, Reggie was the one with more first dates under his belt. Reggie was the one who never seemed close to finding that special someone.

Until Crystal.

It wasn't long after Reggie had begun The Imani Group. He had created the consulting company in response to an assignment in one of his marketing classes for his M.B.A.; it was originally started as an opportunity to bring more local black artists into the Brooklyn Museum's community art school. Reggie had always been vocal about the museum; how all of its magnificent resources sat right in the middle of a diverse neighborhood yet overlooked the artistic diamonds in its own backyard. The formation of The Imani Group allowed him the opportunity to offer organizations and companies the means to make the changes they had all been "meaning" to make for so long: the means to bring black folks in.

Reggie met with the museum administrators and convinced them that by catering more to their neighborhood residents, the museum would see increased membership and greater support by more segments of their community. It worked. As a result of Reggie's consultations, the museum experienced unprecedented growth, adding more people of color to both the museum's membership as well as to its staff. The nature of the exhibits diversified as well, from the Saturday sidewalk chalk art contests for the children to the canvas graffiti exhibition that was lauded by critics nationwide. The community warmly embraced the museum that now acknowledged their existence and cultural contributions. And The Imani Group got a ton of positive press and more work than Reggie could handle in four lifetimes.

It was a sweet and glorious beginning. Crystal had been hired by the museum first as a part-time art instructor, then as an assistant curator for special projects. Reggie had sat in on both hiring panels without a vote, to provide unofficial input. He had been impressed and so had she. They were engaged in less than a year.

"I'm sorry about how I handled the ring thing, Reggie." Seth pushed his glasses up on his nose, then shoved his hands back into his pants pockets.

Reggie chuckled, relaxed. "I know. I was stressed and I know I overreacted. Sorry about that."

Seth ignored his apology. "Embarrassing! I felt like an idiot. But more than that, I was real worried that I had lost you as a friend." Seth glanced tentatively at Reggie, who was looking at the pavement, smiling.

"Nope. Wouldn't happen."

"Well, you sure did give me a scare. The thought of losing our friendship really unnerved me, you know? I mean, I could've replaced the ring. . . ."

"You could not, you lying dog." And they both laughed easily.

"Reggie? How do you think your being married is gonna affect our friendship? You ever think about that?"

"Nope. Never thought about it." Reggie smiled.

"I mean, suppose Crystal says she doesn't want us hanging out any-more . . ."

"Nope. Wouldn't happen."

"Happens all the time, my brother. All the time." Seth looked off in the distance. The DJ was playing the Isley Brothers. A slow jam. "She ain't never liked me."

"She likes you fine. You worry too much. Stop."

"Yeah, I do," Seth said, unconvinced and unconvincing.

Reggie stuck his elbow in his side. "I saw you slip the keyboard player your card. Ever the consummate professional at work."

Seth laughed. "Guilty as charged. Opportunity is opportunity. And hey, guess what? I checked out that lead at that production company I was telling you about. They listened to my demo and if everything is everything, looks like I'm going to be producing an R&B version of one of their jingles pretty soon."

"That's great news, man! Today: freelance producer; tomorrow: who knows?"

"Yeah, but you know, there was something pretty funky going on over there. I heard some conversation about a sister who left rather . . . abruptly. I didn't get any of the details and I didn't ask. Figured I'd go in there and do my job and get the heck out while they're still paying black folks."

Reggie shook his head. "Naw, see, that's the type of attitude that keeps us two steps behind. We *have* to know what happened. And we *have* to get involved."

Seth sucked his teeth and rolled his eyes at him. "Nope. *You* have to know what happened. And *you* have to get involved. That is *your* cause and the nature of *your* business. I ain't Jesse Jackson. I just have to go in there and do my job and wait for my check to clear."

"And what about the sister?"

"I don't know her. She probably did something stupid and militant. Probably walked in there wearing forty pounds of beads on the ends of braids and shouted 'Black Panthers Unite! Power to the People!' to a bunch of white folks who couldn't give a good damn. Whatever it was, I'm not getting involved, okay?"

"You're wrong. You know that, don't you?"

"You have your mission and I have mine. I'm trying to make my way in the world just like you."

"No, Seth, not 'just like me.' I know it's hard to stand by what's right. And look at me now: It's not only me out there on the front lines now; I have to think about my wife."

Seth rubbed his neck. "Oh yeah, rub it in. You know, I'll probably never get married."

"You just got to find the right woman. The perfect woman for you is out there somewhere."

Yeah, Seth thought, standing there weeping and running into the bathroom.

"Reggie, how come I'm just meeting Lauren? Hmm? Why is that?"

Reggie laughed and stopped walking. "Now, why is it that I say something about 'the perfect woman' and Lauren drops into the conversation, like she's on a parachute or something? Hmm? Tell me *that*! Truth be told, I been hiding her from your raggedy apolitical behind." Seth laughed and gave Reggie their trademark wink. Reggie became serious. "She's a good woman, Seth. Don't dog her."

"Reggie! I'm crushed!"

"You know what I'm talking about, my brother. Save her for the finale," Reggie said as he pointed in the direction of the festivities. "Do what you got to do with the other girlies; save Lauren for the finale. When she's ready. When you're ready."

"Now! Now! Now! I'm ready now! Bring her on!"

Reggie ran his hand over his glistening hair. "You are not, you lying dog."

And they laughed and hugged and joked. Just like old times.

"Time for me to get you back to your fairy tale, Prince Charming."

Reggie grew serious again. "And I want the name of that production company."

"I'll give it to you when *and only when* I finish the work and get the check. Come on, I don't want Crystal thinking you ran away and I had to hunt you down to bring you back."

Reggie shook his head. "Crystal knows I'm in it for life. I sure do love that woman."

"Yeah, yeah, yeah. I know. Glad you're happy, blah, blah, blah. Now, get your ass over yonder and get yourself changed so I can take that monkey suit to the tux place in the morning. Oh, and by the way, there is one little detail that I failed to share with you."

"What now?"

"I'm keeping the deposit!"

"You are not, you lying dog."

Seth laughed and led their way back to the ballroom. "Arf."

The mood at the reception was much mellower than it had been when they stepped out. People were quietly coupling off. The little fur heads were draped sleepily over chair backs. Some women held their shoes and danced barefoot. The older men had removed their ties and opened the top button on their heavily starched white ruffled shirts. Some of the little girls had their heads on the tables, hair ribbons untied; some of the older kids were running around on the dance floor; another group was going from table to table collecting unused matchbooks and printed napkins. It looked as if everyone had seen a good time and was all tuckered out. Reggie spotted his beautiful bride on the patio dancing with her dad. He strolled behind them silently, tapped his father-in-law on the shoulder, and politely cut in. Seth watched them from the lobby.

"Baby, where you been? Missed you." Crystal smiled a pout at her husband.

"Taking care of some last-minute business with my best man."

"Oh, your best man. Are you two all right now? Everything okay?"

"Everything is wonderful, baby. Just wonderful."

Reggie held her gently and they danced: his eyes never opened, her eyes never closed.

When the song ended, Reggie took Crystal by the hand and silently led her up the marble staircase to their private dressing room.

Seth walked to the doorway of the Grand Ballroom and looked around for Lauren. She wasn't dancing and she wasn't at the bar. He spotted MommaPatti and walked up behind her.

"May I have this dance?" Seth whispered in her ear.

"Oh my gracious, you startled me, Seth! Don't do that!" He extended his hand and took her onto the dance floor.

"Well, this is definitely the first time I have danced to a song in *this* language!" She chuckled, her eyes twinkling at the nonsensical lyrics of "Double Dutch Bus."

"First time for everything, don't you think?" Seth smiled at her. She smiled back.

"You and Lauren seem to have hit it off, Seth. Am I right about that?" MommaPatti had never been known for being coy about obtaining information.

"I was asking your son why it is that I'm just meeting that young lady."

"And he said?" MommaPatti asked smugly.

"Well, let's just say that he was saving the best for last."

MommaPatti nodded her agreement. "Yes, indeed, Seth. Yes, indeed." And they danced without speaking for the rest of the song.

"She puzzles me, though."

MommaPatti nodded, looking distant, looking concerned. "She needs a patient man, Seth. Can you be a patient man?"

"Of course."

"Good. She likes you a lot, you know. I know it's too soon to be saying that, but I know my niece. She likes you."

"I like her, too." MommaPatti smiled and patted Seth on the arm.

"I think things are just about ready to wind up here. I'd better go and make sure everything is in order." MommaPatti smiled again and patted, patted. "You take care of yourself, Seth. Go find Lauren; she's around here somewhere. And remember, patience is the key."

Seth walked over to the champagne punch fountain and filled a glass. As he stood there and sipped, he saw in the far corner of the darkened ballroom a round table with two people seated: Lauren and some dude who was steady talking. He fought the urge to run over to them, yank Lauren away, and pop the dude in the mouth; instead Seth made the rational decision to observe her behavior. Simply watching how she responded to such a determined man could tell him so much.

Lauren was polite. She smiled at the man, nodded at times, gave him short responses. She didn't gesture much; she didn't play with the glass in front of her. Her body was turned away from the man. The more he turned toward her, the more she turned away. Shutting him out. Seth decided to ask her for the next dance.

As the music ended and the couples left the dance floor, Seth placed his empty glass on a table near the fountain. Not taking his eyes off Lauren, he began slowly walking toward her table. And as the first notes of Stevie Wonder's "Ribbon in the Sky" began to fill the air, Lauren looked up and saw him walking toward her. She smiled at him, oblivious to the man who continued to talk to her.

"Aw, naw, my brother, I have things completely under control over here." The man stood and addressed Seth.

Seth ignored him. "May I have this dance, young lady?" Seth smiled at Lauren and she stood and walked to him.

"Nice meeting you," Lauren offered to the man as she walked into Seth's waiting arms.

They danced with eyes closed. Seth held her tightly around her waist and Lauren offered no resistance. At times, Seth could feel Lauren humming parts of the song. Her being vibrated and Seth accepted her energy. And when he leaned over and placed a feathery kiss on Lauren's neck, he thought he felt her moan.

"I'm sorry about what happened out there," Lauren spoke cautiously, as though she had rehearsed these words over and over. "I want to explain what happened to me, but I can't right now."

Patience.

"It's okay. Tell me when you can. Or don't tell me at all. I'm just happy to have met you . . . to be dancing with you right now."

"And that's enough?" she asked.

Patience.

"It's enough for me."

They danced for a while in silence: she, humming melody; he, wondering about the darkness that had clouded her so quickly.

"So where'd you go? I was looking for you after . . . after I—"

He cut her off. "I was outside talking best-man stuff."

"You left me alone too long, Seth."

Her response caught him off guard. "I shouldn't do that?" Seth pulled away slightly in order to see her expression. But Lauren pulled Seth in closer to her before responding.

"No, Seth. You shouldn't do that."

"But what about the strong, independent, black woman who doesn't want to be smothered with love?"

Lauren looked around her. "Is she here? Show me that hussy. I have a bone to pick with her!" Seth poked her side and Lauren laughed The Laugh.

"You are too much; you know that?"

"I'm also clairvoyant; did you know *that*?"

"Oh, do tell, Madame Lauren . . ."

"Yes, I have this gift. I am given glimpses of the future."

"Well, please share!"

"Mmm, I predict that in mere moments, this song is going to end. The cleanup crew is going to be sent out to move us all along. Reggie and Crystal are going to wave their good-byes and ride off into the moonlight."

The song ended. Holding hands, Seth and Lauren took a step apart.

"Romantic! You're doing pretty well, so far. Please, go on."

Lauren looked deeply into Seth's eyes and then quickly looked away. "It gets a bit fuzzy here," she whispered.

"Well," Seth said as he put his arm around Lauren's waist and walked in the direction of the lobby, "let me see if I can help you out."

"You have the gift, too?"

"But of course. I predict that MommaPatti is going to ask you if you need a ride. But you are free to tell her no."

"Then how am I supposed to get home?"

He turned and faced her, whispered gently in her ear, "May I take you home, Lauren? Please?" Seth looked down at their hands, which were still entwined. So beautiful.

"I'd like that, Seth."

And just as Lauren had predicted, the cleaning crew was sent out in droves to help the crowd move along. Folks were searching for shoes and purses, matchbooks that now held telephone numbers, rice and bubbles to be showered ceremoniously upon the newlyweds. A line of white limousines graced the outside entrance; a red carpet had been rolled out. Lauren and Seth made their way to the front of the crowd.

"Good-bye, everybody! We love you! Good-bye! And thank you!" Crystal shouted out to the crowd of tired, but smiling, family and friends. The crystal buttons on her beige silk dinner suit caught and reflected the light as she moved.

"Thank you all for coming! It wouldn't have been the same without you!" Reggie waved and helped his wife into the first limousine.

"Seth . . . ," Reggie started to speak, but Seth held up his hand to silence him.

"I know, my brother. The finale."

"Yes. The finale." And they hugged.

After the newlyweds had taken off, and the parents had gone home, Seth turned to Lauren and took her hand, leading her into one of the final white limousines in the lineup.

"I wasn't expecting a *limousine* ride home, Seth." Lauren looked around the luxurious surroundings skeptically.

"Neither was I. Sometimes life truly exceeds our expectations." Seth smiled and remained still as Lauren nestled against his shoulder.

Patience.

Five

NIA

Nia didn't need to be a depressed woman anymore. She didn't want to be a victim. As she stood at the top of the stairs outside St. Augustine's, the sunshine warmed her skin and gave her hope. She looked into the crowd of people on the sidewalk and found an unexpected smile coming from a woman who walked by briskly to catch the light at the corner. It was surprises like that that told her all was not lost; life would go on. She descended the stairs quickly and started walking, rediscovering the bounce in her step. Even her backpack felt lighter, less of a burden. And her head felt clearer, calmer. It was amazing, Nia thought, how just a moment of writing could make her feel so much better. No, the writing was a part, an integral part, but this feeling was deeper than the writing alone. At that moment, Nia smiled to herself and felt no anguish, no bitterness, no anger, no regret. Nia smiled and knew she would be all right.

She walked into a small corner luncheonette a few blocks south of St. Augustine's and looked around for a pay phone. The guy behind the counter directed her to the back wall. Nia set her backpack down and dialed the number from heart.

Rome's extension just rang and rang, four times total. Nia hung up the phone promptly after the fourth ring; she didn't want to leave a message on his voice mail. What was she going to say anyway? Hi Rome, I got fired, can we meet for dinner after you get off work? No, things like that were better said directly. Nia decided to give him a call later on, after she figured he would have returned from lunch.

Nia dialed a second number. This time it only rang twice.

"Yeah."

"Hi, Grace." Nia was always caught off guard by the different ways that woman answered her phone. It always varied, but it was never a standard hello. She said that she liked to keep people guessing, hated being predictable. It was only one of the ways in which she and Grace differed: Whereas Grace loved the element of surprise, Nia said that she always wanted to be aware, always wanted to be on solid footing. Always wanted to know and be sure.

"Hi yourself . . ."

Nia could hear the sound of paper tearing in the background. "You working?"

"Chil', I am *always* working! The joys of being self-employed, you know what I mean? Gotsta keep that money aflowing, you know what I'm saying? Why? You got something in mind?"

"Yeah. Come on out of your den and meet me for lunch."

"Your treat?"

Nia laughed. "Yes, Grace. My treat."

"You betcha. Where you wanna meet?"

Nia looked at her watch. It would take Grace a good thirty minutes to make it down here to the East 40s from the Upper West Side. "Meet me at Clothes for My Closet."

"Girl, *tell me* you are not going to buy more stuff. I swear, you have more clothes than anyone on this earth . . . and why aren't you at work anyway?"

"Shut up and get here. I'll give you the scoop when you show up, woman. Bye."

"Damn. Okay. Bye."

Nia had to laugh. As abrasive as Grace sounded, she really was a softie inside. Nia had spent a lot of time over the years trying to penetrate that hard exterior, trying to get to the softness of the woman beneath the shell. Sometimes she wondered why she even bothered. She saw something in her, beyond the coarseness, that others hadn't stuck around to see. And they had found a certain level of closeness over the years. There were gaps in their knowledge of each other, for sure; it was as though they innately sensed their personal boundaries, never treading beyond some undefined level of safety. They had never been the type of friends who would share their every thought with each other, but what they did share had been honest and genuine. Grace would speak her mind and give Nia truth when she needed it, and Nia tried to give her the same kind of space and support.

Grace had always been like that, as long as Nia could remember. Even the way in which they had met was a testimony to Grace's ability to speak her mind.

"So why you reading Sidney Sheldon? You wearing that uniform, so I *know* you ain't reading it for school," Grace had asked her seatmate that morning on the Flatbush Avenue bus. She adjusted the brim of her white baseball cap.

Nia looked up at the girl who had intruded upon her moment. "I'm reading Sidney Sheldon because I like Sidney Sheldon." And Nia returned to reading her book.

"Well, you should be reading something black. Like *The Autobiography of Malcolm X* or *Gorilla, My Love*. Something like that." Grace cracked her gum loudly in Nia's ear.

"Do you mind?" Nia rolled her eyes at the girl, who seemed unfazed by Nia's attitude.

"Naw, I don't mind. But you still ought to be reading some of our people's work. That's all I'm saying."

It was obvious to Nia that this girl was not going to leave her alone and let her have a moment's peace. And since the ride had become full of bumps and jolts anyway, curving around Grand Army Plaza on what felt like two wheels at best, Nia decided she would engage this girl in conversation to entertain herself. She shut her book loudly and held it on her lap.

"So what was the last book *you* read?" Nia leaned back against the window in order to check out her expression. She folded her arms and crossed her legs—away from Grace.

"Right now I'm reading through the works of Richard Wright."

"For school?" Nia asked sarcastically.

"Nope. Because I like him."

"Oh! So *you* can read Richard Wright because *you* like him, but *I* can't read Sidney Sheldon because *I* like him. Do I have this straight?" Nia made a face at Grace and Grace laughed.

"Okay, I get your point. But get mine, too. Read some of your people and not just what 'they' tell you is good"—Grace stuck out her hand—"and the name is Grace. Grace George."

"Hi there, Grace George. My name's Nia Benson. Nice to meet you . . . I think." And they shook hands, sized each other up, and smiled. Friends of the most challenging kind.

They had been on the friendly offensive with each other since that very first day.

Nia hung up the phone, repositioned her backpack, and walked the three blocks down and one block over to get to the crowded entrance of Clothes for My Closet. Grace had been right and Nia knew it; Nia absolutely did not need any more clothes. Especially now that she had no income. But clothes were her passion, her most visible vice, and when she needed a lift, nothing could beat a survey of the coming season's fashion offerings. Some folks drank themselves into a stupor, others got high on illegal drugs. But give Nia a pure silk blouse with panache and she was good to go. Nia stepped inside.

On Fridays the store was usually packed all day, with women taking advantage of the payday specials. Today was no exception. The speakers were blaring Kool & The Gang singing "Get Down on It," and it helped to emphasize the spring in Nia's step. She hummed along and created sexy mental outfits as she went from rack to rack. She was determined to look only—well, maybe try on a little something if it was on sale *and* in her size—but that was it. By that time, Grace would be here anyway, telling her how she was buying into the capitalist political structure that was designed to oppress their people and keep them enslaved to the white blah blah blah. *I deserve this*, Nia thought, and took an armful of treasured finds into the first available dressing room.

"I know you're in there, Miss I-Don't-Have-No-Self-Control." Nia had to stifle a laugh when she heard her buddy outside the dressing room door.

"Hello to you, too." Nia opened the door and stepped out. The floor of the dressing room was a sea of clothes.

"I know you ain't leaving that room like that. Your mama raised you better," Grace hollered after Nia as she walked toward the cashier.

"It was like that when I went in there. And I had a hard enough time just putting my own stuff back on the hangers. Gimme a break."

Nia pulled out a credit card and handed it to the woman behind the register. The total made Grace gasp, then let out a thin whistle.

"Damn, Nia, that's half my rent payment!" The cashier glanced up, first at Grace, then at Nia.

"Good thing she's not my mother, or you might be out of a sale," Nia spoke to the cashier and laughed, breaking the tension.

"You ladies have a good day," the cashier said, shaking her head and smiling.

"You complain too damn much," Nia mumbled, walking past Grace toward the door.

"Can't help it. I'm hungry. And besides, you need a voice of reason when you come into this place."

Maybe she did and maybe she didn't, Nia thought, but once again she hadn't asked the woman for her two cents. This was the part of Grace that she liked least, the caustic, opinionated side that insisted on telling her the right and wrong way of living. Grace didn't even seem aware that she was doing it anymore, just flinging those words out like boomerangs. And just like boomerangs, they wounded the sender most, causing people to run from her and invest their energies in other, less volatile individuals for friends.

Nia had stayed. She had seen through Grace's tough girl exterior and she had stayed. Because even though there were parts of her that Nia found hard to deal with, she knew that if she ever needed a friend, when it was a matter of choosing to go through the fire or walking away, Grace would be in her corner. So a lot of Grace fell to the outside of their friendship, overlooked and tacitly accepted.

Nia didn't say anything. She figured the pain of one more credit card bill had been a small price to pay to feel better about the situation, not to mention *look* better. An hour or two with an analyst would have set her back just as much, and she wouldn't have had the thrill and satisfaction of a new wardrobe.

"You want sushi?" Nia turned to Grace with a tired smile.

"Sure. Sounds great."

The two women walked quietly down the busy street, through the dimly lit entrance of a small Japanese restaurant. They were seated immediately at a booth toward the rear and enacted their personal ritual of pouring tea for each other.

"Okay, so what's the deal?" It was more a statement than a question that Grace posed. She leaned back sideways in the booth, taking up space.

"I got fired this morning." Nia placed her hands around the teacup, letting the warmth of the liquid soothe her hands. She inhaled the green tea's soothing aroma.

"Get out of here! Tell me you're lying—you *are* lying, aren't you?" Grace sat there with her mouth hanging open.

Nia let her lips form a smile that was supported by neither her emotions nor her other facial features. "Not lying. Fired. Jonathan told me to come back after hours and get my stuff—said it would be easier that way. But hell, I ain't going back to that place."

And then Nia proceeded to tell Grace all the gory details of the morning. Here it was, not yet three o'clock, and already it seemed so long ago that all this drama had taken place. Much of the bite in Nia's recollection had been replaced with resignation; much of her anger had been replaced with sadness.

"Oh no, Miss Kum-by-yah. You are not going to sit here and just matter-of-factly tell me that that white girl just screamed and yelled and called you a *niggah* . . . and you're just accepting everything like it's all right! Tell me that isn't what I'm hearing here! Correct me, please!" Grace leaned across the table and still raised her voice.

"Um, could you lower your voice, thank you? I considered filing a lawsuit, Grace. Actually went by a law office to look into the possibilities. But I don't know . . ." Nia played with the top to the teapot, held up her hand to get the waiter's attention.

"Considered. You *considered*—well, there's a commitment to justice for you."

"Grace, I'm not sure that I want to spend the next year or two or five tied up in a legal battle with Feinstein Films. Jonathan gave me a very decent severance check, so I'm thinking that maybe I'll just let things go—"

"He bought you off, in other words."

"Bought me off? No. He gave me what is just and due. He gave me what is mine."

Grace laughed loudly, throwing her leg across the bench of the booth. "Nia, please. This is 1981. When that man gave you the boot, he took away all notions of you getting what was due you. You ain't got no job, right? And with your boy Reagan in the White House, looks like you're not gonna have such an easy time of finding another one."

Nia pulled out the check, waved it in front of Grace's face. Grace grabbed it, held it long enough to read the amount. She squinched up her face and rolled her eyes at Nia.

"And that's supposed to make everything better? Yeah, it's a nice piece of change, but how long do you think that's gonna last? And when it comes time for you to get another job, what about all the time you lost? White girl is gonna have just that much more work experience under her belt—and you up here flashing zeros in my face, thinking you the woman. Give me a break. Don't be so ghetto."

"I'm going to go do temp again. I liked it when I did it before. I ain't concerned."

"Temp work doing what? Moving up in your field? Or doing more of what you were doing?"

"Temp work making money so I can pay my rent! I know it's not a long-term solution; I'm not stupid. I'll be sending out résumés and looking for other stuff at the same time. I'll make it work."

"You stupid if you're gonna take that check and let bygones be bygones."

Nia glared at her friend, who glared back at her. "So you're saying I should run and cash this check and *still* sue Feinstein? Are you out of your mind? If I do that, I can just kiss any thoughts of having a career in this city good-bye. Yeah, you make things sound so neat and clear-cut, but this is not some utopia. There are other things to consider here."

"Other things like what? Suppose Rosa Parks had decided that she didn't want to hassle the ramifications of staying in her seat? Or suppose the SCLC decided to simply support maintaining a *better* status quo? Nia, I don't think you have a choice here. You *have* to sue."

"No, Grace, I don't."

The waiter appeared at the table and cordially took their orders. The women avoided looking at each other.

"So you could just walk away and let her continue living her life? You could let her call the next black woman the same?"

"Grace, not everyone in this world is as militant as you are!"

"Well, they sure should be! Especially those who lose their jobs for being called a *niggah*. I mean, tell me if I'm wrong, but that's essentially what you're telling me, right?" Grace's hazel eyes flashed in anger.

"There is more than one way to fight a battle, Grace."

"Nia, I'm not even sure you're aware of the war!"

The waiter brought elaborate sushi plates to the table, bowed ceremoniously from the waist, and wished them an enjoyable meal.

"Whatever you say," Nia said, pouring soy sauce into a tiny ceramic dish and spilling some on the tablecloth.

"Whatever indeed. You think about that mess some more. You think about the larger scheme of things," Grace responded.

They ate their combination plates silently until Grace took a bite of her tuna roll.

"Ooo, mama, this is *good*!" Grace and Nia looked at each other and started laughing all over the place.

"Woman, sounds like you talking about something that ain't even *on* your plate."

Grace smiled. "Well, speaking of sex . . ."

Nia paused. "We weren't, but go ahead . . . yes?"

"Girl, please. There's a new art director over at *Black Business* magazine. Met him the other day. Tall, super dark, semi-sweet . . ."

"Shoot, Grace, that's what you said about the last morsel you tried to snare. What was that dude's name . . . Boris? Something like that—"

"His name was Gordon. Where the hell did you get *Boris*, woman? Anyway, continue your lie . . ."

"—and you said that *he* was 'semi-sweet' . . . yeah, right. Right up until the moment his boyfriend started calling you and harassing you, talking 'bout 'that's *my* man, honey, now you go on and getchur own.' " Nia snapped her fingers and worked her neck, diva style.

"Now, you know that ain't right, Nia. We did *not* have to go"—

Grace made a circular motion with her right arm, snapping her fingers—"there. But yeah, he was a sweetie, too."

Nia smiled, smoothed her hair into her bun. "So, he's that wonderful, huh?"

"Oooo, weeee, yes! And you mark my words, Nia, I'm gonna have me some of *that* sweetness." Grace adjusted the shoulder straps on her overalls.

"Um, Grace"—Grace looked up from her plate—"have you considered a little revamping of the ol' wardrobe? Might help."

"Haven't given it a thought. I'm strictly jeans, overalls, painter's pants. T-shirts, sweatshirts, sneakers. And if it's a good day, earrings. If not? Baseball cap."

"Do I dare go out on a limb and ask if you've ever tried the lipstick I gave you?"

"I don't like wearing that stuff. We women are incredibly beautiful just as we are. We don't need the products of men to make us attractive. And I don't like nail polish, powders, potions, none of that stuff. You see, all of those concoctions were designed to keep us oppressed, designed to make us feel inferior as women, like we need those things to be . . ." Nia watched Grace's lips move but tuned out her words completely. She thought back to the first time she had tried to hook Grace up, back in high school.

It was right before Grace had transferred into Baxter Academy, September of the tenth grade. The fall reception dance. Nia had known a bunch of the kids from her ninth grade there. Some of them were okay, some were borderline stuck-up, but all of them were pretty decent toward Nia. Everybody was going to unofficially meet up with somebody else once they got to the dance, someone who would agree to dance with you just in case no one else asked, although they weren't officially called dates. Kind of like a safety net. Friends looking out for friends.

Well, since Nia had known that Grace didn't know the guys and the guys didn't know her, she arranged for Tommy Haven to be Grace's standby guy. Grace had agreed, reluctantly, after a massive amount of persuasion. But Nia just wasn't prepared for the drama that would ensue.

"Mom, this is the place; this is where Grace lives." Nia pointed out of the Mustang's passenger window, "758 . . . that's the number." And Mrs. Benson had pulled over and allowed Nia to jump out and go into the lobby where Grace and Nia had agreed to meet.

But when Nia walked into the lobby, Grace sat there wearing white painter's pants and a blue sweatshirt, dirty white sneakers with writing all over them, and a baseball cap turned backward. Nia looked down at her own lavender chiffon dress with the soft pink sash and back at Grace in disbelief.

"Grace! Aren't you coming to the dance? How come you aren't ready?"

"I'm ready! Let's go!" And Grace hopped off the bench beaming and bounded for the door.

"But you can't go like *that*! You don't even look like a *girl*!"

Grace stopped midstep and turned to Nia. "I don't believe you even said that."

"This is a dance, Grace. Haven't you ever been to a dance?"

Grace glared at her friend. "Yeah, Nia. I've been to a *dance*. That's why I wore my sneakers, so I can dance all night long and be comfortable, instead of wearing something that's gonna make my feet hurt and my attitude suck."

Nia kept thinking about Tommy Haven, how he was going to be there wearing a new navy blue suit expecting to see a "cute, light-skinned girl with hazel eyes and dimples and sandy brown hair down to there"—the description she had given of Grace. She wondered what was worse: to picture him being stood up or to see him standing at the punch bowl with Grace looking like one of the guys.

"So, what are you saying, Nia? You embarrassed to be seen with me? I don't look *right* enough for you?" But before Nia could answer, Mrs. Benson walked into the lobby and gasped at the sight of Grace.

"Oh dear, Grace, sweetheart, is everything all right? Are you locked out of your apartment?" Grace just shook her head and walked back upstairs, muttering something about feeling sick to her stomach and not wanting to go anymore.

Nia smiled at the bittersweet memory, reached over and picked up the last of her shrimp tempura. She had long since given up the battle. Grace had her own style, her own way of looking at the world in general and the realm of romance in particular. And while she was a truly beautiful woman visually, Grace did nothing to enhance her femininity in traditionally acceptable ways.

"You haven't heard a damn thing I've said for the past twenty minutes." Grace laughed, shook her head, and slammed down her chopsticks.

Nia smiled. For all of their differences, Grace knew her better than anyone else and loved her just as fiercely.

"I heard the important parts, Grace."

Grace stretched her arm out across the top of the booth and took up lots of space. "Which were?"

Nia leaned across the table and whispered, "I heard *you*."

Six

SETH

Seth sat on his sofa, sipped his coffee, and smiled. He had intentionally waited a week before playing the home movie of the jazz trio that had played at Reggie and Crystal's reception. He knew how good they sounded there, with all the beautiful feelings in the air, but wondered how they would sound without any visuals. So he had turned on the projector and left the room.

The Garrison Walters Trio sounded just as magnificent and polished as they had in the Grand Ballroom of Gramercy Manor. Seth picked up the phone and dialed Garrison.

"Hello?"

"Hello there, this is Seth Jackson. I'm trying to reach Garrison Walters?"

"Yeah, this Garrison," the sleepy voice yawned. "Oh, sorry about the yawn, man. Had a late gig last night."

"No problem, my brother. I met you at the wedding at Gramercy Manor last weekend?"

The phone was silent for a moment. "Oh, yeah, Rex's boy's wedding, right? Wait, wait . . . I remember you! You were the dude who lost the ring, right?" Seth made a face into the phone receiver. Maybe he didn't really want to work with this guy. Garrison chuckled.

"Yeah, you remember. And you remember correct. Anyway, I was wondering if you guys would be interested in doing some work with me. I'm a producer."

He thought he heard Garrison chuckle, but he could have been mistaken. "A producer?"

"Yeah, man, a producer. And I like the way you cats sound."

This time Seth was sure the man had laughed.

"Uh, did I just say something funny? I don't think I did. . . ."

"Man, I'm sorry, I really am. It's just that . . . well . . ."

Seth was getting hot, pacing back and forth, stomping out a path in his living room. "Naw, go 'head, man, spit it out. Say what's on your mind. I want to hear it, 'cause I'm serious about this and you seem to find some serious humor in the situation. Now, I realize that you don't know a whole lot about me—"

Garrison cut him off. "Man, what's a guy like you gonna do for some cats like us? You got money? You got the money to produce us? You got the connections in the business to call somebody up and get us a deal? You hear what I'm saying? We ain't looking for nobody to 'produce' us. We ain't looking to be stars no more. We been down that road a time or two, believe me. And we like where we are right now just fine, thank you very much."

Seth considered ending the call. This wasn't going at all the way he had envisioned it. He thought he'd call the man up and the dude would be grateful that someone was interested in furthering his career. He wasn't prepared to answer the man, wasn't prepared to face the fact that no, he didn't have any money, and no, he didn't have that kind of access to people in the industry who could make the final decision to get this group a deal. He closed his eyes and took a deep breath.

"I hear you, man. And to be honest with you, I have to tell you that I can't make that kind of magic happen for you overnight. But I sure did like what I heard. Everybody who was there liked what they heard. And I can't stop thinking that there must be something I can do to get more people to hear you guys."

"Now that's a new take on an old song."

"What are you talking about?" Seth sat on his couch and watched the film of the wedding guests swaying and smiling.

"Honesty. Most cats make a whole lot of promises and then can't deliver squat. I appreciate it."

"Isn't going to help you *or* me for me to sit up here and lie to you."

Garrison yawned again. "So you're a producer . . ."

"Well, I do some production here and there. I'm a behind-the-scenes kind of man. I managed a group once, back in college, and the bug bit me. Do a little managing now, wrote some music reviews that got published. Worked as a roadie for the Stylistics a couple of summers ago. I love the business and I try to make my way—"

"Ahhh, a man who wears many hats. Good thing to do, too, keeps your options open."

"That it does. I like new experiences. Like learning new things. Too easy to get replaced in this world when there's only one thing you can do."

Garrison laughed. "Now, I don't know that I'm gonna go all the way to saying that. I do one thing: play piano—and I do it well. Ain't worried about being replaced because ain't no one out here can play the same way I do."

"See, that's where you're wrong. You say that all you do is play piano. But I was watching you. Yeah, you were playing piano, but you were handling the business, you were announcing the songs—all of that. And you didn't lose your cool all night long. That takes skills, you know? So you guys play around the island a lot?"

"We play maybe one weekend a month, wherever we can. Wish it was more, but this is just part-time for all of us. The other two cats got regular jobs; me, I'm retired from the post office, so I have more flexibility. But we take the gigs as they come, take the ones we want to take and leave it be."

"So let me put on my agent hat for you. I find you guys work, get you some opportunities, maybe even look for the record deal—things like that."

"And in return, we sign our lives over to you? Man, no offense, but I been all through that end of the music business hustle. And you know what I've learned? I've learned that life is much simpler just doing the local gigs for the local money. It ain't the big money, but it's steady, there's no hassle, and you don't have to lose the shirt off your back. You see, young dude, working for a friend like Rex, the fellas know they gonna be *paid* at the end of the night. Naw, I leave that complicated mess alone. We too old to be going for the glitter."

It was unfortunate that cats like Garrison had to go through experiences like that. It made the honest guys like Seth work doubly hard just to prove they were on the up and up. Seth walked over to the projector and turned it off.

"Garrison, let me show you what I can do. No contracts, no signing, no commitment. If I get you a gig, you guys give me ten percent for my troubles. You don't like my work, we go our separate ways. No questions asked. What do you say?"

"No questions asked? You ain't gonna try to bogart on me?"

"Nope. Hassle-free, man. Hassle-free."

"All right. Let's try it. You get us some work and we'll see how things go."

Seth and Garrison exchanged some details and agreed to meet in a few days to discuss strategies. Seth hung up the phone, smiling to himself. Hey, now. Got himself a client. He made a mental note to call Uncle Rex as soon as he could.

Now if he were only that successful with his phone call to Lauren.

Seth walked into the kitchen and decided to refill his coffee cup. He had theoretically been trying to cut down on his caffeine since he was already a mass of energy, but decaf seemed like such a supreme waste of time. He preferred to just decrease the number of cups he drank a day. But even doing that had been a struggle.

He had taken his time about calling her, looking on a nightly basis at the numbers she had written on the cocktail napkin from the wedding. He had gotten so far as to even picking up the phone and dialing the first three numbers, then hanging up and stretching across his bed, watching the reflection of the streetlamp flicker in his mirror. Sometimes it would flicker for hours and remain on. Sometimes it would flicker and then go out for the rest of the night. There was no pattern to its behavior, it wasn't anything he could predict. Just like Lauren. He wasn't sure he needed the challenge.

He was all for understanding a woman—especially a woman who was new to him, a woman he was just trying to feel. Maybe it was the thrill of the chase, the newness, the discovery that beckoned and enticed him most. But he was sensing hassles on the horizon, big ones. Hassles made him want to run, they always did, and part of him was telling him to take the next thing moving out of this potential situation. The other part of him remembered the softness of the side of her cheek, how easily she found the place to rest her body in the crook of his arm, the feel of her lips as he caressed them with his thumb, the way she had wedged tightly into his thoughts. The way a big part of him wanted to protect her from whatever it was that made her act so crazy.

Call her. No, wait. Reggie was right: He's a dog and should leave her alone. Reggie was right: He isn't ready for a relationship with someone like Lauren. Pick up the phone, she likes that Seth vibe. Call her at work. No, at home. Leave her alone. The choices presented themselves over and over and he was no closer to addressing them than he had been days ago. Well, he knew that if he waited too much longer, the decision would probably be made for him. If he didn't call, he would never know. But if he never knew, he would never hold her again. Yeah, but if he didn't hold her again, at least he wouldn't get hurt.

His doorbell rang, twice—the code ring for Sandy.

" 'S open. Come on in," Seth hollered toward the front door, "I'm in the kitchen." Seth heard the door slam and the sound of Sandy's flip-flops slapping the parquet floors.

"Hey man, pour me some of that coffee you got there, smells good, I'm telling you. Just what a woman needs after a night of don't-ask-don't-tell." Sandy shuffled into the kitchen holding her head and plopped down into one of the mismatched chairs around the kitchen table.

"Rough night, chica?" Seth smiled at the grimacing sight of his neighbor. She had not one drop of Latin blood in her, but Seth had started calling her "chica" as a joke and it just stuck. She would tell you in a hot minute that her mom was Chinese and her dad was a proud black man and don't even start with the Latin beat. But as gorgeous as Sandy was, she could look particularly bad the morning after the night before. "And who was the lucky guy?"

"Sheeet. Shut up and pour me some coffee. Black." Seth laughed and poured as instructed.

Sandy lived next door in the other one bedroom on the floor. She was single, too, but Sandy dated a heck of a lot more than Seth had ever wanted. Men were her favorite pastime, no question about it. She was outspoken and blunt; if she didn't like you, you knew it and you knew why, sometimes in two languages. But if she did, then you were family and, well, you knew that, too. He handed her the cup of coffee.

"Seth, what's with the teacup? Can't you look at me and tell that Sandy needs a mugful? Sheeet."

Seth just laughed and sipped his own. "Mind your manners and watch your French. Refills on the house."

Sandy brushed her waist-length curly black hair out of her face. "Something told me that dog was married, Seth. But did I listen? Heck, no."

Seth chuckled. He had learned over the years that you didn't ever ask Sandy questions about her sex life. She would volunteer information in little bits and pieces as she saw fit. Anything other than that was considered intruding by her. Seth considered it his own personal soap opera saga that he could turn off as he saw fit. Click.

". . . so there we were in the elevator on the way up to his apartment, getting acquainted, if you know what I mean." Sandy smiled and squirmed a little in her seat. "And the elevator door opens and there she is—standing there looking all hurt and all and he's stammering like some ten-year-old schoolboy caught without his homework. Sheeet."

"You pick 'em, Sandy. You have the knack to attract *all* the losers."

"Yeah, Seth." Sandy walked over to the coffeemaker and refilled her cup. "That's because the decent men like you keep telling me no!"

"Sheeet," Seth mocked. They both laughed.

"Yeah, I know you got your little 'streak of freak,' Seth."

But Seth just put his hand in the air and shook his head, backing away. "Naw, I ain't touching that one, chica. Ain't touching that one with a ten-foot pole." They looked at each other and laughed at all the unspoken jokes that could easily have followed Seth's statement.

Seth looked at Sandy and smiled. He had once sought out women like Sandy, the outgoing, carefree, sex-seeking women who didn't pull any punches and let a brother know where he stood at all times. Relationships that had a tendency to be functional, cut and dried. But after a few bouts of having his heart broken, he came to realize that maybe he wasn't only in it for the sex. Maybe there was some deep dark hidden part of him that secretly enjoyed the intimacy, the romance of being in the arms of a woman who truly cared. It had taken him a long time, but Seth had finally learned that he actually *liked* women. Not just having sex with women, but being with them, listening to them, relating to them, understanding them—or at least trying to. Once he realized this, he stopped looking for functional relationships with functional Sandy women. But she sure did make him remember the wild times gone by.

"So Seth . . ." Sandy sipped her coffee, drummed her fingers on the table.

"So what?" Seth was at a loss.

"So, what's her name?"

"Whose name, chica?" Seth thought, sometimes women can be so perceptive.

"This woman who has you thinking serious thoughts. You did recently meet some new woman, right?" Sandy leaned the kitchen chair back on the two rear legs.

"Damn, woman."

"Hey, Seth, Sandy knows these things. Come on, tell Sandy all about it."

"I don't know what you're talking about. But I did just get a new client. Jazz trio." Seth leaned across the table and whispered, "With *no vocalist.*"

"Hey, you think they might gimme a shot?"

Seth shrugged his shoulders. "Let you try out? Beats me. But you know how to work it."

Sandy smiled, tossed her hair seductively. "Oh, don't you wish you knew."

"I'll keep you posted on their gigs. You can show up unexpectedly . . . maybe sit in." Seth stood, leaned against the sink.

"Oh, you know I'll just go and freeze up. But thanks for the looking out. It lets me know you still care." She stared at him, cocked her head to the side, and twirled a wayward lock of hair.

It had gotten way too silent in the room.

"Seth?"

"Hmm?"

"How long are you going to keep running from Sandy?"

Seth always dreaded when the conversation rolled back around to this line of questioning from her. "It wouldn't work, Sandy."

"It wouldn't have to 'work.' It could just 'be.' "

Seth played dumb. Scratched his head. "I don't understand."

"Yes, you do. We're friends, right?" Sandy stood and sashayed her cute little teacup over to the sink.

"Yes, chica. Friends." Seth wanted to walk away: he did, he did, he did.

"So," Sandy whispered as she leaned into him and placed her cup in the sink, "I think we should be . . . friendly."

Desperate times called for desperate measures. Seth was at a delicate crossroads here. He knew he was moments away from proving Reggie right, seconds away from barking "The Lyin' Dog" howl all day long, one nanno-breath away from kissing all his resistance good-bye.

"Her name is Lauren," Seth blurted. He closed his eyes and waited for the storm to pass.

Sandy laughed loudly. "I told you. See, Sandy, absolutely positively knows these things." She turned around, walked back to the table, and plopped down. "So, tell me all about Lauren."

In the past, Seth had never had a problem discussing his relationships with Sandy. She was right; they were friends, close friends, and had shared exciting, painful, and intimate details of their lives with each other. Having Sandy around had been convenient for Seth; it gave him the feminine perspective he lacked, and he appreciated that. But this time he didn't want to share with Sandy. He wasn't sure how he was going to proceed with this relationship, if he was even going to pursue it at all. He really didn't want her input or her opinion or her whatever. But now the truth was out there and Seth felt he had to tell her something.

"I met Lauren at the wedding where I heard the jazz trio."

"That's great, Seth. And is Lauren beautiful?"

Seth wondered how to answer the question. In his eyes Lauren was mighty beautiful. And despite all the rational arguments he had presented to himself, he found himself wanting her, wanting to follow this road, any road, to her. Wanting to even rescue her, if that was what it took. But he knew that this was not what Sandy was trying to find out. And definitely not what she wanted to hear.

"She looks okay."

The answer seemed to have made her happy and Sandy smiled. "Oh, well, that's nice Seth. That's really nice."

Sandy took a step away from Seth, swung her hair around to the front and commenced braiding it into one massive braid. "So have you guys gone out yet?"

"Naw, not yet." Seth looked at the ground. He wondered why this conversation was making him feel so uncomfortable. "Actually, Sandy, I haven't even called her yet."

"What you waiting on, cowboy? How long ago was that wedding? A week? Damn, Sam, she probably forgot about you by now!"

"Forgot about *me*? The debonair delight? Oh, I don't think so!"

"See, that's what I hate about men. They play these silly games, looking at the calendar and all that kind of mess. Now, why couldn't you have just picked up the phone and dialed the digits the moment you got home. Or the next day. Why you got to wait a full seven days before you give her the grand privilege of hearing your lovely voice? That's bull, Seth, and you know it."

"I just didn't want to seem too eager, chica. Wanted to give the memories time to simmer, you catch my drift?"

Sandy just shook her head and looked at Seth like he was pitiful. "I know what you wanted to do. You wanted to give some clown time to move in on your good thing. Sandy knows, Seth. Sandy knows about these things. You don't win the game by sitting on the bleachers."

Seth wondered if maybe Sandy was on to something here. He thought back, remembered the dude at that table trying to get Lauren's attention. She didn't seem happy with his attention, though. He didn't think he had anything to worry about.

"Yeah, I hear what you're saying. But you know, if a woman wants to be with someone, she will, and if she doesn't want to be with someone, she's gonna say no." Seth smiled to himself in satisfaction at his profound revelation.

"You left out one little detail, Einstein." Seth was flattened. "If a woman wants to be with someone who hasn't made any effort to call her or be with her, she gonna do what a woman's gonna do—*if* you catch my drift. Don't go and be counting on your charisma. Yeah, you cute and all. But don't be *counting* on your charisma. Charisma only gets you in the door. The rest is work, work, work."

It made Seth think. "Maybe."

Sandy ignored his indifference. "Okay. Now that that little issue is settled. You're going to call . . . Lauren . . . and ask her out, right? Right. Now, where are you going to take her?"

Seth scratched his head. "I dunno. Dinner and a movie?"

Sandy stood up and stamped her feet. "Dammit, Seth! How you gonna get to know her and talk to her in a movie theater with the sound blasting and popcorn flying everywhere? Hmm?"

She had a point there. Maybe he had been looking at this wrong all along. He thought about Lauren and how exceptional he felt when they were just trying to talk to each other. "Yeah, you're right, but I like the dinner part. The dinner part has romantic potential."

Sandy jumped up and walked over to Seth's record collection, flipping through with purpose. "And where's my Sarah Vaughan? I want my Sarah Vaughan back."

Seth walked down the short hallway to his bedroom. "It's back here. Hold on, I'll get it for you." He walked over to the windows, adjusted the oak blinds. There was just the glow of light cascading through the slots, creating tiny prism beams of color on his sky blue quilted bedspread. He turned on the ceiling fan above his bed and started rummaging through a stack of jazz selections on the floor next to his bureau.

"Seth."

Her voice made him jump and he turned around sharply. "No, Sandy, I said to wait."

"Seth."

The air became thick, you could almost hear the ceiling fan cutting through the possibilities that hovered in the balance. Seth closed his eyes and fought for resolve, searching for the right words to say.

"Sandy, I'm not entertaining in my bedroom. I asked you to wait."

"Seth." And she started walking toward him.

Seth threw the Sarah Vaughan onto the bed and pushed his way past her. "Fine. There you go. Thanks for the loan."

Seth went and sat in the living room. This was so strange. He could think of so many men who would've just jumped at the chance to have such a sexy, vibrant woman just for the asking. An afternoon encounter with no questions and no commitment. What more could a guy want? Seth balled his hand into a fist and pounded the sofa cushion with all the force he could muster.

He could hear the flip-flops coming down the hall, could hear them pause at the entry to the living room. "I'm sorry."

"Yeah, me, too."

The silence was deafening.

"You gonna call her?"

Seth didn't say anything.

"I think you should call her, Seth."

He sighed and shifted.

"Cook dinner for her."

Seth chuckled and blew off her comment.

"I'm serious. Sandy still knows about these things."

Seth just nodded silently without turning around to face her. He heard the flip-flops flapping toward the door.

"And if you need cooking help, I'm here. No games. Hey, I understand—I really do. And if it can't be me, at least one of us on this floor should be happy. Really."

The door creaked open and slammed shut.

Woman Neighbor. Woman Friend. Woman In His House. Woman.

Seth rubbed his temples, trying to unravel the tension that was building. He knew he had just said way too much.

You know, maybe this wasn't such a great idea, getting together today. First, it's silence in the sushi bar and now guilt in the gallery.

Nia muttered under her breath as she fished in her backpack for a tissue. She didn't want Grace to see her cry, especially at what seemed to be nothing in particular. Sure, she had lost her job, but she wasn't feeling angry tears now. Standing around in an art gallery with tears streaming down her cheeks looked weak. She didn't want to have to defend her tears. Truth of the matter was that Nia had simply had enough: reached her emotional limit, been the Strong, Black Woman for just a few hours too many. The least little thing was able to set her off crying and sniffling now.

She stood before a massive canvas adorned with every conceivable shade of blue, thick swirls of acrylics that crested in tips of white, reminding her of waves, turbulent waters. She closed her eyes in front of the expanse and felt herself rocked and swayed by the oceans within her, praying for her personal break from the storm.

"Eh, it's all right. I could do better." Grace tossed the comment out with a flick of her wrist while passing by the eight-by-eight-foot painting, and continued on.

Nia fought the urge to respond to Grace's negativity. At some other time, on some other day, Nia would have rallied 'round Grace and tried to help her to see the positive side of the painting, the beautiful perspective it contained. Being light for Grace helped her to find her own light. But today she had too much darkness in her own sky to illuminate the path for anyone else. Today she needed the elements presented to her as a gift for her own uplifting. She wished for the waves in the painting before her to somehow overtake her life, to consume her pain, to lift her to a place where sky began and dreams dripped liquid like a soothing, cleansing rain.

She wanted to be with Rome.

"Well, I'm ready to ditch this joint. You ready?" Grace took out a filter-free cigarette and a book of matches from her overalls pocket and bopped her way to the gallery door.

Nia took one long, last look at the blueness before her. Such emotion. She didn't know much about art, what constituted a good painting in the eyes of the critics, but this painting moved her. It was as if it knew what she needed and offered it to her in a visual form. She closed her eyes briefly and said a silent thank you for the experience.

"Yeah, I'm ready."

Outside Grace lit her cigarette and took a long drag. "Well dahlin', I really need to get back to the drawing board. Literally. Got to turn in some work in the A.M., and I have a long way to go on it. You heading back to Brooklyn?" Grace talked with the cigarette dangling from the side of her mouth, head cocked to the side, and shoved her hands aggressively into her pockets, looking for change.

"Yeah, but I think I'm going to walk. No rush, you know what I mean?" Nia grimaced and looked off in the distance.

"Yeah, I know. Damn shame. And woman, you think about things while you're off on that walk. If it's back you need, you know I got your back, okay? But don't let those people get away with doing this. If you don't think enough of yourself to file the lawsuit, then think about the next beautiful, intelligent sister who sits at that desk and has to put up with the crap."

Nia continued looking off in the distance and sighed, rolled her eyes.

"I can see I'm making quite an impression on your political sensibilities. Damn shame. Well, call me later. I'm gonna be up, so give me

a call, okay? Maybe we can get together over the weekend, after I finish this project. Oh, man, there's my bus . . . gotta run . . . ciao!"
Grace waved and ran across the street, against traffic, and caught the
uptown bus that had just crossed the intersection.

Nia stood on the corner and watched the bus as it headed uptown
and disappeared in the distance. Sometimes it really was nice to be
alone. Nia had cultivated that ability well over the years: the ability to
be present in the midst of chaos and harried activity and still find quiet
and peace. It had helped her to succeed in school, helped her to study
when her roommates insisted on socializing. It had helped her to survive when her parents had fought in the evenings after work, arguing
violently about bills, neglected responsibilities, and Dad's chicks on
the side. She could always find a corner and a book and escape to
other worlds, find comfort in characters who had problems that un-
doubtedly found resolution and reason at the end of each chapter.
And eventually she had taken up pen and paper and written her way
through the anguish herself. First a moan. A cry. A single plea. Then a
prayer. A poem. And sometimes, peace.

Maybe calling Grace had been a mistake, Nia thought. She really
had not been in the mood to deal with her swagger, to temper all of
her comments with a grain of salt to excuse her arrogance. But perhaps that was the very reason why it was necessary for her to have seen
her at that time. Maybe Nia had to be with her to realize that anger
and sarcasm wasn't what was needed right now.

Maybe now she needed comfort. Understanding. Love.

The time was approaching four-thirty—this day seemed to have
been stretching out forever and she was more than ready for it to end
in a loving way, wrapped inside loving arms. Nia turned decisively and
walked downtown in the direction of Rome's office. She knew that
right now he would be winding up for the day. Or taking a much
needed break if he was still planning on putting in a little overtime.
Rome's schedule was like clockwork. It was one of the things she loved
and hated about him. He was persnickety beyond a fault; if Rome said
he was going to be somewhere or do something at a particular time,
you could bet your last dollar he would be precise. But at the same
time, there was much to be said for spontaneity, and Nia had to admit
that she still sometimes missed the element of surprise. So every once

in a while, Nia had taken it upon herself to inject the unexpected into their relationship and tried to encourage Rome to do the same. She wasn't really great at pulling it off most of the time because it went against her nature. But she tried. That was the important thing: She tried. No, she wouldn't bother to call him again. Occasional surprise, she surmised, is good for the soul.

Roses. Gardenias. Lilacs. Daisies. Tulips. The scents were heady and lulled Nia into the tiny, crowded flower shop several blocks from Rome's office. Nia loved flowers; it was the other indulgence she regularly allowed herself, second only to improving her wardrobe. She never waited for a man to send her a bouquet. If she was in need of the joy that flowers could bring, then she would make the sacrifice and purchase them for herself. Yes, today was definitely a flower day. But instead of buying them for herself, as she usually would, she decided to buy a few stems for Rome. Nia inhaled and blushed. Yes, indeed. Giving or receiving: the pleasure came either way.

Even now, so many years after their first meeting, Rome still had the ability to bring a blush to Nia's face. Nia thought back to the time she met Rome. It was a Thursday, Black History Alliance meetings at the community center had always been on Thursdays. She hadn't really wanted to go in the first place, but she had promised Mr. Shorter that she would, to represent the Brooklyn campus of Baxter Academy. Mr. Shorter was her homeroom teacher, a "righteous brother" as he would say, and would run interference for Nia anytime she needed it. If Nia was late, nine times out of ten Mr. Shorter would let it slide — things like that. So whenever he needed someone to do a little extra work, Nia didn't mind volunteering.

She walked into the boardroom right after her last class and took a seat at the long mahogany table next to Grace.

"Hey, Grace." Nia nudged her as she got herself situated. "Anything worth anything in these meetings?"

"You talking 'bout boys? I know you talking 'bout boys, 'cause that's all you ever talk 'bout. Shoot." And they laughed.

"I'm talking about black history stuff, Grace. Righteous, up with the people, black history stuff. Ain't thinking nothing 'bout no *boys*. The thought ain't even crossed my mind." Nia rolled her eyes at Grace.

Grace leaned over to her and whispered real loud like. "*You are such a liar."* And they continued to giggle and talk about the legs on the junior varsity boys' basketball team.

"Brothers and sisters, welcome to our April meeting of the Black History Alliance. We're going to have some new members with us today. First, we have Nia Benson. Nia is from Mr. Shorter's tenth-grade class, in the Brooklyn academy. Everybody, let's show Sister Benson some love here." Clap, clap, clap. "And then we have, oh, I see the brother is not here yet. Well, it is my understanding that he will be with us soon. Our other new member is Jerome Carrington, a new student from the New York academy. Brother Jerome is a senior. And a transfer. Now, that ought to give you all a topic to start the conversation."

"Transferring in as a senior—now *that's* different," Grace leaned over and whispered to Nia. "Why would anyone want to do that?" Nia shrugged her shoulders and took out her notebook. She'd rather write notes to Grace than disturb the meeting anymore.

And then he appeared.

Jerome Carrington stood at the door, all six feet, three inches of him, smiling slightly and looking extremely comfortable with himself. Grace just about nudged a hole in Nia's side, and Nia returned the pressure. They bit their lips and made giant saucer eyes as they sat there staring at this fine specimen of a high school senior.

"Oh, there he is now, people. Brother Jerome! Just told the membership about you . . . please, have a seat and welcome!"

There was no telling what happened for the rest of the meeting. Nia spent most of the time giving Grace the elbow and attempting to make eye contact with this hunk of fineness from Manhattan. He seemed to be paying one hundred percent attention to what was going on, despite the giggles and blushes and note passing that seemed to have increased since his grand entrance, but Nia heard all the female goings-on. Heard all the whispers and throats being cleared and little feminine hearts thumping. But none of that stopped her imagination from racing way beyond her present surroundings.

She imagined what life would be like to know that this Tootsie Roll–colored guy with the longest lashes she had ever seen—next to that Lawrence-Hilton Jacobs cutie on "Welcome Back, Kotter," of course—was hers, all hers. To have him call her up right after school.

To hear him whisper long and tender good nights to her, good nights that went on and on because neither one wanted to be the first to say good-bye. Maybe to even take her to one of those luscious outdoor concerts in Central Park in the summertime. She could see them now: listening to Deniece Williams singing "That's What Friends Are For," holding hands in the moonlight, lacing fingers, rubbing thumbs. Couldn't get much closer to heaven than that.

The meeting ended and Nia, while having had a wonderful time, had no idea what had been discussed.

"Hi. New guy here. Name's Jerome. What's yours?" Nia stood face-to-face with him, looking down at the ground, trying not to grin, trying not to look stupid or ignorant. "Oh, I'm sorry . . . is something wrong?"

"Oh, no . . . no! My name is Nia." Nia looked up at Jerome and melted in the coziness of his smile.

"Well, good. I didn't want something to be wrong. Being the new person out here, I just didn't know if, well, if . . ." He stammered for the words and looked genuinely embarrassed.

"Hey, it's okay. *You didn't know if . . .*" Nia tried to help him along. She looked at the loose curls of his huge black afro, his dark intense eyebrows, those full kissable lips, and imagined what their children would look like. The thought made her giggle out loud.

"Naw, that's okay." And Jerome turned to walk away.

"Wait! I wasn't laughing at you." He stopped by the door to the stairway, but didn't turn around. "That was just, um, nervous laughter, Jerome. I'm new here, too, and kind of nervous, I guess. What was it you wanted to ask me?"

Jerome turned around swiftly and faced Nia. "You have a man?" Just like that. Straight. Direct. And to the point.

Nia stood perfectly still for what seemed like an eternity to her. Say no, she kept willing her mouth. But nothing would come out. Her knees started to do the jelly thing. Better answer before she passed out. Nia shook her head no and smiled weakly.

Then, in just the time it takes for words to reach the heart, he smiled. He looked at her and smiled that wonderful smile. "Glad to hear that, Nia. Real glad. I was solo, too." Was. He walked over to her and touched her eyebrows. His finger was long and narrow. She closed her eyes, just for a moment. "Here, let me carry your books. I'm parked down the block." And Nia let him. Let him take her books and her phone number and her heart and her forever.

The rest, as they say, was Baxter history.

When prom time came around for Jerome, who was now officially "Nia's Rome," it was Nia whom he asked, of course. He worked afternoons at his cousin's hair salon, sweeping and running errands for the customers, just to be able to buy Nia's corsage and limousine ride, and prom tickets. He even helped Nia buy her gown, because it was blue and blue had always been his favorite color. And Nia was his queen.

After Rome's graduation from high school, after the party his parents gave him at the house, after the relatives had been taken home one by one, Nia sat in the front seat of Rome's daddy's Cadillac. Rome had been smiling all day and winking at Nia. A lot. Nia looked down at the yellow rose corsage above her right breast, and fingered the baby's breath.

"Mmm. They're so beautiful and they smell so good." Nia breathed in deeply and filled her head with the wonderful scent of roses and leather interior. Jerome adjusted his navy velvet bow tie and made the turn using only his left hand on the wheel. He was smiling, but he wasn't looking at her.

"I'm glad you like them, my queen. I know how much you like roses."

Nia blushed. "I'm really proud of you, Rome. Valedictorian! That's quite an achievement."

"Come here, baby." Jerome beckoned, putting his right arm around her shoulder and pulling her next to him. "I want you close to me tonight."

With the other boys Nia had known from school and from the neighborhood, she would have been scared and uneasy. Thinking they might have tried to get lucky. After all, it was his graduation night. It was just about a ritual, wasn't it? But Nia had no apprehensions about being close to Jerome. They had already had that discussion. They had decided to wait to have sex, wait until they were both ready. When it was time. When it was right.

"Something I want to talk to you about." Jerome pulled her closer to him and continued to keep his eyes on the road ahead.

"Okay. What's on your mind?"

"Well, you know I was accepted into Fordham"—she nodded slowly, sensing the apprehension in his voice—"but my first choice has always been Morehouse. I've always wanted to be a Morehouse Man . . ." Jerome's voice trailed off in the distance.

"Morehouse? In Georgia? That Morehouse?" Nia tried to sound supportive and understanding, those were the emotions in her head; her heart, on the other hand, was crying selfish cries and pleading insecure prayers.

"Yeah, *the* Morehouse."

"I don't understand, Rome. You can't just up and change schools like that. You told Fordham you were starting there in the fall. You already picked out your classes. Everything's been set for months."

"But I changed my mind." Just as he had changed his mind only months before, deciding in his senior year that he wanted to be a Baxter graduate.

"You made a commitment to the school. You told them you were going. They're expecting you. You can't just leave them hanging. They believed in you way before Morehouse did and you told them you would go there. You can't just walk away from them and leave them like that."

You can't just walk away from me *like that; you can't just walk away from us.*

"They came up with money at the last minute and gave me a scholarship, Nia. A full scholarship: room, board, books, everything. I got to go. You know I got to go." She pulled away from him, as though the distance in the front seat would give her heart room to explode in silence.

"Of course, Rome. I understand," she said mockingly. But as she looked out of the passenger window, she could barely see the trees they were passing. It was all a sea of watercolor-green meshed with bright white streetlights and muffled, unfamiliar city sounds. A Monet moment come to life. It took such a long time for that first tear to fall. A heavy one, it was. It hit the white and silver ribbon of her corsage, trailed down to the first rose, rested for a moment then spilt onto the baby's breath and rested there with a heavy sigh. Yes, she knew he had to go. She actually wanted him to go, because she knew it was what he wanted. No, that was a lie. She didn't want him to go. Ever. But being supportive was what a strong, black woman did in such a situation. She'd wipe her face, keep stepping, and learn the lesson: the lesson of saying good-bye and wishing Godspeed and giving encouragement and hiding her tears. "It's a wonderful opportunity, Rome. I know you'll do really well there," she finally said.

"Thanks, baby. I swear I'll come back to you. I swear I will."

And Nia held on to that hope through her final two years at Baxter Academy, asking cousins and brothers of friends to stand in for dates at various school functions and family gatherings. Rome was good and did what he said he was going to do and tried to keep things intact. But neither of them had the funds or the energy to successfully sustain a long-distance relationship. When Rome came home for spring break during Nia's senior year, they got together and had dinner in Brooklyn Heights. A celebration dinner.

"So . . ." Nia wiped the corners of her mouth with her napkin.

"So, you're really going to accept this offer?" Jerome asked with just a teensy bit of disdain in his voice, waving the offer letter around without any of the reverence Nia felt.

"Yes! Isn't that wonderful? I got a partial scholarship, some work-study, and room and board!" Nia picked up her glass of ginger ale to give a toast to the future.

"Well, actually, I thought you were leaning toward Spelman. So that we could be together. Scholarships help, sure. But there are more important things than money." Jerome sounded so wise and adult.

"No, I want to go to a women's college in New England." Nia sipped her drink and smiled at Rome. She knew how much he loved her smile.

"This won't be a good move, Nia. Not a good move for us at all." Rome leaned back in his chair and looked at the piano bar off to the left.

"We'll adjust. Just as we adjusted to your being at Morehouse, while *Fordham* would have kept us closer together." Jerome just glared at her, then shook his head.

"You just don't get it, do you? You'll be going to the *white man's institution*." Like that was some kind of brilliant revelation.

"White *woman's*. And they have a wonderful curriculum and a core group of some very supportive sisters. I don't understand, Rome. Help me out. What's the real issue here?" It was now Nia's turn to lean back in her chair.

"*The real issue*," Jerome just about yelled, "is that I want to marry you and it's really difficult for me to do that with you hundreds of miles away."

"Marriage? You want us to get *married*?" She spit out the word in disbelief and Jerome looked at her as though he had been wounded.

"You sound so surprised, Nia. You know you've always been my girl . . ." And he leaned over and took her hand in his. Rubbed her fingers and calmed her.

"I love you. You know that." Nia looked at the dance their fingers were doing in the center of the table.

"But?"

"But . . . I'm not ready to get married. I want to finish school." Jerome smiled across at her.

"Baby, I know that! That's why I want you to go to Spelman, so we can be together. *Married* and together."

Nia withdrew her hand. "I'm not ready, Rome. And I don't want to go to Spelman. I want to go to college with all different kinds of people around me. I love black. I know black. I want to see more." She watched him as he sucked his teeth and picked up his beer. Thought about how understanding she had been when he had made his decision to travel hundreds of miles away to go to college and wondered if she would be able to experience the same. "So, Rome? Are you willing to transfer to Amherst? Or Brown? Or Dartmouth? Or Yale? Are you willing to do that for us to be together?"

"Oh, forget it. Forget that I brought it up, Nia. We'll just go on like we been going on. If that's good enough for you, then that's good enough for me. I thought being together was what *we* wanted." Nia looked at Rome for some hint of where she fit in his equation of what constituted *us*. She had no idea what he was feeling; he just looked vacant. Vacant and unoccupied.

And it turned out that Nia loved the choice she had made. Loved the academic New England environment and just thrived there. She and Rome kept in contact and still professed their love for each other, spoke with each other every Sunday after dinner, and exchanged letters a couple of times a month. She was happy. She went to dances and parties and lectures and readings and concerts. And yes, from time to time, she dated an Amherst man or two. But her heart belonged to Rome. And she fully expected to marry the man once her graduation rolled around.

But soon Jerome started dropping little hints to Nia, telling her things in passing that his mother and other people had mentioned. Things like how uppity a black girl could get going to a white-girl school. Saying that the time would come when she would change and wouldn't be satisfied anymore. Maybe she had changed, Rome would whisper, maybe they both had. But Nia would never respond.

She had actually noticed the change herself. Those Sunday night phone calls got shorter and shorter, then started coming every two weeks or so. Those treasured letters from Rome that once contained passion and fire now spoke of business ventures and graduate pursuits. But the bottom line was that they had agreed to meet in New York once she graduated. To resume their relationship properly, he said. She thought that was a fine plan. And life had just gone leisurely along.

Nia sniffed the flowers. She loved Rome. No doubt about it. When she hurt, Rome was her rock. When he needed, she was always there. For the past few months they had been gently rekindling what had once blazed so fiercely. Everyone needs a sure thing in life, Nia thought. But the fire that had once burned between them had been consumed by compromises on top of compromises. They were an upwardly mobile couple on simmer and the water level had been approaching a dangerous level of concern for some time now. Somebody had best tend to the pot.

Maybe it really was time for them to think about taking that next step. Nia blushed at the thought. Marriage. Whew. Deep down inside, the thought of being wife to Jerome Carrington still made her smile, just as it did on that first day at Baxter.

Nia entered the lobby of Rome's building, glowing. Maybe *she* would propose. And why not? Maybe she would do it tonight. Over dinner. Nia walked her seductive thoughts to the bank of telephones in the lobby and called the main office upstairs. The bubbly African-American receptionist answered immediately.

"Anderson-Moss and Associates . . . This is Lauren speaking. . . . How may I direct your call?"

S eth picked up and put back the receiver a grand total of nine times. It was starting to feel as if he were doing reps with a handweight. Then the sofa cushion was uncomfortable. The music in the background was too loud. He needed a glass of water. With ice. No, without. And it was starting to feel stuffy in the room. He was sure of it.

Just call her. Just pick up the phone, dial the number, and say hello. Gracious. It's not like this is the first time you've ever called a woman. Just go ahead and do it.

Seth tried to understand why it was so hard for him. It was just a phone call. One of the many calls to a woman that he had made in his lifetime. Even back in high school, when he was shorter than most of the girls his age, he hadn't had this much difficulty. He had accepted the fact that sometimes you win, sometimes you lose, and sometimes it's not even your game that's being played. But for some reason there seemed to be so much riding on this call. So much destiny. So much hope. And it wasn't as if he anticipated rejection. He didn't. No, it wasn't the fear of rejection at all.

He pictured Lauren's smile peeling away the layers of his humorous exterior, placing the mountain of protective armor off to the side, and leaving him standing vulnerable and open and wanting. It gets cold when you're out there butt naked and your heart's all exposed; he knew this from counseling his buddies over the years, helping them to get back on track after broken hearts, but he had never allowed himself to be in that kind of a sad situation. He knowingly and consistently pulled the plug on relationships before they got to that desperate stage. It was his rule to never let a woman strip him so completely. But Lauren had that power, Seth could tell. Maybe it was because she seemed so fragile, so in need of protection and warmth. In order to give to her, he knew he would have to step outside of himself and his self-imposed boundaries. And that possibility was scaring him in a very real and intense way.

Maybe it really was time for him to get off the treadmill, grow up, and just commit to one woman. That way, he'd be done with all the game playing, all that unnecessary relationship stuff that takes up so much precious time. He could find focus in his life, just get on with the development of his career.

If he called her now, if he called her today, every fiber of his being told him there would be no turning back. The revelation was like ominous music that played in the background of a tense movie scene: building to crescendo, discordant and captivating.

What the heck.

Seth looked at the phone, picked it up one final time, and dialed Lauren's number.

"Welcome to Lauren's world. There are many beautiful things in my world, one of which is taking my attention at the moment. I want to talk to you: please let me do it at a time when you will have my attention undivided. Please leave a message for me and I will return your call as quickly as I can. Thank you and God bless you."

Seth closed his eyes and swallowed hard. He heard the beep on the machine signaling his opportunity to be recorded.

"Hi Lauren. This is Seth . . . Seth Jackson. Wanted to know how you're doing . . . wanted to say hello . . ." Seth spoke slowly and cautiously.

The phone made another beep. And then he heard The Laugh.

"Hi there, Seth Jackson! It's you!" He could hear the warmth in her voice, the joy in her laughter. It made him smile into the receiver.

"Lauren. You're there . . . oh, am I disturbing you? Were you busy?"

"Well, not too busy for you. Never too busy for you. So, what made you pick up the phone and call me today?"

He sat up on the sofa. He had been so enthralled by the melody of her voice that he had forgotten his apprehension. "I want to invite you to a night to remember. Decent food, pleasant conversation. Exquisite music. Not to mention fine company . . ." He sipped his water and waited for the silence to pass.

"Mmm . . . sounds wonderful. Tell me more!" He could hear her smile.

"More? There has to be more? Did I mention the quality of the company?" She laughed again.

"Well, when is this wonderful culinary event? I know it's not tonight, because you waited over a week to just *call* me! So here, let me get out my book of standard dating etiquette, the Seth Jackson edition. What's the minimum length of time that needs to pass between the time you initially call a woman and the time you actually go out, Seth? Three days?"

"Funny. Very funny."

"Well, I'm just calling it as I see it."

"How about I meet you after work tomorrow. We can go out for drinks. And if we survive the conversation, then maybe we can add dinner into the mix."

"Sounds like a plan, Seth Jackson." They settled on time and place, agreeing to meet at a quiet restaurant not too far from where Lauren worked. Seth wrote her office phone and address in his address book.

"Good . . . good. So I'll see you then?"

Lauren paused, then lowered her voice and whispered through the receiver, "You know, I really missed you. I was wondering if you were ever going to call me. Wondering if maybe I had said too much and scared you away or something."

He closed his eyes and let the moment sink in. She was so honest. He wanted so much to see her, wanted so much to be able to look at the corners of her mouth curl up as she spoke, wanted to be able to reach across the table and touch her hand, feel her face.

"No, it's nothing you said. I was just trying to give you some space in your life, you know? I had a good time with you—a really good time—and I was just enjoying the memories, that's all. And work has been kind of crazy for me this past week. I had shoved a lot of things to the side, trying to help Reggie out as best I could with wedding stuff. Had to get back on the ball and remember where I left off on my own projects."

"So you weren't putting me off?" she whispered.

"No, wasn't anything like that."

"Hmm. 'Cause I was wondering if maybe, you know, when I got upset after the bouquet toss and all . . ." Her voice trailed off and he could barely make out her words.

"No, I understand . . . Weddings are emotional times and they bring up lots of memories. Not all memories are good memories. I'm grown enough to know that."

"Well, I just want you to know how sorry I am that . . . that I let that happen. It wasn't about anything you said or did—"

He cut her off. "I know this, Lauren. Relax. It's not a problem for me, okay? You don't have to explain."

"I want to. I want to explain."

Seth was silent and waited for her to say something, but all he heard was her breathing, slow and steady. He cleared his throat. Silence. A few seconds later he cleared it again.

"I'm sorry. I thought it was going to be easier than this. I thought I'd be able to share this with you."

"Lauren, you really don't have to . . ."

"I've been through a lot this past year."

Seth detected a certain sadness in her voice, not an anger but a pain. As though she had seen too much or felt too much. He wanted to know, he needed to know, but he wasn't sure if he should press her for the recollection. The last thing he wanted was to add another something negative to whatever she was carrying around.

"He was killed, Seth. Someone I was . . . well, someone I was seeing was killed. He was murdered one night a little less than a year ago on the IRT." The way in which Lauren uttered the words pierced him. He could suddenly picture a man sprawled out on the subway platform, fading into a pool of blood, moaning and crying while a crowd of mildly interested citizens hovered and shook their heads in disgust.

"Lauren, I didn't know. No one told me. Aww, man, why didn't someone tell me? I don't know what to say . . ."

"His name was Brandon," Lauren spoke, her voice cracking yet soft. "You know, we were such an unlikely couple. So different. If you can, picture me . . . and a tall, massive, white guy with a southern accent." Lauren sniffled and laughed. "Yeah, a white guy. I still wonder to this day how we could have meshed the way we did. But Seth, he was so full of love. I saw so much more in him than just his color or his upbringing. He was good to me. Really good."

Seth tried in vain to picture Lauren with Brandon, tried to see how she could have allowed her heart to have been taken by a confederate. He tried hard to create the image in his head of this couple; a couple that was as hard for him to fathom as Annette Funicello and Mr. T.

"And he loved me," Lauren continued, whispering. "That was the reason he was killed. Because he was with me. You might expect something like that to happen in Mississippi or Alabama or someplace. Not in Manhattan. And it happened so fast. He leaned down to kiss me while we were getting off the train at Times Square. This group of young kids came up behind us and started shouting all this racist mess. Brandon tried to talk his way out of it, but these kids weren't interested in conversation, you know? So they started slashing him, stabbing him. All of them, eight or nine of them, all at the same time—pushing me around, slapping me. And then they just left. Marched up the stairs and nobody stopped them. He was all cut up and bleeding to death on that platform and I could still feel his kiss. It lingered there on my face for days." Lauren choked. "And the oldest one in that gang was just fourteen, Seth. Just fourteen. Babies."

He listened to her words, listened to her heart. He was sorry that she had seen that kind of hatred in her life and he ached for her deeply. At that very moment, he wished that Brandon had never been killed, that he was still here, able to hold her and love her, give to her.

"You still love him." It was more of a statement, an acceptance, than it was a question. Seth already knew the answer.

"I guess I'll always love him. He was a part of me." She tried to compose herself. "I know that doesn't make any sense."

"Makes all the sense in the world. That's what love is all about."

"We were engaged, Seth. We were going to get married. Worked out kind of like Romeo and Juliet, huh?"

"I really am sorry. And yeah, now I can understand how catching the bouquet would be so traumatic for you. It was brave of you to even go out there and stand in the crowd."

She sighed. "It wasn't the flowers, Seth. Really. I knew the wedding was going to be hard for me to get through and I had prepared myself for that. What I hadn't counted on was meeting someone like you."

"Me?"

"Yes, you," she chuckled, sniffled. "When I saw you standing there, looking so handsome, being so funny and sweet . . . I mean, you really looked like you cared about me."

"I do care."

"No . . . please. You can't care—don't you get it? If you start caring about me, something bad is going to happen. I know it will. That's just how things go for me."

Seth now understood the concern that Reggie and MommaPatti had expressed. Have patience. Don't dog her. Make sure you treat her right. Seth wanted nothing more than to hold her, to clasp his arms around her life, to protect her from all that could ever sadden her or bring her pain. He wanted to love her. He wanted to do that. Now more than he did before.

"Lauren, I'm Seth, and for whatever it's worth, I'm not Brandon. I'm not the man he was and, you know what? You're not the same woman you were then either. History doesn't always repeat itself. And maybe—just maybe—if you give yourself a chance and have a little faith, you might find something different from what you knew before. Something good. And believe me, I know how hard it is to trust another person. And whatever you need, Lauren, I'm here for you. You hear me?" And he meant it.

Lauren sniffled. "Yeah, I hear you."

"Have you ever talked about it with somebody?"

"Professionally? Like a minister or somebody?"

"Yeah. A minister or a psychologist or somebody."

"Nope. Never did. But I'm fine. Really. Life goes on, you know?"

Seth sighed. He couldn't imagine just going on with life so nonchalantly after something so traumatic. It had to have hurt. Had to have scarred her much more deeply than she was letting on.

"If it's too soon and you just need a friend, if you need an arm, a shoulder to lean on, if you need—" He wanted her to know and fully understand, but Lauren cut him off.

"I need to know that if I open my heart up to you, you're not going to walk away from me. I need to know that you're going to be here."

Seth closed his eyes and took the plunge. "I'll be here for you, Lauren. It's going to be all right. I promise."

Seth paid the driver, opened his umbrella, and stepped out of the cab into the river of water that was flowing curbside. He felt the water seep deeply into his Italian loafers, felt the squish with each step upstairs to the commercial production firm. It was going to be difficult to make a smooth impression on such a jagged day, weather-wise. But this was a day of new beginnings. Not only was he ready to impress the staff here, prepared to show them how they would make tons more money by hiring his services, but he was also looking forward to meeting Lauren for dinner this evening. Despite the rain, this had the makings of a very grand day.

"Mr. Jackson, Mr. Jackson! Please come in; we've been expecting you. Here, let me take your umbrella."

Seth gladly handed the man his soaked umbrella. "Jonathan Feinstein, pleasure meeting you again."

"Likewise. Let's go down to the conference room and discuss your association with Feinstein." Jonathan led the way down the hall and through the corridors. "Have any trouble with traffic this morning?"

"Actually wasn't too bad. But you know how it is trying to catch a cab in the rain. It's a challenge. But, being a problem-solver, I welcome challenges. They keep me on my toes." Jonathan laughed, slapped Seth lightly on the back.

"Yes, indeed. I can relate to that for sure. If it wasn't for challenges, most of us would be out of jobs . . ."

Jonathan walked into the conference room, directed Seth to a seat, and proceeded to introduce him to the woman in the room.

"Seth, I'd like for you to meet my personal assistant, Lisa Gold. Lisa, this is Seth Jackson."

Seth smiled and extended his hand to her. She looked down at his hand, rolled her eyes, folded her arms, and took her seat.

"Uh, right. Can we just get this dog-and-pony show on the road, please? I have work to do."

Jonathan spoke up right away, smiling warmly at Seth. "Nothing is more important than the work to be done in this room right now, Lisa. Now, Mr. Jackson . . ."

"Call me Seth, please."

Jonathan loosened his tie, smiled. "Seth . . . that was quite an impressive sample of music you shared with us. Tell us more about your concept. How can you help us help our clients?"

"Thank you, Mr. Feinstein—"

"Jonathan . . ."

"Jonathan . . . in this day and age it simply isn't effective to create one spot and expect it to speak to every segment of the population. This isn't anything new; we make marketing distinctions all the time. We show spots that have more appeal to women during shows that have a greater percentage of female viewers . . ."

"Yes, yes, we do that all the time . . ."

"And the reason these particular spots are effective is because they contain elements that are directly appealing to women—elements that have been proven over time, like the colors used for backgrounds and positive representation."

Jonathan leaned back in his chair and rocked. Squinting. Smiling.

"I propose that this same approach can be used for reaching the black segment of our population. I won't be writing new music for your existing clients, but rather arranging the jingles that you and your staff have already created. Handling the filming portion of these commercials is, of course, your area. But I can be available for consultation if my services in that area are of interest to Feinstein."

"For a fee, no doubt," Lisa groaned.

"No doubt. I'm a businessman as well as an artist."

"Seth, I wouldn't have called you down here if I didn't have something concrete to present to you. We have a current client who is presently seeking to expand into the black community, and we honestly could use some guidance in that area. Our goal is to get this project done as soon as possible; they want these spots on the air and in heavy rotation by early fall."

"Fantastic! What's the product?"

"It's a product from one of our pharmaceutical clients; a new over-the-counter stimulant that has been tested to be safely taken with low levels of alcohol consumption."

"You're not talking about OnTheGo, are you?"

Jonathan smiled and returned his chair to its upright position. "Yes! OnTheGo! You're familiar with the product?"

"A bit. I've heard that there's been some controversy concerning some of the claims of the drug. That true?"

"Yes, that *was* true. There were some questions about the methods used in the effectiveness testing. But all that's been verified. We're back on track now . . . and you don't really have to worry about copy and lyrics, if the arrangements are the only portions of the jingles that will change, correct?"

Seth nodded slowly.

"So are you on board? Can we count on your contribution?"

Seth stood and smoothed his jacket. "I'm going to need a few days to consider this one."

"Oh! Well, if it's a matter of money . . ." Jonathan stood and followed Seth as he walked to the door.

"No, I'm sure that we are talking a fair compensation. Especially since you've already indicated that it's a long-term working relationship that Feinstein seeks. I just need to examine my obligations for the next few months. I'll get back to you in a few days' time. Is that a problem?"

Jonathan pulled out a tiny notepad from his inner jacket pocket, scribbled a figure, and handed it to Seth. "This is the amount I'm willing to commit in order to bring you on board, Mr. Jackson."

Seth looked at the notepad, looked at Jonathan. "This is quite a commitment."

Jonathan handed Seth his umbrella and shook his hand. "Just the beginning, Seth. Just the beginning. Now, you go ahead and think about it, but remember: Time is of the essence for us. Know that we'd love to have you on board!"

The hostess escorted Seth to a table near the back, away from the conversation of the bar. He was glad he had suggested this place to Lauren. Dark but not too dark. A good-sized after-work crowd but not too crowded. The scents of lime and pepper and ginger mingled in the air, confirming his hunger. He had purposefully arrived a few minutes early. This way he could sit back, catch his breath, maybe have a predrink drink. He looked at the people walking outside, a sea of moving black umbrellas.

He ordered a scotch on the rocks.

After downing the first one, he glanced at his watch. She was a half hour late. But it was still raining and still raining heavily; the blare of horns from angry taxis dotting the jazz riffs from the music playing in the background.

He ordered a second.

This one he sipped. Slowly. When he finished it and the waitress walked over to him a second time, he was decidedly agitated. He looked up at the woman holding the chalkboard menu to ask her the specials of the day, and that was when he saw her.

Lauren was looking in the restaurant window, biting her bottom lip, watching him.

"Anderson-Moss and Associates . . . This is Lauren speaking. How may I direct your call?"

"Hey, Lauren! This is Nia. How you doing, girl? They're not working you too hard, are they?"

Nia and Lauren had hit it off immediately when they met at the Anderson-Moss Christmas party last December. They sat off to the side and watched the staff get funky loose; they shook their heads, sipped their ginger ales, and discussed single woman investment strategies—girl talk.

"Nia! Well, they try . . . you know how it is. How've you been?"

I *knew* how it was, Nia thought.

"Yes, yes, yes—that I do. Is Rome around?"

Lauren put her on hold and Nia was graced with the strains of an elevator version of Earth, Wind & Fire's "After the Love Has Gone." That's how you know you're getting old, Nia sighed, when you can hum along with the piped-in generic music. Music from the good ol' days. Nia fished around the bottom of her backpack for her mirror and reapplied her lipstick.

The phone clicked back to Lauren. "Nia, I can't find him. I know he was getting ready to leave, but I think he might still be around here somewhere. You want me to tell him you called if I see him again?"

"No, that's okay. We were supposed to meet later on, but I'm early. Thought I'd surprise him. I'll just hang around downstairs in the lobby so our elevators don't miss each other in passing. You know, you and I ought to get together sometime and go shopping or something. I really enjoyed talking with you at that Christmas bash."

"You know, we really should. I know I should get out more than I do; the last movie I saw was *Greased Lightning*. Got to get out and live life." They exchanged numbers and promises to call.

"I heard that. *Greased Lightning?* Girl, you truly *are* in need of some help." Nia laughed.

"You sure you don't want to come upstairs and have a seat while you wait?"

"No, no, that's okay. I think I'll make a call or two while I'm waiting. You take it easy, okay?"

"You, too, Nia. Nice talking to you. I'm gonna head out of here myself in a minute or two. Bye now!"

Nia said good-bye and hung up the phone, her hand trembling slightly. *Breathe.* She didn't really want to make any other calls at the moment. She wanted the time to select her words of proposal and get those butterflies in her stomach to flutter in formation. She walked to the back of the lobby, near the bank of sixteen elevators. She lingered off to the side, in a shadow, out of the path of traffic but able to see all the comings and goings.

Nia smiled as she looked at the flowers in her hand. It really was a beautiful collection of colors. Colors that would encourage her to just go ahead, to take the plunge and propose. There were so many things that she loved about Rome. His calmness. His peace. Even his predictability. She knew that theirs would not be a marriage of heart-stopping excitement, but maybe that wasn't what she needed in her life. There were other ways in which to approach life. Sensible ways.

Nia looked up at the tidal wave of tired business people newly spilled from the elevators. Women wearing suits, wrinkled brows, worn-out tennis shoes, looking fatigued beyond belief. Men in suits of blue, already loosening their ties and retrieving rings of keys from jacket pockets. Change jingling and cigarettes lighting. They all rushed by her, beyond her. And finally, in the distance, Nia saw her Rome.

Even that far away, he stood out from the crowd. It wasn't just his height, although he was much taller than most of the men around him. It was his presence. Where all of the other people seemed so drained, Rome possessed an incredible energy, an excitement. He stepped off the elevator looking as fresh and as invigorated as most people just starting their day. Nia fought the urge to run over to him and throw her arms around his neck and welcome him with kisses. Instead, she chose to stay off to the side for a moment and watch his walk, his commanding stride, his satisfaction.

Rome took one step, then two. Just two gallant steps before his face broke out in a grin, wide with recognition. He dropped his briefcase on the marble floor; the black leather briefcase Nia had given him just last Christmas carelessly hit the floor and tumbled onto its side with a thud, resonating throughout the lobby. His arms free, they opened wide about him, wide as his smile, wide as the path open to his heart. And then she ran, ran right into his arms, into his heart, the path so visibly clear and open. He reached down and clutched her, brought her up to his level in one motion, agile and swift, consumed her with smiles and kisses, swallowed her happiness, inhaled her wonder. And slowly, very slowly, he allowed her feet to finally, and oh so gently, resume contact with the marble floor.

"I love you." His lips silently mouthing the words, over and over again.

"I love you more." Her lips mouthed in return. She stroked his cheek as though it were cherished antique velvet. And he closed his eyes and caressed her hand in motion.

People departing from newly descended elevators seemed unfazed and unaffected and walked around them without ever looking twice.

They had created a world unto themselves.

And Nia watched it all.

She struggled to find breath around her. But the surreal aura of it all had overtaken the moment. If there was breath, it had escaped her. If there was reason, it had slipped into vapor and detoured this space. If there was anything in this life besides pain, it was only an amazing illusion. Nia was certain of nothing but these things.

And just as it happens when tragedy occurs, Nia saw the moment repeating itself continually and in slow motion. Over and over again, the same series of events leading to this stunning of her senses. She finally heard a voice, her own pained voice, a whimper at first, that found crescendo in its passing. Her body crumpled into itself, and she felt nothing of the woman she was just moments ago. For now she was a woman distanced and detached. A woman broken, like dreams disturbed by unexpected daylight, dissolving into a pool of nothingness. A pool of her own creation.

She should have seen the signs. She should have understood that a man would never be satisfied with the convenient and the sure. Nia thought back over all the years that had gone by. They had been friends and they had tried to be more than friends at times. But there had been so little passion. Just the expectation that one day it would appear. Just the hope.

Nia cried silently. Her tears flowed freely and she refused to wipe them off her face. So many years. She thought back upon their life together and wondered how she could have seen it with eyes so distorted from the truth. They had planned so carefully for the future. They had decided that now was the time in their lives when they could conveniently love; it was there on the agenda, in ink. But Nia's sadness reminded her now that no one had bothered to tell their hearts. And hearts have their own callings to answer.

He had hurt her, it was true. He should have told her. He should have been at least that honest with her. But she had settled for less than the wonderful and the incredible in her life. Nia had dismissed passion, discounted the need for it in living. And that was, by far, the greatest injustice in need of forgiveness here today.

Nia looked up, after what seemed an eternity, to see Rome's eyes upon her. From way across the lobby, his sorrow was unmistakable.

"I'm sorry," his lips mouthed to her. He started to walk in Nia's direction.

But Nia looked away and shook her head in the negative. She didn't want to hear his pain. She was having a hard enough time dealing with her own.

"I need to stop crying." Nia sat on her bed, surrounded by a sea of used tissues. She looked up at Grace, who was pacing back and forth at the foot of her bed.

"He's a dog, Nia. You damn sure ought to stop crying. You need to hire a damn hit man, woman." Grace reached into her jeans' pocket, took out a cigarette and some gum. "Don't worry, I'm not going to smoke in your bedroom. It's a prop, for crying out loud. What a damn dog."

She was glad that she had waited almost a week before calling Grace. She loved her and all, but she had needed the time to grieve the loss of this dream on her own. She thought all the major tears had been shed, but when she tried to relate the lobby scene to Grace, she had started crying all over again. Grace sat and watched her cry, mildly disinterested, and Nia had expected just a little bit more sympathy from her. She was the one person in the world who knew the history she and Rome shared. That was what made it so strange to hear Grace go on and on about Rome and his four-legged qualities. Nia thought back to all the times they had spent together in high school, going to football games and concerts in the park and roller skating— Rome and Nia and Grace and whomever Nia had set her up with that time. Grace had never been really close to him, but she hadn't ever said anything negative about him either. Now the truth was coming out.

"Thought you liked Rome."

"He's a man. And men are dogs. Plain and simple."

"He never did anything to you, Grace."

"Sheeet. He didn't *have* to do anything to me! They're all alike. You just have to use 'em for what you need 'em for . . . and keep stepping. Where've you been?"

Nia looked at Grace. Looked at her posture, looked at her coarseness, looked at her attitude. She didn't ever want to become a woman so callused that every man who crossed her path was subject to her wrath. She didn't want to harbor that kind of hatred for all men for what one man had done to her.

"It's in the genes, Nia. They can't help themselves. They want what they want, and if you aren't giving it to him, your damn skippy he's gonna get it someplace else. Yeah, Nia. He's a dog, but you been living in a dream world for far too long, baby." Grace walked over to Nia's dresser and slowly started picking up her bottles of perfume. "Joy. Halston. Ewww, *Giorgio*? Hmmm. All very strong, heady fragrances. But the question is, do they work? Will any of it make him . . . keep . . . you . . . satisfied?"

Nia stood and faced Grace stoically.

"Yeah, Nia. I think not." Grace cracked her chewing gum loudly.

"You know something? I'm about tired of hearing you telling me about everything that I did wrong in my life. You're always up in my face, pointing out all the mistakes I've made—how I should have said this or should have done that. Yeah, you're really quick to holler out the advice, but where's *your* man? You don't have one. And do you know why you don't have one?"

Grace bristled. "No, woman, tell me why I don't *have one.*"

"You don't have one because you have this arrogant edge that won't let anyone get close to you. Always so quick to tell somebody how to run her life. Always finding fault in anything that doesn't originate with you."

Grace sat down on the bed. "Like you're Miss Accepting and don't go around judging everybody."

"I don't! Not like you!"

"Nia, I have known you forever. I have loved you more than you will ever know. And at times, I have come real close to hating you. I mean, The Dramatics had it right on the money with "Thin Line Between Love and Hate." But if nothing else, I have always let you be who you are. I have never tried to make you into someone you didn't say you wanted to be."

"And I've done the same for you."

"Bull! You never have. See, that's your biggest problem. You just don't see anyone outside of yourself and your own stuff. You've never seen me and who I am. You've never seen Rome and who he really is. You never saw the handwriting on the wall at Feinstein. If it's not slapping you right upside your head, you can't see it. And if you can't see it, then as far as you're concerned it doesn't exist."

Nia sat down on the bed next to Grace and spoke quietly. "What is it that I've missed about you? What is it that you've wanted me to see?"

Grace laughed. "You're funny, you know that? Are you asking me to sum up, what, twenty years of living, in a single sentence? A single conversation? Naw," she said, standing up and puffing on the unlit cigarette, "it's not gonna happen like that, Nia. Just like you didn't just lose Rome overnight. I still maintain that he's Rover material because he didn't have to sneak around and dog you like that, but you played a real big part in that, too."

"Grace, you know I loved him."

Grace laughed again and jumped off the bed. "Sheeet. You did not. You loved the fantasy, woman. And as long as he didn't rock the boat too much, you were happy with things. Please. Be a woman and go on with your life. And clean your house. It's rank." Grace pulled out her pocket watch. "Damn, I got to get out of here. I got stuff to do. And you need to go tend to some stuff, too, woman."

Nia wasn't ready to process everything Grace had just put out there. "Obviously, like you said, it's time to clean up my house."

"There you go. Hey, how's the temp stuff going? You have any success with that?"

"Been putting in a day here and there. You go there and fill in for a day or two and you don't stay in any one place long enough for the people to get all up in your business. Suits me just fine for now. I even put in a day at Vidal Sassoon."

Nia walked Grace to the front door. "Way to go, Nia! Next time you go someplace like that, get them to give you some free samples or a free haircut or something. One-day employee perks. Go for it, woman. It's Nia time now!"

Grace shouted good-byes over her shoulder as she bounced down the block toward the subway. Nia agreed. As much as she wanted to be furious with Rome, as much as she wanted to share Grace's canine sentiments, she knew he was only following his heart. At least he had been honest with himself. She hadn't even acknowledged she had a heart. Way to go, Rome, she thought.

Rome represented a lot of years, a lot of denial. Well, the blinders were off now. And Grace had been right about one thing: It was definitely time for her to take care of her own needs.

Nia walked to the answering machine and looked at the flashing light. There was one new message. She pressed play.

"Hi Nia! This is Lois from Totally Temps, again. We received a glowing—and I do mean glowing—recommendation from Vidal Sassoon about you. Fantastic! And I have something here that might interest you. It's a two-person office, you would be the third, and it's a Gal

Friday type of thing, open-ended. Give me a call either way, and I'll tell
you more about it . . . 555–5683. Bye now!"

She picked up the phone and looked around her apartment.

It wasn't really *that* rank; in the name of a potential new job, she
could clean house another day.

"**S**eth! I'm so sorry I'm late. Got caught up at the office. You been waiting long?" Lauren took off her beige trench coat, folded it, and placed it on the back of her chair.

He leaned back in his chair and smiled. "Been here a little while. I was starting to think that maybe you weren't coming. . . ." He signaled for the waitress.

"Really? I wouldn't do that to you; I wouldn't stand you up." Lauren looked up at the waitress, ordered a glass of sangría.

He paused and nodded. "Okay, so it was one of those days, huh?"

"Actually, it wasn't a bad day, just incredibly busy. Seems like each of the partners was having a meeting with several different people simultaneously. All of the conference rooms were taken by the time I headed out of there. But I don't mind the busy times. I like having work to do."

"Now, I can relate to that! In my line of work, if you're not busy, then you're not working—you know what I mean?"

"You're in the music business, right?" Lauren thanked the waitress for her wine and took a sip.

"Yeah, but I wear a whole bunch of hats. I write music, arrange it, do some production. Then I also do some promotion. A little managing. Lots of hats."

"My. How do you keep it all straight? I mean, how do you keep track of what you're supposed to do for whom?"

Seth laughed. "Well, right now it's not that much to juggle. But I can see how it might become something challenging as time goes on. For instance, just today, I was offered an opportunity to do some work for a television commercial production firm. I've been trying to make my way into that side of the business for a year or so now. It's a hard nut to crack; there's not a whole lot of opportunities for black folks in that area."

"Seth, that's fantastic! Why didn't you tell me that congratulations were in order? We should be drinking champagne!"

"Eh, not yet. I'm having some reluctance about just jumping into this one. It's just not hitting me right. Maybe this isn't the one I'm supposed to take."

"Is it a money issue?"

Seth wrinkled his nose. "No, the money's good. As a matter of fact, the money is great. No, this time it's a race issue. I have to think about it some more."

"Well," she said, playing with the rim of her wineglass, "if it's an issue regarding business and race, maybe it's something you should run by Reggie . . ."

"Yeah. I'm going to do that. Probably call him when I get back home. I don't want to do anything . . . embarrassing."

Lauren laughed. "I know you don't."

"In my wildest dreams, I never thought I'd do something as dumb as lose the ring . . . now, you got to admit, that has to take the cake in terms of embarrassment."

"Wildest dreams . . . I used to have them once upon a time." He watched the smile on her face turn into gloom. And just as fast as she traveled to that space, she shook herself free. "No, no, no. I promised myself I wasn't going to drift there again." She threw her napkin on the table. "I'm sorry. Really."

"Hey, these things take time. I know that. Don't be so hard on yourself."

"Yeah, well, I just hate floating off that way. So tell me, what are your wildest dreams, Seth Jackson?"

He chuckled. "My wildest dreams. Well, eventually, I'd like to be the head of a recording company. A fantastically innovative and successful company. One that I can nurture into being something phenomenal."

As he spoke, he became animated; his speech quickened and his gestures became grand. Lauren watched him, leaning into him at the table, her eyes squinting to see the vision that he saw.

"It's almost as if I can see what you're seeing. You just might make it there."

He nodded. "It's starting to lose its dream status with me."

She looked puzzled. "Oh?"

"Well, once you start breaking down a dream into its component parts, you figure out how to make it come true."

"Wow. Kind of like being your own fairy godmother."

"God*father*, please." He laughed. "But yeah. Then it's not a dream anymore. Then it's a goal. It's not just something you want to happen to you; it's something you're completing the steps to get done. You're taking charge of your dream. You do the homework; you pass the class."

She looked at him as though she just had a revelation.

"What? This is not news to you, I hope."

"I just never thought of things that way."

"Why not? Didn't you read fairy tales when you were a kid?"

"Well, yeah. But I just never saw myself rubbing the magic lamp in my life. I was always the one sitting up in that tower . . ."

". . . waiting?"

She sipped. "Yeah, waiting."

"Well, wait no more, damsel. Get out of that tower and go conquer some dream! These are the eighties, for goodness sake!"

Lauren licked her lips. "Sounds like a productive goal to me!" She signaled for the waitress. "Excuse me, miss? We'd like to see a dinner menu, please."

Seth stroked his chin. "The New Improved Miss Lauren. What have I just unleashed?"

"Live and learn," she whispered, "live and learn."

"Don't even *think* about taking on that account, Seth."

Seth lay across his bed, listening to the scattered notes of SunRa falling all around him.

"Reggie, the money is sweet. And the opportunity is huge."

"This one ain't about the money, bro. Believe me, you are not gonna want to be involved in this one when the community gets wind of this. You get on board with this one now, and more than just ducats are gonna be falling in your path."

"Wait, I know I'm gonna have to verify the claims that the research is on the up and up—"

Reggie cut him off. "It ain't even *about* the research. See, that's the smoke screen that they're using to throw us off track."

"Okay, now you've lost me."

"This is the deal. They want you to come in and give their little jingle a black slant, right?"

"Right."

"And the reason they want to do that is so they can target this drug for the black community, right?"

"Well, yeah. They want to expand their market. Is that wrong?"

"Are they gonna have you come in there and give it some mature, jazzy, classy arrangement? Something you and I might sit down and listen to on a hot, summer night? No. And you watch how they do this, Seth. They are gonna have you go in there and give them something that is new and cutting edge. They gonna have you try to re-create some cutting-edge sounds, maybe rap stuff like 'The Breaks' by Kool Moe Dee or 'Rapper's Delight' by the Sugar Hill Gang. Are you gonna be their spook who sat by the recording studio?"

"Ease up, Reggie. They haven't even gone into details about how they want the spots to sound, but if it's rap, then so what? That's what's happening. That's what folks want to hear."

"Oh? Tell me *what* folks want to hear that, huh? *My* folks?"

"No, the folks buying the records. The young folks."

"Exactly. The *kids*, Seth. They're going to target this drug to our kids. Yeah, I can see it now. 'Go to school or go to work, party all night and get drunk . . . then pop our product to keep you awake so y'all can do it all over again.' That's a not-so-slow suicide they're proposing, testing or no testing. Now you watch. Mark my words: All hell is gonna break loose over this one. Don't do it."

Seth sighed. Reggie could be right about this one.

But still, it was just a theory. And they were throwing a lot of tangibles in his direction to help him make up his mind. Thousands of them.

"I'm changing the subject to something more, um, *pleasant*."

Reggie laughed. "And how was your date with my little cousin?"

"It went okay." Seth paused. "She told me about Brandon. That's some harsh reality to have to deal with, you know? I wish you had told me so I could've been more prepared."

"Wasn't my place to tell you. But I knew she would if she felt she could trust you. Her telling you about Brandon says a lot."

"She's a special kind of woman. And I'm trying. Trying to do her right. Been so long since I've really cared about a woman; I'm kind of out of practice."

"Just be honest with her. That's all you can do."

"That and fix dinner for her. I invited her over to my place next Saturday night."

"Uh-oh. *You* are fixing dinner?"

Seth chuckled and sat up on his bed. "Hey, don't underestimate me and my many resources. I got it all under control. Watch me."

"So this is the big day, huh? Wow, she's a lucky woman, she is."

He barely looked up as Sandy nosed around the living room toting a Bloomingdale's shopping bag, checking out the bouquets of roses and daisies displayed on just about every flat surface available.

"Seth, I'm really sorry about what happened last week. I'm just used to being forward, what can I say?"

He looked her in the eye. She sounded so genuine. And she seemed to be having a really hard time getting the words out. "Hmm. I know. I can tell you are."

"I am." She walked into the kitchen, plopped down the bag, and opened the refrigerator. "Hey, this is some good wine. I see you sprung for the good stuff. What else you got to drink?" She held her two thick braids back as she bent over and looked on the refrigerator's bottom shelf, two tiny dimples peeking out at him as her waistband slipped down.

"You all up in my business, chica, you tell me!" He laughed and continued his dusting.

"Awww, see Seth? See, that's what I've been missing all week! I missed hearing you laugh. I don't like it when we fight." She took a glass out of the dishwasher and poured herself some apple juice.

"Then stop playing innocent." He stood at the door to the kitchen. "This show is not about you and me."

"Maybe not now. I can understand that."

"Never. You and I are friends. *Friends.* You get it? What's so wrong about that? Good friends are hard to find."

"Never is such a long time, you know? And besides, I know you better than she does. Am I right or what?"

"You know me better only because you've known me longer."

"Exactly. And you can be yourself around me at all times. And you know this."

He laughed and shook his head. "Nope. It ain't gonna happen, chica. Ain't gonna happen."

"Sandy's just waiting for the moment when you come to your senses." She walked over to him and handed him her empty juice glass. "And you *will* come to your senses, without a doubt. Sandy knows about these things."

She stood on her tiptoes and let her lips slowly brush against his cheek. Seth closed his eyes because he had to—and opened them because he should.

"Stop . . . I'm not . . . in the mood."

"Well," she smiled, obviously pleased with the reaction she had extracted from him, "I didn't forget that I promised to help. And help I will. A woman always has to check out the facilities," she said, picking up the Bloomie's bag, "whether she has to go or not, so I brought over some candles and incense and flower stuff for the bathroom. Thank me later."

It sounded like a woman thing to Seth, this desire to check out a man's bathroom. Something on the order of going in groups of two or more. Maybe there was an unspoken female law, some subconscious information that a woman learns by finding out a man's brand of toothpaste or deodorant. He waved her on, not really wanting to know the gory details of the female psyche.

She emerged from the bathroom moments later—bouncing, bubbly, and refreshed. "So, did you think about dessert? You need something delectable . . . something absolutely sinful."

"Indeed. I have dessert under control. Chocolate layer cake with raspberries. And just a touch of fresh whipped cream."

He looked around. Everything seemed in order. He checked his watch; there were mere minutes left before Lauren was expected. He had arranged for a limousine to pick her up from her home and bring her straight to his door. This way, she would travel safely in style and comfort, and he would have the extra time he needed to put the finishing touches on the preparations.

Seth walked into his living room, which had been converted into a formal dining paradise. There were tall, leafy plants surrounding the lace-covered table, complete with the finest of china and crystal. Tiny, white fragrant candles glistened in the darkness. For now, the music was Mozart, but vintage Smokey Robinson was next on the turntable. He sat on the sofa and savored the moment. He had truly outdone himself this time.

"Lucky girl. Refresh my memory. What's this one's name again?" Sandy stood at the entrance to the living room, leaning against the wall, her arms folded.

"Her name is Lauren."

"Oh, yes . . . *Lauren.* How could I forget such a sweet and lovely name."

"Sandy? No offense"—he walked to the front door, opened it, and stood aside—"but go home." He didn't think she meant any harm, but he was no longer in the mood for her sarcasm.

She looked at him as if he were knowingly passing up a winning lottery ticket. "Seth, Seth, Seth. You're really funny, you know that? 'Cause I know something you don't know."

"What's that?"

"You'll be back for Sandy. Miss Sweet and Lovely doesn't know you like I know you." She laughed. "Just watch, Seth. Sandy knows about these things, baby."

He closed the door behind her with a thud. He stood there with his back against the front door and breathed deeply. Somewhere along the line he must have given this woman the wrong impression entirely. And it wasn't as if she wasn't a beautiful woman or intelligent or fun to be around. He just couldn't see getting involved with someone who lived just a slab of Sheetrock away. There was no 'get mad' room. No room for escape. And well, now there was Lauren.

Even the thought of her name made him smile.

It had been a whirlwind week, the kind of week that is the stuff of movies. In the past week, he had become captivated by Miss Lauren Montgomery. They had spent much of their weeknights on the phone with each other, gingerly feeling around each other's boundaries. Their conversations had been like a tango in the dark; asking probing questions of each other and apologizing for the boldness when either of them tread just a bit too far into the personal. He figured he was probably seeing exactly what Brandon had seen when he fell in love with her. Seth knew he was falling fast. And the speed with which he fell, well, he knew it didn't make much sense. Here he was, the man who had been deemed King of the Stall—the man his high school class voted the most likely to dodge a relationship and keep it on the light—jumping heart first into this relationship. There was something wildly alluring about her emotional innocence and vulnerability that made him want to take care of her. He wanted to do that. He wanted to be the man who could make life good for her. And now was such a sweet time for them to have met, right when he had decided that he was ready to settle down. He knew it had to be destiny.

Seth heard the muffled slam of a luxury car door and walked to the window in the living room. The limousine driver walked to the passenger's door and opened it, escorted her out. Lauren stood momentarily and looked up and down the block. She pulled the sheer black wrap that graced her bare shoulders tightly around her, smoothed the skirt of her black silk jersey wisp of a dress. And then she smiled. Lauren smiled and waved to the group of children and neighborhood watchers who had gathered at his building entrance. Like an African queen in search of a land to govern, Lauren was here.

He walked away from the window and turned off the overhead lights. Adjusted the music. Buttoned his suit jacket. Picked up the bouquet of long-stemmed red roses. And walked to his apartment door.

When the elevator door opened, Lauren walked out. Her smile told him all he needed to know.

"Lauren."

And before he could hand her the roses, she was in his arms, her arms entwined with his arms, indistinguishable in their oneness. Her lips, so full and Nubian, found his with no effort, so magnetized they were, so drawn to each other. And he pulled her to him decidedly, like a man with a need to be needed right now, right this very minute.

Lauren felt good to him, like a forever finally come, firm in his arms. She was the one who shut the door behind her.

"This week has been the longest week on record," she said to him in between her heavy and long breaths.

"Was it that long for you, too?"

"Mmm hmm. Far too long, baby. Far too long." And she touched the back of his neck and caused a grand river within him to search for the oceans.

"I missed you, you know that?"

Seth wanted so much to have been able to follow the script that he had created for himself. But as she stood here before him, he was reminded of nothing he had to do . . . but love her.

He leaned his body into hers and inhaled the scent of her hair, her skin beneath the perfume. He kissed her, kissed her hard and with purpose, kissed her like it would be his last time of kissing, and found her tongue in search of his. And as he leaned into her and their hips created a smooth, slow rhythm, they danced the dance of tongues, flicking and taunting, teasing with fire. His hands found her hands and they guided his to the tiny white buttons on her dress front. One by one, he unfastened them with the same urgency she unfastened the buttons on his shirt. And they stood there and looked at each other and smoldered and burned: Seth lost his heart's rhythm when he looked at the black lace of Lauren's strapless bra and she smiled when she saw that his desire matched the enormity of her own.

He looked down the hall at the open door to his bedroom and looked at her and it just seemed so far away, too far, and so he lowered her onto the white lambskin rug on the floor of the living room while Smokey crooned "Here I Go Again" and the petals from her rose bouquet flew about them and landed in a circle around them without any effort of their own.

"Lauren . . ." was all he could say, all that could come out in speech, and he reached beneath the hem of her dress and she looked up at him and smiled at his actions. He reached and felt the fullness of her thighs, the smoothness of her bare legs. He reached, like an explorer set to find new land where dreams might live; reached and discovered a hint, just a hint, of black silk and elastic.

"What's for dinner?" she asked, and he gazed down upon her, unbuttoned the remaining length of her dress and removed it from about her; he looked upon the beauty of this woman before him and caught his breath.

"Lobster."

"Mmm, my favorite, yes indeed." Lauren lay in black lace upon the white rug and took his hand into her own, kissed his palm, closed her eyes. "I love lobster, Seth." And she took his fingers, one by one, into her mouth and savored each one, sucking as one would a tiny lobster appendage filled with meat, sweet and delicious.

Seth moaned with each motion, but he could not move, his eyes affixed upon his dream-come-true, his pleasure building and telling his story. "Then we should eat" is all he could say. Lauren nodded and nodded, never opening her eyes, intent on devouring each finger in turn. He fought himself for his freedom, removing his hand from her kisses, and shifted his weight, his hand now both sweaty and liquid in search of her own flowing joy.

And when he discovered it, she, too, found need to moan, as his fingers found rhythm and he whispered to her, "I love you, Lauren . . . I love you, baby," until she gripped the pile of the rug, pulling it into a bunch in her hand, shuddering, calling his name amid blessings, and flowing, flowing like the newly discovered Nile in Manhattan.

He lay next to her and they held each other, stroked each other.

"I can only imagine what you must think."

He turned to look at her, but she turned away and refused to face him.

"You're probably thinking that I do this sort of thing all the time. And you're probably not going to call me again . . . and you're—" He faced her squarely and cut her words off.

"Whoa, where did all of this come from? I thought this was what we both wanted."

"It was," she whispered.

"Then what's the problem? I'm so happy, I really am . . . and I'm so honored that you trust me enough to be so free with me. . . ."

"It just happened so fast. You probably think I'm some kind of slut."

"No, Lauren. No, I don't. I'm not here to judge you. Don't do this to yourself." He stood and carefully handed her her dress. "Let's eat dinner and have a good time, okay? Let's just enjoy each other's company."

She buttoned in silence.

"*Okay?*" He walked over and lifted her chin and kissed her gently on the nose. "I mean, Lauren, you have to know I care about you. *You* are all that has been on my mind. You have to know that meeting you and sharing with you has been very special for me, a once-in-a-lifetime special. And like I told you before: I'm in it for the long haul." Lauren looked at him, with hope in her eyes. "Really, baby. Watch. You'll see," he whispered.

Seth walked over to the table set for two and pulled out a chair and motioned for Lauren to sit. She smiled and warmed up to him. "Okay, okay. That's the old me, thinking the old thoughts. I have to keep reminding myself that these are new times, with a new man who cares."

Seth returned her smile. "There. Now, that's better."

"One moment, okay? Let me just go and freshen up." And Seth pointed the way.

When the bathroom door closed, Seth scrambled into the kitchen to warm the pots and check his culinary creations. He took out the wine and poured it in a decanter, wheeled a cart with the meal into the living room, near the set table. Perfect.

Moments later the door to the bathroom opened again, and Seth heard Lauren's footsteps begin and end. She must be standing at his bedroom door. Seth walked to the hallway and peeked.

Lauren stood at the door to his bedroom and glared at him. Tears were streaming down her face.

"*How . . . could . . . you!*" She stood in the hallway with her fists clenched, obviously struggling to maintain some semblance of composure.

"Lauren! W-what's the matter?" He rushed to her, but she looked at him so wildly that her rage made him stop, stopped him with the force of a brick wall.

"Don't give me that 'what's the matter' crap. Boy, oh boy," she yelled while walking into the living room, picking up her wrap and purse from the floor. "How could I have been so stupid?"

Seth was dumbfounded, unable to move, unable to defend himself from the unknown. She continued to yell as though he were not even present. "I really thought this guy was different. . . . I really thought he actually cared about me. . . . I really thought he considered me *special. . . .* Ha!"

"Lauren! What the hell are you talking about!" And she turned and faced him and slapped him with a force that knocked him off balance.

"Don't you ever . . . and I mean, *ever* . . . call me again, mention this evening again, *think* of me again. Do you understand me?" He touched his stinging cheek in disbelief and reached out to touch her.

"No! I don't! I really don't!"

"You told me I was the only one. You didn't have to go to all this trouble to pretend. I didn't need lies. I *don't* need lies. Now, get out of my way. I'm going home." She walked a wide arc around him, a look of utter disgust on her face, and opened his door.

"No! I'm not going to let you do this. Lauren, tell me what I did! I deserve at least that. Tell me what I did!" He tried to close his door before she left, but Lauren pushed her way past him, walked into the hallway, and pressed the button for the elevator.

"Oh, please. Good-bye, Seth. There's your explanation."

He stood in his opened door long after the elevator had closed and she had gone, trying to understand, trying to be logical, trying to cope. It didn't make any sense. One moment there was so much love and promise in the air, and the next she was gone. Boom. Just like that. In the course of his bewilderment, he looked at the pattern on the floor in front of his door, and watched the tears hit, one by one, heavy and full of pain.

Nothing mattered. He walked and turned off the fire under his simmering pots. He turned off the music. He blew out the candles one by one. Boom. Just like that.

He walked to his bathroom to turn out the lights and extinguish the candles there. And when he looked into the mirror and saw his reflection, the tears on his cheeks, the redness of his eyes, he looked upon the vision that had caused Lauren so much pain.

Draped over the shower curtain rod were three pairs of panties and three drying bras. There were two toothbrushes in the toothbrush holder. Tampons in his medicine cabinet. And on the sink, where his soap dish once sat, was a diaphragm and contraceptive jelly.

Dammit.

He bolted to the front door. Neighbor or no neighbor, this time she had gone too far. But as he stormed down the hallway to bang upon her door and give her a piece of his mind, he heard a muffled sound in his bedroom.

"Ahem."

He heard breathing, movement. He tried to orient his vision to the darkness of his bedroom but he couldn't see anything. He flipped the switch to the overhead light above his bed.

"What the . . ."

Sandy lay upon his bed, facing him. Naked and nasty.

"She left you, didn't she, Seth. See, I told you. I knew she would. Sandy knows about these things." And she took her fingers and scooped and tasted. "Mmm. Mmm. Good."

Seth looked at her writhing and oozing and hated himself, truly hated himself for the way his body was betraying him.

"You're a real bitch—you know that, Sandy? A real in-the-gutter, in-your-face bitch." And he balled up his fist, tight as the tightest tight could be.

But she just laughed. "Aw, Seth, Seth, Seth, Seth. So much tension to be released. Sandy knows you want some of this. It's okay, mmm hmm. Come here," she beckoned to him as though he had been a naughty child to be forgiven, "come to Sandy . . . it's okay . . ."

And in the swiftness that it took for Lauren's slap to reach his face, he found himself grinding this woman, then slipping inside her, thrusting with the force of a man determined to make the moment worth its while, making her scream, making her cry, making her beg to be satisfied.

"Is this what you wanted, Sandy? Huh? Is this how you wanted it to be?" he yelled at her, and she yelled back an incredible, "Yes." His tears spilled upon her hair, her thick black mane spread wild and disheveled upon his pillow, and he grabbed it, grabbed the reins and rode her hard. And she tossed and turned and bucked and thrusted back, meeting his wildness with a fury, her release as fiery as an erupting volcano.

And after he was satisfied, when he was tired beyond belief and could fully realize what he had just done, disgust settled in and he told her to get out.

She nodded and got up, tied on an animal print cover-up, and, without looking back, left his apartment and slammed the door shut.

Boom. Just like that.

Eleven

Nia sat in the middle of her living room floor. The sun shone brightly upon her surroundings, the shades of blues and crimsons so brilliant in the stream of morning sunlight upon her Oriental carpet. Engulfed by pencil-filled sheets of yellow legal pads, opened envelopes, transcripts, file folders, she surveyed this mass of information. Up until this point in time, these records had seemed like something to keep hidden away for safekeeping, nothing to bring out and sort through, nothing to maneuver. But here she was, two weeks into her unemployment, with pencil lodged between her teeth, creating piles, sifting through her past, creating a cohesiveness out of her yesterdays in order to make a way to her future.

The transcript pile. Major: English. Minor: Theater. Four years of so much hard work reduced to just words on a single page. The culmination of incredible amounts of sweat and frustration visible in single letters. Sometimes A's. Sometimes B's. She shook her head and wished that there had been some way to indicate the number of all-nighters that had gone into accomplishing those letters, how many gallons of coffee had contributed to the ink on that page. It just seemed as though someone should know.

And all those theater courses that she had taken, just for fun. It was so funny. She was well into her third year of taking theater courses just for the sheer joy of performing and hanging out, "working crew" when she realized that she only needed two more courses to complete her minor. Theater had been her release, her form of recreation. The fact that she had received credits for her participation was only icing on the cake. It had seemed so wonderfully rewarding then. And her folks had always told her to follow her heart.

Nia chuckled. Yeah, she had followed her heart all right, and just look at what it had gotten her. Here she was, a single black woman in New York City, without a permanent job and barely holding on with an unsteady source of income. She had a pretty decent apartment that she had all intentions of keeping, with a really tiny cushion of financial flexibility. She had done the calculations, and it looked like she only had a couple of months to find something serious—translation: permanent, full-time, *with* benefits—and that only held true if she lived life at a bare minimum.

Her counselor, Lois at the temp agency, had been wonderful, sending her out on jobs regularly. The last job had been the most varied spot; she put in a couple of days at a black partnership in midtown. The two partners had given her a lot of responsibility for someone totally unknown to them, allowing her to make calls on behalf of the company, drafting some letters on her own. Lois had told her it was an open-ended deal, but she and the partners hadn't discussed anything concrete.

Temp jobs were like that sometimes, you just never knew. Sometimes you were only there for a day, other times you could be hanging on in benefit-limbo-hell for months.

It seemed as though the partners were hired as consultants, going into businesses and showing them how they could use affirmative action principles to the company's benefit. It seemed as though they were out of the office much of the time, which suited Nia just fine. They would give her a list of things they wanted done, and then leave her there to do them. No supervisors watching her over her shoulder and no punching the clock. Just a reasonable job where they expected her to complete the items on the list and answer the phones in a professional manner. And when she was done for the day, they didn't mind if she used the facilities to work on her résumé and cover letters for her own job search. As a matter of fact, they had encouraged her to make good use of her time, to her own benefit. But Nia hadn't done so yet; it just didn't seem to be the kosher thing to do, no matter what they said they didn't mind.

Still, Nia hated job searching. In the comfort of her home, she flipped through her résumés of times past, when she had the option of picking and choosing and musing her desires. Now it just seemed that she had to concentrate on getting a J.O.B. And this was not a creative endeavor in the least. She jumped up and grabbed a bright green Granny Smith from the dining table. Things would have been easier if she had known what it was she wanted to do. Easier if the wind hadn't been knocked from her. Easier if the rug hadn't been pulled out from beneath her. Instead, she was sitting here windless, with no rug, and a bad attitude to show for her effort.

She crunched upon the apple with a vengeance.

Life could be kind of hard sometimes.

And even though Grace for sure had her issues, Nia had to admire the fact that the woman definitely knew who she was. Ever since they had been kids together, Grace had never backed away from being Grace, no matter what the cost. She knew she was an artist. She knew she was a woman in jeans and overalls. She knew who she was and what she wanted out of life. While Nia had flitted from one interest to another, and experimented in this activity and that pastime, Grace had remained steadfast in herself and made steady strides in her pro-fession. She was a woman who was creating her own reality. So maybe that was the key to success, Nia concluded. Find one thing in life and master it, do it well. And let somebody else do the other stuff. Nia sighed. Yeah, right. She had tried that method of living before and all it got her was an acute case of boredom. Her calling in life just wasn't to be stable and steadfast. There had to be another way.

When she picked up the *New York Times* classified section and looked through the ads, nothing called out to her. From administration to automotive to banking to customer service, all the ads did was in-duce yawns. They all promised to be such monumental opportunities, with sky-high paychecks and benefits, fabulous locations, and fees paid by employers. But having walked this road before, Nia knew it was all just a ploy. No one she knew had ever gotten a job by answering a clas-sified. She folded up the paper and pitched it across the room.

Nia closed her eyes and leaned back against her sofa. She listened to the silence in her apartment. Total silence. There were no telephones, there was no background music, no radio. Just her thoughts.

What was it that she wanted? What was it that she needed to do with her life? When she closed her eyes, what was the beautiful vision that begged to be brought to fruition?

She saw herself suited. In winter white. A pantsuit. The waves in her hair flowing freely about her shoulders. Her smile leading the way. She was hurrying, walking along with a steady stride. Not because she was late, but because she was sure. Walking along the streets of Manhattan, briefcase in hand, a woman with a job to do, a woman fully capable. There were people who were waiting for her arrival somewhere, waiting for her to accomplish a task, awaiting her personal expertise. And when she arrived, they would be pleased and relieved and relinquish control of the situation over to her. And Nia would take care of the problem, with diplomacy and panache and professionalism.

It felt so right, this thought, this dream of hers. She was on to something good here, and now it was time to flesh it out and bring it to life.

She took out her latest issues of black business publications, looking for any mention of new, up-and-coming enterprises. And then she made a list, drafting letters of introduction, offering her services as an up-and-coming public relations professional, asserting herself as a woman fully capable of getting the job done.

This was hard. She was trying to remain positive and upbeat so she would draw that kind of energy to her job search, to her life. Nobody wanted to hire someone with a chip on her shoulder the size of a Patti LaBelle hair sculpture. But every time she put pen to paper she became more and more bitter. Having to go through these motions just reminded her that she wouldn't be in this situation at all if this world would just spin right and distribute righteousness to righteous people. She read her cover letter and put it to the side—her cynicism was leaking onto the page.

She needed to change her perspective. Maybe create the vision she had seen, go out, get some fresh air, and treat herself to a good meal. This sitting around feeling victimized wasn't going to get her anywhere but down.

Nia walked to her bedroom closet, pushed and pulled and scraped hangers across the metal bar, finally retrieving that winter white linen blend pantsuit that had not yet seen the light of day this year. It was clean, the buttons secure, a brief pressing away from wearability.

Time to create a vision.

It didn't make sense, she kept telling herself. She would probably be better off staying at home and plugging away on those cover letters. But the questioning thoughts didn't keep her from enjoying the lavender gel in her shower or applying a light touch of makeup or styling her waves. She touched up her manicure, adding a coat of clear polish for shine and strength, applied a fine spray of fragrance, and stood before the full-length mirror of her closet door.

Yes.

She walked to the antique mahogany desk in her living room and picked up her briefcase. It was time for The New Nia to emerge: the briefcase-toting, self-assured woman who was ready for her career, not the backpack-slinging, underpaid worker hanging on to comfortable postcollege images. She opened it and looked inside. Yellow legal pads. Pens. Mechanical pencils. Her journal. She reached down, added the marked-up classified section of the *New York Times* for a bit of flavor, then grabbed her purse and stuck it in her briefcase. Cash. Credit Card. Keys.

She slammed her front door shut, locked it, double locked the metal security gate, and walked briskly to the subway. All right, she smiled. Even though anyone watching would swear she was crazy for smiling on the sidewalks of Brooklyn, Nia knew her vision was on the money. The woman was sharp, it couldn't be denied. And this was her day now; her vision had made it so.

When the train arrived she was able to find a seat, able to give in to the sway and rocking of the train ride. From above her, miniature billboards spoke out about the dangers of smoking and neglecting prenatal care, the benefits of this brand of peanut butter, that afternoon talk show. Everyone had something to sell. Everyone was the best. She looked below the signs and saw the faces of people who had long ago abandoned their quest for joy; they were empty, she could tell. There was no joy in the eyes of the woman hunched over in the corner wearing a gray bulky sweater four sizes too small. Or the two boys who took pleasure in pushing each other into the frail man who stood frightened, between them. No joy. No peace in the eyes of the woman sitting next to a man who kept winking at Nia. Nia caught his drift and rolled her eyes at the man and sucked her teeth loudly. She shot the woman a sisterly look of sympathy, but the woman just looked at her, disgusted and empty. Too beaten down and used to the disrespect to even care.

No joy. Nia made a decision to never allow herself to get to the point where she didn't care. She had almost allowed herself to go there after the realization of Rome's change of heart. She had wallowed and she had cried and felt sorry for herself and angry at him and all. But she really believed that everything happened for a reason. Even tears.

Jerome. Nia had tried not to think of him in the past week, tried to concentrate on the practical matters at hand. She needed a full-time job with full-time income. That was her argument to herself. But she still felt an emptiness where Rome used to be in her life. She missed him. Missed being a part of a couple. Missed all that he could have been to her.

And see, that was the crazy part. It was almost as if she was missing a dream that had never been realized. Missing something she had never really had. She and Jerome loved each other. But maybe there was more. She thought back, painfully allowing herself to remember the look on his face as he picked that woman up and held her and clutched her. He had never done anything like that with her. And she hadn't been feeling that kind of passion with him. Yes, there was definitely more. There had to be. She wasn't going to settle for anything less than wonderful in her life anymore. He hadn't. And while she couldn't really blame him, he could've used a bit more tact in the process, she surmised.

Nia looked down upon the dingy blue and gray tile of the subway car, the stray newspapers here and there, the candy wrappers and discarded potato chip bags. The frail man standing between the two youths shouted for them to leave him alone. The boys turned to each other and laughed.

I just don't want to be alone, Nia thought.

She reached into her briefcase and pulled out her journal. Two sheets of paper fell out from between the pages and fluttered to the floor. She picked them up, arranged them in order. Blue ink on gray paper.

Dear Nia,

*How's my girl? Been a long time since I've written, I know,
but I've had some things on my mind. Everything has been getting hectic, and I've had a lot of decisions to make about my future and what path I should take. Trying to decide about grad
school, trying to decide if now is the time. Thinking about us a
lot, too.*

*I know we haven't kept in touch like we said we would, but I
guess you're just as busy as I am. I miss our Sunday conversations. Miss them a lot.*

Nia, baby, let's not get so busy that we lose what we have.

I still have dreams that include both of us. Hope you do, too.

Love all the time,
Rome

He had wanted more, even back then. Nia tried to suppress the tear
that was forming in her soul, tried to ignore it like she had ignored
Rome's plea for attention in the letter she held and had kept close for a
reason she never really understood. And after she swallowed, and
crumpled the letter, the welling tear chose another course, a course of
lesser resistance, and took up residence inside her heart.

Good-bye, Rome.

Some things are better left in the past.

She closed her eyes briefly, not truly understanding the uneasiness
in the pit of her stomach, not sure of what she was anticipating. But
she had decided to get off at the next stop—59th Street.

It was time for her to see the light of day.

Nia glanced at her watch, the goldenness of it attracting the sunshine. It was a little after noon and she was hungry. She decided to
treat herself, to eat an early lunch surrounded by luxury. She walked
briskly downtown on Seventh Avenue.

She didn't even notice how many times she stopped traffic. Cabbies
trying in vain to get her attention. Businessmen walking and craning
their necks to get another glimpse. All she knew was the feeling of the
wind on her face, whisking away her gloom, filling her with an air of
confidence and peace.

Freedom was a stellar feeling, and while it had been a long time coming, today she had chosen to see the best side of her situation.

When Nia entered the Enchantment Café at the Hotel Broadway, she met and returned the smiles of men and women alike. The maître d' greeted her with a respectful nod and she quietly requested a table for one.

She was seated at a table overlooking the small flower garden, a melodic waterfall cascading into a tiny pond with large goldfish and koi. Soft instrumental music played in the distance. Nia sat back in her chair, inhaled her surroundings, and relaxed, closing her eyes.

"So tell me, man, how's this marriage thing treating you? Is it all it's cracked up to be?" Nia opened her eyes and squinted, reaching for her water goblet. The man who was speaking, two tables over, was incredibly loud.

The man to whom the question was directed leaned back in his chair and ran a hand across his hair, wedding band glistening in the light. He smiled, then laughed assuredly, like someone privy to an important secret, and tapped a rhythm on the tablecloth with his two long index fingers. "Man oh man oh man. Is it ever."

Nia sat up. She *knew* that voice.

The other man, the one with the glasses, leaned across the table, like a child listening to his father. "Get outta here, Reggie. The man been bit and swallowed whole."

"I'm serious. I didn't think I'd ever find a woman like her. It's a brand-new feeling to be with someone I can love . . . *and* trust. I don't have to be on guard all the time. That alone is worth it all. And to think that she was able to wait on me, while I went through all my changes. Waking up to her, every morning . . ."

"Whoa . . . whoa . . . whoa . . . *every single morning*? Reggie, my man, whatever happened to that ol' maxim, Absence makes the heart grow fonder?"

"Guess it's maxxed out, my brother. Totally and completely maxxed out. Truth be told, I don't want to be without her in my life." He picked up his coffee cup and whispered over the rim, "Ever."

The man with the coffee cup looked content and serene, sipping and caught up in a peaceful memory; the other man having nary a clue. Nia smiled to herself as she watched the clueless one push his

glasses up on his nose and scratch his head and look off in the distance, bewildered and lost in the relationship world, without a map.
His face was reflecting perfectly the way she felt about men at that moment.

"Damn, Reg, that's deep."

"Yeah, I know. So say, how're you and my cousin making out? You
treating her right?" Clueless With Glasses looked at the floor. And
paused. A long, long time.

"Well, Reg"—Glasses shifted uncomfortably in his seat—"um, actually . . . Okay, I need some brotherly advice."

The waiter came with Nia's salmon teriyaki, distracting her from
her eavesdropping with freshly ground pepper, refills of water, and the
clearing of her appetizer plates. The food was good and she realized
she was ravenous. She didn't mind only catching bits and pieces of the
men's conversation, the whispers and expressions more serious now.
Seemed as though whatever it was should remain within the realm of
privacy.

Men were still a mystery to her. Growing up without a brother had
left Nia at what she perceived to be a disadvantage. She wished she
had grown up with a brother to observe, to get a glimpse of the male
perspective. It seemed odd to her that men spent so much time trying
to appear so together instead of investing time and energy into making
it so.

But maybe that was exactly what they were saying about women.

A man burst through the door with more energy than noise, oblivious to the peace in the place, and spoke with animated and agitated
motions to the maître d'. The maître d' tried to calm the intruder, but
the intruder pointed anxiously to the man at the next table with the
wavy hair, and walked, unannounced, to the men.

The maître d' ran before the intruder and offered apologies to the
dining men, but the man with the wedding band seemed unruffled
and told the intruder to join their table.

"You certainly do know how to make an entrance, Philip." He
picked up his water and sipped calmly. "Problems at the office?" The
two men who had dined together shared a knowing, agitated glance.

That was it. They were the men from the black partnership where
she had filled in a couple of days earlier that week.

The name of the company was The Imani Group, but she couldn't remember their names . . . *what were their names . . . ?*

"Yeah, I'd say we got problems. Thanks to your enterprising buddy here, we got problems up the ying yang."

"Philip, do you always have to be so overly dramatic?" *Philip, that's right* . . . Wedding Band seemed to be aggravated, not only with the guy who had stormed on the scene like a hurricane, but also with Glasses now. Wedding Band was rolling his eyes at everybody.

"Well, Reggie, if you think I'm overreacting, then you tell me how we should deal with the likes of this . . ." Hurricane threw down a newspaper in the middle of their table.

Philip and Reggie, of course, how could she have forgotten that so quickly.

Glasses picked it up and glanced at the front page. "I don't believe this! How did this get to be news so quickly? I just recorded the jingle last week."

Nia's ears perked up at the mention of the advertising term.

"Seth, I told you that you were dealing with fire here. And I just gave you the tip of the iceberg. Listen . . . listen to this." Reggie picked up the newspaper and started reading, "and while the producer of the spot, music industry veteran Seth Jackson, a black man, has been conspicuously unavailable for comment, we were able to interview the president of the production firm, Feinstein Films. When questioned, Jonathan Feinstein denied any allegations of targeting the youth of our community. 'It is not our job to secure airtime for any of the spots we produce. Those decisions are handled exclusively by the advertising agencies who hire us. Our job is to create a commercial that is professional and polished, created according to the specifications provided to us.'" Reggie slammed the paper on the table. "Another prime example of passing the buck."

"I didn't do anything wrong. I was presented with an opportunity to advance my career . . ."

"And you did. Congratulations. You made the front page of the *Amsterdam News*. Now everyone can know about the work of Seth Jackson and what a sell-out he is," Reggie yelled across the table, oblivious to the discomfort of nearby diners.

"I'm sorry, but decisions like this are not about the personal advancement of your career. There's too much at stake," Philip hissed at Glasses.

Glasses threw his hands in the air. "Too much like what? You are acting like I'm the Judas of the eighties! It was one spot! Damn! Just one lousy spot. Get over it."

Philip and Reggie exchanged knowing looks. "Reggie, just go ahead and tell him. You have to now. This guy's a loaded cannon." Reggie nodded.

"Seth, I tried to keep you out of this. Tried to spare you the involvement. But you wouldn't listen to me. Just had to go and do the work. I've been working on bringing down Brooksmore Pharmaceuticals for a while now."

Glasses looked bewildered.

"The makers of OnTheGo."

"And?"

Reggie continued, "Brooksmore developed a flu vaccine back in 1976 around the time of the outbreak of the swine flu. They jumped right on it, responding to a bunch of studies that showed the flu hitting black communities in greater numbers and with higher fatalities. They decided to develop a vaccine targeted to the black communities."

"Isn't that a *good* thing?" Glasses sipped his water.

"Could have been. They had the know-how and the wherewithal to make it happen, but somebody in their camp got real greedy," Philip chimed in.

"Right. After they received FDA approval for the vaccine, *somebody* found a way to increase profits by diluting the drug. Before it was discovered, all of it had been dispensed. And too many heads would have rolled if it became public knowledge at that stage . . . besides, the damage had already been done . . . so no one said anything. Not a mumbling word."

"And we suspect that this is the reason why the flu hit so hard *this* year, especially for black folk. We think they did it again, Seth. And a lot of people died. A whole lot of people," Philip added.

Glasses hesitated. "Uh, yeah, a lot of people *did* die. And you know, I'm all with Power to the People and all that stuff, but I still think you two are overreacting—"

"*Overreacting?*" Reggie shouted.

"Yeah, overreacting. Just a little bit. I mean, come on: I only arranged the music on *one* spot, man. *One job for an entirely different product.* Why are you and Mister Dashiki over here getting so riled up?" Glasses shifted away from the other men as much as he could without actually getting up and turning his chair around.

Philip slammed his fist on the edge of the table, making the water in their glasses ripple.

"Seth, it is always *one*. It will be *one* child who is encouraged to rely on OnTheGo for energy, who will take *one* drink and die because this company decides it wants to cut corners again. We can't afford to play the numbers game anymore! One is just as significant as a million. It may be just *one* person who turns away from his own power *because of you*. One person who could have made a huge difference in all of our lives. Hey, just like it was one woman who had to suffer the indignation of being fired from that joint because she was a sister. Well, I'm *one*, too, Seth. One man who is going to say one thing, do one thing, that makes a difference. That's why *one* makes all the difference between making something right and letting the injustice go on and on."

Glasses glared at Reggie. "Are you quite done? Ain't nothing like a friend on the high and mighty tirade to kick a man when he's down, you know? And I think you're confusing issues here. If you're ticked off at me because of how I'm messing things up with Lauren, then just say so. But don't sit here and go on and on about something as insignificant as some incompetent woman who you and I don't even know who lost her job. How bogus can you be?"

Nia looked down at her plate, her hands trembling. Fancy restaurant or not, she had heard just about enough of this. She stood up, threw her cloth napkin on the table, and stormed over to the table of men.

Glasses looked up, his lip quivering from his explosion. "Excuse me, but this is a private conversation . . . may I help you?"

"Nia? Nia Benson?" Reggie asked, recognizing her immediately.

"You *know* this woman?" Seth asked Reggie. Reggie nodded, beaming.

"Absolutely! This woman came in to Imani and whipped us into shape real fast. Great job, Nia, really great job!" Philip chimed, offering her a seat at their table.

She clenched her fists, trying to channel the rage she was feeling into words. "You . . . you have no idea . . ."

Reggie scooted his chair back, stood up, and extended his hand in one smooth motion. "Whoa, whoa, Nia, what's the matter?" He motioned for her to sit. She shook her head, closed her eyes, and took a deep breath.

"My *name* is Nia Benson. But to *you*," she said, directing her conversation to Glasses, "to *you*, I'm just . . . uh, what was that I heard you say? *The insignificant, incompetent woman who lost her job?*"

All the men stared at her, their mouths gaping.

"Yeah, that's me. Feinstein's Finest. And I realize that you couldn't ask me why I was fired because you didn't know my identity," she continued."But it doesn't serve anybody any good to go around making up the details. It makes *you* look ignorant and it gives me a bad reputation that *I* have to go around defending. You don't even know me! What makes you think you can project like that?"

Reggie stood, and extended his hand in the direction of the fourth chair at the table. "Please, Ms. Benson. Please have a seat . . ."

She looked around her; the waiters were hovering, edgy. Not wanting to cause anyone else anymore grief than she already had, she reluctantly sat. "What?" she said, disgusted.

The men looked at each other, resigned. Finally, Glasses spoke to her.

"I'm sorry. I really am. It was wrong of me to say the things I did, wrong of me to jump to conclusions like that. I don't know you and I don't know the circumstances. I apologize." He sat back in his chair and sighed.

"It's bad enough that I had to deal with the likes of those people there. But it hurts so much more when you hear your own people dragging you down for the sake of interesting luncheon conversation."

"You're right. You're absolutely right," Philip chimed, shooting knowing glances at Reggie, trying to diffuse the situation.

"As a matter of fact, Nia, I've been meaning to have a conversation with you . . . and now is just as good a time as any. You do good work. You like doing temp?" Reggie leaned his elbows on the table.

"It pays the bills," Nia said, losing her edge. "I'm trying to get something entry in public relations. Took the firing as a sign from the heavens that now is a good time to make that move."

"Well," Reggie said, glancing at a nodding, supportive Philip, "as you know, we are in desperate need of someone of your caliber in our organization. If you'd like to stay on, Nia, we'd love to have you." Philip nodded his agreement and smiled at Nia.

"Are you offering me a job?"

"Well, of course it would pay more than you're receiving now because it would be full-time, and you'd receive a decent benefit package . . ."

"That's fantastic! You're offering me a job as a receptionist? Even after I told you I'm trying to find something else?"

"We understand that you want to change fields and we'll understand if something happens and you have to fly, but actually, we need more than just a receptionist. We need someone to run our office and keep us out of trouble." Reggie laughed.

"*And* we need someone to help us get funding for our nonprofit operations. The Imani Group is more than just a consulting operation. We like to go to bat for those who are up against the walls of discrimination. Kind of like the Rainbow Coalition, we have a grassroots mentality, too."

"Sorry, I don't know anything about fund-raising and grant-writing."

"But you're bright and enthusiastic . . ." Philip smiled.

"And a quick study. Listen, Nia. You come on board—on a trial basis—give us a shot, and we'll understand if your dream job happens to fall into your lap, okay? What do you say?"

Nia smiled. This was fantastic. "It sounds superb. Just one thing . . ."

"Yes?" Reggie and Philip asked simultaneously.

"Is *he* a new part of your organization, too? Do I have to deal with the likes of *him* on a daily basis?"

"You know, forget it. I'm sorry, okay? I was wrong. I don't have a decent excuse," Seth barked, then softened his demeanor and continued speaking. "I'm angry and I'm not thinking straight a-and the words just came out. I guess I'm just a little tense with the article and all"—he gestured at the newspaper in the center of the table.

She picked up the folded paper and glanced over the article. "*You're* Seth Jackson?"

Glasses nodded solemnly. " 'Fraid so."

"Hey, don't worry about it. *I'm* not quick to judge. *I* give folks the benefit of the doubt," she said, watching Seth sink into his chair uncomfortably.

Reggie shared more details of his knowledge of Feinstein's activities in the whole Brooksmore scandal, alluding to the fact that perhaps Jonathan may have had some sort of direct involvement with the maneuvers. All of this was news to Nia, but none of it surprised her.

"There was never anything evil or blatantly racist about Jonathan. He always treated me with respect—outwardly, anyway. It was his niece who was the nasty one," she said, accepting the waiter's offer of water.

"His niece. Oh yeah, I remember her," Seth recalled, sitting up. "Real piece of work." Nia frowned and nodded her agreement.

"Well, if it weren't for that woman, I'd probably still be there," she said and gave them the gory details of her last day at Feinstein.

"That's terrible, Nia. The way I see it, even if they aren't directly responsible for Brooksmore, there's still something raggedy going on at that place. They ain't gonna get away with any of this." Reggie crossed his legs and looked pensively out at the koi pond.

"So," Reggie said to her, standing and pushing in his chair, "it would be in our mutual best interest if you would consider my offer. From the work we've seen from you, and from what we know about the kind of person you are, we'd be lucky to have you on board."

Nia smiled and walked toward the exit. It sounded like a win-win proposition to her. She would have that paycheck, those benefits, and the freedom to continue her public relations search—not to mention the opportunity to pick up some grant-writing skills along the way. And if she got lucky, she might even be able to make Feinstein Films squirm a little bit.

"Count me in, gentlemen. I'll see you at work on Monday?"

"Excellent! Monday is fine. Glad to have you!" Philip smiled, pumping her hand.

Reggie turned to his friend. "Seth, man. I'm sorry. I've got to go back to the office now. Catch you later?"

"No problem, man. You need a ride?"

Reggie looked down the block and saw that Philip had already secured a cab. "No, guess I'll ride back with Philip." He turned to Nia. "You okay?"

"I can give you a ride, no problem. I'm parked right at the corner," Seth offered, eager.

Nia smiled halfheartedly and looked at Reggie, skeptical. He laughed.

"Oh, he's okay. I can vouch for him—*I think*. Just don't give him your number. You'll live to regret it!" Reggie called down the block for Philip to hold the cab and ran down to meet him.

"And I get to ride with the infamous Nia Benson." They walked. She glared.

"Infamous? Sounds like a supreme case of the pot calling the kettle black. Tell me, do you always go out of your way to be this obnoxious? Or am I getting special treatment today?"

He laughed at her, put his head back and laughed. "Touché! Okay, okay—truce already!"

She gave him half a smile, her arms folded tightly across her chest. They stood and waited in awkward silence as the attendant raced to retrieve Seth's car. Nia looked him over; he was annoying and had long since rubbed her the wrong way. And she still didn't trust him a whole heck of a lot, especially with his friend Reggie nowhere around. Definitely not enough for her to give him her home address.

"So where to, lady? Just give me your address and I'll have you home in a New York minute!" Seth adopted a fake Brooklyn accent and cracked imaginary gum as they drove out onto the street.

Where to? She had never been much of a drinker, drunk people bored her and she hated hanging out in bars, anyplace where smoke was the pastime of the day, actually. She had been trying very hard to cut down on the use of her credit cards, so shopping was out. She checked her watch. It was getting late. They had been in that restaurant for hours.

"St. Augustine's. You know where it is? I don't remember the exact address; here, maybe I stuck that flyer in my journal . . ." She began rummaging through her briefcase.

"St. Augustine's . . . that's here on the East side, right? So you're a church girl, huh? I love me some *church girls*. Yes, indeed. They know how to treat a man right! And talk about fine? Help me! You know, Reggie really was wrong about me. You give me your number and I'll show you a *great* time . . ." He nudged her with his elbow and she moved closer to the door.

What had she done to deserve this?

"You know, I been a cabby all my life. Ever since I came to this fine country as a young lad. Started driving when I was twelve, ha ha ha. Now, I didn't get my license way back then, no, they didn't let you take the test that young—"

She cut him off, mildly annoyed with his attempt at humor. "Excuse me for interrupting your stroll down memory lane, but you *do* know where you're going, right?"

He howled loudly. "Oh, yes, missy. Sure do. St. Augustine's, next stop."

He continued to whoop and holler, flowing in and out of various accents, giving grand details of the changes he imagined would have been noticed in the city over the past thirty years.

He was not entertaining and she was not in the mood.

When he pulled up in front of St. Augustine's, she unbuckled her seat belt and opened the door before he shifted into Park.

"Thank you," Nia said, her voice dripping with sarcasm. "What a wonderful experience it was meeting you." She climbed out of Seth's car and watched as he grinned, waving to her wildly, and turning the corner with a screech.

What a royal jerk.

He wished she would just pick up the phone and curse him out. It was the silence that was driving him crazy.

Every other moment, Seth was drifting toward the phone, dialing Lauren's number. One night. Two nights. Three nights. And the more time that passed, the more he craved to speak with her, to tell her *something*. He was sure he could find some way to explain the situation if he could just get her to listen. He needed to hear her voice so he could go on with his life and concentrate.

Speaking with Lauren had become a matter of his practical survival.

His apartment was rank, unsanitary, and in disarray. His cherished plants were browning at the tips, the soil as dry as the dirty dishes that sat in the kitchen sink. His dirty clothes were strewn on the floor in the bedroom, the pile of kicked-off shoes growing amid a mountain of magazines on his living room floor. His unopened mail was stained with rings from the bottom of his coffee mug, windowed envelopes and handwritten letters thrown carelessly on his kitchen table.

She hadn't been to work since, well, since she had walked out on him without giving him an opportunity to defend himself.

Sometimes he allowed himself to think in these terms, to allow her to be the unreasonable one. But other times he acknowledged the truth of the situation. Truth of the matter was that she hadn't been to work since he had succumbed to being the man he thought he had successfully overcome. She hadn't been to work since he messed up.

Bringg. Bringg. Bringg. Bringg.

"Yes, this is Lauren and you've reached my residence. I am unable to take your call. Leave a message at the tone. Thank you."

Seth stared at the floor. Well, at least she was honest enough not to promise a return call. But the tone of the message was so different, so altered. The coldness of it slapped him like the February tide at Jones Beach.

Beep.

"Lauren? Lauren? This is Seth. Lauren, if you're there, please pick up the phone. I really need to talk to you. Lauren? Well, I'll just assume that you're not there. I'd rather assume that than assume you're ignoring me. Well, you know my number. Please give me a call. Call me up and cuss me out, if that makes you feel better, but I really do need to talk to you."

Seth pressed the receiver into its cradle. And as soon as he did, it rang.

"Hello!" he shouted into the receiver.

"Hey dude. Been a while, you bailing on me or something?" Seth closed his eyes and tried to regroup.

"Garrison, aw, man, no, no I ain't bailing on you." Seth rubbed his temples and sat down. He had really been lax as far as new business with the Garrison Walters Trio was concerned. He'd been too preoccupied with his love life to devote the time necessary to making it happen. Just something else he allowed himself to blame on Sandy.

"So what's the deal, man? You said you were gonna get us work and then I don't hear from you in a month of Sundays. What's happening?" Seth could hear the striking of a match and the exhaling of smoke into the receiver.

"No excuses. I been dealing with stuff."

"Yeah, man, well, we all dealing with stuff, you know. I'm dealing with *stuff.* I'm dealing with two other cats asking me about the rest of the month and how the summer is shaping up. What should I tell 'em, huh?"

"Tell them it's looking good. Tell them you'll have some word for them soon."

"Yeah, well, *soon* ain't gonna pay the rent, you know what I'm saying here?"

"I'll be in touch with you with something concrete by the end of the week."

"End of the week. That's what I'm gonna tell 'em, Seth. *End . . . of . . . the . . . week.*" Garrison paused and exhaled into the receiver. "Don't make me look bad, Mr. Manager Man."

"I'll get back to you. Later, man."

"Ummm hmmm. Later."

He turned on the stereo, turned it up loud, and let the rhythms of War's "The Cisco Kid" drown out the little voice in his head that was telling him how badly he was messing up this time.

Seth walked to his desk and started flipping through his Rolodex of contacts. He had gone against his own rules, shoving business to the back burner because of his personal life. It wasn't like him. He hadn't established his credibility and growing reputation in the music world as a result of this kind of half-stepping behavior, and he didn't like the way it felt. It went against his grain. He was determined to get the trio at least a little something, just to save face. He stopped the wheel of contacts at the business card of Saleem's. Saleem was one of the nicest guys in the business, always ready to help someone out, always there to give a newcomer a chance. He owned a tiny club in the city, had been there for ages, not too far from where Seth lived. The acoustics were kind of bad, but small bands played passionately on that tiny stage underneath the staircase in the back of the narrow, poorly lit club. Along the walls were autographed publicity shots of everyone who was anyone in the jazz world, with personally written thank-you notes to Saleem. Every jazz group on their way up passed through the doors of Saleem's because the crowd was steady and loyal and wildly enthusiastic. Playing Saleem's was an unwritten rite of passage in the New York jazz scene. And besides, the owner owed him one.

The last time Seth had been there was with Fatima, an a cappella jazz trio that had altered their schedule to accommodate the club. Unfortunately, it had snowed that day, and even the die-hard regulars had opted not to brave the elements that night. They had played to an embarrassing house of four. And performed excellently. Yes, Saleem's was a definite possibility for Garrison Walters Trio. He wrote it down and put a star next to it.

Bing Bong. Bing Bong.

Seth held his place in the Rolodex with his letter opener and walked to the door. He was in business mode, thinking logistically, and absentmindedly threw open the door.

"Seth."

Sandy stood at his door, looking down at her fuzzy blue nondescript animal slippers. Her hair was in eight thick Pocahontas-looking braids, resting on the red plaid flannel of her oversized shirt. Her jeans were splattered with white paint. She stood there, the little girl in her showing, biting her bottom lip, shifting from foot to foot, and shoving her hands into the back pockets of her jeans.

She looked really tired and pitiful to him.

Seth fought the feeling of slamming the door on her, of slamming the door on himself and what he had done. But he was curious. And he wanted to have the satisfaction of telling her no—to whatever it was she was coming to ask.

He didn't say anything, just stood there and looked at her blankly, waiting for her to finish her thought.

"May I come in? Or are you gonna make me say what I have to say in the hallway for all the neighbors to hear?"

"Did you get your stuff? I had the decency to put your diaphragm, underwear, and assorted props in a box and left it outside your door."

"Don't do this here. Come on, it will just take a minute."

"I don't want you in my home."

She looked up at him, looked him in the eye. He could see the hurt that was there. His glare remained fixed and hard.

"Um. Oh, okay, Seth. Okay . . ." Sandy nodded slowly then looked back at the floor. "I just wanted to apologize."

"Apologize?"

"Uh, yeah. I wanted to tell you . . . that I'm sorry for what happened."

Seth had to laugh. He rubbed his forehead, shifted his weight, and pointed at her with his long index finger. "You're sorry for what happened? Or you're sorry for what you did?"

She shrugged her shoulders. "What's so funny, Seth? Is it so hard to believe that I'm sorry?"

"Actually, yeah. It's incredibly hard to believe."

"Well, it's true. I'm sorry for what I did, really am. I want us to be friends again."

He looked at her and wondered how such a physically beautiful woman could be such a wretched individual. "Friends?"

"Yes, friends. Like we were before."

He paused to gather his thoughts. He looked at the black tile in the hallway in front of his door, how it glistened. "I can see now that we were never friends. Friends don't screw their friends."

"Friends do that all the time, Seth."

"No, see, we're not understanding each other here. I said, friends do not *screw* their friends. I know this is a foreign concept to you and that you can't grasp it. But trust me. It's something you need to learn."

She took a step closer to his door and he backed up, like she was contagious or something. She laughed. "Yeah, right. Tell Sandy you didn't like it, then," she whispered.

"Oh, you were a good *f-ff* . . . no. No, I'm not going to say it. Not going to put myself on your level. But don't get me wrong," he spit out the words like bullets, "I know firsthand now that you are good at your *craft*. But friends do not *screw* friends. They just don't hurt their friends like that."

She smiled a quarter smile and turned to walk away. "But I got what I wanted, Seth. Sandy got what she wanted—just like she said she would."

"Did you, woman? Did you really get what you wanted?"

He closed the door, didn't slam it, but closed it and locked both locks. He wanted her to know what it felt like to be Outside and Separated. Just as Lauren had successfully been making him feel.

Seth leaned on the door, closed his eyes, and sighed deeply. Nothing he did took away this spinning sensation that had engulfed his being. Nothing made the disgust he was feeling for himself go away.

And he had gone through the gamut. Trying to justify what he had done, telling himself he had done what any male would have done under the same circumstances. He tried hard not to think of what had led up to his moment of weakness. Tried not to think of the beginning of what could have been a perfect evening. Tried not to think of the scent of Lauren's skin or the simmer of the pots in the kitchen or the sensuous feel of the white lambskin rug beneath their bodies. Tried not to think of how slowly Lauren's tear fell. Tried not to think of how raw and enticing Sandy had appeared in the center of his bed. Tried not to acknowledge how, even now, the very thought of Sandy's naked, writhing body could make him salivate and swallow hard and rise.

Seth hit the door with his fist and his fury. Maybe Reggie had been right. Maybe there really was no hope for him and his having anyone decent in his life. Because after he had gone through all his justifications, he still seriously doubted that another man would have been so rank, have fallen so completely in such a short period of time.

Forget this personal stuff. Forget it all. He would regain control over the parts of his life that he could. He had to concentrate on the music, on the business, get back on track.

Now that the job was done, he wanted his money from Feinstein.

He walked back to his desk, fished the business card from his top desk drawer, sat down, and dialed Accounting.

"Feinstein. Mercedes speaking."

"Hello Mercedes. This is Seth Jackson. I did some work for Feinstein a few weeks back and I was calling to find out when I can expect payment for my services rendered."

"Mr. Jackson, can you hold for a moment while I check our records?"

"Sure." He held on the line for quite a while, listening to a medley of super successful Jonathan Feinstein jingles.

The last jingle, the original Caucasian version of the OnTheGo spot, was interrupted by Mercedes's return. "Mr. Jackson?"

"Yes?"

"Our records show that you failed to comply with the compensable terms of your contract. We show that no payment is pending."

Seth placed call after call to Feinstein Films, trying to reconnect with Accounting for further clarification, or Jonathan for explanation. They put him on hold. They accidentally disconnected him. No one at Feinstein would take his calls.

This made no sense. He tried to calm himself enough to re-create the steps he had taken with Feinstein contractually, tried to understand how something this absurd could have happened. He had gone to the initial meeting, had spoken with Jonathan on the phone for a verbal confirmation of his expected duties. He had signed the contract, sent it by messenger back to them as requested, agreeing to the terms of payment. And most important, he had done the work.

He slammed the phone down and walked to the kitchen, poured himself a glass of bourbon. He took a long swig, the alcohol burning his lips, seeping slowly down his throat. He pulled out a chair, took his arm and swept all the mail that cluttered the spot in front of him onto the floor. This was too much. He put his head in his hands, closed his eyes and tried to remember, tried to think. When he opened his eyes he saw it beneath him.

A letter from Feinstein Films.

He tore open the letter and read it: quickly then slowly, forward then backward. There had to be some sort of mistake.

The letter stated that not only were they refusing to pay him for his work, but Jonathan was now in the process of suing him for defamation of character.

"Hi Crystal, I need to talk to Reggie." Seth paced the floor in front of his desk, holding his glass full of bourbon, pulling the phone cord to allow him movement.

"Seth? Do you know what time it is?" She sounded sleepy and peaceful.

"No, I don't know what time it is. And right now, I really don't care a whole heck of a lot. I just need to speak to Reggie. Put him on the phone." The alcohol was slurring his words, supplying him with an extra dose of crassness and rudeness.

"Reggie is asleep. It's almost five o'clock in the morning. He has a full day ahead of him and I'm not waking him up for a drunk. Go to bed, Seth. Sleep it off." And she hung up the phone.

Seth was livid. He picked up his Rolodex and threw it across the room, picked up his telephone and slammed it on the floor. How dare she. He sunk down onto the floor and dialed their number again. This time Reggie answered.

"What is it, Seth? What is it that couldn't wait until daylight?" He was agitated, his voice conveying no semblance of friendliness.

"It's Feinstein. They're trying to ruin me, man. They're trying to bring me down. I did the work and they're trying to destroy me."

"Seth, it's late and you're drunk . . ."

"No, you don't understand. You're all I have left, man. I don't have anywhere else to go."

Reggie sighed and listened while Seth cried into the phone. Neither man spoke. Neither man hung up the phone.

Seth could hear Crystal in the distance, sucking her teeth. He couldn't make out her whispered words, but he didn't like her. He didn't like the way she tried to get in between him and his friend. Didn't matter much though, Seth surmised. Reggie was still on the phone. As long as he was still there, there was still hope for their friendship.

"Come by the office in the morning. We'll talk it out. Promise."

"Oh hell, Reggie. This is more than just Feinstein. This is more than just a business deal gone sour. You haven't talked to me decent since I told you about Lauren. Reg, please. I really need to talk to you. I need to fix this."

Reggie sighed and cleared his throat, rustled papers, made busy noise.

"How could you screw up on *Lauren?*"

"Reg, come on."

After a pause that seemed to last for an hour and a half, Reg finally spoke.

"I'm going to go work out. Jog. Central Park. You want to come?"

"Yeah, Reg. I'd like that a lot. Meet you at your place?"

"In *front* of my place. Crystal's going to be trying to get some rest, so don't ring the bell or come upstairs. I'll be leaving in a half hour. Later."

Reggie reached up and wiped the sweat off his brow in a feeble attempt to keep the drops out of his eyes. He glanced over at Seth, who was having a really hard time keeping up.

"You're out of shape, Seth."

"Could be the hangover, but I think you're trying to kill me."

"Death by exercise—that would be novel." Reggie increased his speed and his sarcasm.

"Reggie. Stop. I . . . *gotta* . . . *stop*. . . ." Reggie maintained his stride and Seth stopped cold, in the middle of the path. He leaned over, placed his hands on his knees, tried to catch his breath. Reggie jogged around in a small circle, returning to Seth's resting spot.

"Okay, okay, man. Next time. So what was that? Three miles?"

"Three miles, my ass. It was five, if it was a day."

"Whatever you say." Reggie and Seth began walking in the direction of Central Park West. "What happened, Seth?" Reggie looked straight ahead as he spoke. They both did.

"Good question. I've been asking myself that constantly since Lauren walked out on me."

"So you been doing Sandy." Reggie paused. "*Sandy.*"

"No, Reg, I really haven't."

Reggie chuckled. "Man, don't play me for the fool. You know me, I know you. We both know the deal, right?"

"Sandy planted stuff in my bathroom when Lauren came over—all this feminine stuff. Lauren slapped me, walked out."

"I won't ask you how she had the opportunity to do gardening in your apartment."

"I'm too nice, that's how."

"So, sounds to me like it's just a little misunderstanding. Lauren's reasonable. She'll give you another chance. Eventually."

"I don't know if she should." Seth stopped and at looked at Reggie.

"I'm almost afraid to ask, but why?"

Seth shoved his hands in the pouch of his sweatshirt front. Slowly, and painfully, he recounted the discovery of Sandy on his bed, of their encounter, of how his life had been since that day.

And when he was finished, Reggie looked at him blankly a long time in silence.

"Why didn't you just throw her out when you saw her?"

Seth shook his head, recalling the vision. "Reggie, man, if you could have seen her . . . just seen her there. Yeah, I know. I really screwed up."

The men stood sweating, looking at each other.

"Reggie, everything is falling apart. Everything."

"Tell me about Feinstein."

"They're going off the deep end; I don't know what they're thinking about. First, I thought they liked the spot, and now, I get this letter threatening to take me to court and refusing to pay me. It makes no sense at all."

Reggie took a swig of water. "They want to sue you? For what?"

"Something about character defamation. Reggie, I have no idea what all this is about. If this is how the commercial industry functions, I guess I'm just way out of my league."

"It's not you."

Seth looked at him, puzzled.

"They're just shady all the way around. Have you met with them?"

Seth told him how he had called and been disrespected on every occasion.

"Seth, I want you to set up an appointment with Feinstein. Let me know when it takes place. I'll go with you. But don't tell them this."

Seth was confused. "You know these people?"

Reggie shook his head. "Nope, but I know *of* them. Their reputation precedes them."

"Yeah, I'll call . . . try to set it up." Seth didn't press him for details. "And thanks."

"For what?"

"Being here anyway. I know it's gonna cost you with the Mrs."

"Brothers. All the time."

Seth jogged in place, his lower lip quivering, sniffling.

"I think we need another lap," Reggie said, his eyes misting, too, pointing back to the innards of the park, "what do you say?"

"Yeah, I think so. I think that would be great." And this time they jogged slowly, keeping pace with each other, saying nothing to the other, saying nothing out loud.

Thirteen

What a jerk. What a royal jerk.

The man had managed to make her completely lose her composure in the middle of a public place, had insulted her without knowing her, and then, to add insult to injury, had actually tried to get her number and get next to her. Her mama had warned her about men like Seth. *Tip your hat and just keep on stepping, young lady,* is what she would tell her. Sounded like sage advice to follow right about now. Men like Seth would stab you in the back in that New York minute and then try to get you into bed before nightfall. *Negroes,* her mama would call them, then roll her eyes and purse her lips in disdain. *Nothing but common,* her grandmom would say, spitting out the words with venom.

She bought the evening paper from the vendor at the corner, silently handing him payment without making eye contact.

It was a sad state of affairs when you had to have a cuss word, an acrid phrase in your everyday vocabulary, to describe the men who were supposed to love you and cherish you as a matter of course. Nia had given that job to Rome. And from what she had understood, he had accepted the task. He had accepted and now he had reneged. She would take back three cherished memories to keep on her side of the table and make a mental note to make better choices when choosing a partner to play a serious woman's game.

God help the poor man who next crossed her path. Nia knew she was volatile now, nowhere near being relationship-ready material. She wished she could be more like the men she knew and was coming to despise: cold, callous, calculating, and conceited. The same men whom she had adored and welcomed into her life just a few months ago, back when things were predictable and in control. She wanted time when she could concentrate on getting her own life together instead of being expected to give and give, and then, once she had done all that, be ready to give some more.

Nia ran up the steps of St. Augustine's, refusing to turn around and look back at Seth, refusing to see if he bothered to wait until she was safely inside, after he turned that corner, before making his completed getaway. Not that it mattered, because it didn't, but she didn't want any more confirmation of his rudeness and inconsideration. She had just about had it today with playing the Gender Game. The "when he does this, the proper woman responds by doing this" game. She sincerely hoped that no one here at The Poetry Pause would try to smile and cozy up to her and try to make moves. She was not—repeat *not*—in the mood. She just wanted a safe place where she could get away from the likes of all the Seth Jacksons in the world and the memories of Rome-Who-Left-Her-Alone-Carrington and listen to the sound of words.

Words.

Ever since she was a little girl, Nia loved the sound of words. It was hard to describe the effect that listening to spoken words had on her. It was more than the story, more than the content and thought that gave her a rush. It was something that happened between the page and the saying; there was something about the rhythm, the way sound mixed with breath that touched her internally and gave her peace and calm. Her mother had told her stories of how Nia would respond to fairy tales as an infant, her eyes becoming wide, her hands grasping mommy fingers as though she were holding on to the very letters themselves. And her captivation with words continued through elementary school, lovingly clutching the edges of her antique school desk whenever her teachers would read the enchanting poetry of Paul Lawrence Dunbar or the poetic literature of Margaret Walker.

Words. There were not enough.

Since the time she was fired/let go/or otherwise dismissed, she had reread all the books on her shelves, marking up her paperback copy of *I Know Why the Caged Bird Sings* beyond recognition, and cultivating strength from *for colored girls who have considered suicide.* Reading *The Bluest Eye* again only made her angry and frustrated, wanting to let everyone know that she never craved blue eyes that were taught not to see the truth. She could use a good dose of new words tonight and she was looking forward to hearing what the poets had to give her.

When Nia walked inside the vestibule of the cathedral, the woman who had left the flyer for her was placing a Poetry Pause placard on an easel to the side of the main entrance. She looked up at Nia and smiled.

"Ah, you came back." The woman clasped her hands and smiled, delighted.

"Yes, thank you for the flyer. I'm looking forward to hearing the poets."

"Everyone who will be here will be a poet. You are looking forward to hearing yourself."

Nia chuckled. "Oh, no. I'm not going to read. I just want to come and listen to the others read."

"Sometimes it is good to listen, but sometimes it is good to speak up, no?" The woman patted Nia's hand. "Maybe you will be moved to share words with us. Maybe, yes?"

"I doubt it. I think I'll probably just watch and listen this time. Maybe next time."

"We are glad to have you. You are early, the first one here tonight. Go ahead and go inside." She pointed toward the open door. "Have a seat. Relax."

Nia walked inside the room to the left of the vestibule. It was a grand, rectangular room. In the center of the room was a massive oak table with thick, carved legs surrounded by oak armchairs with navy blue velvet upholstery. The windows were stained, leaded glass, depicting a beautiful sunrise with doves flying toward the clouds. In the evening sun the colors from the windows flooded the room, bouncing off the gleam of the highly polished wood, dancing in the beveled crystal of the chandeliers. There was an antique grand piano in the far corner, a well-preserved tapestry of a serene pastoral scene affixed to the wall behind it. It smelled like a museum in here: a mix of old, odd things with modern-day care, ancient fibers and lemon oil.

So beautiful.

Nia took a seat near the center of the table. There were flyers on the table announcing the upcoming Second Annual Open Poetry Competition of The Poetry Pause; she picked one up, read it, and put it in her briefcase. It was something to consider, entering a contest like that. Maybe she would get lucky; she laughed. At the very least, thinking about entering would help her to get her thoughts together and at least attempt to write for an audience. Maybe. She set down her newspaper, removed her journal and pen from her briefcase, and began to write.

"Hi, I see I'm not the first one here tonight."

Nia looked up into the smiling face of another black woman and returned her smile.

"Hi, I'm Nia Benson. Are you here for The Poetry Pause?" Nia shook the woman's outstretched hand and made note of all the beautiful diamonds gracing her fingers.

"I certainly am. Name is Vaughan Gonzalez. I usually try to get here early so I can do a little bit of writing before things get under way. This your first time?" Vaughan sat a couple of seats away from Nia, placing a designer tote bag in the seat between them.

"First time."

"Ah, a *virgin*." The women laughed.

"Well, I don't know if I'd say all *that*. But yes, I'm looking forward to hearing the poets." Nia shifted in her chair, turning more toward Vaughan.

"And we will be looking forward to hearing from you."

Nia shook her head and forced a smile. "Oh, no. Not tonight. Tonight, I'm just here to listen and observe."

Vaughan laughed, tossed her long, black hair over her shoulder. "Dear, no one comes to The Poetry Pause and doesn't participate in the readings. We are more like a workshop than a showcase. *Everyone* reads. We are here to help each other, not here to be *entertainment*."

Nia tapped her pen on the edge of the table. "Hmmm . . ."

"What's the matter?" Vaughan asked as she removed her notebook from her tote bag.

"Sorry, *I'm* not reading tonight."

"Well," Vaughan said after a long pause, crossing her long stockinged legs away from Nia, "I'm just telling you how we operate. Everyone reads. Everyone critiques."

"You don't make allowances for visitors? Suppose somebody comes who doesn't want to read?"

Vaughan chuckled. "No allowances, sorry."

The arrogance of this woman.

"Well, you should. Not everyone wants to read their work, and there may be some people who—"

"I have been coming here for quite some time now," Vaughan said, cutting her off. "We've never had a problem with someone who refused to read. Most people who come here do so because they're *poets*—"

"Excuse me, Vaughan, but you just cut me off—"

"And that's just the way things are."

Nia glared at this woman whom she didn't even know.

Why am I sitting here? I don't have to take this.

It was as though someone had stuck a pin into Nia, as though she were filled with air and wrapped in latex, her resolve and strength exiting through this tiny hole in her armor. She had taken just one piercing too many, had received one push today beyond her daily limit.

Another person she didn't know expecting something she had not consented to give. Another person making judgments telling her what she had to do.

"Fine, well, you know something? That's not the way *I* do things."

Nia gathered her newspaper, shoved her journal and pen into her briefcase, the angry tears of frustration welling and spilling over. She was tired of people and their conclusions. She stood, began walking toward the door, and flicked her wrist, diva style, over her shoulder. This woman should be able to relate to that, she thought.

"Hey, wait! Hey, Nia? I didn't mean to say anything to make you *cry*. Oh, for goodness sake, what did I say? Nia?" Vaughan called after her but Nia kept walking and didn't turn around.

This had obviously been a bad idea.

Vaughan finally caught up to her when Nia was halfway down the steps. Before she could say anything to her, Nia spun around and put her finger in the woman's face.

"*You* do not know me. *You* know nothing about me. And whoever it is that *you* must think I am, *you* are wrong. I came to The Poetry Pause to hear some words that would make me feel better, not to deal with the rantings and ravings of a woman, of a group of people on some power trip. I don't need this. I really don't."

Vaughan looked at Nia, her lips tight. Nia was expecting some fancy retort, was braced for a clever backlash. But instead she saw a softness wash over the other woman's face. "How could I be so insensitive? I mean, really. Nia, please, forgive me? I've had a really bad day, too—I mean bad like you wouldn't believe—and I have obviously just lashed out at the first available subject. I'm sorry, please."

Nia shrugged her shoulders, noncommittally. She had grown up in New York, was used to people going off the deep end all around her, and she had become jaded. She didn't trust Vaughan. But more than that, she didn't even care. She just wanted to get away from this joint. She continued walking down the steps.

"I got to go! Nice meeting you, Vaughan. Take care."

"Nia, please! Listen, just hear me out, okay?" The woman was shouting and starting to attract attention so Nia waited reluctantly for her on the sidewalk. "You know, I have all but ruined your experience at The Poetry Pause tonight. I am so, so sorry for that. Truth be told, I don't really feel like going in there now either. How about we just let bygones be bygones and go and get a cup of coffee—in the name of peace? What do you think?"

Nia didn't respond.

"We can compare horrible days, okay? Please, it's the least I can do . . . my treat."

"Vaughan, we don't *have* any bygones. We don't have anything. So let's not pretend to be girlfriends and nice and just get on with it, okay?" Nia left her words in the wind, making her getaway from the woman.

Nia turned the corner and walked westward, blending effortlessly into the crowd. It was almost seven now, and most of the people on the street were either finally arriving home from work or on their way to dinner. The sun was setting, a few bright rays filtered between the tall office buildings that dotted the landscape.

It could be that the stress was starting to get to her. It wasn't like her to be so snappy with people she didn't even know, even when those people chose to be less than lovely with her. She usually allowed herself a beat to step back and recognize what was actually being said in a situation, what was actually personal and should be taken personally. Her encounter with this Vaughan woman obviously had nothing whatsoever to do with Nia and who Nia is; she didn't even know her. And here she had judged the whole group of poets on this one woman's bad day. That wasn't fair.

Nia wondered how many times in the past day, the past week, the past month, she had jumped to conclusions that reeked with faulty assumptions. How many times had she made assumptions based on incomplete information? How many times had she written off someone or something because of her mood at the time, because of the negative vibe she had brought into the situation? How many times had she done what she often berated others for doing?

In the back of her mind, she heard Grace's voice: *Woman, trust your gut; do what feels good and don't look back.* But she didn't want to be like Grace. She didn't want to turn into an impulsive bundle of cynicism, not caring about other people and not giving them second chances.

She walked into a dimly lit restaurant, a place frequented by a decent-looking crowd, a place where she felt comfortable and they took major credit cards. The hostess seated her at a small booth toward the back and brought her a dinner menu. She ordered a half carafe of Chablis and a seafood Caesar salad.

She took out her journal, her pen, and made a list of areas in her life where she had perhaps slammed the door a little too hastily, places in her life she would reexamine and allow herself to question.

1. ROME

Well, she hadn't even given him the opportunity to say anything to her. Nia couldn't think of any decent response that he could possibly have, but that wasn't the point. She would allow him to speak his piece, let him tell her—in person—what was behind what she had witnessed. It would hurt, she was sure it was going to hurt no matter what his story was, but she would allow him the opportunity to say it. If it was time for her to close the door on their relationship, she didn't want to do it in a huff. She felt she owed what they had built at least that much respect.

2. IMANI

Just because that guy Seth was somehow affiliated with The Imani Group did not mean the entire operation was without hope, she mused. She liked what she heard when Reggie Montgomery spoke. He had vision and he was cool-headed. And she was angry enough and driven enough to perhaps actually provide assistance to his mission. Besides, maybe this was the opportunity to be the positive influence to her people to which Grace had referred.

3. GRACE

Nia wrote her friend's name, underlined it over and over again, drew a box around it all. She sat back in her chair and took in the crowd. There were all sorts of people here. Groups of people, couples, singles on dates, singles chatting with the bartenders. Black, white, men, women. Business types, funky down types. After downing her first glass of wine, she noticed that what they all had in common was that they were all talking; they were all communicating. Talking and listening.

Nia hadn't really understood what Grace meant when she had accused Nia of not listening, of not wanting to hear who she was. All these years of being friends, of setting her up and hanging out. What could Grace have meant? She had told Grace so many of her inner secrets and Grace had been there every step of the way, giving her encouragement, love, and advice. She thought back on the years, trying to think of a time when she hadn't been there for Grace, and came up without a single memory. She had always been there, but it had been Grace who never leaned. But that had not been her fault; that was just how Grace was.

She poured herself another glass of wine and moved on.

4. THE POETRY PAUSE

It was just ridiculous of her to have judged an entire group of people based on the actions of one person, even if she presented herself as though she was speaking on the group's behalf. Nia knew better than that. This one was the easiest to correct: She would return to The Pause next week, walk in as though for the first time, and be open to hearing the poetry.

And even Vaughan. She wouldn't hold this initial encounter against the woman. It was only a brief moment, a truly inconsequential moment, the ending of what Vaughan had admitted was not the best of days. Nia could definitely understand that. She hadn't been the most congenial person either, dragging her nasty post-Seth attitude into St. Augustine's and allowing it to seep into their meeting. First impressions were only lasting if you meant for them to be, and she was more than willing to live a week, go back, and start this anew.

She closed her journal, feeling both purged and full, and finished eating her salad. Nia was pleased with her dinner selection—lightly seasoned, not too overpowering, and delicious—and told the waitress so when she came to clear the dishes. The crowd was thickening, becoming more robust in their laughter, the bar now invisible behind the people two layers thick. Nia asked for the check and took out her wallet. The waitress shook her head.

"Been taken care of, honey. Very generously, too. Hmm, your benefactor was just over there . . . at the end of the bar . . ."

Nia stood and looked into the crowd, looking for Rome but half expecting to see that Seth dude. Instead she felt a tap on her shoulder and turned around.

"I'm really sorry, Nia. Really. Forgive me?"

Nia smiled and nodded that she did. "Have a drink?" Nia motioned for Vaughan to have a seat.

Vaughan sat down, gently placing her precious tote bag on the floor next to her. "I think I've had enough for one evening. I've been sitting at the bar, sipping brandy for the better part of an hour." She looked over at Nia. "Thank you for being gracious, for not making a scene in here."

Nia understood her concern. An hour or so ago she probably would have done just that, having a grand hissy fit in front of all these unsuspecting people. A half carafe of Chablis had made her much more rational and forgiving.

"And thank *you* for generously picking up my dinner tab. It really wasn't necessary, but it sure was good." They both laughed.

"Well, I felt bad about what happened back there. Losing my temper and being dogmatic really isn't my style. I wanted to make it up to you somehow."

"Yeah, Vaughan. I'm sorry for my behavior, too. I am usually more diplomatic."

"Why don't we just start over and put that horrible past in the past?" Vaughan extended her hand across the table.

"Sounds good to me. Truce?"

The women smiled at each other and shook hands.

"Truce. You were just there, catching the remnants of a frustrating day." Nia pointed to herself. "I'm gearing up for a job transition."

"Really? What line of work?"

"I want to move into public relations."

"Any prospects?"

"Not a single one. I decided to just trudge blindly into the murky waters. I'm going to send out a bunch of unsolicited résumés and see what happens."

"That's ambitious. Any companies in particular?"

"Whoever will hire me and give me a decent salary with benefits!" They laughed.

"Actually," Nia said, "I have a list of about twenty-five or thirty companies that will be receiving my résumé. Most of them are connected with entertainment or communications in some way. But yes, it's definitely a challenge . . ."

The waitress walked over to their table. "So is there anything else I can bring you two ladies?"

Vaughan spoke up first. "I think I'd like a cup of coffee. And you, Nia?"

"I'll have the same."

"Two coffees, coming right up," the waitress sang, worming her way back to the kitchen.

"Well, I can definitely relate to frustrating, but not so much work as —"

"Men?" Vaughan chimed in.

Nia chuckled. "Not my favorite topic right now. I keep wondering how it is that I let the gender get under my skin the way I do."

"Maybe you leave the door open, diva."

Nia didn't really understand what she meant by the statement, but it sounded clever and it made her smile. "Maybe I do, I don't know. Anyway, what was your source of frustration today?"

"Oh, job-related issues. I'm a producer over at VisionCom—"

"VisionCom? The black cable network?"

Vaughan laughed. "Yes, that would be the one. I see you've heard of us. So if VisionCom is on your list of prospects, let me know. Maybe I can help you out."

"Thanks! Of course VisionCom is on my list! You know, everyone is sitting around waiting to see how you guys are going to hold up to HBO in the New York market."

"Excellent. I see you *do* know a little something about us. Well, I think we'll do just fine . . . as long as they *listen* to me. We had an issue today regarding a show in development. And actually, part of the problem I brought on myself. I'm trying to develop a talk show based on a magazine concept. The problem is that I'm friendly with so many people affiliated with this particular magazine. And there's truly nothing wrong with having friends, you know. But when it comes to one's livelihood . . . well, friendship is friendship and business is business. Some people just can't understand that."

Nia shrugged her shoulders. "That seems common knowledge to me."

"Well, it gets a little sticky when you have to fire your friends or re-organize or do the corporate shuffle or whatever. No matter what you call the maneuver, it's an uncomfortable one."

Nia could only imagine. She had never experienced such angst on a personal level, but it did sound problematic. Oh, to have the problems of middle management . . .

"If you don't mind my asking, Vaughan, which magazine is making the transition to screen?"

Vaughan laughed, leaned forward, and grabbed Nia's hand. "Oh no, diva! I can't reveal *that* morsel of information! VisionCom has sworn me to secrecy—in writing, no less. I don't know if you know it, but it's absolutely treacherous out there! You can't trust a soul." She looked around for the waitress, who was bringing food to a group of men in the front of the restaurant. "Oh, well, I guess she was just too busy to bring us our coffees. Shall we go elsewhere?"

Vaughan stood before Nia could answer, picking up her tote bag and beginning to inch her way toward the door.

"Actually, Vaughan, I have a meeting in the morning and I'm going to call it a night. But I am glad we got a chance to talk."

Vaughan turned around and all but glared at her. "After I went to all the trouble of following you here, giving you employment advice, *and* purchasing your dinner and libations, can't you *at least* give me the pleasure of a single cup of coffee?"

"I really am getting tired . . ."

Vaughan's edge disappeared as quickly as it had appeared. "Then have a cup of decaf to help you sleep. Oh, come on, diva. Live a little."

Nia exited the crowded restaurant behind Vaughan's lead, acquiescing just this once. She would only stay for one cup of coffee.

Just one.

Just this once.

Seth navigated the rush-hour traffic with ease, weaving the souped-up clunky Continental in and out of lanes with the best of them. He adjusted the radio, switching from FM to AM and back to FM once again. It still baffled him that in a city this size he couldn't find a decent jazz station that played Nancy Wilson unapologetically. And when he could find the occasional song, it was sandwiched in between sales pitches for luxury automobiles that few could actually and honestly afford, and cents-off sales at the local supermarket. Not exactly the most wonderful framing for a national treasure.

He settled on All Talk Radio. It was easier to tune out bad conversation than bad melodies. Bad melodies made him think about bad decisions nowadays, about Feinstein and lawsuits and the blurring lines that divide the personal from the professional. Philip, as repulsive a character as he was to Seth, had turned out to have a wealth of knowledge on issues of retaliation and worker's compensation. He had convinced Seth to allow him to handle any further dealings with Feinstein Films. And that was fine with Seth. One less calamity to occupy his brain.

Seth looked over at the passenger's seat of his car. The scent from the rose and daisy bouquet, heady and strong, filled the air and placed him in a light trance of hope and apprehension. The car smelled like his apartment that night: the smiles and touches . . . *why did he ever have to fall so hard and give in to that woman* . . . and forgiveness and freshness . . . *what if Lauren doesn't want him back* . . . and beauty and life and longing. Never had a bouquet of flowers had so many memories. Never had petals so innocently alive told so many dark and hurtful secrets.

Seth exited the expressway and made three rights, two lefts, and then turned into the circular driveway. Before he could turn off the radio, before he could shut off the engine and remove his keys, MommaPatti came running out onto the porch, wiping her hands on a paper towel and smoothing the Battenberg lace apron tied around her narrow waist.

"Seth! We were getting worried about you. Reggie's been asking for you, dancing around on pins and needles. You run into traffic?"

Seth walked over to her and gave her a hug and a kiss on her cheek. "More like traffic had to deal with the likes of me and the SoupedUp-Mobile zipping and zooming. No, I just had to make a stop or two."

MommaPatti looked down at the bouquet and other assorted packages in his hands. "Good . . . good." She smiled and patted him maternally on the hand. "Lauren's here."

He smiled at her. "I'll brace myself."

She ignored his comment, focusing her attention on the bouquet. "Yes, she'll like these, Seth—or am I being too presumptuous? Maybe these are for me . . ."

"Well, the flowers are for Lauren. But I think you might find something in these packages with your name on it." She took the packages from him and stood on tiptoe to kiss him on the cheek.

"Seth?" she said, her eyes filled with knowing. "Work it out."

He nodded and followed her into the house.

The house was a beehive of activity. There was laughter bubbling from every corner, conversation in pitches from inquisitive two-year-olds fighting sleep to seniors recounting all they had seen and heard, and every happy flavor along the way. A giant banner faced the front door boldly: *Happy Birthday Rex!*

"Now, you just go and do what you came here to do and don't worry about a thing. I'm going to go and make it look as though I've been in that kitchen cooking up a storm all day, sweatin' and slavin'." She motioned to her splattered apron. "Don't you go and tell these folks that I'm just a make-believe five-star cook. I know how to pick up a phone and call a caterer and get my husband to whip up a batch of barbecue sauce. But that's just more than they need to know, you hear me? If information like that gets out, it could make all the women around these parts jealous!"

Seth smiled and hugged her once again.

"Go on, baby. Reggie and Crystal are out back with Rexxy. But you go on and get that woman and work it out. You're already family, but we want you as an in-law."

MommaPatti braided her way through the crowd, hugging and laughing while intently kitchen-bound. Seth walked slowly behind her, saying hi to everyone, remarking on wellness or growth or beauty, as appropriate. But he wasn't present in the moment, wasn't actually absorbing the welcoming smiles that were delivered his way. He wondered how many could hear his heart pounding in fear, how many realized how close it was to catapulting right out of his chest.

Someone shouted out that the ribs were done and hitting the table any minute and folks just started gravitating toward the kitchen en masse, mumbling about how hungry they were and how good a plateful of ribs would be right about now. Seth was swept up in the current, carried downstream, still clutching a handful of daisies and roses, still searching for Lauren's face.

"I knew I'd see you in the kitchen."

Reggie leaned over Seth's shoulder and then gave him a brotherly hug.

"They smell about ripe. You going to grab a plate?" Seth looked up at Reggie, and Reggie gave him the once-over.

"Yeah, unless you need us to have a conversation first."

Seth shook his head. He didn't want to monopolize his friend's time here. "I haven't seen her yet."

"She's here. Last time I saw her, she was deep in conversation with Crystal."

"Oh, great. Once Crystal gets through with her, she'll be sure never to speak to me again in life."

Reggie laughed. "I don't know why you feel that my wife doesn't like you. I've never heard her say anything negative about you."

"Stop lying."

"No, really. I mean, after the wedding, once that ring was on her finger, she's never made *any* comments about you. You're being overly sensitive. She's probably telling Lauren to give you another chance."

"Yeah, okay. And it's gonna snow through the rest of July."

Seth didn't want to press the issue. His friend was obviously in love up to his wide-open nose. But Seth could feel the animosity flowing from that woman every time they met.

"Hey there, husband." Crystal walked up behind Reggie and gave him a squeeze around the waist. She looked blankly at Seth. "And hello to you, too."

"Hi, Crystal. Good to see you again."

She nodded at Seth, picked up a plate, and stood in the newly formed line, next to Reggie.

"Well, you know what? I think I'm going to go and track down the recipient of this bouquet before I try to carry anything else, you know what I mean? Crystal, you're still as radiant as ever. Reggie, I'll catch you later, okay? Thanks . . ."

He moved swiftly out of the kitchen, not waiting for a response, eager to get away from Crystal's glares and silences. Fear or no fear, he had to find Lauren. He had to try to talk to her, try to get her to listen to him. And even if she refused, he figured that at least she would know how he felt. At least he could say he had done all a man could have done. He began walking through the dining room, surveying the family room and backyard, walking back toward the front of the house.

And then he saw her, tucked away in a corner of the living room. At first he wasn't sure; it was as though he were looking at the outline of last night's dream, remembering how her cheek glowed satin in the shadows of the dream sequence. But when she moved, when she turned toward him, he knew she was no dream, no apparition, but flesh and feeling before his eyes. She looked at him briefly, lowered her eyes, and turned her back to him. It was the way she looked at the floor that made the waters flow inwardly in Seth, the slow turning away that made the waters pool and remain languid in his eyes.

"Lauren, don't."

There was no way she could have heard his whispered words as they emanated from his lips, the crowd had made that impossible. But she turned as though he had spoken directly into her ear and faced him squarely.

Her tears flowed freely, and she made no effort to brush them aside or hide her emotions from those who marched in between her and the anguished man who watched her from across the room, on another shore of her life. He extended his arms to her, he opened them and offered their comfort. And when she didn't move, he offered her the bouquet.

"Baby, please," he called to her.

Lauren took no steps toward Seth. None at all.

They stayed like this, paralyzed and muted, long enough for a child to run by them saying how good the ribs were this year.

Seth refused to cry all out in the open like this. Not standing in front of her, not holding flowers, not begging for audience, not relinquishing dignity. So when the first tear fell, he turned abruptly and gently placed the bouquet on the coffee table and walked, defeated, down the hallway and out the front door.

He tripped his way to his car, his keys a surreal blur of color beyond his tears, and tried clumsily to find the keyhole and get inside before he totally lost it. He was so sorry he had come. Sorry he had hoped. Sorry he had given in to the notion that Lauren would even think about forgiving him. And as it was, she didn't even know the truth of the matter. She didn't even know how far he had actually fallen.

So he really couldn't get too angry, Seth thought as he wiped his face dry and sat in the driver's seat of his car. She was just a woman functioning on that intuition thing, probably sensing all the garbage that was reeking beneath the surface. He bit his lip and balled his fist and thought about smashing it into his window with force, a *manly* force, but then his common sense made him reconsider—such madness might hurt.

Might hurt and he had already caused himself enough pain to last a little while. Chuckles welled up from the pit of his stomach, made him shake his head and lean back against the seat, close his eyes. He might be a man in love—a *rejected* man in love even—but that was no reason for him to be a fool, too.

Seth reached over and turned the ignition key toward him, allowing the cassette player to be activated. He reached for a tape, shoved it into the player, and turned it up. It was a tape of the Garrison Walters trio, a demo they had made the year before, the only positive thing that had come out of their last managerial relationship.

That is what he would do. Concentrate on his career. On business. Be professional. Get his act together. First thing in the morning, that is what he would do. Get serious.

The music was transforming. It was good and it was soothing. The upright bass plucked notes deep inside of Seth, made him nod and moan in time. He didn't recognize the tune as anything he had heard before, but he knew the song. It was a song his heart had been singing for a while now, a song of sadness, of longing and pain. A song of loss. Yeah, he thought, not Sandy's fault, and certainly not Lauren's fault; he had messed this one up on his own. Nobody to blame this on but himself.

"Seth . . ."

Even through the windows and even with the music playing, there was no mistaking Lauren's voice. He opened his eyes and saw her standing just beyond his window. She held the flowers. They looked at each other for a time, looked at eyes that mirrored pain and hopelessness and fear, looked for answers. He opened his door and stood and waited.

"I'm sorry, Lauren. Really, really sorry."

"Me, too."

The silence was charged. Seth did the hands in the back pocket thing and shifted his weight back and forth.

"I've been hurting, Seth."

He couldn't even answer her, just nodded.

"Nice flowers. The roses, daisies . . . nice, thank you."

He thought he was going to cry. There was so much that he wanted to say to her, so many emotions he needed to convey. But nothing would come. No words were adequate. "You deserve better, Lauren. You deserve more than explanations and excuses."

"And you deserve a chance to explain. That was something that Crystal reminded me; you deserve at least that."

Crystal had reminded her to give him a chance. He was shocked.

Lauren looked over at the car. "Nice music thing you got going on inside there."

He had forgotten that he had left the cassette playing. "Yeah, remember them? Garrison Walters Trio."

"I remember." Lauren smiled, walked over to the passenger-side door and slid into the front seat. "I remember lots of things."

He turned around at that and was surprised to see her smile, watched as she beckoned him to come and share the song.

The pluck of the bass wasn't sounding half as sad anymore.

Seth sat behind the wheel and slammed his door shut. He pushed his glasses up on his nose. "Trying to get them a gig at Saleem's. You ever been there?"

"Little-dark-musty-hole-in-the-ground Saleem's?"

"Yeah, same one. Owner owes me one. It's a start."

"Starts are good, Seth. Everyone has to start somewhere. But you know something? Fresh starts are even better."

He wanted to look over at her and assess her mood, but he was afraid to break whatever was happening here. It felt too good.

"Want to go for a drive?"

"Sure."

Seth pulled around the driveway and navigated the streets, making rights and lefts, weaving through wilderness, drawn toward the ocean. Lauren opened her window, rolled it down all the way, and enjoyed the cool salt-filled air on her face.

He parked the car across the street from a dune, a slightly hidden area that reflected the moonlight and the crest of high tide. The sand here was coarse, gravel-like, and embedded on the shore were massive rocks that were home to seagulls during the day and crawling, close-to-silent things at night.

Seth got out of the car and walked around to Lauren's door and opened it. She stepped out and stood, both of them taken by the beauty of this place.

"I didn't think I would speak with you at all, let alone here. I came all prepared to say nothing to you tonight. Wow, this is beautiful, Seth."

He took her hand and they walked toward the shore. "Nothing, huh? I'm glad you changed your mind. So what made you?"

Lauren squeezed his hand and laced her fingers in his. He liked the way they fit together. "My conversation with Crystal. I guess loving and forgiving a person really mean the same thing. I missed you. More than you need to know. And I realized life is short. Brandon taught me that," she whispered, bending over and picking up her sandals. "I guess sometimes we temporarily forget our lessons. Even the hard ones we swear we'll never forget."

Seth smiled and looked off in the distance. *Thank God for Crystal.* "I used to come here sometimes with Reggie, as a kid. We used to say it was easier to talk here, because the waves were silenced by the dunes. We could hear stuff better here."

"Well, if that's true, then I'm glad this is where you brought me. Because I'm ready to listen. Okay? Talk to me."

He swallowed, wondered how much of the truth he should let escape, how much she could handle.

"I love you, Lauren."

It wasn't the first time he had told her that, but it felt new, felt different and right.

"I believe you, Seth. So what's going on?"

He sighed and dug his heels into the sand. Do or die. Now or never.

"I'm sorry about what happened. I'm sorry you had to see that stuff."

Lauren walked off a little by herself, and spoke to him with her back toward him. "Well, it hurt, Seth."

All he could do was nod. No words were coming out. And she couldn't see his actions.

"So, her stuff was just *there.*"

"Yes."

"And you and she hadn't been having a relationship?"

"No, just neighbor stuff. She would come in and have a cup of coffee and talk about her dates and all. But nothing that would require her to have underwear and personal stuff there."

"So why do you think she did it, Seth?"

He knew exactly why she had done it. Knew that Sandy was a determined woman who was out to conquer and enjoyed the quest most of all. She wanted him, and she had set her mind on having him. And she had gotten her way, just as she had predicted.

"Not sure. Maybe she was jealous."

"Jealous of what?"

Seth walked toward the shoreline. "Jealous of you. Of us. I used to talk about you all the time."

"Used to?"

"Yeah, I would share lots of stuff with her. How much I cared about you, how much I wanted everything to be right when you came over for dinner. I guess I just talked too much. She didn't have that level of caring in her life, looked for it all the time. Guess she figured that if she didn't have love in her life, then no one else should."

"A hurting woman's game."

Seth picked up a rock with seaweed wrapped around it and threw it into the water. It made a deep plopping sound. "Yeah, it is."

"Is she pretty, Seth?"

"Lauren, don't."

"No, I just want to know. I mean, I know that I'm not the most glamorous woman in the world, that was never an issue. I just want to know."

"Her looks could never compare to your beauty, Lauren."

"Hmm, I see. She must be gorgeous."

Seth walked over to her, stood behind her, and put his arms around her shoulders. He inhaled slowly, his nose on her neck, remembering the scent that he missed so much, the moment mixed with salt and sand and the faint remembrance of sweet cologne. He felt her moan, felt her shudder and lean against him. He felt her relax into his arms. And if he allowed himself the very thought, he thought he could feel her hips move, creating heat.

"If you say you weren't having a relationship with her, if you say she planted that stuff in your bathroom, then I believe you, Seth." She sighed and laughed at the same time. "I don't know if it's the moon, or the water, or the fact that I've been missing you, but tonight . . . I believe you."

Seth closed his eyes and prayed for the strength to tell her the truth. The truth beyond omission. He knew it would hurt her, he knew that if he told her it might be the last thing he would be allowed to say. He looked down upon her hair, how it reflected the moonlight in a beautiful, muted sort of way, and opted for the words.

"Lauren, I have to tell you something. I have to let you know—"

She cut his words off with a finger to his lips. "Is it about the past, Seth?"

He nodded.

"Is it about something *I* did?"

He shook his head in the negative. "No, Lauren, no, it's—"

"No. Then I don't need to know."

"Yes, you do."

"No, I don't. A new life for us begins tonight. A new life. Let's leave the past in the past."

Lauren took his hand and led them over to the car, supported herself against it. She took her palms and cradled his head, then pulled him into her kiss. Her hands played in the hairs at the back of his neck, her tongue searched for his, unafraid.

"I couldn't believe how much I missed you, Seth. I really did. I missed you bad," she whispered, his moans crashing upon the night like relentless waves. She reached for him and felt swelling, quickening at her touch.

"See what you've done to me?" Seth spoke softly.

She parted her lips and called to his tongue, surrounded it with her mouth tightly and found a night rhythm that neither of them desired to control.

His hands found their way to the hem of her blouse, reached beneath the cool, starched cotton to the smoothness of her flesh. His hands traveled skyward, making slow tender circles upon the curve of her waistline, migrating toward breasts that rose with her heavy breaths, the hardness of her nipples pronounced through a thin layer of lace.

"I want my Seth back. *All of him.* I want him back and I want to know he's mine."

She reached and unzipped him, with a determination he had not seen from her before, unzipped him and reached beyond denim and silk, freeing him, holding him, closing her eyes and calling his name.

"We don't have to do this, you know. We can wait. We can take our time and wait until we're—"

"Now," she said.

Now.

And sometime in between the first time she found release and the second, Seth closed his eyes and reluctantly allowed himself to remember the vision of Sandy on his bed, the saltiness of her skin, the way she had to have it rough, how their bodies had sounded together. He listened to the waves of the ocean, reminding him of the waves in Nia's hair, reminding him of how forcefully that woman had spoken her mind to him and then receded from him like the tide. And then he came inside Lauren and moaned, afraid to call her name, afraid of what he might actually say.

"**N**ia, please, can we talk?"

She stood at her front door and looked out through the ornate metal security gate. Stood and looked at him, as though she were looking at a stranger. As though she wasn't sure that he wouldn't cause her harm again. A man of questionable intent. A man she didn't know.

"What do you want, Rome? I had a long day at the office and I don't feel like engaging in idle chitchat." It was the truth; it had been a long day and she had been at the office. Just not at the office he recalled. She never had the opportunity to tell him about her ordeal at Feinstein. And in light of everything that had happened, she doubted if he really cared to hear it.

She was tired and beat from riding the subway home during rush hour. She had just walked in the door moments ago from her first day as a regular employee at The Imani Group, going through old files and trying to understand the various dealings of the company. It looked as though it was going to be an interesting interim job. They were so diversified; the scope of their business made her head spin. Not only were they involved in implementing affirmative action, but Reggie had a really soft spot for any black person who had suffered any form of discrimination. He regularly went to bat for those who needed muscle behind them to fight the powers that be. And most of that stuff he ended up doing without any thought of remuneration to The Imani Group.

But now, safely within the confines of her home, she didn't want to deal with the problems of The Imani Group. And, truth be told, she didn't really want to deal with the likes of Mr. Two-Timer either. She had all but forgotten that positive self-talk she had written in her journal about giving Rome time to articulate his indiscretion. Now that he was here, standing right outside the private entrance to her street-level apartment, all bets were off.

He faced her, looked at her, the same expression that he had used when he wanted his way with her, when he told her how much she had meant in his life. He leaned against the side of the brownstone, pouted a bit, and smiled.

"Aren't you going to let me in, sugar?"

"I don't know yet. Convince me. Is there a reason why you can't say whatever it is right here?"

His laugh surprised her; he shook his head and looked off in the distance.

"You aren't going to make this easy for me, are you?"

She just stared at him. Stared and waited for him to finish his thought.

"I want to apologize, Nia. Apologize and explain. I owe you that much."

He did owe her. She wanted to slam the door in his face, tell him to be gone and forget her, but the urge to hear his words stirred her, and got the better of her. She clicked the gate open, stepped aside, and ushered him into her space.

Rome walked to her living room, as he had so many times before, passing the gallery of sepia-toned photographs that graced both sides of the long hallway. His presence intruded upon the vanilla bean scent of her home, his musky cologne mixed with the faint smell of sunblock. He sat in the blue overstuffed easy chair where he always sat, played with the silver magnetized toys on her coffee table as he always did. Nia watched him, watched his actions. The familiarity of it tore at her senses. She had missed him more than she thought.

"Yes?" Nia stood, her arms folded, her armor intact.

He put the toy down, quieted the silver balls that had found their momentum, and created stillness. It took a long time for him to look up at her, a strained pulling of silence and feelings too close to the edge.

"I'm sorry." He turned away, continued to speak. "I should have told you. I wanted to tell you, Nia. It just never seemed to be the right time."

"I'm sure. I mean, how do you tell someone that you don't love them anymore." Nia looked him in the eye, his eyes so large and brown and piercing. He had eyes that had never been able to lie to her, even when it would have been convenient. He looked down, his thick, dark lashes creating a shelter, a haven for himself.

"Nia, I never stopped loving you."

"This is not love. You do *not* love me. Don't even try it, Rome."

Rome clasped his hands, sat on the edge of the sofa, and looked down at the carpet. His intense discomfort began to melt away her anger.

"You looked so happy," she said.

"Yeah." He nodded, never looking up from the floor.

"When I saw how you looked at her, saw how happy you were that she was there . . . I didn't know what to do. It was like my whole world started spinning."

He paused and looked pained, looked into the silver balls at his own reflection.

"Maybe if you had decided to come to Spelman . . ."

Nia changed the subject. She didn't want to play a game of what-ifs. "How long have you been seeing her, Rome?"

She expected him to tell her the story of a whirlwind romance. How she had come into his life and knocked him off his feet before he had even known what had happened to his will. Either that or the story of a hot one-night stand, a story of a man who was about to apologize for a regretted night of passion and beg her forgiveness. She was prepared to hear these stories. Prepared to forgive him, prepared to rectify whatever shortcomings may have been present on her side of the fence.

"Nia . . ." He stood and walked over to her, placed his hands on her shoulders and looked into her soul. "Nia . . ."

"I just thought we were always going to be together, Rome."

"I know that's what you thought." He nodded in agreement and massaged her shoulders as he spoke.

"And I thought that we were . . . that we were going to . . ." Her heart began to sink.

"Nia, her name is Claudia."

She broke away from his touch, walked past him into her tiny kitchenette. "I don't want to hear it. I don't want to know."

"And she's my wife."

She turned to him and waited for the retraction. It had to be a joke, a cruel, practical joke. But Rome just looked at her, his eyes red and truthful, his pain now so incredibly visible to her.

"Claudia and I got married last weekend. In Maryland."

"You're *married?*"

He nodded.

She didn't want to, but the tears came too quickly, there had been no warning. She stood before her sink and stove, and sobbed. Her body betrayed her and her knees buckled, she sank, clutching the countertop for support.

"Nia . . ." Rome walked to her, rushed to her, and out of sheer habit she reached out to him, her world spinning, her vision clouded and distorted. He sat next to her and rocked her on her kitchen floor, held her and rubbed her back, soothed her.

Her mind was asking questions, a million a minute, but her body reached for the comfort it had always known. It was so unnerving, to crave the arms that could only deliver pain now, to want to be held by the man who was no longer free to hold.

"I don't understand" was all she managed to get out. "Is she pregnant? Is that what happened?" Rome held her hands and sat back, creating distance so she could see his face plainly.

"No."

"I don't understand. Rome, help me to understand."

"Claudia and I met last summer. She was an intern at the firm, very bright and very eager to learn. She wasn't working with me, she was under the supervision of clerical when she first came on board. But we struck up a friendship, a working friendship." Nia shifted and tried to pull away, but Rome turned her head gently and continued his eye-to-eye gaze. "I need to say this, Nia . . . and you need to know."

"No, forget it. I don't want to hear any more."

Nia broke away from him and walked into her bedroom. She stretched out across her bed and buried her face in her pillow. She could feel his presence follow her. The chimes on the back of her bedroom door jingled.

"Nia, it just wasn't there between us."

"Maybe we just stopped looking."

"No, we were just going through the motions, that's all. And you deserve more than that. You deserve a man who's crazy about you. And . . . and I deserve to feel that way, too. Life is too short to settle for less than wonderful."

"I loved you, Rome." She sat up and wiped her wet face with the back of her hand.

"I loved you, too," he whispered, "but it just wasn't enough this time."

They looked at each for a while, the distance between them growing with every moment. She could hear him breathe.

"I need to go, Nia."

She turned her back to him and waved him on.

"Go on. You don't want to be late for dinner."

"Nia . . ." He tried to reach for her, but she avoided his touch.

"Good-bye, Rome."

She heard his footsteps slowly moving toward her front door. It wasn't until she heard the wind blowing outside so wickedly strong, the wind that carried his voice, that she heard him tell her good-bye.

"Rome said *what*?"

"He's married."

"See, Nia? Why wouldn't you listen to me? And I know I don't hear you cryin' and snifflin' over there, not over Rome. Nia?"

Nia reached for another tissue, cradled the phone on her shoulder while blowing her nose. "What."

"Woman, you ought to be right glad that I'm out of town. 'Cause if I were there, I would kick your butt from here to the South Pacific. Cryin' over some nig who didn't even have the decency to tell you he was in a serious relationship. *He couldn't find the right time to tell you.* That's a crock, Nia, and you know it."

"You know, Grace. Sometimes you can be real insensitive. Bordering on bitchdom."

"Um, excuse me? Did I just hear somebody call me a bitch?"

"You know, sometimes a woman just needs a little support, a little sympathy from her sister friend. You know what I'm talkin' about, here? No. No, you wouldn't know. 'Cause you're just too damn busy judgin' everybody else in the world and condemning them for living their lives according to a scenario other than the world according to Grace."

"I don't believe this. Let me see if I have this straight, okay? Please do me the honor of correcting me if I'm wrong—will you do that for me, Nia?"

"Shoot."

"You are telling me that I am nonsupportive and unsympathetic because I'm not joining your little pity party for Rome? Is that a fair assessment of the situation?"

"Sounds like a real good start, Grace."

"Hmm, okay. I guess I should try to be more like you then, huh?"

"Why not?"

"*Why not?* I'm trying to remember the very last time you were supportive of *me*, okay? When was the last time you asked *me* about the state of *my* heart and *my* feelings?"

Nia was silent.

"Okay. Well, if that moment in time is too difficult for you to pinpoint, let's just widen the scope, why don't we? When have you *ever*—and I mean *ever*—allowed me to tell you about something or someone who mattered to me? I mean, really allowed me to speak without dismissing me, without taking everything I said to you as a big joke."

"You're being ridiculous. I always listen to you."

"Then answer me this: Why am I out of town right now?"

Nia paused. "You're out of town on business?"

Grace laughed. "Is that a question or a statement?"

"I don't know, Grace! I figured that if you wanted to tell me why you were out of town, you would."

"And I figured that if you really *cared* you would ask."

Nia started pacing the floor in front of her bed. "Okay, you're right. I'm wrong. Why are you out of town?"

"I'm out of town because someone I thought really cared about me turned out not to give a good damn. I needed some space—a whole lot of space. Not that *you* give a better damn."

Nia chuckled, relieved. "Oh, you could have told me that! I *obviously* would have understood. Men are not high on my list of appreciated beings right now either. It just hurts when you start hurling insults around at me and my choices."

Instead of hearing Grace bounce back into the conversation, Nia only heard more sighs come across the phone line.

"You and your choices . . . Nia, do you ever sit back and listen to yourself? When are you going to stop making all these leaps and assumptions about me? No, no, forget about me and my situation, let's concentrate on you. Sometimes I don't even know why I try . . . Rome is a dog. I've said it before and I'll say it again. And *you* are disillusioned."

"Grace, what are you talking about? Try what? You're not making sense and I'm tired of guessing."

"Forget about it, Nia."

"Forget about *what?*"

"We can't even have a simple conversation where I can be honest about who I am and speak my mind. I can't even tell you what I see when I look at you and Rome. You don't want to hear it, so I'll just shut up and go along with the program."

"You know, I thought we were friends . . ." Nia was beginning to shout into the telephone.

"We *are* friends, Nia. And that's why I have to tell you the truth."

"Your truth."

"It would be your truth, too, if you took off your rose-colored glasses sometimes. Rome doesn't care about you, pure and simple. If he cared about you, you wouldn't be sitting on the phone boohooin' and trying to justify getting messed over like this."

Forget this.

Nia hung up the phone. No good-bye. She didn't want to hear this spin on logical. Didn't want to examine where she had gone wrong in the relationship or its aftermath. All she wanted right now was to be heard. She wanted to let the hurt out. Just talk to someone who would listen, vent a bit. She didn't need the anger, the vengeful spirit that hovered around Grace. She just wanted to let the pain ooze itself away

for a while. Let it drain out of her system like an abcess too long neglected.

She grabbed her journal, her bag of stuff, and headed out the door.

"Here you go, diva. Drink the chamomile," Vaughan whispered as she
tilted the ceramic teakettle and filled their cups. "That is a very low
blow. You just have to be devastated."

Nia leaned back in the booth, took a deep sigh, and finally relaxed.
She nodded and tapped her nails on the tabletop.

"So are you hating him yet?"

The word *hate* got her attention. "No, I'm not."

"Hmmm. Well, aren't you angry at all? You must admit, diva, that
your friend was just wrapped in folds of endless deceit. A man does not
just up and get married. No matter how wonderful the sex may be.
There was a long-term relationship going on there, many nights that
he should have been spending with you that he chose to spend with
her. Doesn't all of that long-term deception disturb you at all?"

Nia sipped her tea. "I don't see it as deception, really. Now that I
look back on our relationship, he really didn't deceive me. There were
just some things he chose not to tell me. There were things I chose not
to tell him, too. We were living an illusory relationship. But he was
right about one thing: We *were* just going through the motions."

Vaughan put her head back and laughed heartily. "My, my, my. But
aren't we the magnanimous one. To mutually take blame for the de-
mise of the relationship. Diva, omission . . . deception . . . it all adds
up to the same thing. A lie is still a lie. He lied to you. It hurts to be the
recipient of a lie. And right now you are hurting. And you know how I
see it? The sooner you admit how much you are hurting, instead of trying to pretend that the hurt isn't there, the sooner you're going to heal.
Do you understand?" Nia nodded.

"Good. Now, let's have ourselves a fabulous dinner. Top of the line,
superb, elegant, and lovely! It shouldn't be long now," Vaughan waved
her hand high above her head, her diamonds glistening, in a successful attempt to attract their waiter's attention. She pointed silently to the
nearly empty teapot and the waiter smiled, moving quickly to the
kitchen entrance.

"Your diamonds are beautiful. Your husband must have loved you very much."

Vaughan stopped midwave. "My husband? Oh, no, diva. Did you think these were *presents* from my former? No, no, no!" She leaned back, gently fingering the edges of her linen napkin, allowing each diamond to catch the light and reflect color.

"Well, from wherever they came, Vaughan, they certainly are lovely. Exquisite. Someone has wonderful taste."

"Isn't that sweet and polite! I know you want to ask, diva. Let me tell you, straight out. If there is something that you want to ask me, ever, just go ahead. I have no secrets. I bought these diamonds for myself. One ring for each affair of my former. He would have an affair, find happiness here and there, and I would go and buy a diamond. I wouldn't say a word to him about his exploits. He would just receive a loving bill at the end of the month. Payable in full."

"That's kind of rough."

"You think so? I would have imagined that after a while, he would have caught on to the pattern and stuck with the same bimbo for a time. But he was a man who craved variety. And"—she waved her hand in the air—"variety *costs!*"

"Rough. Effective, but rough."

"A lesson more women need to learn, diva."

"What would you have done if he *had* stayed with the same woman?"

Vaughan lowered her eyes and sighed. "Well, that's eventually what happened. See this?" She pointed to the empty ring finger on her left hand. "I actually gave it back to him. Told him to take that band, take his life. I liked the way my skin looked without the shadow."

The waiter came with their entrées. They ate in silence for a while, heavy in thought.

"I don't think I could be that vindictive."

"Vindictive? I didn't seek revenge. I wasn't out to hurt him. But I wanted him to know that the price of happiness can be very high."

"So you bought your happiness?"

Vaughan set her fork down audibly. "The rings were just *things.* Stuff. Back then, I would have traded it all in for a man who loved me."

"I don't know you that well, but I just don't see you as a woman who would trade anything for a man's attentions."

Vaughan smiled. "You are right, diva. You don't know me very well. There was a time I would have done it in a heartbeat. But now I just concentrate on Vaughan. Loving Vaughan. Doing what makes her happy. I love going to museums and galleries. Love Off-Off Broadway. Concerts. Poetry. And those are the things I choose to do with the time I have in my life."

"Well, you have to admit it's nice to have company on the journey."

"Yes, sometimes it is, but at what expense? My former hated going out. But when we first met, he would take me out all the time. He would take me and smile and hold my hand, the whole nine yards. But you know, once we got married, he said those things were *unnecessary*. Those were things a man did to *get* a woman's attention."

"Sounds like he lost *your* attention."

"Sometimes they learn, diva, and sometimes they don't. But your job in life doesn't end. You still have to be true to yourself and honor your own happiness."

"Rome was the same way. The things I liked to do just bored him silly. So I ended up going out by myself a lot of times, or going with girlfriends."

"Well, good for you! I say, life is for living—not for hanging around, being a lady-in-waiting."

"Come to think of it, most of the time when I needed support and understanding, it was my friends who were always there for me. Not Rome."

Vaughan shook her head in agreement. "Mmm hmmm. I know just how you feel. I went through the same revelation."

"It's crazy. Spending all this time putting energy into a relationship with a man and all he does is cause you grief, betray you time after time after time, give you a ton of broken promises. And we want to be strong and positive and all that. I mean, I know that life goes on, and I don't want to live life being alone, but making all these concessions . . . making all these compromises . . . all we end up doing is growing apart from who we were in the first place." Nia shook her head, disgusted. "I just don't want to have to slip into some man's expectation of who his woman is supposed to be. I want to see things, and go places, and feel things—with or without a man on my arm."

"That's it! You finally understand. Make sure you write about it, put some of this into your poems. How are you coming along with that job search?"

Nia sighed and told her more of the details of her dismissal from Feinstein, her efforts on the way to that new career in public relations, and her new job with The Imani Group.

"Very interesting! Sounds like you have some prospects, some *good* prospects." Vaughan sipped her wine and looked at Nia over the rim of her glass.

"Well, so far I've received nothing but rejections from that list of po-tentials—though only three. And I'm enjoying my work with Imani," Nia said with hope in her voice.

"Fabulous! Let me take a look at the list, see if there's anyone on there I might know."

"I'll make sure I get a copy of it to you this week." Nia smiled.

"Tomorrow, diva. Things move fast in business! Send me a copy of the list, let me make a few calls. I might be able to provide some assis-tance in your search."

Nia was elated. "You would do that for me? Vaughan, you don't even know me! And you certainly don't know what I can do in a pro-fessional environment."

Vaughan put her head back and laughed heartily. "Oh, quality pre-cedes itself, diva! I would be honored—really, I would. That's what the *old girl* network is all about: women helping other women. We don't need that stinky golf and cigar stuff to make a good deal stick."

"I mean, now that I think of it," Nia leaned across the table and whispered, "there really is only one thing a woman *truly* needs a man for."

Vaughan tossed her glistening hair behind her shoulder, smiled a million-dollar toothpaste-commercial smile, and drummed her mani-cured nails on the rim of her wineglass.

"Well, diva doll, *that* is an *entirely* different conversation."

"All right, let me make sure I have this straight. These are invoices that need to be paid . . . this is the list of thank-you notes that need to be written and mailed . . . this is the list of cold-call prospects . . . and"—Lauren waved a piece of notebook paper in Seth's face—"and what's this again?"

"Those are clubs that have called asking about booking the Garrison Walters Trio."

"Okay. I guess there really is some sort of organization to your mess, then. So, what do I do about those? You want me to call them, too?"

"You know, maybe you should call Uncle Rex on those. Keep him informed, you know? Let him keep track of his investment. It's a good thing he's decided to help them out, especially since he likes those jazz sounds so much. He seems happier." Seth picked up his briefcase and walked to the door, patting the pocket of his suit jacket. "I am so, so lucky to have you."

"And don't you ever, ever forget that. When will you be back, baby?" Lauren set her pen down and rocked back and forth in the leather desk chair in Seth's home office that actually *looked* like an office now.

"Shouldn't be long. Just need to sign the contracts, run an errand or two, and firm up some equipment issues. Probably no more than an hour or two." He walked up behind her and whispered in her ear. "Why? You gonna miss me?"

"Mmmm hmmm. Yeah, that . . . and I want to know how much time my boyfriend and I have before my boss gets back."

"Well, from what I've heard, that poor excuse for a boyfriend only needs a minute or two"—he tickled her—"so just make sure he's gone by the time I return—and save the best for me."

It had only been a few months since Lauren starting helping him out with the business, and the difference in his productivity had been phenomenal. She understood how he functioned, understood that he had to be free to work on whims and spurs of the moment, and how that often translated into what could politely be deemed disorganization. But he wasn't disorganized. He was creative. Lauren understood that and helped him to deal with that quirk in his personality.

She taught him the value of a memo pad in recording his activities during the day, and how he could transform his notes into usable records at his leisure. She shared her business acumen with him, helping him to visualize and create possibilities. And those activities that usually tripped him up, those dreaded tasks that usually made him procrastinate to a dead standstill, Lauren took on herself. She became his cheerleader, coach, and quarterback all at the same time. And Seth was grateful and loved her for her lessons. All of them.

"You are bad, Seth Jackson. Wretchedly bad." He tipped her chair backward and nuzzled his nose in the curve of her neck. He felt her purr.

"I try."

"Go on. You're going to be late. I've got it under control, Seth. Really. Be gone!"

Seth moved swiftly to the door, taking the self-assured strides of a man about to clinch a deal. He blew Lauren a kiss and let the door shut loudly and securely.

"Seth Jackson," Jonathan said, extending his hand in introduction, "I would like you to meet our counsel, Manny Horowitz of Horowitz and Fletcher. Manny, Seth Jackson."

The men nodded at each other silently and took their seats around the conference table, Manny taking the seat directly next to Jonathan, Seth sitting on the opposite side of the table, the battle lines obvious.

"Seth, I'm glad you could make our meeting, glad you could keep it just between us, confidential. I always knew you were a man of reason." Jonathan addressed him from the head of the table and glanced at Manny huddled over the yellow legal pad of notes before him.

"Are you going to give me my money, Jonathan?" Seth asked calmly.

"Direct and to the point. I like that. I like a man who can speak his mind." Jonathan sat back in his chair.

"Jonathan, if I'm not going to get the money due me, I really don't think we have anything to discuss here." Seth made the motions to stand up.

"Seth! No, no, relax, sit down. Of course we brought you here to discuss your money. We recognize that you put a great deal of work into that spot and we want you to be paid for your efforts. Isn't that right, Manny?"

Manny stopped writing long enough to look up at Seth blankly. "Absolutely."

"Manny, why don't you detail the compensation package we're proposing for Mr. Jackson."

Seth was lost. "Compensation package?"

"Yes, package. We realize there has been a delay in payment and we want to compensate you—not only for the lapse of time but also for any inconvenience you may have encountered in your business as a result of our inadvertent delay. So to that end, we are prepared to offer an amount far in excess of our initial agreement. How does that sound, Seth?" Jonathan was flashing that Ivy League smile. It wasn't working. Not in the least.

"Excess is good, Jonathan," Seth said skeptically, "but to what do I owe this change of heart? Last I recall, you were threatening to sue my ass for . . . what was it?"

"Breach of contract and defamation of character. Your contract specifically forbade you to say anything negative about our client," Manny chimed in, never looking up, never removing pen from paper.

"That's bogus."

"We have it right here—*Amsterdam News*—you were quoted as stating that 'OnTheGo might not be the way to go for the hip folk truly in the know . . .' "

Seth was so sorry he had ever answered his phone and issued a statement to that reporter. Looked like everybody in the world had a beef with at least something he said in that one tiny interview. And folks thought that no one actually *read* black newspapers. He was living proof they did.

"And it's not. No one product is for everyone," Seth said, trying to be diplomatic.

"True, but it's not *your* place to say that. Let the consumer decide for himself."

Seth sucked his teeth. Please. How was the consumer going to decide for himself when all he sees are celebrities endorsing the stuff? When all he hears are top-of-the-line singers singing about the stuff? He leaned back in his chair. All he had been trying to do was to even out the playing field a bit. He wanted the money. He needed the money. But he needed to be able to sleep at night, too.

He shot Jonathan a look that let him know he was a man who was not buying the hype. "Jonathan, exactly what is it that you want from me?"

"Pure and simple: We want to avoid a lawsuit," Jonathan said.

"Fine. Are you going to pay me?" Seth asked.

"Absolutely," Manny chimed in.

"Give me credit for my work?"

"With glowing recommendations in the business," Jonathan added.

"Perfect," Seth said, standing. "Then we're in agreement. Draw up the papers and I'll sign them as soon as I have *my* counsel look them over."

Manny and Jonathan exchanged glances. "Uh, Seth? There's just one assurance that we need from you." Manny stood and faced Seth, looking him in the eye.

Seth met his stare and returned it. "Yes?"

Manny leaned across the table and whispered, "Get your dogs off Brooksmore. Get that investigation dropped and we sweeten your personal pot in excess of a million dollars, tax free. Untraceable."

Seth's mouth became as dry as J.J.'s jokes on "Good Times."

"And if I don't? If I *can't*? I'm just the jingle producer. I don't have any control over what other people do."

The men snickered and stared at Seth.

"Give it your best shot."

Seth left Feinstein and walked across town to the signing—the real one—the one Lauren expected him to be attending, his mind not focused enough for anything but the most amicable of contract negotiations. Luckily, Fatima, the first group Seth ever managed, was now ready and eager to work again, their lead singer newly recommitted to the vision of the group after ditching her gangster ex-boyfriend and giving birth to a set of twin boys. The signing between the individual members of Fatima and Seth, their on-again manager, had gone off without a hitch.

Counting Fatima, Seth now had three groups that he needed to handle and groom. When Fatima called him, back in town and raring to work, he had been all prepared to tell them no. He wanted to tell them he didn't have the time—or the energy—to try to rekindle industry interest in them, but Lauren showed him how he could organize himself to handle the extra load. And Fatima had proven to be the easiest group to book; folks were still impressed with their tight a cappella harmonies and sophisticated haute couture appearance despite the nasty rumors that had been circulating about their gangster ties. They had been playing to sold-out audiences for their last few gigs, and were moving in the right direction—financially and creatively—to make a high-quality demo in a month or two.

The other act that Seth was handling was a little boy, a ten-year-old jazz pianist who went by the name of Torch, who was lighting up the five boroughs as though he were a wildfire. The only problem had been with his guardians: He lived with his maternal grandparents and they were a bit overprotective of him, not realizing the heights he was destined to achieve. In this case, patience was indeed a virtue, and Seth spent more time grooming Torch than he did trying to convince his folks to give him more liberties. It would all come together soon enough.

Lauren had given him so much vision, had enabled him to see how he could juggle and manage and get it all done. That was her professional strength. She had been very concerned when her employer had restructured, giving her a new supervisor. She thought it would translate into more work for less pay, as most of those "kinder and gentler" Republican-type takeovers did. But amazingly, Lauren was plucked out of the reception area and promoted to a more lucrative position with less busywork. Her new position was in management and organization, and traffic was where she seemed to naturally thrive: distributing and tracking new assignments to the lower-level line accountants.

"It only takes a system, you know?" Lauren had said, bouncing through Seth's home office on that first Saturday, a week after Rex's birthday party. "Now, I can give you my Saturdays and maybe one other night a week, for now." She never waited for his response, just got to work and kept working on those days, working until his desk was cleared and the tasks for the day had been accomplished.

And he had told her that he loved her, that he loved how she loved him, but she had lovingly threatened to file charges of sexual harassment and so he refrained from such conversation until she was done at the end of the day, paycheck firmly in hand, monetary transfer completed from employer to employee.

And then they would make love all night. Physically, verbally, spiritually, emotionally. Make love and talk about good things. Dreams. Goals. And sometimes fears.

"I hope you never up and get married on me, Seth," she had whispered one night. After she had moaned and shuddered and clutched him twice.

"Married? You want us to get married?" He hadn't brought it up, but the thought had occurred to him more than once lately, and it didn't frighten him anymore. Maybe it was time.

"No . . . well, yeah . . . but that's not what I'm talking about. You know, my boss, my *new supervisor*, did that. Up and got married one day and the woman he had been seeing didn't even see it coming."

"Didn't see it coming? That's kind of weird, don't you think?"

She leaned her head upon his chest and breathed heavily. "Happens sometimes, baby. Guess sometimes it happens just like that."

It had seemed strange to him, that it would bother her so much. He couldn't see himself doing something so heartless. More than likely that boss of hers had been stepping out for a long time on the woman he ditched. Or maybe the ditched woman was just a little diversion for the man and she just took the whole thing way too seriously. Guys vacillated between playing around and settling down all the time. But it wasn't sudden; it was never sudden.

He had looked down at Lauren's head on his chest; she was biting her bottom lip. He hated having to defend himself for another man's actions. He hadn't done any of those things, but he still had to calm the fears this other man's actions had instilled in her: His sudden and unprovoked leaving was one of her greatest fears. It was strange to him, and he didn't understand it, but he never made light of her fear.

"I'm not going anywhere, Lauren. Relax."

She had smiled and closed her eyes, allowed him to rock her to sleep that night while he stroked her hair and thanked God for all the undeserved blessings in his life. But he himself could not sleep. It was often the case nowadays, that even after months of Lauren's consistent presence in his life, he was still plagued by his own fears of abandonment. So he never took her love for granted. Never lived as though tomorrow was promised.

Even Reggie had noticed the change in him. At his final farewell to summer gathering, Reggie had pulled Seth to the side, promising to Lauren to bring the man back soon and intact.

"You've grown, my brother. It's a good thing to see," Reggie whispered, slapping him on the back. The two men picked up their glasses and walked onto Reggie's balcony, while Crystal and Lauren sifted through a tall stack of classic jazz LPs.

Seth took a seat on a lounge chair and looked out over the tops of the trees in Central Park. "She matters to me."

"She's good for you."

Seth nodded. "More than you know. More than you will ever know." Seth sipped his wine and exhaled loudly. "Reg? It just might be that time."

Reggie smiled and looked at the trees and beyond. "Might be, my brother. But there is one thing I've got to make clear to you, man to man."

"Shoot."

"This time, *I'm* keeping the deposit on the tux."

Seth made up his mind that day that he wanted to marry Lauren, that he would propose to her soon, but properly, with ring in tow. And it couldn't just be any old ring. It had to be an exquisitely beautiful one, one she would always treasure and remind her of how valuable she was to him.

Reggie had told him of a jeweler friend of his, a former client, who designed engagement and wedding rings with an Afrocentric flavor. He was based in Chicago, with another office in Los Angeles; since Seth was scheduled to go to the West Coast before Christmas, he had made it a point to get his phone number.

Now, almost two months since he had made the decision, he still had not called the jeweler; he still had not proposed. He told himself it was the stress of the workload—trying to get new business, trying to keep old business—the business was taking its toll. And now, he could add to that list his dilemma with Feinstein. Now just wasn't the right time to propose and move into something new and unknown. He would—he knew that—he would do it soon . . . just not now.

Seth left the Fatima signing and took a cab home. He had too much on his mind, too many issues clamoring for immediate attention, too many monumental decisions to make. But he didn't want to deal with any of it tonight. No more business. No more crucial questions and answers. Just a good dinner, some good wine, his good woman, and some peace and quiet.

"Lauren?"

His door was unlocked when he entered the apartment. Lauren never left the door unlocked. Never.

"I'm in the kitchen."

"In the kitchen?" he said as he set his briefcase down in the office. "I'm taking you out tonight . . . so don't even think about cooking, baby."

But as he reached the kitchen door, he saw much more than he wanted to see.

"You have company, Seth."

Lauren sat at the table with Sandy who was clutching tissues and nursing a cup of tea.

All of his internal organs panicked. He stared at the women stoically.

"Have a seat, Seth. I have some things that I need to take care of, so I'll just run along." Lauren stood and went to walk past him. He stammered, said something that didn't make any sense in any language, and tried to reach out for her, but she avoided his grasp and her eyes iced over when she said, "Sandy might seem very quiet right now, but she can be very talkative when she needs to be."

"Lauren, you said the past didn't matter to you."

She chuckled. "Yeah, I did say that, didn't I? That was dumb. Well, you know what? When the past catches up with the present everything changes. *Everything.*"

Seth stood, unable to move, and stared at Sandy, who never looked up at him, never said hello to him or good-bye to Lauren as the woman he loved and cherished whisked by and slammed the door behind her. He wanted to run after her, to tell her that whatever it was, it was all a lie, but it wasn't and so he didn't run, he only stood and felt worthless and caught, felt condemned to relive life's errors over and over again.

"Why, Sandy? Why . . . after all this time?" The gentleness in his voice surprised them both.

He watched her tears drip onto the table and occasionally into her cup, not understanding, not wanting to understand.

"I was happy," he said to himself, in something less than a whisper. She nodded.

"I'm pregnant, Seth."

He laughed. Laughed for what seemed like forever. And the more he laughed, the more she cried.

"So that's the lie you were laying on Lauren?"

"I didn't tell her that. I only said I had a problem and I needed your advice."

He finally said, "So why are you telling me?"

And she finally said, "Because it's yours."

He laughed some more, a venomous laugh. Said sonofabitch about a million times.

"How can you *know* it's mine?"

"Because you were the only one I was with."

And then she looked at him. Straight in the eye. It sent a chill up his spine.

"That's a bunch of bull, Sandy. You were doing it all the time. With every man who had a moment and a story to tell. You told me so your-self."

She sniffled and wiped her nose. "Yeah, I talk a good game, don't I, Seth?"

"I . . . don't . . . believe . . . you," he spit out.

But she just shrugged her shoulders and held her teacup like a holy chalice of wine.

He looked at her and realized he had no idea who this woman was. The woman seated here was vulnerable and exposed and in need of protection. Like a wet kitten in February.

"You planned this. You planned this all along."

"You know, you can point fingers and blame me and call me all the names you want. I wanted to sleep with you, yes. But you never both-ered to ask me why, never took the time to see that this chica here really cared about you. I wanted your closeness, Seth. For years, I have."

"Please, spare me, okay?"

"Ask yourself then: Why do you think I stayed away?"

And she had. He had seen her only a handful of times since Lauren had come back into his life. And never when he and Lauren were to-gether.

"So why are you telling me this? What is it that you want from me?" He shoved his hands in his overcoat pockets and looked around at the walls of his kitchen. There were no good answers.

Silence.

"I just wanted you to know."

Silence.

"Seth, you're not making this conversation any easier, you know."

Silence.

"Seth? I don't know what I want."

Silence.

He finally spoke. "Well, if it's a money issue . . ."

"It's not."

Silence.

"Help me out here, Sandy."

"You know, maybe we should talk about this some other time—sometime when the hate isn't so thick." She stood to leave and he no-ticed that she seemed somewhat different to him somehow. Maybe it was just his imagination. Or maybe it was just time.

He saw her eyes. He had seen that look once before, in another pair of eyes, in another time and place. A look of pain beyond the realm of tears, where women have been destined through the ages to suffer in silence. A place men just don't feel comfortable trying to reach, no matter how sincerely they may strive.

When he was a child it had seemed easier to reach inside of himself to find the tenderness. He could look at his mother's tears and remember his own. He could remember his tears and he could relate them to hers, but there was nothing he could do to make her pain go away. He remembered the helplessness he felt then, feeling too young and too powerless to offer relief.

He remembered.

"Mama? Is there something I can get you? I cleaned my room. I did my chores." Seth put his arms around his mother's neck and tried to get her tears to stop. But during the days that followed his father's death, nothing anyone did could make her stop crying. And nothing Seth did could make her smile.

All he knew then was that his father had died and not died at home. It wasn't until years later that his mother would tell him how his father had taken his last breaths in the arms of a woman who had given him pleasure throughout his parents' marriage. But she didn't have to articulate to Seth the depths of her depression. He had been there. He had lived it.

He looked at this woman and saw the eyes of his mother's pain. The loss of hope; the look of walking death, empty that way. He didn't see a neighbor scheming. He saw a woman dying here. And maybe, this time, he could somehow try to help.

He walked over to her and put his hand on her shoulder and softened.

"No, chica. I'm sorry. Sit down . . . sit. We have to work this one out."

He couldn't sleep for many nights. Every time he closed his eyes and started to drift, he had nightmares, the same one actually, over and over.

The dream took place in shades of brown, like a photograph found torn and forgotten in the corner of an attic. He was wearing a suit and a hat and was seated on a train of shiny, polished chrome. The train traveled at a steady pace and then sped up, going faster and faster, until it hit some soft billowy obstruction and then fell . . . down down down . . . into some dark abyss. And there was nothing he could do to control it or stop it. Nothing.

And each time his perspiration would pool in his bed and awaken him, and he would sit straight up and wonder why the hell he had gotten on board that damn train, knowing it was going to crash.

Seventeen

NIA

Nia sat on the edge of her bed, trying to figure out her Rubik's cube. No matter what she did, she was only able to align one color side at a time; all the other sides reflected a hodgepodge of colors. It was frustrating, nowhere near the relaxing alternative to thumb twiddling the saleswoman had promised.

She did this whenever she got the urge to pick up the phone and get herself into trouble. At first, the only time she picked up the stupid toy was when she thought about dialing Rome. Turning around the sides of the square was preferable to listening to him apologize for being blissfully happy and brazenly honest with her. She missed hearing his voice. She hated the feeling of loss that washed over her without notice, misting her eyes and taking her breath away.

When the feeling started to hit her, she told herself it was what every woman felt when she was betrayed by a man: that kind of hurt and disillusionment, that level of pain. But this felt like something different to Nia. This loss was deeper, more internal, the kind of loss one feels when a part of oneself has been shifted away from the core.

All of the blues on one side, or all of the yellows. And once, there was that time when she had all the whites *and* all the greens. But that only happened once. No matter what she did, she simply couldn't get all the colors to align.

Today she concentrated on the red side while reading the card she received from Grace. Short and to the point, all it said inside was *Call me*. The front of the note card was a collage: a torn-up strip of four photographs the two of them had taken years ago at a photo booth in some mall, glued grains of sand, and lengths of white thread. It had been more than a couple of weeks since they had spoken, a longer silence than they had ever experienced in the past when they had disputes. Maybe it was time to break the silence. When one side was red, and nothing but red, she picked up the phone and dialed the numbers. Grace answered on the first ring.

"Your dime."

"Nice card."

"Yeah? You like it? I was cleaning out some stuff and ran across the photographs. I was hoping you wouldn't take it the wrong way."

"The wrong way?"

"Yeah. I had to rip the photos in order to make the point I had to make, which was that you and I shouldn't be torn up like this . . . shouldn't let our friendship sift away like grains of sand. We have to hold on to all the threads between us that we can find."

Nia smiled. "I got the message . . . and I agree. It's beautiful, girl."

"But you know something, Nia? I broke the ice and spoke my mind about how I felt about Rome, but I really do think it's time for us to talk about some other stuff, too. Woman to woman. There are some things I need to say to you."

"Uh-oh, should I be scared?" Nia joked. "You going to tell me about you and that cutie pie guy at that magazine? You know, oh, what was his name, Grace? Or you going to cuss me out again?"

Grace didn't laugh. "I'm serious. I need to sit you down and tell you some things about me that you probably don't want to hear. In order for me to remain true to myself and who I am—and be honest in my relationship with you—I need to do that. Is that something you can deal with?"

Nia felt a wave of panic rising but fought it. "Sure. We can get together and talk anytime."

"Good. You busy this coming Saturday? I went to Saleem's a few months ago and heard this really tight trio and got on their mailing list. They're going to be playing at Scattz and I wanted to check them out. Maybe we can check out the early set and then go and grab something to eat in the Village."

"Sounds good. Been a while since I've been there. They still over there by NYU?"

"Yeah, same place. Listen, I need to run, but I'll take care of the ticket thing and meet you there at seven. The set starts at seven-thirty, I think." Grace paused. "Yeah, I'm pretty sure it starts at seven-thirty. So seven it is?"

"Seven at Scattz. See you there?"

"See you there."

"Grace?"

Grace sighed. "Yes?"

"Thanks."

"No, don't thank me yet, Nia. Just hear me out, okay? That's all I'm asking. Just hear me out. *Listen.*"

Nia exited the subway at West 4th Street and walked the few blocks over to Scattz. The winds were whisking all the trash out of the corner bins, newspapers were flying wildly above the grass at Washington Square. People were beginning to hunch over themselves and walk briskly, gathering scarves at their necks, donning gloves. It felt as though New York was going to experience a wicked winter this year.

There were groups of two and three huddled outside the entrance, single people pacing, everyone waiting. It was way too chilly for all of that, Nia concluded. She walked inside the tiny, dark lobby, removed her leather gloves, and looked around.

Grace was not here yet. Nia glanced at her watch; it was only a quarter after. They both had a history of running late, so this was nothing new. Nia walked over to the bulletin board listing the coming attractions, stuck her gloves deep into her coat pocket.

"Well, if it isn't Nia Benson. Fancy meeting you here." She turned around at the droll mention of her name and looked into the face of the less-than-charming Seth Jackson. She hadn't seen him since that lovely meeting at The Enchantment Café.

"Hey, Seth. How are you?" Nia asked, disinterested.

"Working hard. Are you here to see the show? Great line-up tonight, if I must say so myself." Seth jumped, grabbed his ear, and immediately adjusted the volume on his headset. "*Great Googamooga!* Why do people feel they have to scream whenever they get in front of a microphone? Sheesh."

Nia laughed.

"What? You think it's funny that the guy just blew out my eardrum? What kind of sadist are you anyway?"

"Masochist."

Seth looked at her over the top rim of his glasses. "Ahh. You're a masochist, too? Very interesting . . ."

"No, no. I'm neither. But the word you *meant* to call me was masochist. Someone who enjoys inflicting pain on someone else. That's a masochist not a sadist."

"A woman who has to be right all the time, I see. Nia Benson you *are* wrong this time. But I'm not going to argue with such a lovely lady on such a lovely night. When you get home, look it up." He put his hand on the earpiece. "Oh, okay, I'm in the lobby . . . okay, hold on, I'll be there in a minute, hold your horses!"

"Not good to talk to your boss that way."

Seth chuckled. "No, Nia Benson. That was one of my *assistants*. I'm producing this show here. So if you like the sounds, look me up. I'm the man who takes the kudos."

Nia rolled her eyes. "Yeah, sure. I'll do that."

Seth started walking toward the house entrance and paused. "Nia, do you have your tickets already? We're close to being sold out tonight . . . thank God."

"I'm supposed to be meeting a friend here. I don't know where she is . . . we usually run late, but not usually *this* late—and *she* has the tickets."

Seth didn't miss a beat. He glided over to the box office, obtained two reserved house tickets, and handed them to Nia. "The warm-up act is getting ready to go on. Group named Fatima—they're good, you don't want to miss them. Go on inside, sit down, and relax yourself. Hey, those are great seats, too, by the way—pretty front, pretty center."

"This is really nice of you, but like I told you, I'm meeting a friend here."

He motioned to the pay phone in the corner of the lobby and spoke

to her in a tone more befitting the scolding of a young child. "Well, go
call her. Leave a message. If she comes, she comes. If not, no one
misses out, you know? Then call a *different* friend, leave the ticket at
the box office and go inside. Life is only as complicated as we make it,
Nia Benson. Enjoy yourself!"

Maybe he was right. Nia walked over to the pay phone, called
Grace and left a brief message on her answering machine: "I'm here,
you're not, I have a ticket, I'm going inside." She then took out her
phonebook and dialed another number.

"Evening greetings."

"Vaughan? Nia here. Feel like being . . . spontaneous?"

"Diva, this group is simply fabulous!" Vaughan leaned across the
dime-sized table, their long legs crowded and touching. "I'm so, so
glad you thought to invite me. I've been working too hard and am
really down about that job situation."

"Yeah, I remember you mentioning something about that before."

"Yes, well, my *friend*, the one I have to let go, is giving me a great
deal of personal grief. She is not taking the news well at all."

"I can understand that. No one likes to be fired . . . and especially
by a friend."

"Business is business . . . and she should have at least expected that
we would bring our people in on some levels, in some capacities."

"Yeah, it's got to be a tough call on your behalf. Friendship on one
hand, business on the other."

"Well," Vaughan said, smoothing her hair, "not such a tough one. If
she were *truly* my friend, she would always be there for me, no matter
what."

"Maybe you can find her some other position on the show?" Nia
asked.

"I don't think so. There's just too much animosity there now. Best to
just move along, move along." Vaughan flashed Nia a smile and patted
her hand. "I'm so glad you thought to invite me. That was so nice of
you! And *that's* what friends are for!"

"I'm just glad you could come. I figured that since you live in the
Village anyway, you might make it here before they started playing.
Plus, I like your company."

Vaughan picked up her glass and sipped her drink. "I like yours, too."

The place was packed. There was a whole school of we-just-want-y'all-to-think-we're-single men standing against the bar profiling, other folks hugging the walls in the back. The room smelled of stale cigarette smoke and hot sauce, old wood and polished shoes. Excitement crackled in the air right along with the sound system crankings, the dust particles floating in the stream of blue hazed spotlights.

The two women sat, legs crossed and sipping their drinks, loudly responding to the excellent display of harmony by the three polished women on the stage. Everyone seemed to be caught up in the fervor of the newly arranged Billie Holiday medley, snapping their fingers, boppin' to the beat, carried away to another time and place.

"Miss Diva, I think I see my former over there."

"Ex-husband?"

"Indeed. Right over there." Vaughan tipped her head to the back of the room, and Nia observed a tall, seriously handsome older man, smiling and raising his glass in their direction.

"He's smiling at you, Vaughan." Nia nodded and politely smiled back at him.

"We went out last night. He ought to be smiling. I don't know if he really did, but he *said* he had a good time."

It was the first time Nia had witnessed Vaughan anywhere near being unsure of herself. Nia could barely hear her words.

"You and your ex? You still date?"

"Well, we went out, ate dinner, and ended up having sex. Does that constitute a date?" Vaughan looked at the floor. "Every woman has her weakness. Guess you just tripped upon mine."

"You're not married to him anymore, Vaughan. You don't need to do anything with him. And you definitely don't need to give him your power."

Vaughan gave her a nasty look, rising above the cowering stance she had just exhibited. "It isn't a one-way street. I get something good out of the deal. And besides," she said, taking out a cigarette and lighting it with elegance, "I have ample opportunity in my life to be the woman on top—figuratively speaking, of course."

Nia coughed and looked around the club. She decided not to ask for details. If Vaughan wanted to share with her, she would have come right out and said what she was going to say. Nia wasn't going fishing for information.

There were so many couples there, it looked like Date Central. Everyone seemed so happy, so into the music. Seth had been right this time about the group; Fatima really did sound wonderfully good. She wondered what else about the man she had misjudged. The emptiness was rising again.

Vaughan was smiling at her. She smiled back.

At the end of the song, the pianist announced that they would be taking a short break; everyone should freshen their drinks and clear their minds for the goodies yet to come.

The two women stood to stretch their legs. Nia noticed that more and more people were beginning to look their way. She smiled at the various eyes she met, but no one smiled back. And then Vaughan touched her arm and she turned around and was face-to-face with Grace. A glaring Grace.

"Girl, what happened to you?" Nia asked her with genuine concern.

Grace looked at Nia as though she had never seen her before.

"Grace?" Nia asked, walking toward her.

Grace took a step back, removed her white fedora.

"Grace, what's wrong?"

"Nia Benson and Vaughan Gonzalez. Never thought I'd see the day."

"Hello Grace," Vaughan said, her voice icy.

"You two know each other?" Nia asked.

Vaughan and Grace stared at each other silently.

"I would invite you to join us, but as you can see, there's only room for *two* at this table," Vaughan hissed, moving closer to Nia.

Nia turned and looked at Vaughan, puzzled. "Hey, I'm sure we can find another chair in here, look, there's an empty chair over there; I'm sure they won't mind if we bring it over here . . ."

"You've got to be kidding me, Nia. I wouldn't even consider intruding here." Grace turned and walked away.

"Grace! What are you talking about? Honestly, it's no intrusion," Nia called after her, her voice trailing Grace's quick movements toward the lobby.

"What was *that* all about? For goodness sake," Nia said, speaking more to herself than to anyone else.

"Let her go. She doesn't want to be here. Let her *go*." Vaughan sat back down and crossed her legs away from Nia, picked up her drink, and sucked forcefully through the stirrer.

None of this made any sense to Nia. She felt as though she were in the eye of an invisible storm. She picked up her purse, excused herself and tried to catch up with Grace.

When she walked into the lobby, Grace was there pacing, fuming. It was almost as if she was waiting for Nia, as though she knew Nia would seek her out.

"So Nia, how long have you been seeing Vaughan Gonzalez?"

Nia stood speechless.

"I mean, correct me if I'm wrong, but that *is* Vaughan 'Firing Squad' Gonzalez in there, is it not? You know, it's bad enough that you and I were supposed to hang out tonight and you decided to stand me up"—Nia tried to interject, but Grace was determined to have her say—"but then I have to come here and see you with *her*?" Grace walked away from Nia. "And here I was . . . all worried about finally coming out to you. Isn't that ridiculous? You're out here sipping mai tai's with the woman who chumped-me-dumped-me-and-left-me-for-dead and I'm concerned about shocking *your* sensibilities!"

They stared at each other for what seemed like forever, Grace refusing to say anything more, Nia searching for words of response.

"You're so wrong and so off base, I don't even know where to begin. I'm not *with* her, Grace. The woman and I are just friends. I invited her to come down here when *you* didn't show up."

"Nice try, Nia. Nobody—and I do mean *nobody*—is just friends with Vaughan Gonzalez."

"Well, I am."

Grace nodded, adjusted her hat, and put on her shades.

"So I guess that means you haven't slept with her yet. Yeah, I guess that's what that means," Grace said to herself.

"You are nowhere *near* to being right."

"I see. And I suppose now you're going to tell me that you just happened to have had a couple of front-table tickets to a sold-out performance just fall into your pretty little lap. Or did Ms. Gonzalez pay your way? Let me see—seats like that go early so you or she must have been planning this little outing for a long time. You know, I paid a lot of money for those tickets, the tickets that just went to waste, and I didn't ask you to give me a dime."

Nia was sick of hearing the conversation about the money. She reached into her purse and pulled out two bills. "Here, Grace. Take the money and your accusations and your nasty attitude and leave me alone. If you don't want to hear what I have to say, then I guess there's no point in my saying it."

Grace snatched the money out of Nia's hand.

"You thought I wouldn't take it, didn't you? I deserve this and so, so much more. You and Vaughan can both kiss my black ass, Nia."

Grace bopped out of Scattz and caught one of the cabs that were waiting outside the door. Nia stood at the door and looked out onto the sidewalk.

"You give up on the concert, diva doll?" Vaughan walked up behind her, her voice soft and caring. Nia had no idea how much she had heard.

"I'm suddenly not much in the mood."

"Oh, come on. The music might be just what the doctor ordered. They sound good . . . I'm telling you . . ."

Nia shook her head. She hadn't wanted to, but the tears came anyway. She wiped them away with the back of her hand.

Vaughan handed her a scented embroidered handkerchief.

"This is beautiful; I can't use this—I'm wearing foundation."

Vaughan laughed and gave her a hug. "Use it. And use this," she said, pointing to her shoulder, "that's what they're both here for."

"I don't want to go back in there," Nia said.

"I'll tell you what. I'll slip back in there, pick up our coats. We can go someplace else, have dinner or something. Have you eaten?"

Nia shook her head.

"Then it's settled," Vaughan said, opening the door to the seating area. "Problems seem much smaller when your stomach is full."

Vaughan went inside. The music did sound tight. Vaughan opened the door again a little while later, holding their coats, accompanied by Seth.

"Problem ladies?" he asked, concerned.

"Seth, I have to go. I'm sorry. They sound fantastic and the seats are great but . . ." Nia took her coat from Vaughan and put it on.

He looked at Nia, his hands on his hips. "But what? Service issue? Anything I can do?"

"She isn't feeling well," Vaughan chimed, buttoning her own coat.

"Oh!" he said, looking from Nia to Vaughan, from Vaughan to Nia. "Oh, well, I hope you feel better soon, Nia."

"She will," Vaughan interjected before Nia could answer him, "I'll take good care of her and see to it that she gets home safely."

"Thanks, Seth," Nia said over her shoulder, Vaughan's arm around her waist, leading her out the front door.

The winds howled around them, carrying large, cold raindrops that stung the face no matter which direction was taken. The streets were slick and cars were sliding, stopping beyond intersections and swerving to avoid rain-filled potholes. On nights like this everyone drove as though they operated a taxi. Vaughan and Nia walked with their collars up, heads facing down, arms linked for strength and warmth.

"Where do you want to go eat?" Vaughan shouted above the winds.

"Someplace cheap. I'm a little short on cash now."

"You like seafood?"

Nia nodded and did the mental calculations: a seafood dinner in the Village. She wasn't that solvent, but she could deal with an appetizer and something to drink.

"I know just the place. Not much farther," Vaughan said, clutching Nia's arm tighter.

It was cold. Nia returned Vaughan's clutch with one of her own.

The rain was beginning to turn to sleet. They walked silently, conserving their breath and energy. This storm had not been predicted. It had come up from out of nowhere and hit with a vengeance. Not that knowing would have changed anything, Nia mused. She still would have gone to Scattz. She still would not have been able to use an umbrella; the winds had eliminated that possibility. She still would have left the concert, argued, and cried. No. Nothing would have changed.

"Over there," Vaughan said, pointing to an apartment building across the street from where they walked, "my place is over there."

The women crossed the street in the middle of the block, ignoring the crosswalk, and entered a small courtyard. From the courtyard, one could enter any of three buildings. There was a small, fenced, grassy area with park benches, stone checkerboard tables, and matching squat, stone stools.

"Guess which door," Vaughan asked, fishing around her bag for her keys.

Nia looked at the entrances; they all looked the same to her. "The one in the middle?"

Vaughan laughed. "No way. I would never be caught in the middle of anything."

Vaughan led them to the entrance on the left.

"You cook a mean meal, Vaughan. If I could cook like that I'd never bother going out to restaurants." Nia dabbed her mouth with the linen napkin that had been placed before her. "And you set a beautiful table, too."

Vaughan smiled, moving around her kitchen like a dancer onstage. "Thank you. I love a good meal, love entertaining my friends. Did you have enough to eat? Ready for dessert?"

"Dessert? Girl, you've got to be kidding me. I couldn't eat another bite."

"Well then, how about some coffee? A spot of espresso?"

Nia smiled. "You know, I've never been a big fan of espresso; I never liked the way it smelled. Always seemed too pungent. But why not . . . it's a new day. One espresso, please."

"One espresso, coming right up. Why don't you go into the living room? I'll put on some music and we can relax and sip in there, okay? Make yourself at home."

Nia walked into the living room and admired the decor. Vaughan was an avid art collector; there were life-sized bronze-and-wood sculptures of women warriors in the corners, beautiful oils of black women and children on her walls, all the pieces flooded by spotlights and beautifully showcased.

On the wall behind the cream-colored, sectional, leather sofa was an exquisite historic collage of hand-tatted lace, sepia photographs of proud-looking black women, authentic slave records, vintage 45s of songs stolen by popular Caucasian artists of the day, and a replica of the Emancipation Proclamation, singed around the edges. The piece was beautifully affixed to a backdrop of burgundy velvet and framed in antique gold. It was wrenchingly beautiful, the hideousness of the truths behind the piece taking a backseat to its artistry. Nia squinted to see the name of the artist. It was created by Grace George.

"I commissioned that piece," Vaughan said, standing in the kitchen doorway. "First time I had ever done anything like that. She did a splendid job, didn't she?"

The women stared at each other in silence.

"So," Nia paused, unsure of how or why or even if she should approach the subject, "so you and Grace . . ."

"Grace and I . . . Grace and I," Vaughan chimed, annoyed, "yes, Grace and I were lovers. But that was a long time ago. All of that is water under the bridge. It's over. We've moved on."

"And you've done business together . . ."

Vaughan sighed, bored with the conversation. "Obviously."

Nia remembered the look that Grace and Vaughan had shared earlier that night. So much pain. So much emotion. Maybe Vaughan was telling the truth, maybe not, but one thing was certain: It had definitely not looked like a "water under the bridge" situation.

Nia felt everything was changing around her and nothing was making sense in her life anymore. Her man was not her man, but another woman's husband. Her best friend was not her best friend, but a woman she didn't even know. And her newest friend was standing before her, handing her an aromatic cup of spiked espresso, gently caressing her hand. And Nia was not pulling away.

A million thoughts crossed her mind as she took the cup from Vaughan.

"Go ahead, diva," she whispered in Nia's ear, "*taste it*. If you don't like it, you don't have to finish it."

Nia smelled the espresso and closed her eyes.

"But you won't know how really good it is until you taste it for yourself . . ."

Vaughan kissed her gently on the cheek while Nia sipped, inhaling.

Seth sighed and took a swig of beer. Put his feet up on the dark wood chair next to him and watched as the crew disassembled the sound system wiring. Great show, they had yelled to him. More than one person had complimented his professionalism, had told him that he was, indeed, The Man. He had smiled back and lifted his bottle to them, in a silent toast.

They didn't know his pain.

He was there and not there. Happy and disgusted. One step removed from everything that had been going on around him. He was solidly living on the brink of madness, the businessman and the personal man within him both clamoring for his most immediate attention.

A few women sat off by themselves, good-looking older women, whispering and laughing, waiting for men in the crew or, maybe, in the band. They adjusted their clothing, checked themselves in hand-held mirrors, giving each other approval or suggestions for improvement. They seemed happy. Seth looked and wondered why.

"Seth."

He turned around and stood at the voice of Garrison, a smiling Garrison.

"Naw man, don't get up. I know you got to be beat. I just wanted to tell you that you done a good job."

Seth shook his head. "Nope. You guys were the ones who turned it out here tonight. I owe it all to you."

"You mind if I have a seat? You have a little time?" Garrison asked. Seth dragged a chair over to his table, resuming his semireclined position.

"Yeah, I got time. Always have time for you, Garrison. You want a beer?"

He shook his head, "Naw. Just had a few in the back . . . got to watch my gut." Garrison patted his totally absent belly with an almost bony hand. They laughed.

"Seth, I got to hand it to you. You said you were gonna come through for us, and you have. You're a man of your word. That means a lot to me. The guys and me, well, we been knocked around a lot over the years, you know what I mean? So we weren't the most trusting group of cats you'd ever meet—and I know that. Kind of made life difficult for you, I know."

"You didn't make life difficult for me. If anything, you made me get up off my butt and get some work done! You started the trend, my man."

"You've done more for us in these last few months than all our other managers have done for us throughout our careers. And you know why? Because you had focus. Honest focus."

"Focus? I don't know about that, Garrison. I mean, I've just been trying to get from step to step. When I think of focus, I think of zeroing in on a goal or something. I didn't do that. I was just trying to get you guys out there. As much as I could."

Garrison slapped his knee, leaned back in the chair, and adjusted his hat. "Aw man, you young cats! Don't you see? That's what focus is all about! For us, that was it! That was what *we* needed."

Seth didn't quite understand why he had chosen to make a reference to his age. "Something wrong with being young, man?"

The jazz man laughed loud and long. "Naw, man. Youth is a wonderful thing. A wonderful thing. But you know what the difference is between youth and an old cat like myself? Naw, don't answer that . . . 'cause I know you don't, but I'm gonna tell you. The difference is knowing when to fit stuff into the mold and when to find a mold to fit the stuff!" He laughed like it was the funniest revelation in the history of man.

Seth looked at Garrison and wondered how his words of wisdom could apply to his life, could give him vision. He thought about Nia leaving in the middle of the gig with her friend. Maybe she had found a different mold.

"Women can make us do some crazy things—believe me, I know."

Seth nodded his agreement. He knew that truth all too well. The men looked at each other and tripped off into their separate memories.

"I know we ain't never had a personal kind of relationship, where we could just talk about things, man to man, and I don't mean to be prying or stepping on any toes. Just wanted to let you know that I been around the block a few times," Garrison pointed his head toward the waiting women gathered around the table, "and if you need to talk, I'm here for you."

Seth smiled at his genuine offer of friendship. "I got a lot on my plate, Garrison."

"I can tell, my man."

"It's not getting in the way of my work, though."

"Oh no no no. I wasn't trying to imply that, nothing like that. I'm just saying that the stress is starting to show, man. And no matter what, you got to be true to Seth. You a man—you want to do the right thing and be righteous, I know, but you got to do what's best for Seth. That's how you be a man. You always have to be your own man before you can be someone else's."

Seth listened to the jazzman's words. They struck discord and Seth winced inside.

"Anytime you want to talk to an old man, Seth"—Garrison stood and walked away—"remember, I'm here."

Seth rode back to his place alone in a cab. It cost him a fortune; with all the freezing on the road, all the traffic moving erratically. He was grateful that the driver wasn't talkative; he wasn't in the mood.

Success. It wasn't supposed to be like this. Whenever he had pictured success in his mind, he had been smiling, content. Not feeling this strange, uneasy feeling of forgetting something, of incomplete-ness. It was more than just traveling home by himself in a cab that was triggering these thoughts. For the first time in a long time he felt truly alone. Cliché after cliché bombarded his mind: Success is nothing without someone to share it with. No man is an island. A man without a woman is like . . . is like . . . Seth without Lauren.

Seth without Lauren.

She had been putting him through a living hell. By being there and being distant all at the same time. Being around her the last few weeks had been his personal torture. He wanted so much to turn back the clock, to undo the things that had so quickly been done. He thought back to the first time he had seen Lauren after Sandy had come back into his life.

"Hello Seth." Lauren had stood at his door, holding her briefcase, wearing jeans, a white T-shirt, and a blazer. Her face scrubbed, devoid of makeup. Her hair pulled back into a ponytail, unpretentious.

The woman was beautiful.

He hadn't known what to say, just stood dumbfounded and grateful, and offered her entrance.

"So, what's on the agenda for today?" She walked straight to the of-fice, set down her briefcase, and looked over the documents on the desk.

"Baby, oh baby, I'm so glad to see you," he said, tentative and per-plexed, shoving his hands into his back pockets, following her into the office. Her office.

"No," she turned to him sharply, pointing an accusatory finger at him, "not *baby*. The name is Lauren. And stop acting as though you're surprised. I *do* have a job to do, right?" She removed her blazer, walked to the closet, and hung it up.

"Yes! Yes, of course you do. Always." He followed her as she walked authoritatively from room to room.

"Well, let's take it one day at a time, shall we? So, where are the re-ceipts for the week?" She shuffled through the papers scattered upon the desk.

"Baby? I mean, Lauren? Damn, I hate this! We have to talk."

"You lost the receipts?"

"Lauren, please. Don't do this." He reached for her, his hand reach-ing to touch the side of her face.

"Seth," she breathed, clutching his hand before it could reach her cheek, "tell me . . . what do you want from me, huh? I am doing the very best that I know how."

"I want to tell you what happened with Sandy. I want us to talk."

"And I *don't* want to talk. I don't want to hear it! I just want to do my job. That's all I came here to do. So if you let me do my job, I'll stay. Otherwise, I'm out of here. I'm not being paid for conversation."

He felt so much for her. He loved her integrity and her strength and the way she held a pen, so honestly, and her fragility and her pain and all the elements that comprised who she had become over a lifetime of living. Part of him wanted to run, to give her the space, the chance to find a man worthy of her caring, but the greater part of him was selfish and clung to the hope of the chance of her forgiveness. And it was this part that spoke from the dark, unbridled segment of his soul when he stood before her and whispered, "Believe that I love you, Lauren."

She surprised him, too, when she looked up at him and told him that she knew this.

"I love you, too, Seth. Very, very much."

"So why are you being so cold?"

She looked away and shrugged her shoulders.

But it was the way she looked away and the change in her posture that made him nervous. It made him wonder if maybe—just maybe—he should have just come on out with it and told her flat out that Sandy was pregnant. Instead, he left that thought unsaid and the piercing silence gave way to her slow, creeping smile. It was an eerie smile, a smile that jolted him, teased him. A smile that said to him, *Well maybe she knows already. Maybe she's just waiting for the right time to go to the kitchen and get some large, sharp utensil.* It was a smile that made him think that maybe she was planning to kill his ass and get it over with once and for all.

"*I'm being . . . cold?*" The chill in her words frightened him more than watching Mother turn around in *Psycho.*

He gulped. He stammered. "Yes, why are you being so cold?"

She raised herself out of the chair, leaned over the desk, and eye to eye she said, "Because I love *me* more. Now, if you'll excuse me, I think I'll fill my water glass."

He paced the office, listening. Footsteps, slow and deliberate. The cabinet door opening. Slamming shut. The refrigerator door opening.

Water pouring. The refrigerator door closing with a thud. And then, more footsteps. Slower and slower.

He closed his eyes. He was losing it. He knew he was losing it.

"Something wrong, Seth? You seem . . . disturbed," she asked him, leaning on the wall outside the office.

"No, nothing's wrong. Nothing at all."

"Good," she said. "Now that we understand each other, let's get to work."

So much had been accomplished that day. All the preliminaries for Garrison's concert at Scattz, all the media kits prepared and mailed. Tons of business. But there were no hugs, no whispers, no kisses or touches of any kind. And in the days and weeks that followed there had been no dates after work and no nonbusiness-related telephone calls between them.

It had been that way ever since. Professional, productive, and one hundred percent unfulfilling.

Seth entered his apartment and secured the two locks on his front door. He was grateful that he had left the radio on, playing softly, the soothing strains of slow love songs calling out to him, welcoming him home. He was a man who was used to being alone. Solitude was never something he feared or shunned. But now he was beginning to see the absence of love in his life.

Now that love was gone, it had left a hole. Gaping and wide.

He walked to the office and set his leather briefcase down next to the desk. The glass desktop glistened, creating prisms in the dark, reflecting the streetlamps that shone through the white translucent curtains hanging at his windows. The plants were growing, adding life, the palms and the ivys, lush and thriving under the touch of their devoted caretaker. Thriving under her touch just as he had thrived.

Seth sat at the desk, the chair not even feeling comfortable anymore, not supporting the contours of his body. It had become not only her office, but her desk, her chair, her plants. Lauren had come in and brought life to all of the things that surrounded him. He smelled her cologne, the scent of White Linen woven firmly into the fabric of his life now. Lauren had come in and breathed purpose into his existence. And now, in a movement just as purposeful, she was depriving him of the chance to enjoy.

Now, no matter where he was, he was uncomfortable.

It wasn't always that way. There was once a time when, no matter where he was, he felt comfortable . . . as long as she was there with him.

"I feel so safe around you, Seth," she had whispered the words to him, holding his hand tightly, trying to look composed and failing miserably.

It had been the first time they had ridden the subway together. A gesture of trust on her behalf, a symbol so strong that said how willing she had been to get on with her life. It had seemed that way at the time.

"You are." And he had clung to her hand and laced his fingers tightly with hers. "No one is going to hurt you. And no one is going to tear us apart."

She snapped her head in his direction. "Don't promise me that. Anyone or anything can tear us apart at any time. You don't have control over what other people can do."

"I don't have control over their actions, but I have control over my reactions. And I'm telling you, I'm promising you—right here on this subway train—that I will always love you. No matter what, Lauren. You'll always be a part of me. The good of me . . . the all of me."

The train rocked and reeled, jerking and bouncing its passengers haphazardly, without consideration. Like an aching whale with unsettled human cargo. The noise level so high that he wondered if she had even heard; her expression remained so fixed and unchanged. But instantly, Seth knew his words had bonded them together in a spiritual kind of way. Did she feel the change? He didn't know. But it had transformed him and carried him to a place he felt sure he had wanted to go. The oneness had felt so delicious back then. It had seemed the right thing to do at the time. But now, in the confines of his aloneness, he wondered if he would ever be free of her presence.

She hadn't come to Scattz. He didn't think she would. But every five minutes he had paced the lobby, checked the backstage area, and looked over the audience for any sign of her arrival. He knew she wouldn't be there for him, but maybe in spite of him, she might have boldly walked through the doors, perhaps with some good-looking guy on her arm, for jealousy's sake. He had been prepared for that. He had hoped she would want to see the fruits of her labor, her sweet efforts, payoff in impeccable organization and smiling couples and nodding heads, and round after round of robust applause.

They were applauding you, too, Lauren. Loud and strong. And you didn't even come to hear it.

Seth went into his bedroom, removed his clothes, laid them upon the easy chair in the corner, and walked to the bathroom. He closed the door, turned the shower water to hot, and stepped inside the tub.

It didn't take long for the steam to cloud his vision.

It didn't take long for the tears to rain freely from his eyes.

So this was success, he thought. This is how it felt to have finally arrived.

He stayed in the shower, allowing the water to redden his skin, until the stream of water began to run cool. He dried off, leaving no trail of water as he walked to his bedroom.

The answering machine flashed red. He pressed play.

Beep.

"Seth. This is Rex. Call me as soon as you can."

For the first time in a long time, Seth decided to end his evening and begin his morning with a good stiff drink. He walked to the bar in his living room and picked up the much-handled letter from Manny Horowitz. The letter lived on his bar, reading it and drinking seemed to go hand in hand. He knew the contents by heart. It contained Feinstein's final offer in writing and they wanted his answer this week, yea or nay.

Get your dogs off Brooksmore.

He poured himself a double shot of brandy, sat nude on the lambskin rug, and drank until the sun came up.

Nineteen

NIA

I t felt good.

Nia opened her eyes in response to a stream of hot sunshine poured upon her face. The sun usually wasn't this strong this time of the year, especially so early in the morning. The warmth felt delicious; she stretched her lithe body like a cat beneath a windowsill and pulled the sheets up to her nose. They smelled like a field of wild lavender and made her think relaxing thoughts about freedom and running without restriction.

It felt good to feel so free. She tossed awhile, reveling in this quasi-dream state, reliving the good parts of every dream she could remember. In her dreams there was no discord or misunderstanding or deceit. In her dreams she could fly above the turbulence to the clouds that existed only for their beauty. She, once a raindrop, now wrapped within the friendly clouds of white down, was frolicking in this moment of solitary nudity.

And then she remembered. This was Vaughan's bed.

She thought back to the beginning of this, how she showered and dressed for the concert at Scattz, how the train came late, so full of people, how she exited the subway station and walked through the wind. She remembered the people in their coats, the ones who were smiling, the ones outside smoking cigarettes and leaning against the wall. And then there was Seth and his kindness, Vaughan and her company, Grace and her conclusions. She remembered the sleet, the walking to shelter and seafood, the sofa, the silences.

If only she had said yes to Vaughan's offer to dessert, then maybe none of this would have happened. Maybe then she wouldn't have accepted that espresso and brought it to her lips, that hot steaming liquid, pungent with lemon twist and rich Italian coffee. Every time she sipped, Vaughan kissed her, gently at first, a grazing of her cheek. And with every sip of the cup, Vaughan would add one more kiss, gentler still, until it really didn't feel like human kisses at all, but being loved by air.

She hadn't come here for any of this. She hadn't come here to do anything but spend an evening getting over an evening she wanted desperately to forget. With every kiss to her cheek, Nia justified the moment as something that was happening to her, something outside the realm of her control. With every kiss to the curve of her neck below her dangling silver earrings, Nia melted into thinking that she wasn't doing anything but sitting on that couch, closing her eyes, and being wonderfully entertained.

"I'm not going any farther, diva," Vaughan whispered in her ear, sending chills right through Nia. "I can't."

Nia didn't understand why she would stop now. Every nerve ending in her body was alive and fully charged; *she knows this*, Nia thought, *as a woman, she knows what she's doing to me*. She looked at Vaughan, puzzled.

"You have to tell me what it is you want," Vaughan said.

Nia smiled, closed her eyes, and started to pull Vaughan closer to her. Vaughan resisted.

"No, Nia. This is not about what you will let me do to you. This is not about me being the big bad lesbian and you being the sweet innocent straight woman who just happened to fall into my clutches."

"Give a woman a break, Vaughan. I've never been here before," she breathed. "Come on . . . help me . . . meet me halfway."

"No."

Nia watched Vaughan as she stood up from the sofa, smoothed her slate gray sweater dress, and walked slowly into the hallway leading to the front door. Moments later, the Friends of Distinction singing "I Really Hope You Do" filtered through the room. Nia closed her eyes and listened to the soothing voice of that glorious alto, that woman singing to her, someone chosen above all the potential someones, being totally up-front with everything she was feeling.

Singers always made it sound so damn easy.

She wished she had been drunk or high, out of her mind and out of control. She wished there had been something outside of herself that she could blame and to which she could point, something external. She understood fully what Vaughan was saying and she had been right. It would be really easy for her to walk into this situation of her own free will tonight and then blame it on the boogie in the morning. But Nia was in no way incapacitated; there was nothing but her own oozings on which to blame this wanting.

Vaughan walked back into the living room, slowly. She was holding Nia's coat in her hand.

"I think you should go."

Nia didn't move from the sofa. "And suppose . . . suppose I don't want to go?"

Vaughan chuckled and held her coat out to her. "Nia, please. You want to go. Believe me. You do."

Nia stood up and walked over to her. "I really don't."

"Just take your coat, okay? I don't have time to play your little game. Take your coat, walk out the door, and go home."

"Well, if that's the way you want it, Vaughan."

"Dammit! This isn't about what I want. *I* know what *I* want. If I had *my* way I would make love to you all night long and bring the sun up with you in my bed. But if you don't know in your heart what it is that *you* want, then you're more dangerous to me than a loaded gun without a safety. And I don't need the stress, okay?"

Vaughan put Nia's coat into her arms and walked over to the living room window.

"Go ahead and let yourself out."

Nia draped her coat over the back of the sofa. She walked up behind Vaughan and hugged her around her waist, hugged her closely, nuzzling her nose into the back of her neck.

"No, I won't go. I want this."

"You want *what*, Nia?"

Nia turned Vaughan around, held her face in her hands, and kissed her gently, as though she were afraid, then stood back and looked at this woman. Vaughan's demeanor changed before her, losing its hard-core edge, its barracuda bite, her guard dissolving under Nia's fingertips. Nia let her hands explore the contours of Vaughan's velvety smooth face: lovingly studying her and wanting to know her, touching those deep, dark eyelids and long, thick lashes, her arched eyebrows, the beautiful bow of her sweet, sweet lips. Nia kissed her ears and whispered into them that it was time for them to please, please, please stop standing.

"We can sit down on that sofa, right over there . . . or . . . we can go elsewhere," Vaughan said.

"Elsewhere, Vaughan, let's go elsewhere."

Vaughan walked down another short hall and turned into a room swathed in hues of winter white and gold. The mahogany bed was large and inviting, draped with an ethereal netting of white, the satin comforter reflecting the soft lighting from the ceiling.

It was a room containing the look and feel of St. Augustine's Cathedral.

Nia walked in behind Vaughan pulling off her own sweater and stepping out of her snug leather jeans. She stood in front of Vaughan and smiled in her cream-colored satin bra and bikini, matching the bed linens as though all of this had been planned. Vaughan watched her silently, her mouth slightly open and ready to kiss, watched her as she unbuttoned the tiny pearl buttons that stretched down the front of her dress, watched her as she helped the cashmere fall away from her shoulders and onto the floor, watched her as she kissed her lovingly, head to toe.

Their movements became fluid and synchronized, one woman's pressure becoming the other woman's release, over and over and over again, like ocean waves that never stop coming until the tide recedes and the morning finds dawn.

All night long they found new ways to make each other scream for a savior.

Nia awakened slowly and realized she was alone in the bed. She felt incredibly fulfilled, her body more satisfied than she could ever, ever recall. She smelled food cooking in the distance, and it made her stomach rumble. She wondered how long she had been asleep. She reached over to the night table to look at her watch and knocked something onto the floor. It hit with a thud and she reached down to pick it up—a heavy, intricately carved, mahogany frame. She turned it over and set it back in its place: a photograph of Vaughan and Grace kissing on a beach.

"I don't know why you're getting so upset. I told you that whatever was there is gone!" Vaughan put the breakfast tray down on the bed in front of Nia.

"You just don't get it do you? Grace is my *friend* . . ."

"Well, if she's your *friend*, she would want you to be happy. She wouldn't want you sitting here letting a perfectly good omelet go to waste."

"You know, Vaughan," she said, standing and searching for her underwear, "I don't know if the rules are different in your kind of lifestyle, but where I come from friends don't sleep with other friends' lovers."

"In my kind of lifestyle? Is that what I just heard you say?" Vaughan walked up behind Nia, grabbed her shoulder and spun her around. "As I recall, *you* were giving just as much as you were getting. Do correct me if I'm wrong, diva."

"One night isn't going to make me . . ." Nia looked away from her.

"Going to make you what, Nia? One night isn't going to make you *gay*? Isn't going to make you admit that you enjoyed every single thing that happened between us? Oh, come on, Nia. Stop the B.S. You and I both know the truth: You *knew* about me and Grace and you made the choice of your own volition. Friend or no friend, you went for the woman. So be a woman now and deal with it." She walked over to the ivory damask chair in the corner, scooped up Nia's clothes, and threw them at her. "Grow up, get dressed, and get the hell out of here."

The streets looked different to her now.

Nia retraced her steps and walked to the subway. She must have looked like holy hell, not stopping to brush her hair or look into a mirror, just grabbing all she could find that was hers and walking out the door. She took the stairs down to the lobby, walked past the old men who were sitting in the courtyard playing an early-morning game of chess. They broke their concentration to say good morning and tip their hats to her but she didn't respond.

If I just keep moving, maybe I'll actually get somewhere.

Nia opened the doors to her apartment, picked up the mail that her landlord had dropped in her mail slot, and walked down her hallway to her living room. She felt at first as though she were walking into foreign territory. It seemed as though it had been so long since she had smelled the vanilla bean and cinnamon fragrances of her home, and feasted her eyes upon the blues and greens of her familiar and cherished upholstery, much longer than the single day that had actually passed. She wanted to be here, to be grounded and sent to her room, wanted to sweep and dust and vacuum and have her hands touch things that belonged to her and stayed steady. She wanted to reacquaint herself with the tangible, go back three steps and not collect $200 this time. She wanted fresh flowers in her space again, she was ready to be around living things again. She was so, so glad to be home.

Sifting through the mail, she separated the bills and advertisements from the pieces she wanted to read. A letter from her aunt. A letter from a potential client in Los Angeles. And another envelope with no stamp and no return address. She began opening this one first and took a seat at her desk when her telephone rang.

She sat there and stared at the phone, reluctant to answer and deal with anyone at all. There weren't a whole heck of a lot of people she wanted to hear from at the moment. But it could be an emergency. And then again, it could actually be something good. She doubted it strongly, but it could be. She picked up the receiver.

"Hello."

"So you finally made it home."

Nia closed her eyes and searched for strength. "Hi Grace."

"I was wondering if you were going to come home today. Wondering if you'd spend the day in bed."

"Grace . . ."

"Yes, Nia? What could you possibly have to say to me?"

Nia was silent.

"You know . . . you know, this is a really twisted scenario here. Be-cause, usually, *you* would be the person I'd call to lean on. I'd call *you* for a shoulder. And I guess old habits just die hard, you know? I'm feel-ing pissed and used and hurt and betrayed . . . and the person I always call to help me find my way outside of those feelings is the one stick-ing it to me. Go figure."

Nia was weeping, dripping tears on her unopened mail.

"Now, you notice that I haven't asked if you sexed it up with Vaughan. You *do* notice that, don't you? Because, you see, if I don't *di-rectly* ask you, then there's always the possibility, small as it may be, that you did the decent thing and slept on her couch or went to a fancy hotel just to think about who you are or something." Grace's voice began to crack. "So I'm not going to ask you what you did or where you were . . . or what I did to you . . ."

They cried.

"Grace?"

"I don't want to hear the bull. Save it, okay? I really, really don't want to hear it today."

"She still cares about you."

"Did she pay you well to say that to me?"

"No."

Nia wanted to tell her about the photograph on the nightstand, tell her that Vaughan hadn't put it away. She wanted to tell her that Vaughan had not moved it—hadn't even turned it around—no matter what had transpired between the two, not even for Nia. But she couldn't get the words out. She couldn't even admit to Grace that she had been in a position to see it.

"I love you. You're my sister. That's all I can say," Nia whispered.

"You have a really funny way of showing it."

"I guess . . . I guess I was looking for something."

Grace sniffled. "Well, do tell. Did you find it under the satin com-forter?"

"I don't want to have this conversation. It . . . it just hurts too much."

"You know, you break up with somebody and you think you're all over them. In your mind, you know that's it a no-go and you need to move on. But then something happens and you realize that the person is still all inside of you, reminding you of all the good times you had. And that's where I am now. I know she's toxic and bad for my health, and she probably always will be. But I saw the good parts of her, too. When I saw the two of you together . . ." Her voice trailed.

"I wasn't lying to you either. We really were just friends. At least, that was my reality. I don't know what happened, Grace. I don't understand how things ended up the way they did . . ."

"Open arms are real inviting, aren't they?" There was no bitterness in her voice, no accusation, just the pain of a woman who knows the cost of curing loneliness.

The two women listened to each other's silences on the phone.

"Especially when you've been running on empty for so long," Nia said, closing her eyes. "Grace?"

"Yeah?"

"I am so sorry."

Grace sighed. "I know. So am I. I don't want to go into a long list of shoulda-woulda-coulda, but maybe one day we'll learn how to be more honest with our friends. I need to go now, I really do. You . . . you take care of yourself, Nia. Don't take any wooden nickels."

Nia heard Grace hang up the phone and held on to the receiver until the dial tone came on.

Grace's words resonated long after she had hung up the phone: *Maybe one day we'll learn how to be more honest with our friends.*

She placed the receiver in its cradle.

"And maybe one day I'll learn how to be more honest with myself."

Worcestershire sauce. Tomato juice. Aspirin.

None of that stuff worked in real life. Seth walked gingerly into the kitchen, massaging his temples, trying to coax his hangover to flee as quickly and as completely as possible.

Now he remembered why he didn't drink brandy. That stuff took away brain cells faster than a surgeon performing two-for-one lobotomies. And that madness about having a taste of the dog that bit you? The same rabid dog that had already torn you up without mercy? He had always believed it was a remedy concocted by some warped advertising executive going for a promotion on some alcohol account. Someone about as warped as Feinstein. It didn't even sound right.

Exactly what had he been thinking?

He felt through his fog and managed to turn on the faucet, allowing the water to run, filling the teakettle. Tea. Herbal. Naturally decaffeinated. Strong. It seemed the sane thing to do first thing in the morning. But first thing had come pretty late this day. The black-and-white kitty-cat clock on the kitchen wall indicated that it was a quarter past two. And each swish of the tail signaled another second past and gone.

He tiptoed to his room and grabbed some clothes, just sweats today, nothing fancy. A glance outside revealed a silver sky, a sky sullen and heavy with clouds, hinting that the storm had not totally passed. This Sunday after Thanksgiving was a good day for reflection. For reading and sorting. Figuring stuff out.

He had to call Rex and he had to give Feinstein an answer before the end of the week.

Rex had been a good partner for him. He hadn't thought it would work out so well at first, with Rex being so much like a dad to him throughout the years. But this was beneficial, relating to him on an adult level, partner to partner. Rex knew how those older jazz guys thought, had been there to see how badly they had been treated through the years, and could relate to them in a way Seth just couldn't replicate. And the fact that he had lots of time and money to invest didn't hurt the situation either.

The one aspect of their relationship that had been fuzzy had to do with Seth's relationship with Lauren. Whenever her name came up, Rex seemed to shed the professional demeanor and take on a paternal edge. His favorite niece. There was no objectivity there. So Seth took special pains to leave her out of his conversations with Rex, at least in a business context.

"Look at the quality of these contracts, Seth," Rex had mentioned to him as they were riding in the cab to the Scattz signing. "And to think that my Lauren did these. The woman should have gone to law school—this here shows some kind of smarts, I'm telling you."

"Yeah, Rex. She did a real good job. Had my lawyer look 'em over, and he said she covered just about all the bases. He just had to add a touch here and there to make it all come together."

"You don't say? Well, that's my niece! She ain't no dummy."

"Nope. No dummy at all."

Rex flipped through the contract pages. "Mmm hmmm, make some man a dynamite wife."

Seth looked away. He didn't want Rex to see the sadness. He didn't want him to read his pain. "Without a doubt, she would. Dynamite wife."

But Rex wasn't letting the topic go. "Oh, absolutely! But not just any man, mind you. Got to be the right man. Got to be someone really special, someone who would not only be right for Lauren; got to be someone who would fit into the family, too. That's something you young folks don't consider much anymore. The concept of family. You all think it's just two people that get married and run off by themselves. But I'm living and breathing to tell you different . . . that couldn't be farther from the truth!"

"I hear you, Rex. We should go back to the time of arranged marriages, huh?"

"You joking over there, but mark my words, Seth. A man leaves his mama and daddy and takes on a wife and her whole laundry list of relatives. Read the Bible, it'll tell you. And remember"—he jabbed Seth with his finger—"ain't nothing in there talk about the wife leaving none of *them* to be with him. Not a one. Hmmpf. You find it in there, you let me know!"

Seth laughed. "If I find it in there, I'll let you know first thing."

Then Rex got serious. "She's good for you, Seth. And you're already a part of the family. You know that, right?"

Seth nodded. He had wanted to be able to share his pain with Rex, but he didn't know where to start. Did he start with the fact that he was going to be a father or the fact that Lauren and he were barely on speaking terms or the fact that he didn't know how to make anything better anymore? He didn't know where the circle began, couldn't find a thread to begin the unravel. So he just nodded. Kept silent and nodded.

"I know there are problems."

Seth looked over at Rex as the cab took a swerve to the left to avoid another wild and crazy cabbie.

"Yeah, Seth. I know there are problems. Take a blind man not to see that you and Lauren are having problems. But the way I see it, there always gonna be problems in a relationship. You just got to hang in there and work at it and keep working at it, till it's not a problem anymore. Till you either die trying or get too old to remember what the heck the problems were!"

They had laughed together and Seth nodded his agreement. But he wasn't convinced then and he wasn't convinced now.

Some problems were just beyond the reach of hope.

Seth sat at the desk with his tea and dialed Rex.

"Hello?"

"Awww . . . hi there MommaPatti. How's it going?" Hangover or not, she still brought a smile to his face.

"Seth! I'm doing just fine, yes, I am. Just fine. You missed Rex. He headed out of here in a hurry, said he had some business to take care of. Have you recovered from that fine, fine concert of last night?"

"Well, not quite." He laughed. "But I'm starting to get it together over here."

"Good. I sure did have a wonderful time! And thank you so much for allowing Rex to have a hand in things. He will probably never say a mumbling word to you, but it means a lot to him. You know he's not the fishing/hunting type of man, and it's not good for a retired person to just sit at home with nothing important to do—you understand what I'm saying, Seth?"

"Well, he's been more help to me than I've been to him, I'm sure. Thank *you* for sharing him with me!"

"Oh, stop! I'll tell him you called and have him get back to you first thing. You take care, sweetie."

He hung up the phone, laced up his running shoes, grabbed his gloves, his scarf, and his hat and opened his door.

Rex stood there, hand poised to ring the bell.

"We got to talk, Seth." He pushed by him and walked into the apartment. "And we got to talk *now*."

Rex walked quickly into the office, his footsteps resounding on the wood. He hovered over the desk, his face full of darkness and concern.

"Sit."

Seth unwrapped the scarf from around his neck, pulled off his hat, and dutifully plopped into the desk chair.

"Yeah, Rex?"

"Time to talk." Rex sat in the chair opposite the desk, and drummed his fingers on the armrest. "On two different levels, Seth."

Seth braced himself. He felt the tidal wave coming.

"I want to talk to you about the concert. I was up all night. Couldn't sleep."

"Yeah, Rex. I know the feeling." Seth put his head in his hands.

"Patti finally told me that whatever was on my mind had to come out in the open. That's why I'm here. I have to speak my piece."

"Okay."

"First, the business issue. I have in my hand a business card. Dude gave it to me last night after the Miles Davis medley. Said his name was Sammy Diggs. He's starting a new jazz label out in L.A. And he's real impressed with the things that he saw up there on that stage last night."

Seth was beaming.

"Well, he said he doesn't have a ton of money. But he's a young guy like yourself and I got a good feeling 'bout him, Seth. He wants to talk to us about signing the group on. Wants us to come out to L.A. to talk a deal, Seth."

"That's great! When are we heading out?"

"I was hoping *you* would take charge on this first step. You make the trip." Rex handed him the card.

"Sure, Rex. Sure, I can do that."

"Now, the personal. I was real surprised not to see Lauren there last night. At first I was worried, thought something had happened to her and all. Then I called her house, and she answered the phone. She was crying."

Rex got up and started pacing. The window to the door. The door to the window. Like a caged lion.

"That angel was crying. After all that work she put in to making that concert happen, she wasn't even there. I was real disturbed. She didn't want to tell me what the problem was. She gets quiet like that sometimes when she gets upset."

No kidding, Seth thought. Seemed as though it had been months since they had enjoyed a meaningful conversation.

"I know, Rex. I've tried to talk to her about what's bothering her. But she won't talk to me. Nothing but business."

"Well, Seth. That's because *you* are the problem. She finally did open up to me." Rex faced the window and looked outside. "So who's Sandy?"

Seth felt the brandy remnants and the tea and the tension dancing around in his stomach, making him want to heave like a rookie sailor on an unstable ship. "Sandy?"

"Yeah, Sandy. Tell me about her."

On one level, he really wanted to share. He wanted to share with Rex, the Man, the man of years and wisdom. But he knew he'd never be able to reach that man, not with Rex, the Protective Uncle standing watch. "Rex, I made a mistake. And let's just leave it at that, okay?"

"No, not okay. Tell me about her."

Seth surprised himself by pounding his fist, his frustration spilling all over the desktop. "Why? Huh? Why should I bother telling you or anyone else about her? What difference would it make? I made a mistake! I did something I shouldn't have done and nothing I do or say or feel is ever gonna change that! Nothing is ever going to take that away."

"Do you love her?"

"Love who?"

"Sandy."

He was all ready to shout out his emphatic no, to deny that he had ever felt anything about her. But he thought back to a moment, a brief moment, when he saw her vulnerability and wanted nothing more than to protect her, to shelter her and her unborn child. Maybe his unborn child.

Was that love?

"I care about her as a person."

Rex nodded slowly and looked suddenly peaceful. "Lauren's afraid, Seth. She's afraid she's lost you to her. You know, when Brandon died, she went through this whole thing then. Rejecting anyone and everyone who tried to get close to her. Reject them before they had a chance to reject her. She puts up walls so that no one can touch her. She feels she'll be protected that way. You hear what I'm saying to you?"

"Yes."

"So what you need to do is to tell her."

Seth looked up at Rex, threw his leg over the arm of the chair. "Tell her what?"

"Tell her that the whole thing with Sandy was just a mistake. Tell her it's over. Tell her she's out of your system, out of your life. Tell Lauren that she is the woman of your future, and Sandy was just a woman from your past."

It sure did sound nice. Sure would have been ideal if life presented itself in such wonderfully neat little packages. But there was no way he could say that to her. Not with a baby on the way. A baby that he was believing more and more each day was actually his. And despite the circumstances of the child's conception, he was determined to not leave her to raise the baby without his influence.

Rex raised his eyebrows, questioning, waiting for Seth to provide him with some assurances.

"Thanks, Rex."

"You ain't gonna do it, are you?" Rex resumed his pacing. He was going to wear a groove in the floor. "You gonna blow the whole damn thing. Seth, I had so much more faith in you than that."

"Then know that I'll do what's best, Rex."

"Best for who? For Seth? For Lauren? For the business? Who, Seth?"

That was the question. That had always been the question.

Seth cleared his throat and walked to the kitchen, signaling the end of the conversation. "Okay, is that it?"

"Yeah, all right. We can play it like that. For a minute. You got any coffee in there?"

"Sure do. Instant. Cream and sugar?"

"Instant's fine—and I take it black. No bullshit." Rex followed behind Seth and stood in the doorway. "Well, that was some performance last night, huh?"

"Sure was. Garrison was in rare form. They were playing, I tell you."

"Yes, they were. And the audience seemed to really appreciate where they were coming from."

"You did a good job, Rex."

"You, too."

Rex was skirting, Seth could tell. Just passing pleasantries to keep the conversation civil. He handed him the coffee. "So ask whatever it is you're trying not to ask me."

He sipped. "Okay, I will. Was that Sandy—the woman who had you running in and out of the lobby at Scattz? The one on the verge of a catfight?"

"Nope."

"*Another* woman, Seth? For Pete's sake, man. Business is business!"

"And I handled my business! It wasn't like that. Truth be told, she was an acquaintance of Reggie's." And as soon as he said it, he was sorry.

"Reggie?"

"No, you don't understand. Reggie introduced me to . . ."

"My Reggie?"

"Rex! Listen to me!"

"Damn, does Crystal know?"

"Why won't you listen to me, huh? Why won't anyone listen to the things I have to say?"

"Okay, I'm listening. But you know something? I don't like what I'm hearing here, none of it. I really don't. You young guys think you have it all figured out, think that a dip here and a dabble there is going to go unnoticed and get over. But you don't want to listen to reason. You don't want to—"

"Oh, forget it Rex! Now I know why people shut down. Gets real tired having to explain yourself all the time. Having to defend yourself against people's runaway imaginations."

"No, no . . . talk! Please! I want to hear it all! Go ahead!" Rex sat down carelessly in the kitchen chair, his coffee sloshing all over the rim, the blue vein on the side of his face throbbing dangerously.

"Why bother? I'm already guilty, right? Reggie's already guilty, right? Lauren is God's perfect angel. And Sandy is a pregnant conniving bitch, right?"

The words hit the air like a one-two punch leading to a TKO. Neither of them breathed. Neither of them moved. The teakettle whistled. The clock ticked. Rex and Seth locked eyes, neither willing to break the stare. But Rex's expression told the story.

He hadn't known.

All this time, Rex hadn't known.

"Lauren didn't tell you about Sandy being pregnant?"

And in an instant, Seth replayed the moment in his mind, from the second he walked into the kitchen until the time Sandy left. She had told him straight out that she hadn't said anything to Lauren. But Seth, skeptic that he had been, had never believed her.

Sandy had told him the truth: She hadn't told Lauren she was pregnant.

"I got to get out of here." Rex stumbled to the door. "Got to get out of here before I do something I'm gonna regret for a long, long time."

"Rex . . ."

He paused at the door. "No, Seth. She didn't mention it. Too caught up with thoughts about her own pregnancy, I suppose."

A lesser man would have left town by now. Left town and left woman and left baby one *and* baby two behind, with a "Gone Fishing" sign tacked up on his door for good measure. It was more than he could handle in a drunken stupor, more than he could handle without a friend or a sound mind.

Lauren was pregnant. Lauren was pregnant with his child and had not seen fit to share that information with him. Just gone on with her days and nights and conversations and professional correspondences as though the sun that now rose held no special significance for them. It was the sun warming the life inside of the woman he loved who harbored his unborn child.

When Rex slammed the door on his way out, Seth had remained in his chair in the kitchen for hours, trying to understand, trying to feel. For hours he tried to pray, to ask for an explanation. But all he heard was the hollowness of his own voice, the *why* that never seemed to go away.

It took seventeen shots of brandy, and several wrong numbers for Seth to reach Lauren's extension.

Bringgg.

"Hello?"

Her voice sounded light, unencumbered.

"Lauren?"

"Yes. Seth?"

"Lauren? How could you . . . I mean, I want . . . umm, Lauren?"

Silence.

"Lauren?"

"Seth, you're drunk."

"Very much so. Drunk and I want to talk."

"Bad combination. We'll talk when you're sober."

"No, see I want to talk *now*."

"Later, Seth. We'll talk later." And she hung up the phone, without emotion or drama.

He had half a mind to go over to her house and bang on her door and make her listen, make her talk. But he couldn't find his left shoe. It had to be here somewhere. After all, the stove was where he had left it, so why not the shoe?

He crawled under the table to get on the shoe's level, to see if he could find it easier that way. And while he was crawling about his kitchen floor conversing with the dust bunnies, he fell asleep and slept through a good part of the day.

The linoleum was cool and calmed him, inviting dreams to come and give him insight. He found himself in a field, a meadow lush and green, surrounded by thick floral scents. Tiny birds chirped and flew about the blue and cloudless sky. A brook gurgled in the distance. He found himself drawn to the water, finding himself thirsty and craving. And so at first he walked to the brook, then ran, his urgency growing and becoming controlling. The water appeared to retreat from him; the more he ran, the farther away it appeared. Sweating, heaving, he stood steps from the edge, looking in horror. No water was flowing, instead it was blood, red and thick; his cries giving rise to tiny voices calling his name over and over and over.

"Seth? Seth, are you all right?"

Seth found his way from his dream back to the kitchen, welcoming the sight of the floor, appreciating the hand upon his shoulder.

"Huh?"

"Seth, you were screaming. I came in because you were screaming."

Sandy crouched next to him and stroked his hair. It felt good to him.

"Damn. Was I? That was some dream. Hey, what time is it?" And he tried to get up, not realizing that he was under the table. "Ouch!"

Sandy giggled. "That's nothing compared to the pain you're gonna feel when all of this alcohol wears off. And you smell bad. It's seven."

"Seven—A.M. or P.M.?"

"Wow, you really are out of it, huh? How long you been drinking like this? It's seven o'clock at night. And I bet you haven't eaten all day, right?"

He felt the rumblings in his stomach. "Yeah, guess you're right. Sandy?"

She looked down.

"You didn't tell her you were pregnant."

"No. Was I supposed to?"

He shook his head. "I just figured you had, that's all."

"No. Wasn't my place." She changed her tone and changed the subject. "So why don't you go on and get cleaned up and I'll fix you something to eat. Okay?"

"Sandy, that's really nice of you, but you don't have to do that—I have it under control."

She opened the cabinets, took out a package of pasta, and looked around for pots and miscellaneous ingredients.

"Too late. Go on."

Seth stood up slowly, feeling the effects of the brandy leaving his brain, and nodded. He felt too bad to argue. And the company would be kind of nice. For a while, anyway.

"Seth?"

He turned around, rubbing his temples. "Yeah."

"Just a dinner between friends. Real friends. I could use one tonight."

"Yeah. Me, too, chica. Me, too."

The shower water felt good on his skin, warm and soothing. He half expected Sandy to burst into his bathroom, to open the locked door with a hairpin or paper clip, so he kept his towel within reach, never totally relaxing. But the intrusion never happened. His space remained his own.

When he opened the bathroom door, he was hit by the aroma of garlic and heaven, the sounds of Isaac Hayes's *Hot Buttered Soul* and the clanging of dishes. His stomach growled audibly from the hallway.

"Seth? We gonna pass on the wine tonight."

He walked into the kitchen and sat at the table. "You get no argument from me, chica. That smells great. I'm starved."

It felt good to sit and eat with her, felt like old times, before things got all complicated and serious. Seemed as though she sensed it, too, both of them keeping the conversation on subjects that were safe and light and easy, free of controversy and decision.

"I have to take a trip to Los Angeles. Good news. Looks like someone wants to record the Garrison Walters Trio."

"Hey! That's fabulous!"

"Yeah, yeah. Looks like it's gonna happen for them."

"Even without an incredibly shy premier vocalist. Amazing, huh?"

He laughed. "They don't need a vocalist to work their magic. They're complete just as they are."

"Interesting. Is that how the business works?"

"Well, think about it. If they can do it on their own, why add to the whole?"

She seemed to fade off into some other plane of existence, leaving him alone.

"Sandy? You okay?"

"Oh, I'm sorry," she said, pulling herself back to the present. "That was kind of deep, you know? 'If they can do it on their own, why add to the whole.' Makes me think. Makes me think about a lot of stuff."

"Okay," he said, concentrating on his concrete example, "just look at it from an economic perspective. Why split the pot with four performers when you can split it with three?"

And he went on, eventually explaining the role of the manager and the agent and royalty calculations in grand detail. Sandy nodded from time to time, asking a question here and there. But her focus had changed. She closed her eyes. She looked like she was praying, centering herself.

"What's wrong?" he asked, alarmed.

"Nothing. Here," she said, placing his hand upon her stomach, "feel this?"

He withdrew his hand quickly.

There was movement in her womb.

There were a total of six messages on his answering machine.

Seth tried to understand why they needed to move so fast. Sure, he knew the recording company wanted to meet with him and bring the Garrison Walters Trio on board, but the folks had left four messages on his answering machine in the last twenty-four hours. This was only Monday. Slight overkill, Seth mused. He'd get it in time, get to it all.

Lauren had called and left a message that she wasn't coming to work Monday evening. She said she probably wouldn't be coming in at all this week. It was strange; when he called her, he only reached her answering machine. Maybe they both needed the time apart to think about things. Maybe he had botched things up sufficiently. Maybe maybe maybe. His personal life was in shambles and his professional life was threatening to tumble right along with the mix. On the machine, she spoke softly and slowly, assuring him that she would be there soon, saying she had it all together and she just needed a little time off. But time was exactly what he didn't have. The work was piling up and he had decisions that required her input.

So rather than suffer the repercussions of looking bad, he returned the frantic calls himself.

"Seth! Great to hear from you! Sammy Diggs, here."

"Yeah, man. I've heard some good things about you. Good things happening out there in California, huh?"

"Well, we want to make good things happen that include you and your camp. I'm very impressed with the Garrison Walters Trio."

"Polished group, aren't they? Polished and ready to go."

"Looked that way to me, Seth. So when can I get you out here? Now, before you answer I want you to know that I'm trying to do a big tie-in with some festivals coming up in late summer, but in order for that to happen, we need to start the ball rolling by the beginning of December."

Seth looked at the desk calendar and shook his head into the phone. "No, I can't do that. Have another client who won't be done recording before then, and I need to be here."

"Okay, okay—we'll work something out. We can start on the preliminaries, lay some groundwork . . ."

"That'll work. And I'll see if I can get my assistant to fly out there first to personally answer any questions that you might have before I get there. Then I'll meet up with you around the second week or so. Would that work?"

"I think we could work that. Check out the logistics and get back to me. I have a good feeling about this, Seth."

"Me, too, Sammy. Time to do it."

"Definitely."

Seth hung up the phone. The last message was from Manny Horowitz.

He decided to call Lauren.

"Seth, can I talk to you later? I'm not feeling well."

"This won't take long. Really."

"What is it?" She sighed into the phone, her voice sounding sleepy and in slow motion.

"I need you to go to California for me."

"When?"

"As soon as possible. In a couple of weeks, at the latest."

"Okay. If I can get the time off from Anderson-Moss, I'll go." He could hear her shifting. She moaned. "Let's talk later, okay?"

He wanted to talk to her now.

"Hey, since you're not feeling well, why don't I come over there and fix you some soup and—" She cut him off with a whisper.

"No, Seth. There's nothing you can do. I'll be fine."

Lauren sounded so different. She sounded like another time to him, as though he had stepped into a movie and was watching himself doing the things he knew were supposed to be right and proper. He was saying the things he expected himself to say, trying to feel the things that were expected of a man who cared about a woman. But the distance was killing him. He couldn't do this anymore, being both actor and spectator, critic and performer.

Maybe he cared because he was a man and he was expected to care.

Maybe he cared only because he had said that he would.

He wanted to talk to Reggie.

Twenty-one
NIA

It was a bad habit that she had slipped into, not opening her mail right away. A habit that started way back in college, when there had been so many more bills than money available to distribute. She didn't see it as avoidance, just a matter of practicality: Why waste time and energy with an immediate impossibility? It had allowed her to relax through college and concentrate instead on poems and theories, but these were no longer innocent college years. And the letter that sat unopened on her desk was no bill. Nia discovered the letter there, days after its delivery, underneath the unrequested advertisements for glazed ham dinners in a box and tom turkeys free with a shopping cart full of purchased groceries.

Her public relations services had been retained by Staccato Music in California.

She read the letter several times, a few brief paragraphs outlining their needs, requesting her to come to Los Angeles to meet with the staff as soon as possible. She called to speak with Gina, one of the partners and the woman who had written the letter.

"Nia! I'm so glad to hear from you! We were so impressed by your materials, impressed that you had taken the initiative to contact us. And that wonderful endorsement by Vaughan Gonzalez just wowed us like you wouldn't believe. You know, we are a brand-new organization here . . . just starting out . . . but we're growing. And we'd love to have you on board to grow right along with us!" Gina's bubbly attitude was highly contagious.

So Vaughan really had done what she said she would do. Amazing.

"I'd love the opportunity, Gina. And I'd love to take a trip to Los Angeles to see how I can best serve the needs of Staccato. Perhaps I can meet some of your artists and learn more about the beginnings of the label."

"Sounds good. How soon can you get here? We need you last Thursday afternoon!"

Nia laughed. "Well, let's see, that would have been Thanksgiving, according to my calendar. But let me call my travel agent and see what I can do, all right? I'll let you know as soon as I have the specifics."

"Sure thing. Oh, one formality, I almost forgot. You mentioned that you were doing some work for . . . The Imani Group, is it?"

"Yes. Have you heard of them?"

"Of course. Strong company. I've always liked how they take a stand and go out on a limb. Edgy and gutsy, two great qualities in a successful company, don't you think? Listen, if you could have them jot down a brief recommendation it would make my job a whole lot easier, just to make personnel here happy. You think you could do that for me?"

"I don't think that will be a problem."

"Grand! Well, Nia, I look forward to hearing from you with your itinerary. Bye now—and thank you!"

Nia hung up the phone, sat back on the sofa, closed her eyes. This was the beginning, the chance for which she had been waiting and hoping, her big break. And now that it was here, it didn't feel anything like she thought it would feel. This was scary. Someone actually wanted to hire her, sight unseen, to do a job she had never done before, for money. Someone wanted to put their money behind her promises, someone had enough faith in her to trust their careers, their professional lives, to her efforts.

All at once she realized that this was what she had been meant to do. All those nights of studying, all those papers and exams, diversifying her knowledge, all of it was a path to this very moment. Because every single time she had risen above her expectations, every time she

told herself that she could forge ahead in the face of the seemingly impossible, she had been moving toward this moment.

She had put one dream in front of the other and ended up being offered a public relations job in a new record company.

Nia walked over to her table of mail and surveyed the array. Bills.
Requests for donations. Solicitations for credit cards she didn't need or
want. Bills. A December *Essence* magazine. An alumni newsletter
from Baxter Academy. They were rather benign missives in the grand
scheme of the world.

Of what had she been so paralyzingly afraid?

Nia stood outside the door, took a deep breath, counted to ten, and
knocked.

"Come on in . . ."

"Hi Reggie." Nia walked into his office and smiled. "You busy?"

Reggie put down the newspaper he was reading and sat back in his
desk chair. "Just checking out the climate of the world on this fine
Monday afternoon. What's on your mind? Have a seat . . ."

Where to begin?

Nia sat in one of the two leather chairs facing him. "I've been offered a job. I have an interview in Los Angeles next week."

He didn't smile at her the way she had envisioned him smiling at
her news.

"Well, it doesn't surprise me that someone else wants to scoop you
up. You do great work."

"Thanks."

"You think you'll take it?"

Nia chuckled. *What an idiotic question. Of course I'm going to
take it.*

"They want me to fly out to California and talk strategy as soon as I
can swing it."

"Well, I have some good news, too," Reggie said, rocking back and
forth. "One of the grants you wrote was funded. They called me at
home over the weekend."

Nia beamed. "Really! Which one?"

"Hispanic Hope."

Hispanic Hope was a philanthropic organization that gave money to small businesses and organizations that were seeking to enter the Latino market. Nia had written a proposal that would allow The Imani Group to research incidences of employment discrimination against the New York Hispanic population.

"Reggie, that's great news. I remember that one; it was probably the hardest grant for me to write because I was so unfamiliar with the subject matter. I'm glad we pulled it off."

"*You* pulled it off, not *we*. I guess I was assuming that you would be here to monitor the project. It's going to be hard to replace you."

"That's nice of you to say, Reggie."

"Nice nothing! I'm looking at this from a practical point of view."

Nia sighed. "But you knew I was looking around for something in my field. You knew that months ago . . ."

"Oh yeah, I know what you said. I guess we were just hoping you would have a change of heart and decide to stay on here. Yeah, I know you have an interest in public relations—you've made that quite clear from the get-go. It's an exciting field and you have the outgoing personality that will go the extra mile and get the job done. But Nia, not everyone can write a grant. That's a skill that's hard to come by, a skill that will have a direct impact on gobs of people. It may not be as glamorous a field as what is beckoning to you, but it *could be* if you decided to make it that way. And you have a gift for it. Really. I'm not just trying to flatter you. We'll miss you and we'll miss the work you do."

Nia wanted to cry. She couldn't remember ever feeling so torn at leaving a job. She knew Reggie wasn't just saying these things, she could tell he really meant it all. He and Philip had allowed her to take all the grant-writing seminars and workshops and classes that she wanted, grooming her at no personal expense. And she really had loved it, drinking up the information and writing grants for the sheer fun of it. Writing grants was like solving jigsaw puzzles to her, finding just the right words to convey the urgency behind the request, balancing budgets that looked feasible, infusing her proposals with enough emotion that the funders could feel that the match would be right.

"You've given me so much. Letting me come here as a temp, keeping me on as an administrative assistant, a *real* ad assist, not just on paper—I almost feel guilty coming here like this and asking you for a recommendation."

With his finger Reggie outlined the edge of the silver frame that held his wedding photograph. "You want a recommendation? By all means, I would be honored to write one for you. I have nothing but stellar things to say about you and the way you handle your work. You learn fast, you stay the course, you apply yourself, you get the job done with style and diplomacy."

Nia was beginning to blush. "Gracious, Reggie . . ."

"You know, Philip and I had been discussing you and your contributions here at The Imani Group. And we agreed, without hesitation, that we owe you a lot. We were going to wait until the new year to have this discussion with you—you know, the holidays and all. But you've come in here and forced our hand, my sister."

Nia looked puzzled.

He leaned across his desk, clasped his hands, and looked her in the eye. "I'll give you an option here. I will write you the most glowing recommendation you could ever imagine and wish you luck on your new journey into the world of public relations . . ."

"Thank you." Nia smiled.

"*Or*, you can go out to LaLa Land, wine and dine with the plastic people, politely tell them *no, thank you* . . . and come back here to join us at The Imani Group as a full partner." Reggie stood and put his hands on his hips. "Now go out there, enjoy the sunshine, and make a good decision."

Nia sat at her desk that day, distracted. No matter what she tried to do, she had a difficult time concentrating. This was a new feeling, a new dilemma. She had never been so in demand, never been torn between two wonderful paths. It had always been about struggle before: struggle to get the interview, struggle to get the job, struggle to keep the job, and struggle to be recognized for the job well done. Now, all that negativity was falling away, she wasn't sure what she truly wanted other than simplicity. She had imagined that one would simply arrive; that once she had achieved her immediate professional goal, life would just unfold in some sort of static state of bliss. She hadn't counted on feeling this tug, this wanting and needing, this desire to be happy, fulfilled, and responsible, too.

There was a knock on her partially open office door.

"Hello?"

It was Reggie, wearing his overcoat. "I'm leaving early today and going home. There's a neighborhood meeting taking place at my house tonight and I want to help Crystal get things ready. You feel free to leave whenever you want; the weeks between Thanksgiving and Christmas are always really slow around here. Here . . ."

She walked around her desk to the doorway and took the document from his hand.

"It's your letter of recommendation."

"Reggie, you didn't have to type it up right away. I'm not leaving tomorrow."

"Yeah, yeah, I know. But I wanted you to be able to read it over and over and over again and feel guilty as hell for as long as possible." He laughed. "Think about things, Nia. Okay?"

Nia felt tears coming to her eyes. "I will, Reggie. And thank you."

He turned to leave and then stopped as though he had forgotten something.

"Yes?"

He looked at her and smiled. "No matter what you decide to do, *be happy*. Do not pass . . . joy. Do what's best for *Nia*."

It was quiet. Many of the offices in the building across the street were already decorated for the holidays. Nia could see the tiny white lights glistening through the windows, tinsel and artificial evergreen garland hanging from cubicle to cubicle. This time of year had always made her happy and festive. But this year she looked around and saw so much that had changed in her life. There was imbalance. She felt professional, polished, and very, very alone.

Last year at this time she had been celebrating with Rome. She had gone to the party at Anderson-Moss and had a wonderful time. She had been a part of a couple: a he, a she. It had worked for her then; it had been good. She didn't question things the way she did now. She just lived. One foot in front of the other, one party at a time, one obligation after another. It was predictable, it was life, and everyone was doing it.

Things seemed so different to her now.

Now she wondered why the evergreen had to be erected, why the tiny white lights that were so pretty had to come down after the first of the year, why she had gone to so many parties where no one really wanted to be at all.

Why had she gone to the trouble of working so hard to create the illusion of something that wasn't there? What had she gained? What had anyone gained?

Why was she playing at life instead of actually living it?

Reggie was right; she would go home and read the letter over and over again until it sunk in that someone else considered her worthy. She would make a copy of it and keep it in her files. Make another copy and frame it, hang it in her bedroom and repeat it like a mantra until it became part of her mind-set.

She started packing up to go home for the day, thinking logistically about what a move to California would actually entail. She was putting on her coat, making her mental checklist when the phone rang.

"Good afternoon. You've reached The Imani Group. Nia speaking."

"*Nia Benson.* Seth Jackson here. How *are* you?"

She smiled. "Hi there. I'm fine, thanks for asking. How are you?"

"Me? Oh, I'm doing okay. How are you? The last time I saw you, I believe you were ill . . ."

She thought back, trying to place his reference, and then it struck her. The lobby of Scattz. Vaughan. Grace.

"I'm feeling a lot better now," Nia whispered.

"Good, good. I'm glad to hear that. I was . . . concerned."

She tried to change the subject. "I don't think I properly thanked you for helping me out. It was really nice of you. You went above and beyond, as they say."

"Well, believe it or not, from time to time I've been known to do a good deed or two. I just wish you had stayed for the entire show. Fatima was good, they always are, but the Garrison Walters Trio had the crowd on their feet."

"You must have been really proud."

"I was glad that I was able to help those guys out. They've been playing for decades and no one knows about them. And they're just as good as Ramsey Lewis Trio and some of the older cats out there. They just needed some exposure and someone in their corner who wasn't going to rip them off."

"Enter Seth Jackson."

"I just tried to help them out, that's all."

They paused.

"Well, I know you didn't call Imani to talk to me. Reggie's not here; he's gone for the day."

They paused again.

"Actually I did call to speak to Reggie, but I'm glad I got the opportunity to talk to you. I've been meaning to call for a long time. Life has just been so . . ."

"Crazy?"

They laughed, sighed.

"Yeah, very crazy. Hey, I hope I'm not keeping you from your work, Nia." His voice softened.

"No, not at all. I had been sitting here looking at all of the Christmas decorations going up. They don't waste time anymore. We live from holiday to holiday."

"From one purchasing opportunity to the next."

Nia smiled. "Does it make you sad, too?"

They paused once again.

"A lot of living makes me sad. But then, I guess I'm just a played-out player looking back on his life. And you know what?"

"What?"

"I'm not sure the world is going to change just because we say it should."

"That's interesting, Seth Jackson."

"Why's that?"

"Because I'm not so sure that it won't."

The city was covered with a layer of brown. A thick smothering of smog that kept the illusions of the city close to the ground, permeated only by the planes taking off and landing. This was Los Angeles. She had heard that it was a wonderful place.

Her plane landed roughly, making Nia gasp and clutch her armrest.

"First time landing at LAX?" The overweight man next to her asked, sharing his breath, which was reminiscent of four hours of salted peanuts and imported beer, his girth bulging over the armrest that defined his seating area. She hated flying. Hated breathing in stale air for hours at a time.

She nodded, closed her eyes, and prayed as the plane applied its breaking mechanism. She had successfully avoided conversation for most of the flight, content with sleeping and dreaming, reviewing her itinerary for the next ten days.

"So, you out here on business or vacation or what? Me, I'm here to visit my son and daughter-in-law. First grandson was just born last Wednesday. They say he looks just like me. Got to see for myself, you know?"

She smiled at the man, who was already taking on the role of the proud grandfather. "I bet you're going to spoil that little boy silly."

"Oh, I can't wait! I have seven granddaughters! But now, I have a *grandson*." The pride he was feeling made the man's chest poke out and made Nia want to cry.

"Well, I wish you all the best. A long and happy relationship with him. With all your grandchildren." The FASTEN SEAT BELT sign was turned off and Nia stood to retrieve her bags from the overhead bin.

"Thank you, lady. And you, too. The best of everything! Life is short—remember that! We're only here a little while and then we're gone. Got to do all we can while we're here."

Nia reached out and shook the man's extended hand. "You know, you're right. Sometimes we get all caught up in the technicalities, in all the little daily stuff. But we have to remember why we're here. Thanks for the reminder."

The man guffawed and then blushed a bit, loosening his shirt collar and picking up his duffel bag. "Full of toys, this one is," he said, trying to hide his embarrassment, "toys for the boy!" He looked at Nia and smiled.

"Nice meeting you," she called back at him, as she was swept in the current of the exiting passengers.

Palm trees. Wide streets. People exposing their arms and baring their knees in the days before Christmas. And so much sky topping off a horizontal landscape. In New York she hadn't noticed the sky as much, camouflaged by the skyscrapers and sidewalk commotion. Her focus had been on the ground. It had been a long time since she had looked up and seen anything of natural magnificence. This was nice.

Even the smog seemed to disappear, becoming a haze, now that she was no longer above it but beneath it, herself a part of the landscape. Nia was glad she had opted for the convertible, paid the few extra dollars for the zippy red luxury, and been brave enough to take on the freeway system. It seemed like the California Woman thing to do.

She was told to take the 405 North to the 101 South, but only if it was between noon and two P.M. and then only if she had flexibility in her schedule. Her hotel was in Hollywood, a quarter mile or so from Sunset Boulevard they said, tucked neatly away on a side street but still central to lots of things, if she didn't feel like acting like a native and taking a drive around the corner to shop or get some dinner.

"Welcome, Ms. Benson! We've been expecting you! Did you have a pleasant flight into Los Angeles?" The woman at the registration desk smiled at her and politely waved away Nia's offer of her credit card. "We won't be needing that; the room and all related expenses are entirely taken care of, ma'am. We have a suite for you on our sixth floor. The bellman will meet you upstairs with your luggage in just a few moments. If you have any questions or need anything, please feel free to call upon me personally. My name is Ren."

Gina hadn't mentioned the five-star service to her, and Nia hadn't expected it, with Staccato being such a new company. But she had to admit the extra attention made her feel wanted and pampered and special. A woman could get used to this, she thought. Nia walked through the opulent lobby, an exquisite example of art deco at its finest, and boarded the waiting elevator. Once inside, she smiled to herself, enjoying the smoked glass and brass that cocooned her, humming along with the gentle melodies that escorted her to the sixth floor.

She had decided to stay in this evening and remain quiet, get acclimated to the time difference, maybe create some notes for her meeting with Gina in the morning. She just wanted time to think, time to reflect. Maybe she'd just take it easy and order room service, put on her slippers and enjoy her surroundings.

This had been her plan. But as she opened the door to the room, the scent of flowers greeted her, a heady and tropical fragrance she could not recall ever smelling before. She walked over to the table, and opened the envelope attached to the vase.

It's all right . . . I forgive you, diva.

Diva. This was Vaughan's doing.

She picked up the flowers, placed them in the trash, and set the can outside in the hallway for housekeeping to retrieve.

"Now why would you do something like that? After all the trouble and time and expense that I went through to surprise you? I think *I'm* the one now deserving of apology."

Nia looked up at Vaughan, standing in the doorway to the bedroom, holding a flute of champagne, and wearing a white lace negligee that reeked of too much perfume and too little fabric.

"How did you get in here?"

"It's my room, diva. Welcome. I've been expecting you."

Nia stormed toward the door, throwing it open without a word, and bumping right into the bellman.

"Ma'am? Is there a problem?"

Hot, angry tears came streaming down her cheeks. "I'm not staying here. Please, take my luggage back downstairs. Now." She found the elevators, pressed the button, and turned her back to the bellman.

This was a nightmare in living color, complete with setting and props. Leave it to Hollywood to create a horror so realistic.

"I need another room." Nia found herself breathlessly talking to the person at the desk.

"I'm sorry but we're sold out this evening. Is there a problem with your room?" the young man graciously asked.

"You're damn right there's something wrong with my room! *I* am not the only person in it!" Nia dispensed with all forms of pleasantries and banged her fist on the marble counter. "I want to know how this happened. I call here for reservations, I reserve them with my credit card, and now, I have to put up with a *roommate*? What kind of sense does that make?"

The man pursed his lips, and began flipping through a stack of filed papers. "I don't know what could have happened, ma'am. Please, give us a moment and we'll take care of the problem. I am so sorry."

"Where's Ren? I was checked in by some woman named Ren."

The man looked up at her over imaginary glasses. "Ren is gone for the day, I'm sorry, ma'am. But my name is John and I will definitely take care of the matter. No problem."

Nia began pacing the area in front of him. "I'm tired. I'm hungry. And I have a ton of work to do. Why is this happening to me?"

"I'm sorry, ma'am, I really am." John flipped and sorted frantically. "I can't find anything."

Her anger rose, meeting up with her fears, culminating in sobs—uncontrollable sobs.

"Ms. Benson? Please, for your troubles, while we are sorting through the problem, please, have dinner at our expense in our dining room. And then, by the time you're done, I'm sure we'll have the situation under control. Is that all right?"

Nia removed a lace handkerchief from her purse and wiped away her tears. "Sure. It's not your fault. You weren't even here. And I *am* hungry."

"Yes, ma'am. Here, let me introduce you to our maître d' . . ."

The clerk walked her to the hotel restaurant and explained the situation. She was immediately shown to a table in the corner and offered a wine list. The waiter appeared soon after.

"Good evening, madame. And what would be your pleasure this evening?"

Please let "peace" be on the menu, Nia thought.

The dinner proved to be superb. She dined on lobster, steamed to perfection, and sipped a dry Chardonnay until her problems seemed to melt before her eyes. She even allowed herself the luxury of a decadent chocolate dessert. By the time she set down her napkin, her problems seemed minuscule.

She walked to the registration desk a calmer woman, having returned to her state of rationality. John greeted her with a troubled expression. She returned his look with a mildly intoxicated smile.

"Ms. Benson? I'm so very, very sorry for the mix-up. It seems as though someone called in, from Staccato apparently, and canceled your initial reservation. They then insisted upon reserving our premiere suite for you and another individual."

"And that was probably a Vaughan Gonzalez."

"Yes, Ms. Benson. That was the name."

Nia laughed.

"Well, sir, she is not affiliated with Staccato Music in any way. I don't blame you or the hotel. But just as a matter of business dealings in the future, you really should confirm any cancellations of this sort with the person who initially contacted you."

"Yes, ma'am. We will, ma'am. This sort of thing won't happen again in the future, believe me!"

She nodded. "Now. Let's deal with the fact that I have no room."

"Well, that's a problem that we haven't found a suitable solution to as of yet."

"Oh?"

"We have no available rooms in our hotel here for the next three days. There are a lot of filmings going on this week for some reason, and most of the hotels in the area are booked."

"All right. Well, I suppose I'll call my contact at Staccato and see what solutions they suggest."

"Feel free to use the telephone in our lounge area. And, once again, Ms. Benson," his said, his eyes softening, "our most sincere apologies."

Nia sat in the black brocade chair in the lounge, her body sinking deep into the cushions. She explained her situation to Gina, leaving out the most incriminating parts, just saying there had been a mix-up of some sort.

"Oh, Nia! I'm so sorry to hear this. Yes, I know about the hotel room shortage, it happens here often. There's always *something* going on here! But let me make a few phone calls. Give me your number and I'll call you back in a few minutes. And don't worry! It's not always like this!"

Nia sat back in the chair and closed her eyes briefly. The alcohol had done its job, perhaps a tad too well, and she found herself drifting off when the ring of the telephone awakened her.

"Nia, I think I have a solution. It's not ideal, we know this, but I hope it will be acceptable to you. My partner has a beach house out in Malibu, it's a small two-bedroom right on the beach, and he'd love for you to stay there."

She loved the beach and had heard so much about the waters of Malibu. "That would be fine! I have no problem with that!"

Gina chuckled. "Well, wait a minute. Let me continue. See, you would be sharing the space with another person."

Nia held her breath, waiting for the other shoe to drop. "Yes?"

"A woman. You'd have your own bedrooms, but you'd have to share the other facilities."

"Can you tell me her name?"

"Sure! Wait, I have it right here . . . goodness, I need to clean off this desk! Okay, here it is. Her name is Lauren . . . Lauren Montgomery. She's here from the East Coast also, on another business matter with Staccato. I haven't met her personally yet, but she seems very personable on the telephone. Do you think this will be a problem?"

Nia breathed a sigh of relief. "No, I don't think it will be a problem at all. That is, if she doesn't mind the company."

"I don't know if I'll be able to catch her actually. She's already in transit. But don't you worry about it. You just go on over to the house tonight and get yourself situated. And I'll meet you in the morning, all right?"

"Will the beach house be difficult to find in the dark? I'm not used to these freeways; this is my first time here."

"You know what? With everything you've been through today, let me just take that one little burden away from you. I'll have the company car come over there and pick you up in a few minutes. How does that sound? Leave the rental there and we'll make arrangements for you to pick it up tomorrow."

"Thanks, that would be great. I'm usually not so much trouble."

"Please, relax. You're in good hands now."

The limousine driver drove her through Hollywood, giving her a mini-tour, showing her the office building of Staccato Music. All the bright lights and elaborate billboards excited her and made her catch her breath. The car took on the curves and bends of the streets, finally ending up at the Pacific shoreline, stopping in front of a beautiful house, set upon sturdy-looking wooden stilts, built upon the sand.

"I'll be here for you in the morning, Ms. Benson. Have a good night," he said, tipping his hat to her. He had already refused her offer of a tip, reassuring her that his compensation had been taken care of.

This was no little beach house. It was opulent. The shape of it was unusual to her, with expansive ocean frontage and not much depth, allowing each room a picturesque view of the surf from its floor-to-ceiling windows. She chose one of the bedrooms, decorated in blond wood and colors of white and beige, and changed into her nightgown and bedroom slippers. She removed her notes from her briefcase and sat on the bed to prepare for her morning's meeting. But even with the soothing sound of the surf in the distance, it became hard for her to concentrate, her thoughts drifting to Vaughan and wondering why.

Maybe Vaughan was one of those people who only wanted what they felt they couldn't have, pursuing things and people until they were just within the realm of possibility, and then abandoning them when there was no more chase to be had. Maybe she didn't feel she deserved anything that wasn't a hassle.

Why had Vaughan gone to all that trouble? She had wondered if Vaughan had an emotional problem when, after throwing Nia out of her house, Nia started receiving phone calls several times a day, breathings and hang ups. Nia didn't like to think about Vaughan. She didn't like to think about That Night. She had seen too many sides of herself that night that went against all her notions of who she was, and it unnerved her. It wasn't just the sex; the sex she could dismiss if she tried hard enough. But when she thought about how much she had hurt her friend, when she remembered the pain in Grace's voice, the memory just made her cry. What had she been thinking, to do the things she had done? She would never have slept with her friend's ex-boyfriend, under any circumstances. What did she feel was so different with Grace and Vaughan?

Who did she think she was?

She wanted things back to where they had once been, her notions of who she was and what she wanted out of life clear-cut and compart-mentalized, unchallenged. It seemed as though when she opened her-self up to choices, she walked in a cloud and couldn't find the right path to take. Other people navigated this thing successfully all the time, so why couldn't she?

Nia had just resumed another attempt at reviewing her notes when she heard the doorbell ring. The sound made her jump, caused her heart to beat frantically. She reached for her robe and walked gently past the living room, and stood at the door.

"Yes?"

"Hi, I think I'm your roommate? My name is Lauren Mont-gomery."

Nia opened the door cautiously.

"Lauren? Lauren from Anderson-Moss?"

The women smiled at each other, both of them relieved beyond belief.

"Hey, girl! You gonna let me in or what? This woman here is tired. Flying just wears me out."

Nia stood away from the door, ushering her in. "I know the feeling. This has *not* been the most ideal of days for me." Nia showed Lauren to her bedroom.

Lauren looked approvingly at the ornate brass canopy bed dressed in soft blues and greens. "Yeah, I heard. Gina told me there had been some snafu at your hotel. And I for one am glad! This is going to be fun. It has been entirely too long, girl! What have you been up to? Did you and Jerome ever work things out?"

It had seemed so long ago that Rome had walked out of her life. His memory had become dreamlike, vibrant yet undefined at the edges. She shook her head. "Once he got married, there wasn't anything to work out."

Lauren looked blankly at her. "But you gave him a piece of your mind, right? You let him know how much he hurt you, yes?"

"I tried to understand how I could have been in so much denial, to have not seen it coming. What he did was heartless, but what I did to me wasn't very loving either. Never again will I settle for less than wonderful in my life. But see, that's what happens when you stop believing in love. Besides, I'm not really into revenge and that kind of stuff."

"Yeah. I guess those things have a way of catching up with you. So, when Rome got fired, you probably didn't lose any sleep, huh?"

"Fired?"

"Oh yeah, girl! You didn't know? That's old news. Jerome got fired behind some kind of under-the-table-dealings with one of our clients. A pharmaceutical company. Something about some fancy accounting that he had authorized to cover up some ugly shade of fraud. There were a lot of heads that rolled behind the Imani incident. He was let go right around the time I spoke to you last. I figured you knew."

Nia shook her head in amazement. "Imani?"

"Yeah, that was the name of the whistle-blowing company. Some kind of grassroots activist concern. Word was out that Imani was doing a great job of convincing the media of the fraud before the company ever even saw the insides of a courtroom. When the word of our client's shady dealings reached us at Anderson-Moss, we conducted our own in-house investigation. I thought it was funny, myself. I wanted to shake hands with all those Imani folk; that was a public relations move for the textbooks. Because when all the dust settled, I found myself with a big promotion, a wonderful raise, and time for a part-time job that landed me right here, right now."

Nia extended her hand.

"What's this for?" Lauren questioned, looking at her hand.

"Meet that Imani PR person."

"Get out of here, girl! You?" Lauren questioned, walking to the kitchen. "You know, we need more companies like that, companies that care about the people as well as the profits. Not too many people are real enough to do that though. Folks get all caught up in the glitter of the almighty dollar."

Her work at Imani had made an actual difference.

"So what's your connection with Staccato? Is that your part-time job?"

Lauren poked her head in the refrigerator and pulled out some brie and cheddar. "I've been working for the manager of a group they want to sign. I'm just taking care of some prelims until he can get here." Her mood seemed to change, becoming more pensive, more serious.

"Well, that sounds good, Lauren. You like the work?"

She nodded. "Oh yeah. Never had a problem with the work."

"Well," Nia said, deciding not to pry, "I would say that this deserves a toast, dear." Nia removed two glasses from the cabinet, took out a bottle of ginger ale from the refrigerator.

"Yes, I would say it does. It's nice seeing you again . . . amazing . . . but really, really nice!"

"So, to life—and all its amazements!"

They clinked their glasses and smiled. "Cheers!"

Seth loved flying. Especially the take-offs and landings. It gave him a rush that made him feel as though he was going great places, doing great things. It made him think about his youth, when he was a little boy, holding on to his balsa wood airplanes and running down the hills in the park, screaming *zoooom*. It was full of excitement. Full of potential.

He had spent so much of his life just keeping it light, going from woman to woman, job to job, never getting serious or attached. He never saw the need for any kind of commitment in his life. Everything had always been about the thrill, the taking off, the landing. Others around him had seen the need to put away that toy airplane and dispense with childhood fantasies. He had just been slow to leave the fantasy behind. One by one, all his childhood buddies had taken the plunge and selected The Right Wife and The Normal Life, a life of predictable comings and goings. But Seth watched from that hill and stomped his feet, his toy airplane still in hand, as his friends traded in their model airplanes and Lego houses for station wagons and co-ops. They selected wives who could entertain and not embarrass them in public, women who never wore gold lamé to a silk organza function and knew their way around a Tupperware catalog.

And what was love anyway?

Maybe love was having these things, these trinkets of a life well lived, a home and a woman in it who didn't make one miserable. Maybe that was all it had ever been about. Maybe it was the naive search for more that had brought him so much misery. Maybe it had been the hoping that had been the cause of his sadness.

Lauren wasn't bad for him. She was a good woman; she was smart and professional and loyal and pretty and she seemed to care about him deeply. No, that wasn't bad at all, considering all the horrible things he had done in his life. And Rex was right: When he married her, he would be marrying into his own extended family. He would be entering familiar territory, formally gaining a family that knew him and loved him and welcomed him anyway.

He made the decision to make Lauren his wife.

So he was feeling so positive about this trip, being in a neutral environment with Lauren, both of them together to see all their hard work pay off. He was glad she had agreed to come, glad she had agreed to wait for him to arrive and get settled a day or two before returning to New York. It would give him the time he needed to meet with Reggie's jeweler friend and finalize the arrangements for the ring he had selected by way of detailed telephone conversations.

Seth felt the same way he did when he took the last final of his senior year in college: He had done the work, put in the time, and just wanted to be handed the degree so he could go home. Reggie had assured him that he was just having typical, about-to-give-up-the-little-black-book jitters.

"Man, we *all* go through that 'want to run in the other direction' phase. It's part of the process. Believe me. This is going to work out for you and Lauren; you have the best of family behind you guys," Reggie had said on the phone that night after his community meeting.

"I don't know, Reggie. I don't know if I'm feeling . . . I don't know if I should go through with this."

"What? So what's the alternative, my man? You two date and date until it's time for Social Security?"

Seth didn't even want to think that far in advance for his own living, let alone someone else's. But Reggie had a point. He wasn't getting any younger. And Lauren was pregnant with his child.

Sometimes timetables just weren't of your own making.

So he had it all figured out, how he would pick up the ring

tomorrow after the initial meeting with Sammy Diggs and present it to her after a romantic dinner, walking along the beach. The thought made him feel tired and mature, his palms sweaty. He was eager to give the ring to her, couldn't wait to watch her expression once she realized how much he was willing to invest in their life together.

When the FASTEN SEAT BELT sign was turned off, he was the first one jumping out of his seat and standing at the door, waiting for it to open and set him free. He bounded down the jetway, unstoppable. He was determined to bridge the gap that was wedged between them. He had decided that no longer would he hold back; he had promised himself that the moment he saw her standing there, waiting for him, he would run to her. Run into her arms and hold her and kiss her and tell her he loved her and he wanted to try again to make it right.

That was what a man about to get engaged would do.

But when Seth reached the waiting area, after he had navigated through the crowds of people, he didn't find her standing there, waiting. There were no arms for him to rush into. No stubborn mind for him to convince. He stayed at the gate, waiting for her, looking for her in every direction. But she didn't appear. Even after ten minutes. Twenty minutes. Forty-five minutes. An hour later, Seth walked slowly to the baggage claim area and retrieved his bag. He placed a call to Sammy Diggs.

"Hey, man! Glad to hear you made it in all right! Cannot *wait* for us to meet. Now, you settled at the house and all?"

"Hey, Sammy. Actually, I'm still at the airport. I was waiting for Lauren to pick me up, but I haven't seen her. How do I get to where I need to go?"

"You know, we ran late here this afternoon and I heard there was a traffic jam on the freeway. I know you want to get out of there ASAP, but hold on for just a few more minutes. I'm sure she'll get there. If you don't find her in, say, another half an hour, give me a call back and we'll take it from there."

Seth found a bench right outside the baggage claim and sat. The fumes from the buses and taxis and jets and cigarettes all meshed to create a stench in his brain, extinguishing what little joy was left. It wasn't her fault, he kept telling himself. She didn't plan to be late. A panhandler asked him for five dollars and he gave it to him. Maybe it would help the man think his luck had changed.

He saw her in the distance, crossing the street, looking at her watch and stomping her foot at the red light. She ran across at the hint of green, looking for him, looking frantic. He stood and waved his hands high above his head.

"Lauren! I'm over here!"

She heard her name and stopped and found him, her expression relieved, exhausted. He picked up his bags, and walked toward her, meeting halfway between where they had been and where they could be going.

"I'm sorry, Seth."

She looked uncomfortable, like there was something she was supposed to say but couldn't. He smiled at her and shrugged his shoulders, forgetting about the hugs and kisses and confessions he had expected them to share. It seemed out of place now. It always seemed out of place nowadays. They walked to the parking structure, she asking questions about his flight, he answering as pleasantly as he could.

"So, how do you like California?" he asked as they drove toward the shore. She seemed calmer now that she was behind the wheel. He looked at the people in the cars passing by, some singing to music he couldn't hear, some not.

"I've had a really nice time. Thank you for the trip. I needed it."

"I wanted it to be more than a business trip for you, Lauren. I was hoping that maybe we could get some good conversation in there . . . talk like we used to talk."

"Yes, I have a lot of things to catch you up on. Sammy and I met and went over the terms of the contract and—"

"That's not what I'm talking about. I'm talking about us."

She sighed heavily and then glanced at him sideways. "Look."

Outside, the setting sun was causing the ocean to glow in intense tones of orange and red. It was beautiful. Enough so to change the tone of the conversation and to soften up the edge.

"When we get to the house, Seth. We'll talk then."

They rode the rest of the way in a peaceful silence.

"And this is your room."

Seth whistled at the opulence, setting his bags down at the bedroom door. "I like. I like. But, you do mean *our* room, right?"

Lauren took his hand and led him toward the living room. "Come. Let's walk on the beach."

They walked down the stairs that led from the living room balcony onto the beach below, her hand clutching his, his fingers laced with hers. They removed their shoes and socks and walked barefoot toward the shore, the wind blowing wisps of her pulled-back hair, the sand feeling good sifting between his toes.

"I remember the water, Seth. How magical it always was for us."

"And it can be that way again, you know. You act as if it's over."

"Well, I'm leaving, Seth."

He looked at her puzzled, unsure of what she was saying. "I was hoping you could stay at least *one* more day. Lauren, I just don't understand. It's been a long time since I've understood."

She faced him and looked him in the eye, her face pained. "I know. And I apologize for that. I shut down. I know I do."

He softened just looking at her. "Just talk to me. That's all you have to do. Just talk to me, baby."

She looked at him and tried to speak, but the tears came before the words. "I'm leaving you, Seth. Leaving the job. Leaving everything that used to be. I'm going back to Virginia. Time for me to work on my dreams for a change. I've been thinking about opening a restaurant or something . . ."

It hit him unexpectedly. "Why? Is this about Sandy? Is this because you think—"

"No, Seth. It's about me. This time it's about me. Lauren's time."

Her words sounded so strong but her demeanor was so unconvincing. "I don't love her, Lauren. I never did. It was a mistake and I'm sorry if I hurt you and all, but it was never about her."

"Seth, I don't know how to tell you this, I . . . I . . ."

He placed a finger upon her lips and kissed her eyes, kissed the wetness that dripped from them and held her.

"Baby, I know you're pregnant. I know and I'm happy . . . and I'm not going to leave you. I'm going to stay with you through all of it. I told you I'd be here for you and I will be. And," he said to her as he kneeled in the sand, "if you'll have me, I want to marry you. I'm loving you, Lauren. We can do this. We can make this work. Just say yes. All the drama with Sandy is something that we can work out together—as husband and wife. Say yes."

He hugged her thighs and felt the sobs racking her body, waiting for her to say yes, waiting for her answer. It wasn't how he had wanted to propose to her, it hadn't been his plan. But the time was right, ring or no ring. He had needed to show his conviction right then and there. She stroked his head and helped him reluctantly stand.

"No, Seth. It's too late. Maybe if we had tried before. Maybe then. But now, it just wouldn't work."

He watched her break away, walking toward the beach house, shouting over her shoulder. "And I changed my mind. I'm leaving tonight. My flight leaves in a couple of hours. I made notes for you, so you won't be lost in the negotiations and all. Thanks . . . but I got to get out of here."

"Why Lauren? Why are you doing this to us?"

Lauren stopped and faced him, faced the ocean. "Seth, there is no *us*. There's you and me and the business. That's it. I need more than pretense in my life. I need more than appearances and what looks good. I need more than posing pretty for the camera. Just because you or I might want it to be love doesn't mean it is . . . or ever will be." She turned back around and continued walking toward the beach house.

"I deserve more than this brush-off. What about the baby? *Our* baby?"

She turned around clumsily, losing her footing in the sand, like a person numbed by drugs or cheap wine. "I had an abortion, okay?"

"An *abortion*?" He was numbed.

"It seemed the sensible thing to do, under the circumstances. So now you can be with Sandy. Unencumbered. Without having to think about me and my infant reminder. Went against everything I ever believed in to do it, too. And it hurt. It still hurts. All up inside of me hurts, Seth. And every single time I see your face and hear your voice, I relive those moments of pain. I got to get away from you, Seth."

He was crying. The tears washed over him before he could control them. Now they controlled him. He walked over to her. "It was never about me and Sandy, Lauren. I thought it was about me and you; I thought *we* were going to create a life together. I thought you knew this."

"And I thought you wanted to be with her. I thought you'd be relieved."

"Why didn't you just *talk* to me, Lauren? Instead of *thinking* all the damn time?"

She shoved his hands away from her shoulders and resumed her walk to the stairs, mumbling to herself over and over, "I got to get away from you. Men. You ain't nothing but pain."

"I thought you loved me," he said.

"You know what, Seth? Maybe the problem is that we both think too damn much. I guess you just can't intellectualize yourself into loving someone, huh? I mean, you can go through the motions for a whole lifetime, I guess, but one day you'll realize that there just isn't anything there. Maybe we should be grateful that it happened for us when it did—before we made it legal."

"I love you, Lauren."

She laughed through her tears. "No, you don't. You don't *love* me. You admire me. You maybe even like me a whole lot. But this isn't love. See, you forget, Seth: I've seen love before. This isn't it. This hurts."

"We can make it work."

"No, we can't. You're going to leave me. Sooner or later, you will. You'll crave that something that's missing. You'll miss what isn't there."

He walked after her, shouting in his frustration. "I love you! I'm not going anywhere! I want to marry you!"

She faced him squarely. "No."

"Why, Lauren? Why don't you want us to try?"

"Because I deserve more. We both do." And she resumed her walk to the beach house.

She must have heard him screaming and shouting, asking her why she was doing this, but she never turned back around to face him. She only stood on the stairs and tossed words to him over her shoulder.

"We both deserve so much more," she said.

Lauren was gone by the time he got back to the beach house hours later. He had stayed on the beach, walked along the shore, trying to make sense of all that had just happened. As he walked from room to room he noticed that almost nothing of her remained. No crumbs. No lingering perfume. And he was glad. Relieved. It was better this way. He didn't know who this woman was. She certainly wasn't the woman he had conjured up in his mind, but that had been his fault, not hers. He had been looking at her through eyes that had never been his own.

He had cried most of the anger out of his system, all that was left now was fatigue and sorrow. He stretched out on the bed, and closed his eyes, trying to make sense of his life.

Looking for love. Always, always looking for love.

He heard the key turn in the front door lock, heard the footsteps coming to his door and a familiar voice.

"Lauren? It's me. How'd things go with you today, girl? You hungry? I was thinking about going to that restaurant down the beach, The SeaFarer? I heard they were . . ."

"Nia?"

"Seth?"

"Guess I'm your new housemate." He sat up on his bed. They smiled at each other, each weary and emotionally spent in their own way. "And dinner sounds great. I accept. Graciously."

"Hmm. So *you're* Lauren's boss."

"And you're the PR wonder of wonders."

"Okay, okay . . . so I'm sure there's a juicy story behind your being here, right?" Nia said, grabbing her purse and walking toward the door. He slipped on his loafers and followed behind her.

"Just as there's a juicy story behind *your* being here." They looked at each other and nodded through the unspoken thickness.

"Okay, I gotcha, Seth. I don't want to go there either. Let's just eat, okay?"

"Food and neutral conversation, coming right up, ma'am!"

They walked down the road in silence, glancing at each other from time to time, feeling comfortable enough to be silent in each other's presence. After they arrived at The SeaFarer and had given the waiter their orders, Nia spoke.

"I never properly apologized to you, Seth."

"Apologized for what?"

"Sadist. Masochist. I looked it up. I was wrong. You were right."

He nodded slightly.

"And for leaving Scattz the way I did."

"Forget about it. *You weren't feeling well.* Things happen."

"Not like that. Not to me. For a long time afterward I tried to figure out what happened that night. It was a night chock-full of mistakes for me. I'm just sorry that you got all caught up in it."

Seth nodded, feeling her pain. "Did everything get . . . resolved?"

"I wish I could say yes. Not really. I gave up my power that night. And I gave up my self-respect. Sense of self." She played with the salt shaker. "I wish I could say that I'm one hundred percent back to me, but I'm still traveling the road. Uphill. Uphill all the way."

"Well, you're honest, if nothing else."

"For whatever *that's* worth."

"It's worth a whole lot, believe me." He laughed and looked at her, sitting there across the table. The candle on the table gave a golden glow to her face, softening what already looked mighty soft. "I've told myself a whole lot of lies, taken the easy way into and out of a lot of situations. It takes guts to be honest with yourself."

Nia sat back in her chair. "Sounds like maybe that's what you've learned in your travels to Oz."

"Hey, men do it, too, you know. We just try to finesse the painful parts away."

"But you all don't generally give your power over to others. Power means way too much to you guys."

"We may not *give it up* like you mean, but guys look to other stuff to make us feel more like men. We got to have the right car, or the right job . . ."

"Or the right woman . . ."

They both fell silent and looked at each other's eyes.

"Yes," he whispered, "sometimes."

"She's not here now. You miss her?"

"So, you know about me and Lauren, huh?"

"I finally put two and two together. 'The manager of the hot new group . . .' "

"No," he said, shaking his head, "I don't miss her. Just miss the woman I thought she was—actually, the woman I thought I could *make* her be. I miss the relationship we only pretended to have."

"Boy, do I know *that* feeling."

When their food arrived, they ate and chatted about their connections with Staccato, loving the beach, their temporary home, the coming days of work. It was easy conversation, unstrained. By the time the dessert cart was rolled around, and the second carafe of white zinfandel had been consumed, laughter abounded and they were totally at ease.

"So whatever happened to Seth, king of the commercial jingle world?"

"Please, that is one area of my life that I *never* want to relive. I hope I never do another piece of music just to sell something."

"You ever get your money?"

"Naw. They made me an offer but it was a buy-off, pure and simple. It was a lot of money and it made the kid sit down and think; I could have done a whole lot with that piece of change. But there was more than money at stake there. It wasn't worth it to sink into the muck and mire with Jonathan and his henchmen."

She smiled. "I'm proud of you."

"Yeah? 'Cause I'm stupid and poor?"

"It takes a strong man to leave the money behind on the high and mighty road to Principle."

"Funny! *You* pick up the check then! Nia, girl—why is it so easy for me to talk to you?"

"Well, could be two reasons. First of all, you probably still think I like girls."

Seth spit out the remnants of his last swallow of wine, shocked at her candor. She laughed at his expression. "No! I wasn't thinking that! See! Now, look at what you made me do. Sheesh."

"Yes, you did. Isn't that what you thought?"

Seth eyed her sideways, the wine releasing his inhibitions. "Well? Do you?"

"Guess."

"Guess?"

"Yeah, guess." She smiled at him slyly.

"Okay, whatever whatever. That tells me nothing, absolutely nothing, but I'll leave it be for now. And your second reason?" He rolled his eyes at her, wiping his shirt. "Sheesh."

She laughed. "Second reason is that you don't have any reason to lie to me."

"Now, that one makes sense. But see, I don't have any reason to lie to *any* woman."

"Whatever, whatever." She smiled. "That ain't what *I* heard! But you don't have anything to lose opening up to me. There's nothing at stake. I'm not a part of your life, so I can't hurt you. I'm on the outside of it all."

"Inside, outside—it's more than that. I feel comfortable with you."

"I feel comfortable with you, too, Seth. But I don't think that's all of it either. Maybe we just finally feel comfortable with who *we* are."

They stumbled back to the beach house slowly, enjoying the salt air and crashing surf, cracking corny jokes that only drunk people could possibly understand, sharing bits and pieces of their lives. First she, then he, back and forth, peeling back the layers of fear and hurt and protection that they had erected in memory of who they once had been. It felt good to Seth. Felt good to be himself and not face judgment, by her or anyone else.

And once all the lights had been turned off and it was dark in the house, once they had said their final good nights, they ran from bedroom to bedroom, tucking each other in, kissing each other on the nose and the forehead, acting like little kids on a Friday night sleepover, and laughing themselves to sleep.

Twenty-three

Nia traced the veins in Seth's hand as he slept, counting his breaths, grateful.

The flight back to JFK had been smooth and unremarkable, the movie dull, the food unimpressive. She hadn't been able to sleep the entire flight, too caught up in the work that faced her in the coming weeks, too excited about her life. Her head was spinning, deep in creation mode, trying to figure out, trying to sort through. It had been a good trip in so many different ways.

She had swept through her time in California with new confidence and conviction, ready to accomplish tasks, take risks, and make things right. It was the old Nia revitalized, a glance back in time at the woman who once knew who she was and wasn't afraid to show it or be it. And she had learned that she missed that woman, the person she had once admired and cherished, the friend she had neglected for too long.

Seth stirred in his sleep and she leaned upon his shoulder, calming him. He had become a friend to her, a lover of her life and dreams, a person in her corner. She didn't have the need to prove anything to him; he had seen her at her most vulnerable and cared about her anyway. It was nice not having to pretend. It was nice to be able to be herself.

"Guess we're back in Kansas now," she said to him after they had re-trieved their bags from the revolving carousel and found their way to the commuter bus stop.

"You think? Look down there . . ." He pointed toward the entrance to the expressway, flowing with cars in a hurry. "It still looks like the Yellow Brick Road to me."

"You're sweet, you know that?"

"Yeah." And he laughed and held her closely. "Let's meet for dinner tonight."

But Nia shook her head. "No, not tonight. Tonight I have to take care of some business. But soon. Very soon."

"Are you brushing me off?" He stepped away and touched her cheek. "You don't have to do that."

"Not brushing you off, Seth. Call me tomorrow. And the day after. And the day after that. And the . . ."

He dropped his bags to his side, slid his hands into her coat pockets, and kissed her on her neck, on her chin, and then on her lips. "You are such a gift. *Thank you.*"

She searched his eyes for truth, troubled. "You sound like you're saying good-bye to me . . ."

He smiled faintly, then held her and whispered, "Listen harder."

She watched him walk away to a different bus, one meant to take him where he needed to go.

She had so much work to do. And it felt so good to know it.

The city was slushy, harboring remnants of an early holiday storm. Slick ice patches hid beneath fallen leaves. It had been a surprise to the city, this snow and ice, catching everyone off guard. But they were all trying to adjust; the women in pumps who strived to seek balance, the rosebushes with late fall blossoms too fragile to survive, and the children who shivered in clothes too thin to withstand the winds. All trying to adjust in their own way to these unexpected things.

She took the bus to the Upper West Side of Manhattan, and then took a taxi to the familiar apartment building, carrying her own bags into the dimly lit exterior lobby and dialing the security intercom. No one answered the phone, but a buzz allowed her entrance, the elevator lifted her to the fourth floor. She rang the bell on the door and before she could remove her finger from the bell, it opened.

"Well."

Nia set her bags down at her side and pushed past the pretense, hugging her friend and apologizing.

"Come inside."

Nia slid her bags before her and walked into the space, took off her shoes at the door, setting them on a straw mat designated for that purpose. Grace seemed more serene than Nia remembered her being. Centered. Her home reflected that peace: George Winston played a piano solo that was soft and graceful, there were candles burning that smelled liked baking apples.

"I'm fixing hot chocolate. Whipped cream, mandatory. It's nasty out there still. You want some?"

"Yeah. Sounds good."

Grace bopped into the kitchen, glancing at Nia from time to time, demanding nothing specific. "So, Miss Nia Benson, what have you learned?"

Nia leaned against the sink. "A friend . . . is a friend . . . is a friend."

"Well, yeah, except when she's not."

Nia took her mug from Grace and sipped, getting whipped cream on the tip of her nose. "Yeah, I learned that, too."

"I don't think you'll ever know how much you hurt me. Not only by what you did but also by what you didn't do."

"I got lost, Grace."

Grace looked her in the eye. "Yeah. You did."

"And Vaughan—"

Grace cut her off. "No, I don't want to hear anything about Vaughan. This isn't about Vaughan. She has her own issues, believe me. You didn't come here to talk about her, did you?"

Nia shook her head. "I came to say I'm sorry."

Nia walked out of the kitchen and into Grace's studio, a room adjacent, filled with light, paints, papers, and canvases. It always smelled of rubber cement and acrylic paints no matter what she did; dabs and splotches here and there that had fallen on the straw mats and been captured, refusing to come out.

"So now you know I'm gay."

Nia ignored her. "What are you working on now?" Nia peeked at the drawing board, a pencil rendering of a beautiful black woman standing in a body of clear, calm water. She stood there majestically, lifting her head toward a brilliant dawning sky, embracing herself, with extra hands and arms surrounding her, reaching for her.

"You going to ignore me forever? Do you think that will make it go away?"

"No."

"Nia, I'm not going to pretend for you—or anyone else—anymore. I've done that all my life, even with you. I am who I am. This is it. This is what you get. Take it or leave it."

"I miss my friend."

"Well, she's still here. And she's still the same person you knew before, mostly. This is just the new and improved version. And if there are things you don't want to hear about, details about who I love and all, hey, I can deal with that. But I'm not going to live a lie anymore."

"And I won't make assumptions."

Nia traced the rendering of the woman's form.

"So what do you think of that?" Grace leaned on the wall and sipped her hot chocolate, nodding toward the artwork.

"It's beautiful." Nia stared at it, appreciating its potential. "It makes me think of me."

"My, aren't we the humble one." Grace laughed.

"No, really," Nia said, unfazed by the slight, "it does. It's hard for me to articulate what I feel when I look at it. Maybe I'll write a poem or something. You mind if I sit here and write to it for a while?"

"That'll be a first for me. Someone writing a poem to one of my works in progress. But hey, be my guest. I have some phone calls to make anyway."

"Grace?" Nia called out just before she left the room. "I love you, sis."

"Love you, too, Nia." Grace smiled. "Go on. Do your work."

It felt really good to be able to come all the way back home.

"These are some serious stairs, woman," Grace complained. "You sure they didn't add some since you been here last?"

Nia laughed and took the flight up in stride. "You need to get more exercise, that's what your problem is!"

"Listen, you need to just be glad I came out here at all. Been a heck of a long time since I've been to a poetry reading. They gonna try to convert me and all? Try to fill me up with cappuccino and biscotti?"

"You know, Grace, they just might! But you know the right way to swing, huh?"

They stood at the top of the steps, looking down upon the headlights in the distance. It was a magical sight.

"Nia, I hope you're ready for this. I hope you know that it could get kind of nasty in there." Nia nodded. "You sure you want to do this?"

"Come on. I want to get a good seat."

The two women walked into St. Augustine's and went to the room used by The Poetry Pause. The room was set up differently than Nia had remembered; tonight it was organized auditorium style, with five short rows of chairs facing a beautifully carved lectern.

A man walked up to them and Nia gave him her name.

"Nia Benson. I'm so glad to finally meet you. My name is Myron and I'm one of the organizers here. I'm so glad you could come."

"I'm glad to be here."

He escorted them to the first row, and offered them seats. "I was a little bit concerned when we tried to reach you by telephone and learned that you were in California. We were hoping you were just there for the holidays or something. I'm just so glad you were able to get back in time."

Nia smiled at him.

"Well, I see that some more of our members are coming in the door. If you'll excuse me . . ."

They watched him walk into the vestibule to hand out programs to the people just arriving. He seemed to be greeting everyone with the same level of graciousness that they had just witnessed.

"Nia . . . there she is . . ."

Nia turned around and saw the woman walking toward her.

"Well, never thought I'd see the day. Nia. Grace."

"Hello Vaughan," Nia said dryly.

"Grace, you don't seem like the poetry type. To what do we owe this grand honor?"

"Hello Vaughan," Grace said, nudging Nia.

"Did Nia tell you she's on the list of The Poetry Pause finalists for this year's competition?"

"Yes, Vaughan."

"And did she also tell you that I, too, am one of the finalists?"

"No, Vaughan."

"Well, I am. And since they have always given the award to an insider who knows how to play the game, I'm sure she won't be terribly disappointed when my name is called and I walk away with the prize."

"Vaughan, don't talk about me in the third person. I'm right here, in front of you," Nia said calmly.

"Of course. Well, if you ladies will excuse me, I think I'll go and take a seat nearer the lectern."

Grace and Nia rolled their eyes at each other, watching Vaughan scoot her chair, which was parallel to theirs, inches closer to the lectern.

"What is she trying to prove?" Nia asked Grace.

"That she's good enough."

"For what? For whom?"

Grace shook her head. "I guess for Vaughan. Who knows."

"Ladies and Gentlemen, I thank you all for joining us this evening here at The Poetry Pause. Tonight is a very special evening. Tonight we will be honoring some of the most beautiful poems to have been entered into our yearly contest. We find it appropriate to have this celebration in the beginning of the new year, because we see this as a new beginning. We looked for poems that made us think of fresh starts and new hope and we want you to sit back, relax, and enjoy yourself. First, we will hear all three of the winning poems, and then we will award the prizes: first, second, and third prize. So relax, sit back, and enjoy. As is our custom, we first hear from our membership. This year, we have one finalist who is a regular contributor here at The Poetry Pause. Her name is Vaughan Gonzalez and the poem she will be sharing is called 'Nourishment.' Vaughan?"

Vaughan stood and walked with paper in hand to the lectern. Her fingers rustled the paper as she set it down, her lips quivering.

"Thank you, Myron. And thank you all for coming tonight. I wrote this poem to a friend, but I never sent it—I'm sure some of you know how that is. Sometimes we get so caught up in how to say we're sorry that we never actually get around to saying it. Okay. 'Nourishment.'"

I have the most incredible dreams
when I go to sleep hungry. I dream

about places that I've never seen. I speak
languages that I've never heard. I see

faces that have no eyes. They look
at me and ask me questions to which I have

no answers and ask me to do things that have
never been done. All of this, but only when I am

hungry. When I am full, I dream of nothing, not
dreamless sleep but dreams of void. It is

what happens when one has something and leaves
it alone to tend to itself. Maybe all of life

is this wanting. Once the wanting is gone, then so is
the life. I have taken and taken

to staying up and creating dreams that feed me
all the time. Dreams where we can all go and be full.

I am at a party and no one has come:
I miss the table, satisfied or hungry.

When she finished reading her poem, Vaughan picked up her paper and sat down in her chair. She didn't turn around and acknowledge the people who were applauding her efforts, just sat stoically looking straight ahead. Myron walked to the lectern.

"Our next winning entry was written by a woman who is not a member of The Poetry Pause. When I finally caught up with her, I learned that she had come to visit us a while back and read a flyer announcing our contest. She almost didn't make our very stringent deadline." He laughed. "But we are so glad that she did and thought enough of us to send in her beautiful, uplifting entry! Ladies and gentlemen, Nia Benson reading her poem 'In the Arms of One Who Loves Me.' "

Nia walked to the lectern. She was grateful that she had memorized her poem so that she could close her eyes and just feel the words as they washed over and anointed her. She gave herself no introduction.

> *Emerging out of water,*
> *I walk a maze of your design:*
> *Turn here, you say; walk there.*
> *And I follow because you say*
> *you know the way.*
>
> *This way to loving arms.*
>
> *I navigate a web of flies*
> *They are silent.*
> *Their silken captivity no testimony*
> *to one intent upon the journey.*
>
> *This way . . .*
>
> *I travel underground tunnels.*
> *You hand me a map. X lies*
> *the treasure, beyond these markers, you say:*
>
> *When you pass the first, give me your smile;*
> *when you pass the second, give me your confidence;*
> *and when you pass the third, relinquish the lines on your palms.*
>
> *This is the way to loving arms.*
>
> *But then I see the water, reflecting who I was.*
> *I stand in stillness and hug myself preserving warmth*
> *You shake your head, point to the map. But I am clear.*
>
> *Finally and at long last, I am in the arms of one who loves me.*

When Nia finished reciting her poem, she opened her eyes and looked out onto her audience. Grace was nodding her head, smiling at her, looking proud. Some of the people were dabbing their eyes, shedding tears. Nia hoped she had touched a heart in this place. It hadn't always been that way, but now she wanted people to hear her words and maybe be inspired to find their own way to whatever was right for them.

She looked over at Vaughan as Myron was walking to the lectern. She was smiling, looking at the floor, with tears flowing down her cheeks.

Nia took her seat, amid applause, next to Grace.

"Is that the poem you wrote to my drawing?" Grace asked.

Nia smiled. "How could you tell?"

"Because the poem sounds just like the drawing looks!"

"Thank you, Nia Benson," Myron said, smiling at Nia. "And now, our final finalist. This must be the year of the woman, because all our finalists are women! We received this entry from a new poet and we just loved it. It rang so honest and true to us; we just had to meet the honest woman behind the honest words. Reading her winning entry, 'LocoMotive,' I present to you Mercedes Lucero."

"I don't believe it," Nia said.

"You know that woman?" Grace asked.

"I sure do. She works in accounting at Feinstein." Nia folded her arms. "And believe me, there is nothing *honest* about that woman."

Mercedes walked to the lectern and rested her manuscript on it.

"Thanks for selecting my poem as one of the finalists in your contest. I see that I am in grand company this evening and I'm excited just being here. I wrote this poem last year. Sometimes people do things and say things they think are the right things, you know, and then, *wham*, you end up getting it right in the kisser! Hey, and don't I know it; nobody's perfect. Anyway, I wrote this little poem to try to explain, to myself, what I had done. The title of my poem is 'LocoMotive.' "

These are
Eye level, they bring pain
too long then look

bright lights.
to those of us who stare
the other way

I thought they were
the kind to be followed
that lead the way
I chased it

the beckoning kind
and chased
to peace.
went that way . . .

But not all brightness   *leads to heaven*
Sometimes lights   *give way*
to whistle's blare   *to cargo and caboose.*

When Mercedes finished reading her poem, she sighed and sat down next to Vaughan, resigned. Nia wondered what had prompted her to write the poem. Myron was right; it did seem honest—so unlike her impression of what the woman would write.

"Please, another round of applause for all our finalists. You ladies did a fantastic job! Simply wonderful!" The audience applauded loudly, whooping and hollering like they were at a sports event. "And now, the announcement of our prizes. Our third place prize this year goes to our very own, Vaughan Gonzalez! Vaughan, won't you come up here and accept your prize?"

Vaughan stood and smoothed the skirt to her power-red business suit. She walked regally up to the lectern and spoke into the microphone.

"Obviously there's been some sort of mix-up, Myron. Perhaps you were reading from the bottom up."

Myron looked over the list in his hand and shook his head.

"Well, in that case, I decline the award. Obviously, it's been rigged or something. There's no way I could have received third place with poems by those two novices in the running." She turned and walked down the center aisle toward the door, "Thanks people, but no thanks. Vaughan Gonzalez never takes third place in *anything*!"

The crowd tittered. You could hear tiny gasps and people clearing their throats and shifting in their seats. Myron seemed unfazed.

"All right, all right. Settle down. Artists can sometimes be . . . well, *artistes*!" He laughed. "If you know what I mean, and I'm sure you do. Moving right along, our second place prize is awarded to Mercedes Lucero. Mercedes?"

Mercedes stood beaming and walked the few steps to the lectern. She shook Myron's hand, and accepted a beautiful certificate and a small plain envelope from him. She was visibly moved by the applause. "Thank you. Thank you so much. I've never won anything like this before. I can't believe I won." She held the papers in her hand as though they held the answer to the question of life.

"Well, I guess the surprise is over! Our first place prize in the 1982

Poetry Pause Competition is Nia Benson for her poem 'In the Arms of One Who Loves Me'!"

Grace nudged Nia. "Go on, girl. They're calling your name."

Nia could barely see the lectern through the tears that had gathered in her eyes. "I owe so much to the people in my life for this poem. This past year has been so full of experiences—both good and bad. I guess we never really see the good in the painful parts until it's over. I'm just glad I made it through *alive*. Thank you."

"Amen!" Mercedes shouted out.

She accepted the certificate and the envelope from Myron and returned his hug. "It's our pleasure, Nia. It really is."

"So how does it feel to be an award-winning poet, Miss Nia Benson?" Grace asked, holding an imaginary microphone in front of her face.

"I can't believe I won. This is fantastic." Nia sipped her punch.

"Maybe one day you'll stop being so surprised at yourself. This is only the beginning; I hope you know that."

"You always were good for my ego."

"I'm just speaking the truth over here. The truth as I sees it, woman. Once you decide to spend some of that precious energy loving Nia, everything else is going to fall into place. Watch, you'll see."

Mercedes walked up to them. "Nia! That was some kind of beautiful poem! When I grow up, I want to be just like you!"

"Hi Mercedes. How are things at Feinstein?" Nia asked, disinterested.

"Oh girl, I left there months ago. Jonathan moved Lisa into Accounting, to keep an eye on the books. Ridiculous, right? The woman didn't know a number from a noodle and here she comes trying to tell me how to do my job."

"I thought you and Lisa were tight."

Mercedes looked uncomfortable. "I've wanted to apologize to you for a long time. For the way I acted and all. I wasn't very nice; I know that now. I thought that by getting in with the boss's niece, well, thought things would be more secure for me, you know? But I did learn something in the whole process. I learned there ain't no fool like an old fool. She ran over me just like she ran over you."

"Yeah, that's Lisa all right. I'm really sorry you got fired."

"Fired? No, I didn't get fired. Once the FBI started coming in and hanging around, I read the writing on the wall and decided to hightail it out of there!"

"The FBI?"

"Our Jonathan Feinstein was involved in some shady stuff. They tell me he was a major shareholder of a drug company that was under some major investigation for fraud. I don't know the details; it got too complicated for me."

"Was the name Brooksmore?"

"Hey, yeah! That was the one."

"That's pretty amazing. Were you able to find other work?"

"No, I'm hanging up the towel. Retiring. I'm no spring chicken, you know. It's time for me to go and spend time with my kids and grandkids. I'll probably move down to Miami sometime this year; they keep hollering for me to *come on down!*"

"That's nice, Mercedes," Nia said and meant it.

"Yeah, it would be real nice. What are you up to nowadays?"

Nia sighed. That was a real good question. "I was just offered a job in L.A. heading up the public relations department for a new record label."

"Ooo! That's sounds perfect for you, Nia!"

"*And,*" Grace chimed in, "she's also been offered a partnership at one of the hottest consultant groups in New York City."

"Nia? Is that true?"

Nia nodded, smiling.

"So which one are you going to choose?"

"I've been asking her that question for the past week!" Grace said.

"I think I'll just look behind me . . . and then look in front of me . . . and follow my heart."

"You get no straight answers from this woman," Grace said, sucking her teeth.

Nia rolled her eyes at Grace.

"Well, whatever you decide, you take care of yourself, okay? You're good people, Nia. And keep writing; please keep writing. Again, I'm really sorry," Mercedes said.

"You, too. Thanks, Mercedes."

They hugged.

As Mercedes walked away, Nia whispered to Grace, "You think Vaughan is coming back for the grand showdown?"

"Not on your life. If she can't be the star, she's not going to be in the show."

They laughed and remembered and got refills on their punch.

He stood and watched the commuter bus carry her off into the distance, feeling complete. Watched it until it was barely a speck in the distance, watched it until his feet felt frostbitten. He hadn't noticed the icy wetness seeping through the seams of his shoes. He hadn't noticed that he was standing in a puddle of slush. Infatuation will do that to you sometimes.

The feelings of kinship had sneaked up on him this time, sometime between the days when they had shared secrets and the moments that she appealed to the little mischievous boy in him, playing a week's worth of practical jokes on him just as a good buddy was prone to do. She made him laugh, made him think, allowed him entrance into her world and tread softly into his own storehouse of memories. And he, on the other hand, felt drawn to her presence, magnetically so, as if any time spent away from her was too much to risk in an uncertain world, a world where either one of them might be redirected to follow another course at a moment's notice.

The bus let him off within walking distance of his apartment, the walk refreshing him and giving him a view of his life and surroundings. It seemed a lifetime ago that he had walked these streets, ages since he had seen his building or turned the key in his front-door lock.

He was another man now, trying to place his past in context with his present.

When he entered his apartment he felt a reconnection, a coming home of sorts, but not a true reunion, just a stop along the way. He walked his suitcase back to his bedroom, noted the number of calls on his answering machine, and walked to the kitchen to pour himself a glass of juice.

He had expected that there would be more mail awaiting him, more bills, more flyers, more reminders of his absence. The dust had not even accumulated to a thickness. And yet so much had changed within him.

He came across a letter, not a bill or an ad, a handwritten letter that beckoned to be opened. Cursive words written on lined notebook paper took on the voice of their author and spoke to him as he read.

> *Dear Seth,*
>
> *I don't expect you to understand. I don't expect that you ever will.*
>
> *You're probably thinking that I don't love you. I do. I love you enough to know that I have to let you go to pursue your relationship with Sandy. I was never much for fighting it out over a man. Case closed. She wins.*
>
> *Please do not try to contact me. I need to make this a clean break in order to go on with my life and make a fresh start. A neat good-bye . . . that is all I ask.*
>
> *Take care of yourself, Seth. I'll be praying for you, for your safety and for your health.*
>
> *Good-bye.*
>
> *Love,*
> *Lauren*

Reading her words, he didn't even feel the sting anymore. He didn't feel the gripping pain that had swept over him on that California beach or the anger at her refusal to listen to his heart. All he felt now was a dull sadness at a life discarded for a reason he didn't understand. He wished he had had more of a say in their life, wished he had known more *of* her to give more *to* her. But that is what happens when life is rushed through: The end is achieved but the core remains hollow. He picked up the letter, and tossed it in the trash.

"You're home! How was your trip?" Sandy stood at the kitchen entrance, twirling the keys, smiling. "As you can see, your plants are still thriving!"

Seth smiled back at her. "Yeah, I see. Thanks, chica."

"No problem. No problem at all." She shuffled her way to the fridge, opening cabinets on the way. Seth laughed.

"You hungry or something?"

"Seth, I am always hungry! Gonna be big as a house by the time this is over. Sheeesh. And you don't have anything fattening in here either."

He looked at her, in her fashionably torn jeans and oversized sweatshirt that hinted at her rounding belly. She was starting to show.

"You look cute, Sandy." He leaned back in his chair and watched her rummage through the second shelf of his refrigerator.

She turned around and frowned at him, turning her baseball cap around. "Oh, shuddup." She found a jar of pickles, brought it to the table and sat down. "Men."

She stuck her fingers in the jar and pulled one out, accepting the paper napkin Seth handed her. He smiled at her. "Seth? What gives?"

"Chica, we gotta talk."

"Okay, you talk. I'll eat. Deal?"

"I want to talk about the baby."

Her mood changed immediately, from carefree to burdened, and she braced against the fear, preparing for the worst.

"Okay."

"Naw, see, Sandy? Don't do that. Don't switch gears on me. It's not like that. I want to be there for the baby."

"Go on."

"That baby didn't ask to come here, I know that. And it certainly didn't have a say in how it was conceived. That was our decision. And I don't want to make any child of mine pay for a mistake that I might have made."

She looked away, far beyond the confines of Seth's kitchen. "A mistake . . ."

He stopped, surprised by her emphasis. "Chica, it wasn't something we were supposed to do. We weren't a couple. You and I both know it was all about the sex, all about the conquest. There was no love involved."

She stared at him, her eyes filled with sadness and hurt. "There was for me."

And in another time and another place he might have found remnants of truth in her words, might have found himself swayed by the lilt in her voice or the moisture in her eyes. But he had seen the eyes of love. He knew now what it looked like, knew what it felt like. It wasn't about conquest or power or good memories pulled like golden threads scattered haphazardly in a quilt made mostly from pain. Love felt good all the time, not just moments in between angst and fear and control.

She left him that night and, after that moment, he expected she would. She told him she was going west, to find her mother's people in New Mexico. He assured her he would always be there for the child, providing financial support and co-parenting as much as she would allow. He told her he was glad they had developed a friendship, a real one, a relationship based upon honesty and truth, and how he had hoped the friendship would remain and develop through the years. But she wasn't even listening anymore. She had stopped listening as soon as the fantasy died, the truth being just too hard for her to take.

He watched her load up her station wagon with boxes and household furnishings, nomad style, refusing his offer of assistance. She was gone within the month, her apartment unoccupied for another two. The landlord was renovating, adding more windows to bring in more light.

"Seth! It's so good to see you again! I've missed you! But see, that's what happens. People go off in the world and make a little name for themselves and they just don't bother with us little people anymore!" MommaPatti greeted him in the lobby of Staccato East Recording Studios.

"Awww, MommaPatti . . . you will never be one of the 'little people' in my life." He gave her a big hug and a kiss on the cheek.

"Now, wait a minute, I'm not sure I like that reference!" She stood back and put her hands on her hips, looking down at her torso.

Seth laughed. "Women! I'm telling you, you just can't say the right thing!"

She held his hand. "They're all in Studio A, setting up, getting things in gear. This is so exciting . . . recording Garrison's first major release! I'm so glad you guys were able to convince them to let you all record in New York. Glad I can be here to witness this. Rexxy is so proud, Seth. Thank you. He may not ever say these things to you, but he is. You've given him back his *zest*. He needed that. Trust me: We both did."

"I couldn't have done this without him."

"And Seth? I'm really, really sorry about you and Lauren."

He tried to dodge the conversation. "Hey, things happen."

"Seth, no." She looked at him in his eye. "I *know*."

He tried to look at her puzzled, as though he didn't understand, but the way her eyes penetrated him cut through his pretense.

"I was with her when she had the abortion and I know."

All of the feelings he had thought he had dealt with successfully came rushing to the forefront, the pain sweeping over his face like sand over driftwood during a storm.

"It hurt, MommaPatti. She didn't have to do it that way. I kept telling her . . ."

She held him, her son by friendship, and patted his back, his pain finally getting the better of him. "I know, baby. I tried to tell her. We all did."

"All?"

"Rexxy and I . . . and Reggie and Crystal, too. But I was the one there with her. She had made up her mind that it was the best way. There wasn't anything any one of us could do. She wasn't herself."

"I know you all blamed me for hurting her. And I'm sorry for that."

"No, Seth! No one blamed you. Lauren should have had counseling a long time ago. She had been through a lot, and there were a lot of things in her past that she hadn't dealt with—we knew that. That's why we were all so fearful. For her, yes, but also for you. We knew that you loved her. And we knew that, with love, the possibility was there that you would get caught up in the crossfire. And even though you're a big strong man, I know there is a fragile core deep inside of you. I'm sorry it had to happen this way. I really am."

They held each other, swapped tissues, and gave strength to each other.

"How is she now?"

She patted his hand, and smiled up at him. "I think she'll be okay in time. She has a lot of work to do on herself." She paused. "When she's ready, she'll do it. But for now, I believe that your presence is needed in Studio A, Mr. Co-Producer!"

"Thanks." He walked confidently toward the door that read STUDIO A.

"I have loved you since you were goofy and silly, Seth. And no matter what happens, none of that is going to change, you got that?" she called after him.

He stopped midstride and turned back to her, a troubled look on his face. "MommaPatti?"

"Yes?"

"You mean to tell me that I'll *always* be goofy and silly?"

She missed when she threw her magazine at him.

"Seth."

"Hey."

Seth stood at Reggie's door, holding two bottles of water, wearing his workout gear, maintaining a slow jog in place.

"Get your gear—we're long overdue."

Reggie smiled at him, looking kind of puzzled. "Well, sure. Hold on a sec. Let me tell Crystal."

Moments later the two found their pace, a mutual pace. It felt good to be back in step.

"Been a long time, Reg."

"That it has. A lot has gone on."

Seth nodded. "Life is like that sometimes."

"Tell me about it. A group of neighborhood people are trying to get me to run for City Council."

"Reggie! That's fantastic! You going to do it?"

"Hmm, I don't know. Crystal's pregnant. Due in the fall."

Seth stopped jogging, punched his friend in the arm. "Get out of here! Oh, man! That's great!"

"Yeah. You're gonna be an uncle."

Silence.

"Seth?"

Seth looked his friend in the eye, unable to look away in time to miss the sympathy pouring from his eyes.

"I'm sorry about Lauren."

Seth didn't know how much Reggie knew, whether he knew about the baby or the abortion or any of the intricacies of the past year. He looked at Reggie, at his happiness bubbling just beneath the surface. He could tell that Reggie was genuinely concerned for him, his life-long buddy. But the details didn't really matter now. This was a joyous time.

"Yeah, well, life is full of lessons, my man. Let's talk about you . . . gonna be a dad! You ready for that?"

Reggie didn't even acknowledge his question. "I'm sorry, man. I was so concerned about Lauren, thinking about everything she had been through, that I didn't even see what was going on through your eyes. She hurt you pretty bad. I know she did. I didn't know how to bring it up. You holding up okay?"

Seth nodded. "It's okay. Really. I dealt with it. I had a lot of help. Remember Nia?"

Reggie smiled.

"She's been a good friend to me."

"Friend? I can't even imagine Seth Jackson having a woman as just a friend."

Seth didn't take the jovial way out of the conversation. "She's fun. We can talk to each other. Share stuff. And the best thing about it is that she doesn't judge me, there's no pressure. It's nice."

"Doesn't surprise me much. She's good people."

"Yeah, she is. I guess I really let you down, huh? I was supposed to make it work with Lauren and keep the family in the family, so to speak."

"Seth, what is it going to take to get it through that thick skull of yours that you're *already* family? There's nothing you can do or say to become any *more* family than you are!"

"Yeah, but you and Uncle Rex and MommaPatti . . . everyone was expecting me to hit it off with Lauren."

"Well, you know, it would have been nice, but I don't think any of us wanted you to be miserable doing it. You got to do what's right for you. You got to stop playing at living and just live, man. Stop trying to love and just love. I don't know if you loved her or Sandy or Nia—and it doesn't really matter to me *who* you end up loving. Or even if you decide to go off and be by yourself for the rest of your life. As long as Seth is happy and doing it for Seth. You dig me, man?"

"Maybe you were right. Maybe Lauren was good for me."

"You're not hearing me—"

"No, no . . . ," Seth cut him off, "not in a romantic sense. But maybe she was good for me in that being with her made me see how much I play around at love. It's a hard lesson to learn. So many people get hurt."

"And now there's Nia."

"My friend."

"For now."

For always. Seth smiled. He felt no need to contradict him, no need to explain how he was feeling. He would just allow time to speak for him and Nia both.